THE PRETENDER

THE PRETENDER

Jo Harkin

BLOOMSBURY PUBLISHING

LONDON • OXFORD • NEW YORK • NEW DELHI • SYDNEY

BLOOMSBURY PUBLISHING
Bloomsbury Publishing Plc
50 Bedford Square, London, WC1B 3DP, UK
29 Earlsfort Terrace, Dublin 2, Ireland

BLOOMSBURY, BLOOMSBURY PUBLISHING and the Diana logo
are trademarks of Bloomsbury Publishing Plc

First published in Great Britain 2025

A catalogue record for this book is available from the British Library

ISBN: HB: 978-1-5266-7834-8; TPB: 978-1-5266-7835-5;
EBOOK: 978-1-5266-7833-1; EPDF: 978-1-5266-7831-7

2 4 6 8 10 9 7 5 3 1

Typeset by Integra Software Services Pvt. Ltd.
Printed and bound in Great Britain by CPI Group (UK) Ltd, Croydon CR0 4YY

To find out more about our authors and books visit www.bloomsbury.com
and sign up for our newsletters

'The same Duke purposing to accomplish his said false and untrue intent, and to inquiet and trouble the King, our said Sovereign Lord, his Liege People and this his Royaulme, now of late willed and desired the Abbot of Tweybury, Mayster John Tapton, Clerk, and Roger Harewell Esquire, to cause a strange child to have be brought into his Castle of Warwick, and there to have beputte and kept in likeliness of his Son and Heir, and that they should have conveyed and sent his said Son and Heir into Ireland, or into Flanders, out of this Land, whereby he might have gotten him assistance and favour against our said Sovereign Lord; and for the execution of the same, sent one John Taylour, his Servant, to have had deliverance of his said Son and Heir, for to have conveyed him; the which Mayster John Tapton and Roger Harewell denied the deliverance of the said Child, and so by God's grace his said false and untrue intent was let and undone' –

From the Attainder of the Duke of Clarence

'Some carp at men of worth, others approve of them: the lower class aren't spoken of at all' –

Anonymous Theognidea fragment

John

'This song for young men was begon
To make them true and steadfast;
For yarn that is evil spun,
Evil it comes out at the last' –

How the Wise Man Taught His Son,
Anonymous

… Was this the first thing he wrote of his own?

> *I am John Collan*
> *today in the yere 1483 I will defeat the goat.*
> *In the name of honnour and glory to god highest & for reson that it*
> *knocked me in the mud again today*
> *& has TRODDEN churlishly over my back*
> *has despoiled*
> *!*
> *an insult that cannot be borne.*

John has made a plan of battle. According to the ancient art of the famous Vegetius who set out in his book how the Roman Empire toppled and suborned all enemies. According to his brother Tom.

Tom did not read that book, but he told John what he was told was in it.

Tom had a favourite military stratagem of his own. This was the goose trap. He'd stand in front of something and call: little John, oh little Johnny John John! You are a pink pig's arsehole, a hairy ball sack, a shitbeetle – and then when John, sore wroth, would charge at him, Tom would dodge and John would run into that thing he was standing in front of which was usually a cow shit. And then Tom would shout: *goose trap!*

Now Tom is gone to be an apprentice and John is goose no longer.
John is a general.

The wise general uses the ground to his advantage when laying his snare. He positions his light infantry (himself) ahead of the enemy's advancing cavalry (the goat), with the stream at his rear. From this position, the infantry will make a feint attack with an artillery of pebbles. The cavalry, incensed, will charge – whereupon the infantry will leap up, take hold of a willow-tree branch, and swing to safety above the water. The cavalry, unable to halt his charge, will plunge headlong into the stream, and be thusly carried away, probably ending up in the sea.

Toppled and suborned.

And the wise general shall obtain the victory and pass unmolested through the farm to fetch water and weed the herbs and feed the chickens ever after: praise be to God.

John walks with his water bucket and a bag of pebbles toward the stream, whistling.

There are primroses on the bright grass edging the mud tracks, which have dried and cracked. The pigs trample through the richly fetid midden.

Bluebells in the wood; wood pigeons flapping on top of each other; blossom crowded onto branches, silky, lavish, deeply pink.

Above it all the sky a flawless blue, intensely perfect, like a lid that could be flipped, to show God looking down saying: *go forward, my son.*

This spring you are a man.

This spring you show the goat who is master.

John goes into the kitchen, a small room leaning against the main house like a labourer taking a nap. It's hot in here, and smells of baking bread, meat cooking in the iron pot above the fire, and a bitter scorch of something starting to burn, because Jennott, as she always tells them, is a head dairy maid and not a fucking cook.

4

John stands in the door with the water. Jennott's growling at the bread, which she shovels out of the oven and piles onto the table. The rising heat waves the lines of light and dim that divide the room. She turns around and sees John.

'Old Gaspard got you again, did he?'

Her pretence is that the goat is French. She mislikes the French. They killed her dad.

She takes the water from him.

'You're covered in scratches. And so *wet*. Did you fall into the stream?'

John isn't going to discuss military strategy with plebeians, but calling Jennott a plebeian might get him one of her blindingly fast smacks around the head, so he doesn't say anything.

'He knows you're frightened, that's what it is,' she says. 'You've got to steel your balls, stand up straight and stare him out.'

'You can't stare something out when its eyes go in different directions.'

Jennott laughs. She picks up a loaf of bread and puts it on her head, tucks her lower lip under her teeth and says, 'Who am I?'

'Sir Nicholas,' says John.

Sir Nicholas the parish priest and John's father Will are enemies. In the past John's dad said some heretical-flavoured things and Sir Nicholas accused him of being a secret Lollard and threatened to get him burned.

And it's true, said Will Collan, that my grandfather was a Lollard who didn't see why knavish priests like Sir Nicholas should be called Sir any more than a cobbler should, or why they should take the confession of honest men, nor their sweated-for money neither – and then he joined the revolt of the peasants, and was killed just before his own son, my dad, was born.

Will didn't hide his bitterness when he said it. But it's not for any turdly priest to accuse him of *sympathies*. So Will Collan put manure through Sir Nicholas's windows. The act was anonymous but also, in a small village, completely nonymous, or whatever the word is. (John, small village boy, is often short of words.)

'Correct,' says Jennott. 'The old fart-smeller. That's what he does in Confession. Smells farts.'

'Is that lawful to say?' asks John.

5

'It is if you cross yourself after and say "Hail Mary, full of grace, the Lord is with thee",' Jennott says, and as ever, John can't tell if she's joking.

Things John Collan's father shouts at him in the daytime:

For God's sakes John pick up your feet stand straight stop bothering the women stop bothering the cows stop bothering Jennott where in the holy hell were you don't wipe your mouth on your sleeve don't blaspheme quieten down stand straight how many times where the devil is he now—

Things his father says at night:

Get to bed, my boy, sleep sweetly (and a pat, on the head).

Our Father in Heaven
Hallowed be your name

My father on the farm
Will Collan be his name
The cows come
The cheese be done—

Dear God, I am very sorry about the prayer I said in school it was heresy and I was rightly beaten. Please forgive me I know not what I did. Thank you, God.
    Amen.

King Edward is lateward dead.

'Deadward,' says Jennott. She says King Edward was a right goodly-looking man who never turned down a tumble, even with low women. She looks sad, then, as if at a lost opportunity.

King Edward's little son, also called Edward, is going to be king. He's only twelve, a few years older than John. His uncle Richard is Lord Protector for now.

John tries to imagine being a boy king. His first act: the beheading of Gaspard, for divers villainous buttings-over – and no sign of repentance. Those uncanny slotted eyes say: God is not my master. And Gaspard's death would be a warning to all goats, and all the little children of England would cheer King John, safe from treadings-on and trampling evermore.

Like King Edward, John's mother is dead. The only thing he remembers of her is the rosemary she used to scent her hair – or maybe he only remembers it because that's what Tom and Oliver remember. His brothers say she had a mole on her cheek and dark eyes and a creaky but tuneful singing voice. They added once that their mum sang like a dove and Jennott like a crow, and Jennott said, if you fight like a bear you can sing however the fuck you want, and threw a pan at them.

(John crushes rosemary in his fingers sometimes, holds it up to his nose.)

Tom and Oliver aren't dead. But they are gone, in a way that's almost as permanent. Tom is an apprentice to a tailor of fine clothing in Bristol. Oliver is learning to be a goldsmith in London. The latter is a passing expensive apprenticeship, and the cause of many meaningful glances in the village.

Will Collan is known to be *doing well*. Tom and Oliver told John that he hadn't always done so well. They said that when they were John's age the farmhouse was half the size it is now, with only one room for sleeping; that there were oilcloth coverings over the window instead of wooden shutters; no pewter ewer and bowls on the table. Their beds were hay, they said, not wool.

John wasn't sure if they were lying or not. They liked to tease and jape him.

He said, How did our father have so many fields and cows if he was so poor?

Tom laughed and tapped a knockaknock on the top of John's head.

Think! Tom said. He didn't have all that back then. He got the fields next to ours when old Allerwych died with no sons. And he bought the cows.

This herd of cows is a curiosity in the village. Nobody has so many as Will Collan – nobody in the county ever *thought* of having so many, it's not at all how farming is done, but now they think he was pretty sharp, because he sells his cheese in Oxford.

(Maybe – lowered voice, here – *unnaturally* sharp.)

So where did he get the money to buy the fields and cows? said John.

Oh, yes: he thought he'd got Tom then. His crow of triumph was already vibrating in his throat.

Tom shrugged. Investment from a rich merchant, he said.

Who?

Some Oxford man. Probably the one who wanted the cheese.

John opened his mouth. The caw collapsed out of it, soundless. Tom and Oliver laughed.

Don't be wroth, Little John, Oliver said. Anyone would think you weren't the lucky one. The one who gets beef for lunch.

The third son, said Tom.

The one who goes off to seek his fortune, said Oliver. Ey, cheer up, Little John, maybe you'll fuck a princess.

Little Johnny's so pretty he could *be* the princess, said Tom.

John ran across the room with his fists up, shouting, but they were waiting for him and they wrapped him up in his fancy wool blankets and sat on him. Through the hot layers of cloth he heard them telling him that this was for his own good, that he has to be wrapped because he's bitten them before, hasn't he (sad voice), but once he lies still he'll be released.

Most days ended with John being sat on. He'd always tell himself he wouldn't attack his brothers again, but they'd jape him until he'd lose his wits and throw himself at them. He wasn't properly in occupancy of himself at these times. His calmer John-minds, once lost, would fly up and perch somewhere, like the painted angels in the church, watching sorrowfully as his apeish body gibbered, howled, bared its monkey teeth – until his brothers bundled the unholy creature up and squashed it.

His brothers are also the ones who taught him to read and write. They show him how to make ink and sharpen a goose-feather quill and how to write j o h n c o l l a n and then a sigil, which they tell him means John but even he can see is a drawing of a penis and two balls. They are proud of him for realising.

'He's a clever boy,' says Tom, patting his head. 'Now, verbs and nouns.'

He likes the twins at those times.

And all of which is meant to say why, the day that Tom and Oliver left, almost half a year ago, John jumped and hooted and ran laps of their shared room in celebration – then found, on his bed, a whittled boat with a little man inside, with *John* carved into the boat, and had what his father called a womanish fit of tears—
—which took him again whenever their letters home arrived. But not in front of his father. He'd leave the fireside, mannish-chin jutting, mannish-eyes dry. He'd make a tent of his wool blankets and sit under it and weep in secret.

The knowledge that the blankets would never oppress him again was no comfort.

Jennott, despite being a woman, is not given to womanish fits of crying. Especially not concerning the departure of John's brothers.

She has blonde hair, thick and unshining as hay, and blue eyes, which she puts down to a Saxon lineage. The twins used to do impressions of her behind her back.

Oh, this? It's just my Saxon lineage, don't mind it. An unbroken line from Alfred the Great, not that I like to mention it.

John, hearing but not understanding, asked Jennott why she was a dairy maid if she came from Alfred the Great. A ringing ear, that's why, said Jennott.

What? ... Ow.

Aside from the whittled ship, John's favourite thing is a fairy arrowhead. He found it last year, in the ploughed furrows of the wheat field. A flint bitten into the shape of a leaf, glossy brown in the centre, clear honey glass at the edges. He held it; ran his fingers over the scalloped face.

In the Widow Tolley's alehouse, the men say John's father got his gold from the fairies. That Will Collan went over the hills to the fairy barrow on Midsummer night, set down a pot of ale and called out: What a right savoury ale this is!

And a door in the barrow opened up, and in the door was standing a fairy princeling. Diamonds on the buckles of his shoes. A cloak embroidered with the moon and stars. He looked at Will and curled his lip.

Give me your ale, Englishman, he said.

(John, hearing this from his friend Rolfe, was suspicious of this story.

Why would a fairy want ale? he asked.

Use your head, said Rolfe. How are they going to make ale, living underground? They drink from underground rivers and eat raw mole, envying us our ale and pottage.

Anyway.)

Hold now, there's a price for my ale, said Will. I want your fairy gold. And the fairy smiled, and said: Follow me into my palace, and you'll have all the gold you can carry.

But Will knew that if he went into that barrow he'd never be coming back out again. So he said to the fairy: I think not. And the fairy said, Well then, I will conjure you some from the treasure house, here! And there it was. A whole glistening heap of it. But Will laughed and made the sign of the cross over the gold, and it turned into a pile of dead leaves and acorn shells.

Oh, he knew that princeling's games.

He knew well. And then he seized that wretched fairy and turned him upside down and shook him until gold tumbled out of his purse, and rubies too, sapphires, emeralds, and before he let the princeling go he took his diamond-buckle shoes. Thank you very much.

Ha!

But as soon as he got home he put iron at every threshold and up the chimney too, and he wore a piece of iron as protection, because he full knew the fairy prince was after his blood now, and evermo.

Did you steal a fairy's diamond buckle shoes? John asked his dad.

God's bones, said his dad. They're still telling that story?

Rolfe's dad told it.

Rolfe's dad is a cunt.

You *did* get your gold from the fairies, though, John asked. Didn't you?

He wanted it to be true. An upside-down fairy prince, not a cheese-buying Oxonian merchant.

My arse I did, said his dad. And – listen to me – forget about gold. Don't be noising anything about gold around the village. You hear me? Good.

After John picked up the arrow, a *feeling* came over him. He looked around, as if whoever shot it might be following after, looking for his father – or maybe his father's son.

He couldn't see any living thing out here on the fields. Afternoon had collapsed into dusk; a warmish September night. The line of hedge and the trees beyond it were silent. The heaved-up earth was dark under his feet. Smoke rose helically into the purple sky from the low farmhouse in the distance. John had a feeling that eyes were on him; a cool pressure, not friendly, not unfriendly, a gaze from – what? How could he name it? He hadn't got the words. But he became conscious of not wearing any protective iron.

He put the arrow into his jerkin, not knowing if it was good luck or bad; started back toward the house.

3

It is today.

John is crouching on the ground to the side of the house, looking at the early-morning grass. The sun has just come up above the beech treeline and everything is luminous. Across the grass spider webs are interlaced, strung with dew crystals. Where are the spiders? The network of webs is an abandoned city.

He hears Jennott and his dad's voices. They're coming up the puddled track carrying some sacks of malt; they've been to the neighbouring Mylton farm, which has a malthouse and kiln.

'John,' his dad says. 'What are you doing here? The stream is the other way. Where's the water? Have you been sitting out here all morning like a baby pigeon?'

'The pail's full,' Jennott says. 'John comes around this way for water, just to avoid the goat.'

John picks up the pail and hies to walk beside them.

'The Myltons said the young Prince Edward was arrested by the Lord Protector, his uncle Richard of Gloucester,' Jennott tells John. She's in a jovial mood; the sun and the walking have put a shine on her. 'What's Richard up to? Claims that the queen and her family were scheming against him, purposing to kill him, and so it was best he take hold of the little prince. And Richard's men killed some of the queen's kinsmen too. In self-defence, he says. And now the poor queen's had to go into sanctuary again at Westminster Abbey with her other children.'

'Where did they put the young prince?'

'In the Tower. They want to put his brother in there with him.'

John tries to imagine a high view across London. But he's never been in a city; he's never been anywhere above the ground floor.

'Will there be another war?' he asks.

'No,' his dad says. 'Maybe. It shouldn't touch us, either way. Wars are for soldiers and nobles. For the rest of us they're just a shitting nuisance. Pray they never decide to do any warring near Oxford.'

'Those two boys will never get out of that tower,' Jennott says. 'And Lord Protector Richard will make himself king. I've seen his type before.'

'What type?' Will says.

'*Men*,' Jennott says.

Will laughs. He and John go into the house, the dim closing over them. Jennott quits them, hauling the sacks off toward the kitchen.

'I'm glad I'm not a soldier,' John says. 'What *am* I going to do? An apprenticeship? Can't I be a scholar instead? And stay here? Can I be a scholar and make cheese?'

He isn't allowed anywhere near the low stone-floored dairy where the butter and cheese are made. It's always cool in there, and clean, everything sluiced with water and scoured with sand; the shining leads, the churns, the vats and milking bowls. It smells intoxicating, a creamy tang that he's come to associate with the white-armed women, working the white milk.

John's too dirty for the dairy, according to Jennott. She thinks he'll get mud on the floor and stick his fingers in the cream. John considers this an outrage. He only wants to see what goes on. Once he secreted himself inside before the dairy maids arrived, talking loudly.

Sarah was saying, The better one is short and fat, rather than long and thin, but long and fat is obviously best.

Only if you've got a big hole, said Mary, and the other women laughed.

Sarah says, Ho, Mary's just wroth because her husband has a baby's penis. He does. I've seen it. It's like a button mushroom. Like a wren's egg in a big nest.

When did you see it?

Jennott's voice: She's seen them all, from here to Oxford.

General laughter. Then:

What's this?

An earwig!

A boy, where he ought not to be!

John was routed, chivvied, chased out. He stopped red-faced in the doorway, shouting:

It's not fair I'm not the dirty one you women are the dirty ones...

Jennott caught up to him and gave him a slap on the cheek, not too hard. She was more amused than angry. Out, she said. And mind your beak.

'Make cheese?' his dad says now. 'Women make the cheese.'

'Just a scholar, then,' says John. 'At Oxford. Nor far, like Oliver and Tom. Then I can come back and visit.'

Maybe it's the mention of his brothers, but his dad has a strange look. John isn't sure what the look means, because he hasn't ever seen it before. He's gazing at John as if John's a... (he can't find the right word)... a *foreigner*. Not the French kind of foreigner: the look isn't disgusted. It's more a mystification, the kind that might be provoked by a visitor from a very distant land, like Babylonia or the dragon-rid East.

But then it's gone.

His dad waves him out. 'Less thinking on the future, more on the weeding,' he says. 'Go.'

It's July, and there's a morality play on in Banbury. It's the first time John's been out of the village: he was too excited to sleep last night. They travel there in the cart, noisy and jolting, its wheels churning through the fallen honeysuckle petals on the muddy tracks.

Will is talking about buying some of their neighbour Mylton's land, Mylton having just died of a cow kick – but he's not sure the Widow Mylton will sell.

'Won't owning two farms make you rich?' John asks. 'I thought you hated rich people.'

'He's warming to them,' Jennott says drolly. She's wearing her good gown, green with embroidery at the neck, and looks at her most Saxon.

'I hate the ones that abuse their position,' Will says. 'Which is most of them.'

'Do we know anyone in Banbury?' John asks.

'They know our cheese,' Jennott says. 'Banbury cheese is famous across England, and I make the best of it. It was Banbury cheese that crossed the channel with the Duke of Bedford, to fill the men who'd be killing the French. God bless them.'

'*Your* cheese went to France?'

'What? You turd-egg. I'm not that old. This was fifty years ago.'

'Was that when they killed Joan of Arc?'

'Yes. A fucking nuisance, she was. I like to think Banbury cheese had a hand in her downfall.'

The cart bumps along the Salt Way – an ancient road, the work of Romans – under a canopy of trees, the sunlight flickering greenly in the leaf gaps – and then, finally:

Banbury.

John, never having seen a town, marvels at how it fills his vision. Wool-rich, cheese-rich, ale-rich, the town seems expanded to brasting point; the beamed faces of the houses tight against each other, the thick embanked walls of the castle sitting fatly in the centre like a moulded pudding. The press of people! The smells! Blood and loaves from the stalls under the Bread Cross; ale from the taverns; baking pies; roasting meat.

The play is so dazzling that it arrives in pieces. Brightly coloured clothes, explosions of smoke, bells, voices. John only understands that there is a battle between the evil characters – Nowadays, Nought and New Guise – and the good character, Mercy, for the soul of the human farmer, Mankind.

Nought says, 'Listen, listen. A Pope's Indulgence guarantees the following. If you bury your nose in your wife's socket you will have forty days of relief from your sin.'

Everyone laughs. John has no witting why.

Mercy doesn't jape. He just talks about avoiding drunkenness and temptations of the flesh, and being Christ's own Knight, as the crowd starts to shift and shuffle. Then the three villains come back, with a song:

Nought:
'Let's all sing! You, good people, join us:

'"*It is written with a coal,
He that shitteth with his hole,*

Unless he wipes his arse clean,
On his hose it shall be seen!"'

'Is it right to sing along?' John asks Jennott.

'Yes, of course, it's for morality,' she says, clapping.

Mischief arrives, plotting with the others to call up the famous, the one and only, the wonderly abominable devil Titivullus—

—if only the audience can put up some money, for Titivullus is a demon of considerable importance.

'That's right, no small coins, no buttons, if you want him to grace us with his infernal majesty… count it up, count it up… heads of the households – yes, you – hands in your purses! Curse all you like: you won't see the devil 'til you pay his fee!'

'Don't!' says John, alarmed, as his smiling dad drops some coins into the passing bowl.

But here is Titivullus anyway, entering through smoke, teeth bared, his face monstrously painted. John shuts his eyes. He doesn't open them again until Titivullus finishes tormenting Mankind into a life of sin, and leaves. Mercy is back now. He tells Mankind he can still be saved.

Mankind cries, 'It is not right to offend and beg mercy, offend and beg mercy, over and over again. God will surely not forgive such a man as me.'

'Nay, it is not so,' says Mercy. 'Raise your voice to the Lord, beg him, "Have mercy on me," and he will forgive.'

As Mercy gives his final speech, on grace and perseverance, Jennott starts casting her eyes around. 'It's getting very theological. Oh, look—' it's the pie-seller, making his way through the crowd ' – over here, good man!'

After the play they're joined by some of his dad's friends. Will's eyes are genial crescents. He smells of ale. They walk through the busy streets; the sun overhead hot now, hovering at the top of its parabola, about to begin the slow dive into the hills. John dodges a man staggering by, toasting people with an imaginary cup; cranes his head to see back into an alley, where a couple are intriguingly knotted.

'… making a fortune,' someone is saying.

'I don't begrudge it, not for proper actors. Better than the mumming, when Farmer Mylton was St George and got beaten by the dragon.'

'That was an unholy riot,' says Jennott, with relish.

'Anyway that's my favourite morality play, the others are much drier.'

'Altogether too sermonical.'

'This one does the job far better, of educating us and fixing our minds on salvation.'

'Ho, here's the alehouse.'

When the day is over several people come back with them; squeezed woollen bodies and yeasty breath in the newly cold, blue-purple air. Only the irregular jounces of the cart keep John's eyes open; his eyelids an impossible weight. The voices around him break into fragments between the noise of the wheels:

can't say that, he's the king now, they crowned him in London

thunk

killed the queen's kin, all them Woodvilles

thunk

both the little princes in the tower

thunk

probably dead

thunk

the queen must be right doleful, imagine

thunk

the poor cow

—John closing his eyes at last, his head on Jennott's shoulder, the sounds of the human world calling after him as he heads into the land of dream; reaching, falling short.

4

Hard to say when Will Collan and Jennott stopped speaking to each other. It's much easier to measure when speaking starts. But how can John remember the beginning of a not-happening?

When did they *last* speak?

John thinks back. There was a night of drinking, not long after Banbury: Jennott and Will and the farmhands and dairy maids sitting around the hearth. John was noticed and sent to bed.

He said, to reprove them, I don't know *what* Mercy would make of this drunkenness and lewd storytelling.

Nobody was reproved. In fact, they all started shrieking with mirth. John waxed wonderly wroth. Jennott wiped her eyes and said, I hope that play isn't going to make him into another Sir Nicholas. He's in mortal dread of that Titty tit whatever his name was.

Well, *you're* in mortal danger of going to hell! John shouted.

Furious as he was, he had been Vegetian in his timing. He'd picked a moment in which Jennott's cup was full of ale, and she wasn't likely to throw it at him. But Jennott, a superior military strategist, took off her shoe instead and got him on the back of the head as he ran.

It's this moment he remembers now, creeping back a little, peering around the corner to see, everyone laughing again, and his dad pulling Jennott to sit in his lap.

So.

They were talking then.

Have they talked since, other than to communicate the business of the farm to each other? In anything other than a formal voice – formal yet angry (Jennott), formal yet evading (Will)?

John doesn't think so.

He is outside, in the dead-leaf, summer-earth-smelling shadow under a beech, well out of the goat's usual route. It's another sunny morning. Everyone's starting to get nervous about the lack of rain. There's only one cloud above him now, a long strip stretched white across the blue sky, like a pennant without a crest.

He's supposed to be feeding the horses. Instead he's trying to compose a nursery rhyme on his tablet.

Wash your hands and your feet
And Titivullus you defeat…

After a little while he looks around. By now his dad or Jennott should have come into view and shouted at John for idling. But he hasn't seen anyone.

He goes into the house and is surprised to see his dad, in smart clothes, sitting very straight-backed with the Widow Mylton and her father the miller. The good cups are out; the good beer. The Widow Mylton smiles at John. She's a slender woman, with an uncertain manner. John bows to them all.

'What cheer?' says the miller. Then, to Will, 'A fine fellow, your boy.'

'Thank you,' says Will. He seems inquiet; his eyes tick between John and his guests, not finding a comfortable place to stop. Then he says to John, 'Did you feed the horses?'

'Not yet, I—'

'Well then! Go do it right anon. Lazy rascal.'

(In a tone not so much of condemnation as relief.)

On a Sunday after Mass the adults talk, while John and his friends play football in the churchyard with a pine cone, it not being pig-bladder season. John kicks the pine cone accidentally into the face of his enemy, Jack.

It *was* an accident.

Jack won't believe it. Makes mourn out of all measure. Has it that his eye has nearly been dashed out. Shouts, finally, 'At least I'm not scared of a goat.'

'What's he talking about?'

'Collan's scared of his dad's goat. It knocked him into the stream.'

John looks at his friend Rolfe, who'd sworn to keep the story privy until his ending day, and beyond.

'Sorry,' Rolfe says. 'It was just... too funny.'

'John bows when the goat comes by,' says Jack, and now the others are starting to laugh. 'John's the servant of the goat!'

Hot wroth overtakes John. His vision narrows. He's about to hurl himself at Jack, but the adults are coming, his father is in view, talking with the Widow Mylton, her father, and – surely not? – Sir Nicholas. Jennott is walking behind, arm-in-tight-arm with her best friend Red Moll.

'On my oath, I'll kill you tomorrow,' John says to Jack, quietly hissing. Then he joins Jennott.

'... fucking turds, fucking cunts,' she's saying. 'Oh, hello, John. You're full red. Been fighting?'

'Not yet.'

Jennott smiles grimly.

'My advice is, don't hold off,' she says. 'When you know there's a fight coming, just get in there and brain the other fucker, before they get a chance to break your heart.'

John can't tell what she's talking about. Red Moll shakes her autumn-coloured head, and makes a sympathetic mouth.

'Can I have a goat put on trial?' John asks them.

'By the Saints, can you what? You mean Gaspard, I suppose.'

'They do it on the continent.'

'They swive their sisters on the continent,' Jennott says, 'and birth babies with tails. What would you accuse it of anyway?'

'Murder. It wants to murder me. Fore-murder. And now blackening my reputation in the village.'

'I made a milk pudding once,' Jennott says, reflective. 'And forgot the nutmeg and cloves. You know what it tasted like? Nothing. That's what. That's what *she'll* taste like.'

'He'll be full of regret,' Red Moll says.

'The goat?' John asks. He is ignored.

'Oh, he will. He's got a standing pintle for money,' Jennott says, 'like all men, but afterwards he'll be sick at what he did. Increasing his *estate*. Lollard, my arse. I won't be abiding here for any second thoughts, I can tell you that. They can search the country up and down for *me*.'

Not the goat, then. Nobody's listening to John. As usual.

'What are you *talking* about?' he asks Jennott, frustrated.

'Oh, you'll know. Soon enough.'

John comes to know that night, by which time he's forgotten all about it. He's kneeling on the rushes next to his bed trying to remember all the bad things he'd done that day so that God would forgive him. The speech of Mercy has inspired him to be more diligent in this. (John's a demon for seeking forgiveness, Jennott said. He's barely finished farting before he's begging God's pardon.)

His dad comes in, interrupting him. It's hard to tell in the stop-start candlelight, but he looks almost furtive. His eyes fix on a point above John's head. He says, 'I'm marrying the Widow Mylton. She's a decent, mild woman. And it'll be less to do for Jennott. So. This is the best decision for the household. You'll be pleased to have her here.'

'Oh,' says John. There doesn't seem anything else that he could say. But his dad seems grateful. He comes over; bestows the brisk ruffle of the hair that is Will at his most tender.

'Night then, son. Sleep well.'

On the day of the wedding feast it rains in the morning, and Jennott says to Red Moll that Milky Pud (as she's taken to calling Emma Mylton) will be dissolved in the downpour. But it dries up by midday, leaving the sky a radiant light-flecked grey, bright as a live fish. The grass is extra green and squishy underfoot; mud flecks the hems of the guests' best kirtles.

Emma Mylton wears a blue dress and looks like the church painting of the Virgin, somewhat faded.

You can... call me Mother if you like, was what she said to John after the banns were read, with a faltering expression, as if not convinced by the thought of herself as a mother.

John thought it was a bit late for him to be getting a mother now, what with his being on the cusp of being grown and overthrowing the goat.

It's alright, he said, and gave her a reassuring pat on the hand. She looked relieved.

He wonders if she's happy to be marrying his father. She's been quiet all day. But then she was quiet when she was wife of Mylton. And she's decorated the trestle tables with cornflowers and honeysuckle, the sweet scent drowning now in gusts of ale. Which must mean she's happy. But then happy women don't look like they'd rather collapse and die than be led by Will to dance. But then as she dances she starts to smile, her headdress flapping, feet stumbling in the wet grass, looking at John's dad, so maybe:

happy?

John doesn't dance. He sits under a table, dazed with fullness. There was a feast of bread, mutton pottage with mint, stewed apple in spices, a whole smiling pig on its spit. Every now and again he pats his belly, proudly, thinking of everything he's fitted into it. He watches the piper, the fiddler and the drummer driving the village feet round in a ring, faster and faster.

Above table, where nobody has noticed John, the talk goes like this:

'He's not that keen to breed then. She's had two stillbirths only. I'd say there's nothing more in her.'

'There'll be something in her tonight.'

'Yeah, Jennott's knife.'

'Well, a stabbing of some sort. Ha.'

'He must want to leave the farm to the boy. The elder two won't be back. They were book-spoiled. I've seen it before. People get book ideas and then nothing here's good enough anymore. They'll be earning a fortune now. Just to keep themselves in books.'

'A sad sight.'

'Did you hear they tried in London to rescue the two little princes out of the tower? Set fires round the city.'

'King Richard will have to answer to God for locking them in there.'

'What's this?' (Jennott's voice)

'The princes trapped in the tower. Little angels.'

Jennott laughs. It's not a mirthful laugh. 'What little boy did you ever know that was an angel?' she says. 'Even if they were, they turn into men in the end.'

'Those boys are different. They're *princes*.'

'They're bastards now. So says the king.'

John, bored, wriggles wormish out from under the table and joins the other children, zigzagging and shouting in a game of their own under the beeches.

'John!' calls small Mary. 'Is it true? That kings have a groom of the stool who watches them shit and then takes the shit and looks at it?'

'Of course it's true,' John says. 'There's a groom of the stool right here in the village.'

'Who!'

'Jack. He waits by the midden to collect everyone's turds. He's probably got one in his jerkin now.'

'I do not! You cock-egg! He's a liar! I do not!'

'He does! I can smell it!'

'Check his jerkin.'

'Get him!'

'Get off!'

'Get him!'

John watches Jack run back to his mother. His mother's skirts! The shame of it. Jack will never come back from this.

A triumph, he thinks. John is in the ascendant. Watch out, Gaspard! Your downfall will be next.

Evening comes. People dance on. A few people fall asleep at the table, or are dragged home. Jennott, drunk, tells the Widow Mylton – no, John corrects himself: she's Emma Collan now – 'Good luck', with immense dignity.

Emma looks confused. She thanks Jennott, and Jennott looks like she might say something else, but then Jennott's friend Red Moll hies over to them, and bears Jennott away.

5

There are savage dog-headed men on the island of Andaman, and unicorns in Lambri.

So says Marco Polo.

The village boys take their lessons with the priest, Sir Nicholas, during which they try to tempt him into leaving off grammar and reading from his only book: a printed edition of the *Book of the Marvels of the World*. Sir Nicholas won't let their grubby little peasant hands roam over the precious pages, and he's unsure about letting their grubby little peasant brains roam over the precious learnings, but what it comes down to is, he loves the travels so much he can't resist reading his favourite passages aloud, and all it takes is for someone to say,

Didn't Marco Polo say there were pygmies in the Indies?

For Sir Nicholas to say,

Saint Mary, no! That's a detestable lie. The venerable Marco Polo is very disparaging of nonsense such as the existence of pygmies. Listen to this, you dullpate, and *learn* something.

'I'm going to go to Cathay,' John says now. 'And the Indies.'

Sir Nicholas snorts, as if irritated, but says nothing. There's a misliking truce between Sir Nicholas and Will Collan on account of the Widow Mylton (as John can't not think of her) and her horror of quarrels.

By St Francis, she's a trembling blade of dry grass, said Jennott. Can't even watch a cockfight!

Another reason for the truce: Will Collan is now the richest man in the parish save for the local squire, Sir Havill – who doesn't count, being of a different order.

'Collan *can't* do that,' says Jack. 'Sir Priest, can he?'

'I don't know what these farmers are capable of anymore,' says Sir Nicholas. His eyes go to heaven, accusing. 'Or what they might become. These times are disordered and upended. Why not an ape in the university. Why not a pig for a judge?'

'Hear that?' John says. 'That means I can go.'

As she was meant to, the Widow Mylton fills the outline of her predecessor, John's mother.

'This is an improvement, hey?' Will says of her fragrant ale, her unburned bread, her vegetable garden, her wool-spinning, her gentle treatment of the housemaid, her laundry, her shopping at market, her sewing of undergarments, her recital of prayer.

John doesn't say anything. Loyalty is important. So while he might eat all his bowl of newly savourly pottage, and ask for more, he will not catch his dad's eye over it, and give the look that says: yes, much better.

That's *honour.*

August ends.

The harvest is on. Everyone goes out to the wheat fields, even John. They work as the sun rises until it slips out of the purple sky. Then afterwards they sit and drink ale.

Jennott is seen with a man who comes to help with the harvest. They stand under the cherry tree out of sight of the farm and the man draws a long piece of Jennott's yellow hair from under her headdress and winds it around his finger.

In the land of Oxfordshyer, writes John (privily, in case he's told to stop wasting time), *there are monsters such as loathely hairy devvils in goat shape & also fairyes who are maybe or maybe not purposinge us large evil.*

School is over for harvest – may be over forever, because John is almost ten. He asks his dad what happens to him next.

Will tells him to gather the eggs; weed the vegetable garden; go help Emma. Stop asking so many questions.

The King of France dies.

Jennott hears it first, from the man she knows. She puts a pan on her head, holds up a carrot afore her, puts black spots on her face with soot and crosses her eyes.

'Who am I?'

'A demon?' guesses John.

'Close. I'm the King of France, off to hell!'

She's been in an excellent mood lately.

Everybody thinks now that the two princes in the Tower are dead. People are noising that King Richard killed them, and yet Richard says nothing. If they were alive, wouldn't he show them? Wouldn't there be a proclamation?

He's smothered them in their beds, thrown them out of the high windows, drowned them in the moat.

Or else they escaped, but not many people believe that.

The summer heat turns very still now, as if suspended, like the moment before a ball in the air decides to stop going up and start coming down. The swifts and turtledoves are already gone; soon the swallows will disappear.

John can remember the positions of everyone in the farm the afternoon the unknown nobleman arrives.

Will Collan: ploughing with his men, small shapes in the field.

Jennott: in the dairy with the women.

The Widow Mylton: in the house.

John: up the apple tree, trying to reach the ripest fruit. From which vantage point he sees a man on horseback, coming down the track.

A nobleman, John thinks, as he approaches. Then he thinks – making out the man's plain cloak and drab hat – not a nobleman. But still: the man has an *air* of being well dressed. His countenance is both ordinary and striking: a pale brown beard and eyebrows, a long, thin jaw, penetrating eyes. He uses these sharp eyes to fillet through the land, the farmhouse, the distant men. The way a noble-man would.

And look at his horse. All its copper surfaces smooth and shining.

And his simple cloak now looks like very good wool.

And his skin is as white as a priest's.

The closer the man gets, the more confused John is, and the more adread, seized by the feeling that something is wrong in this man, who isn't one thing or another – and maybe not of the earth at all. He doesn't want the man's eyes to fall on him, peel and chop him, but he's stuck in his tree. He holds himself very still as the man passes below, and for a moment it seems like the man hasn't noticed him, but then, almost directly beneath him, the man looks up. He smiles at John.

Then he rides straight on, toward the farmhouse.

Jennott comes out of the dairy and sees the man's approach. Sarah is close behind her, mouth open, and Jennott gives her a shove. John can't hear them but he can see Jennott's mouth moving. Saying something like,

'Go fetch Will. Run, now.'

John stays in the tree, feeling suddenly unforward-coming, while his dad is fetched. Will comes out of the field at a half-run and immediately folds himself into a bow that John hasn't seen before – not for Sir Havill, not for anybody. His nose sweeps as low as it could go without Will turning himself upside down. John would do this kind of bow (scornful, overdeep) if he were mocking one of his friends but, though he can't see their expressions from here, he can tell his dad isn't japing.

The nobleman in the drab hat dismounts from his horse, revealing himself to be taller than Will, though more thinly built. He hands the reins to Will, who ties the horse up for him. Then Will Collan and the man go into the house. The man walks first, purposeful – only looking down once, as if checking the likelihood of stepping in some shit.

Once the two men pass through the door, the Widow Mylton comes out, quite quickly. As if sent out. She looks like she's not sure where to put herself next. Seeing John, she comes over to him with a look of relief.

'What's happening?' John asks her.

Jennott joins them too. She tends not to pass much time with Mistress Milky Pud, but these are exceptional circumstances.

'Yeah, what's afoot?' she asks Emma.

'He didn't tell me,' Emma says. 'By Saint Mary! I wasn't expecting anyone. Do *you* know who that man is, Jennott?'

'Some gentil fucker in poor man's clothes. Beyond that...' She shrugs.

They all stare at the copper horse, which crops the grass, keeping its counsel.

'Is it the man who buys the cheese?' John asks.

'What? Saint Peter, no.'

Which leaves John's other, deeper suspicion.

'Is it a... *fairy prince*?'

Drawn here, years later, still wroth over his stolen gold. Is Will Collan wearing any iron? Or has it been so long that he's forgotten?

'Shut up, John,' Jennott says. 'This is serious.' She frowns at the dark doorway of the farm. 'What *is* he about?' she says, under her breath.

But that question isn't answered, at least not to Jennott's satisfaction.

After a little while the man comes out of the house again, watched sidelong by Jennott (weeding the pristine vegetable garden), Emma (scattering corn for the just-fed chickens) and John (lying hidden in the long grass, clutching a horseshoe).

The man gets on his horse. He nods politely to the women. Then he rides away. His horse's hooves make the same dull thud on the track as those of any horse. Iron on mud.

Will comes out now, squinting in the sun, or frowning. It's hard to see his expression; the sun has made him into a child's drawing. Two lines for eyes, a line for a nose, a line for a mouth.

'So what were *those* doings?' Jennott says immediately.

'I've got a tutor for John,' Will says. He's increased the authority of his announcement, by making his voice louder than usual and not looking at Jennott. He squints down at John. 'A *tutor*,' he repeats. 'So that he can become a scholar and go to university.'

Speech has fled from John – how funny, when he's being offered the chance to live a life of words, that all the words he might think of have taken to the air, circling like swifts, too high to reach.

'What are you talking about?' Jennott cries. 'That's a *tutor*? That flashy turd who just trotted off on a charger that cost more than the farm? How do you propose to pay *his* rates?'

Will looks annoyed. Possibly he had expected his authoritative tone to subdue Jennott. An overlarge task for any tone.

'That's not the tutor. And it's none of your concern, but that man is John's... benefactor. A very *private* man. Very behind-doors. You understand? No jangling in the village about his visit today. So, John, what do you say? Have you turned into a post? What do you make of your future? You're a smart boy and you've got a love for books, so I thought I'd do you a good turn. But what say you? You'd rather be a dairy maid?'

One swift: caught.

'No!' shouts John.

Not a fairy, then. A man who – though he might have first seemed somehow threatening, and maybe not kindly-meaning – actually is a good man who wants to pay for John to become a great scholar, maybe even for him to travel to Cathay and write books about it. (After which, he thinks privily, he'll come back and make cheese with Jennott, because his dad will be old and John will be able to do what he wants).

His delight sparks; roars; gets so hot he can't help but hop a little.

'There we are,' says Will, patting his shoulder, looking above him at Jennott, putting weight into it. And now, remarkably, Jennott says nothing. 'A bright future! But secret for now. Remember.'

'Oh, this is remarkable!' Emma says. There are tears in her eyes. 'God has blessed John. We must give thanks!'

Jennott gives her a look that John can clearly interpret: scorn.

Then a look for his dad: suspicion.

But Will isn't looking at her, he's looking at John, smiling, and it's hard to know everything in his dad's look, the elements of it are too many; flashing by too fast: pride, doubt, affection, sorrow, triumph, and a flicker – only a flicker, but distinct enough to cool John's joy – of that old particular expression, as if Will's looking not at his son, but a stranger from a distant land.

6

In October the talk is all of the Duke of Buckingham's rebellion against King Richard. On a Sunday afternoon the men walk around the countryside — ruby, gold and amber now, the trees crowned kings — practising their archery. The duke carries them between their marks: gateposts, tree branches, stumps.

'Richard proclaimed him rebel and traitor.'

'Buckingham says the king killed the two little bastard princes.'

'I heard noise that Buckingham did it himself and blamed the king.'

'I heard the French did it, on behalf of the Tudor, Breton Henry.'

'I never heard of a Tudor before.'

'Welsh, aren't they?'

'They have nobles in Wales?'

'Any man without a harelip is a noble in Wales.'

'Isn't Breton Henry allied with Buckingham now? What's he doing?'

'On the continent, acting the twat.'

'He could end up king.'

(Laughter)

John dreams that he's lying in a field, and his dad is watching him, with the strange look he has sometimes — and then it isn't his dad, but Titivullus, his jaws stretched open to the ends of his face, and all his teeth exposed.

'John! John!' says Jennott. She's kneeling on the bed, shaking him. 'You're shouting.' She prises his hands away from his wet face. 'It's only a dream. Same thing as before?'

'Yes.'

'Listen. Just make sure you say your prayers and the demons won't get you. It's as easy as that. I promise. I've had demon visits of my own, I know all about it.'

'You do?'

'Remember when Sir Nicholas told us about the priest who had a vision of his dead mother in hell with toads and snakes hanging from her paps? As punishment for the adulterous offspring she'd nursed there? Well, I had my own night visions about that. Because I wasn't my father's child. That's why I left home. And I was sore doleful, thinking about my mother suckling toads in hell. So what I did was, I sold her things at the market, and bought enough indulgences to save her soul. And so it did. I had a dream that night that my mother was forgiven and in heaven at last.'

She kisses him on the ear; a loud noise like a thunder-crack.

'Back to sleep. And don't go telling anyone that story about my mother, or I'll put you in a churn and roll you down the hill.'

But Jennott isn't staying around to roll anyone down any hills.

She's marrying the man who wound her hair around his finger at the gate. Thomas Urry is his name.

Not that it matters, because she and Thomas are going to Southampton and John will never see either of them again, let alone call out to them on the street, *Hi, Jennott and Thomas Urry!*

The days are getting short and dark.

Jennott is going, then gone.

John can't cry womanishly about Jennott leaving, not even under the blankets. He's too old now. He asked her, before she left, why everything had to change.

It's like that morality play, she said. Men can't say no to New Guise. Not now, not evermo.

John imagines Jennott as Mercy, making her exit. Her final speech:

Listen, I've given up on Mankind: he has no need of me. But I'll give you some advice. Be a decent man. Don't fight, unless someone is really asking for it. Don't aggravate the rich. Don't try to get your hands up the girls' skirts. Unless they ask you to. Don't be a monk with one mouth and a devil with the other. Don't make bargains with people you don't understand. Don't let that goat make a cunt of you.

Got it? Good.

The problem is that Mercy is... well... not very merciful.

Though she does embrace the son of Mankind – a fierce enfolding – before she quits the stage. And over the top of his head, he thinks she might be crying.

(He can't know, because she doesn't look back.)

Buckingham is dead.

The weather undid him and he was beheaded in Salisbury marketplace.

Talk at the alehouse:

'No display of the head.'

'Well then, he got off lightly. Think what happened to Simon de Montfort, back when the Normans had the rule of us. Handless, footless, balls hung over his nose. That's what kings do when you aggravate them.'

'So what happened to Breton Henry?'

'Landed then unlanded in a hurry and gone back to the continent. Didn't even make it out of Plymouth harbour.'

'What a cock.'

'King Richard the Hog's full on the warpath now. Hear he had his dead brother Edward's mistress, Jane Shore, marched through the streets of London in her undergarments?'

'I heard. I wish I'd seen it.'

'*I* saw it. I was visiting my auntie. It started to rain and her shift was soaked through, stuck to her fine large breasts and her belly and even underparts, and you could see her dark cunt hair like a water vole.'

'She's a blonde, you lying turd.'

'Can I be tutored in Southampton?' John asks his dad. (Thinking he'd visit Jennott there.)

'What? No. You're to Oxford.'

Jennott in Southampton.

One brother in London, the other in Bristol.

His father in the village.

John to Oxford.

One night before bed Will Collan comes with a candle, to sit with John.

'For someone whose fortune is made you've looked right heavy lateward. I wonder if I've done a good thing?'

He laughs, but he looks evasive too. The evasiveness arrived earlier that autumn and settled like a light fog around him, and now his expression is always partly blurred.

'I'm very thankful,' John says. 'Thank you.'

He doesn't think his dad wants any other answer. Like: You're heavy too. Or: Why doesn't a good thing feel very good? Or: I miss Jennott, who you betrayed.

He notices Will is looking at the side of the room where Oliver and Tom's beds used to be. There's a silence. John thinks his dad is feeling the weight of absence now too, and the weight becomes not lighter but heavier.

'At Christmas I can tell them that I'm not Little John anymore,' he says.

'Christmas?'

'When they come back. Because I'm bigger now.'

His dad is silent again. Then he says, 'Little John *was* big.'

John is confused.

'Robin Hood's friend Little John was a giant man. Remember the May Day games of Robin Hood?'

'Yes. Not much. No.'

'Well, Robin Hood was a yeoman, who robbed bad noblemen and corrupt bishops and the like. And looked after the poor. That's what the ballads say.'

His eyes lift rightwise, his voice changes, and he says:

' *"Thereof no force," then said Robin*
"We shall do well enow;
But look ye do no husbond harm
That tilleth with his plough.

'*"These bishopes and these archbishops*
Ye shall them beat and bind
The high sherif of Notyngham
Him hold ye in your mind."'

Then he stops, coughs, and looks embarrassed.

John is startled and impressed, then slightly aggrieved.

'You've never recited that to me before,' he says.

'Well. Singing… poetising – all that's longwards behind me now. Ballading's for young dandelion puffs who don't know the world. There was never any Robin Hood, not like that. He would have been hung within the month. And anyone who gets money has to keep it, not give it away, because money is the only advantage any common man gets in life. And even when you get it, someone will come after you for it. But if you don't have it, you're everybody's dog. Understand?'

John doesn't understand, but it's maybe the longest conversation he and his dad have had, and he doesn't want to spoil it.

'It's late,' Will says now, getting up. Out of the wobbling range of the candlelight, his face disappears. 'Time for prayer and sleep. Ask God for favour for your dad, will you? Ask for His good grace.'

7

John tells his friends that he's going to Oxford to be tutored, and it's being paid for by a rich man.

Silence follows the news, and confusion.

'You aren't,' says Jack.

'I am.'

'Why?' asks Rolfe.

John doesn't know why. There's a silence.

'He's lying! He's been sold for a bugger's boy!' shouts Jack. 'Bugger's boy! Bugger's boy!'

Nobody takes up the chant. Uncertainty zigzags in the air. John's story is just too far out of the usual way of things. Nobody calls it truth or lie. Nobody wants to touch it at all.

'Why *is* that rich man paying for me to study?' John asks his dad.

'I told you,' says Will. 'Charity. Rich men often found schools and so on.'

'Then you were wrong. You said rich men were greedy misers. But now a rich man is paying for me to study, out of kindness.'

A flare, here, of Lollardish heat: 'It's not for kindness the rich give to charity,' Will snaps. 'It's to keep themselves out of hell.'

John is alarmed. He hadn't seen kindness in the nobleman in the drab hat. But he'd been told it was there. Given assurances.

He *needs* those assurances.

'Can fairies disguise themselves as humans?' he asks. 'And fool everybody?'

Will looks confused, and frustrated. 'Does this blaver have a point? What are you looking so pale and buckish about?'

'They won't do anything despitous to me, will they? The rich?'

'Oh. No. Don't distrouble yourself over that.'

Will rubs his face as he says it, tiredly. John feels he's been churlish then, and takes his dad's elbow.

'I'll work hard,' he says, 'I'll read many good learnings, I'll make you proud of me.'

'That's a good lad,' his dad says.

Looking, as is usual these days, uncomfortable.

John's running down the track to the farm. It's morning and the frost has turned the grass blue. White spines crystallise on twigs and leaves; fine lace threads over the dark earth of the naked fields. He can't smell the soil, or leaves, or any flowering thing, or the milky smell out of the dairy door, or the midden; he can't smell anything except frost, an absence of smell that burns his nose. His breath flies behind him in clouds.

It's the first day of December. Fifteen days until Oliver and Tom come back for Christmas and he can tell them all about his tutor, the rich benefactor; Oxford; his bright future—

—that seems nonetheless hazy, the way heaven seems hazy when you try to fix it in your closed eyes.

It will come clear in time.

Then there is the matter of the goat. This is a difficult one. In one way of perceiving it, John has mastered the goat by means of cunning.

In another way, John has won the good graces of the goat by giving it his lunch.

And so it could be said that, despite Jennott's warning, the goat has, ultimately, made a twat of John.

Maybe he'll tell it like this: the goat knows better than to mischief with me now.

Leave the rest to their imaginations.

Yes. He runs across the crackling grass, swiping at enemies with his stick. The redwings gathered on the firethorn scatter as he runs below them, clattering his stick on the trunk. Die, wretch! Villain!

Ha!

He runs past the kitchen; catches sight of the Widow Mylton and the maid in the doorway; slows. Emma is crying.

'It's just so *soon*,' she says.

John's confused, and he's more confused when he sees three strange horses tied up outside, but between the horses and the house a kind of witting descends on him: that inside the house will be answers, and inside he finds his father, standing with two men, one of whom he recognises.

It's the unlocal lord who came before. The nobleman of the drab hat. The rich man paying for John's study, to keep himself out of hell. The man who is kind – and yet still has that inquieting look about him, that sharpness of eye, like he might do something perilous, if he wanted, and he hasn't decided yet if he *does* want.

John, suddenly adread, bows very deep.

'Ah, here he is,' says his dad, shifting on his feet and looking as distroubled as John feels. 'John, this is Maister Richard Simons.'

He's not indicating the nobleman of the drab hat, but the unknown man of the two: a younger man, in his middle twenties. Though – looking closer – the nobleman of the drab hat is only about thirty himself. It's the manner of each man, not their age, that gives the sense of a great distance between the two visitors.

Nobody offers the name of the nobleman of the drab hat. He speaks without being introduced.

'So this is our boy,' he says. Not to John but to Maister Richard. His voice is medium-low and deeply gentil. The tone too dry to identify anything in it beyond dryness. 'Look at the colouring. That pale hair. The height, yes. Farmish manners, but that's to be expected given the circumstances. Skinny, though.'

'He's only ten, my lord,' says Maister Richard.

'Yes. Though I was a wide creature at ten. I was like a bookcase.'

'He'll fill into those shoulders, by the look of him.'

'Perhaps. Clarence had no shoulders to speak of.'

John, silent with fright, wonders if Jack was right and he's going to be a bugger's boy after all. He looks at his father, who is looking at the floor.

'Well then, John,' the nobleman of the drab hat says. He smiles widely, showing a foxlike number of teeth. His eyes, at least, are ordinary-looking: dark brown and human – though not reassuringly so. 'Maister Richard is a scholar and priest. He'll be taking over your education. Your father's told you about this, yes?'

'Only that, sir,' says Will.

'We can cover the rest on the way.'

There's a short silence, in which they become gradually aware of a soft, watery sound. The Widow Mylton has come in and is crying quietly behind them.

'She's of a tender disposition,' Will says quickly, 'and sees John as a son.'

'Please forgive me,' Emma says. 'I only… I'll get his things ready, in a pack.'

The younger man laughs, then, and the older one sends him a quelling glance.

'That's very kind of you,' he says to her. 'But he'll have everything he needs in Oxford. Clothing and effects more… suited to town life.'

John's alarm has kept him low and still, like a frog in a frozen pond. But at *town life* he finds a voice.

'I am to go today?'

Emma puts her hand on his shoulder, and his dad finally looks at him. But it's not the look John was hoping for, the look of good-night, son and stop daydreaming and Christmas ham and spiced cider and brothers and blind man's buff and the memory of his wife's rosemary-smelling hair.

It's the other look.

You are a stranger, says the look. *And it's time for you to go.*

Whether or not they're suited to town life, John goes to his room to get the fairy arrowhead and the little boat his brother carved for him. They rattle inside the bottom of his bag, pitiful cargo.

Will comes into the room. The look of earlier has gone and he's John's father again. Looking squashed-in and folded, like a sat-on hat.

There's a silence.

'The bag is too big,' John says, to end the silence. 'I think I'll leave it here.'

39

His dad looks confused at first, and then he goes into his own room, coming back with the soft leather purse he uses for his coins.

'Here you are,' he says. 'I'm sure you'll get a finer one. But.'

'I don't want a finer one,' John says. His fingers clench themselves on the purse.

'Well. Whatever you like. You're going to be a rich man. Do you know that? An important man.'

'Like Sir Nicholas?'

His father snorts. 'Far beyond that windy turd.'

John remembers what the man downstairs said: *like a bookcase*. He's never seen such a thing as a bookcase. He's never seen more than two books in the same room: Sir Nicholas's Bible, Sir Nicholas's *Marco Polo*.

There's something cheering in the idea of a bookcase.

'When I'm back I can bring you a fine money purse,' he says. 'And books, and other goodly things. And when I'm a man you can come with me to Cathay – even further – and I'll write my own book, *The Travels of John Collan and Will Collan His Father*. You would come, wouldn't you?'

'Sure,' his father says. There are tears in his eyes.

John's never seen such a thing. He didn't think his dad *could* cry. The sight is alarming, then lovely. Will must be passing happy to see that his son's bright future has arrived. And maybe, given the circumstances, it's not womanish for John to cry too, and so he does, gratefully.

The future, while bright, is also a little frightening. It's an inquieting thing to pass out of the bounds of the farm, out of sight of the waving Emma and his father. The men beside him terrify him. Even his horse is intimidating, as beautiful as it is. Its hooves are oiled and its mane traps the light in tiny pieces. The only reason it hasn't bucked John's grubby body off its elegant back is because it's too gentil.

(Maybe he will be allowed to keep this lovely polite horse?)

His fright only drops as they're riding through the village and he sees his friends playing in the road. They all stop and stare. Their obvious astonishment counterweighs his own. Here he is, high on his horse, unbucked, with two fine gentlemen at his side. He slows up, to give what he imagines is a lordly wave.

'Don't forget us, John!' calls Rolfe.

'I'll try not to,' John says, grandly.

'God bless you!' they shout. 'Goodbye! Good tidings!'

Except for Jack, who rolls his eyes, so John calls, 'Don't worry, Jack. When I need a turd inspecting, I'll be sure to send for you!'

And rides out of the village, to general applause.

His merriness doesn't last. When he catches up to the two men, Maister Richard is saying,

'…a proper ruffian. Left a long time on that farm. It'll be a lot of work to whittle him into shape.'

'There was no good time until now,' the nobleman says. His tone is unfriendly. The peril John first imagined embodied in his person seems more tangible now. 'If you've decided you don't want the job…?'

'Oh, no, my lord, I didn't mean it that way. I'm wonderly grateful for this privilege, I didn't mean to say—'

'Alright,' the nobleman says, clipping him short. He turns to John.

'That's enough shouting at your peasant friends. We ride quietly, understand?'

'Sorry,' John says, abashed.

'Take this.' The nobleman passes him over a flask. It's made of silver; it feels warm and living. John can see his face in it: flushed, agape, peasant-like. He closes his mouth.

'Have some,' the nobleman prompts.

He drinks. It's more savoury than anything he's ever tasted.

'Sweet wine from Greece,' says the man.

'May I have another sip?'

The nobleman inclines his head. 'See, Simons, there's that natural gentilesse.'

'Of a sort,' says Maister Richard.

'Now, John… This is the last time anybody will be calling you by that name. You *were* John Collan. Your real name is Edward, but we can't use that yet. In letters we've coded you Lambert, so we may as well stick at that. You are Lambert Simons. Understand?'

He doesn't.

'Yes,' he says.

Lambert

'There saw I first the dark imagining
Of Felony, and all the compassing' –

The Canterbury Tales,
Geoffrey Chaucer

'Good,' says the nobleman of the drab hat. 'You *don't* understand, of course, but it's good that you're tractable. So, Lambert. The truth of your birth is that you're the son of George, Duke of Clarence.'

A jape. Some strange nobleman's jape. Lambert waits patiently for them to laugh.

'You are the Earl of Warwick by title,' the man continues. 'And, after the present king and his progeny, you're next in line to the throne.'

Nobody laughs. They're both watching him, unsmiling.

'Nothing to say, Lambert?' says the nobleman.

'Maybe he's lightwitted, my lord?' Maister Richard says. 'He could have been kicked in the head by a cow.'

'Shut up, Simons. He's just astonied. Drink some more of that wine, boy. You'll find your tongue there.'

It takes a few gulps for Lambert's tongue to surface. It comes up flapping with panic.

'There's been a mistake, my lord,' he says, in a rush, 'I'm just a peasant. I'm a charity boy. I'm to be tutored. I'm not an earl—'

'But you *are*,' says the nobleman. He looks amused now, but not in a japing way, only in a tolerant way. Amusement from a height. 'Do you know anything at all about the House of York?'

'Sorry, my lord... uh, not large knowing, no.'

'Then let me explain. There are three brothers in the House of York. Edward, Richard and George. You're the son of George, Duke of Clarence. You look struck... have I lost you? You know our king is Richard, yes? Good. He's your uncle. And you know our last king was Edward? Excellent. He also was your uncle. Edward's sons, the two little princes, were your cousins. God rest their souls.'

'The princes in the Tower? They're dead?'

'Tidings move slow out here,' the man observes. 'Yes, they're dead.'

'King Richard really killed them?'

'We don't speak it that way,' the man says sharply. And here it waxes again, the feeling of peril, radiating from his tall person. 'We say it thusly: after an unfortunate illness, both boys now sit at the right hand of Our Lord. Anyway, your father Clarence was plotting against his brother King Edward, and, rightly or wrongly, he thought the king and queen were plotting against him. So, he was in fear that you'd be murdered.'

'… I?' Lambert says.

Just the slenderest of words, barely squeezed out from his compressed throat. Shock has its hard hand around his neck, lifting. His feet kick. What are they telling him? Everything he remembers and knows and *is* adds up to… nothing? Oh, little John, little John, where are you?

As dead as the two princes, apparently.

The nobleman, taking in Lambert's state with a sidewise look, calmly carries on talking. He says Lambert's father, Clarence, had spent most of his life scheming to overthrow Edward and become king himself. Clarence schemed like drunkards drink. Scheming was the marrow of his bones. And one of his schemes was to send away his infant son to live as a common boy, and raise a common boy in his place. So Clarence's men brought the baby to the Collans' farm, to live secretly there.

'A changeling,' Lambert says.

'Exactly like a changeling,' the nobleman says, smiling. 'You see, Simons. No cow hooves have belaboured *this* lad's pate. He understands all.'

(He does not.)

'Where… where is the Duke of Clarence?' Lambert asks.

'Well. Heavy tidings there. He's dead. Your mother also, in childbirth. Clarence was executed by King Edward, for excessive plotting. He was drowned in a butt of malmsey wine, by all accounts—' he sees Lambert's eyes go to the flask '—no, not *that* wine.'

'Then why are you—'

46

He wants to say *Why are you here?* but is scared to.

'Why are we here?' guesses the nobleman. 'Here now, so late? We didn't know about your existence before. King Edward claimed your father had failed in his child-swapping scheme. And, being dead, Clarence couldn't speak otherwise. We found out lateward, from one of his confidantes. And now the boy raised as the Earl of Warwick has been in place for near ten years, and you've been on this farm for nine years. Longer than anyone meant.'

'My dad – he always knew I wasn't his son?'

'You mean the farmer Collan? He knew. Blessed be God, he's an honourable man. When the instructions stopped coming, he thought you'd been forgotten aright. Some might have drowned you but he set about raising you as his own.'

'Did my mother... I mean, Mistress Collan, did she know? Did my brothers know? Jennott?'

'Collan said to me nobody knew anything about it except his own self and his late wife.'

There are tears in Lambert's eyes now. He holds fast, keeps them in. But his voice comes out quiveringly anyway:

'Then, if I'm not going to Oxford to be tutored, where *am* I going?'

'Oh, you are going to Oxford to be tutored. We have to school the farm out of you, lad. Maister Richard Simons here will be instructing you in all knowledge and manners meet for a gentil man. Now: you do not have any further questions. By which I mean, there is nothing else you can ask me that I am going to answer. How long you'll be in Oxford; what will happen after that; who am *I*, even – none of these things are your concern.'

Lambert hadn't thought to be concerned about that. His thoughts are on his family; suddenly not his family. Dark-haired father and dark-haired brothers. Pale John, the odd one out. He'd thought his mother must have been blonde. But nobody ever said she was. He thinks of the fairy gold, the fairy princeling turned upsodown. The tears come to his eyes again.

'So, Lambert, have you any words?' says the nobleman. Playful tone, warning eyes. 'No questions, now.'

'No, my lord. But... Wouldn't I know who I was, if I was... wouldn't I *feel* it? Like an earl?'

'Feelings follow the thoughts,' says the nobleman. 'Your minds are disordered at present. Calm contemplation will salve you. I recommend you reflect now, as we ride, on God's grace, His restoring you to your correct place, and give thanks for it.'

'Thank—'

'Thanks to *God*. By which I mean: in silence.'

In silence, then.

Praise God, for all the—

Thanks be to the Lord my God, for—

It isn't working.

Lambert's breath is coming in irregular little pants. Heh *heh* Heh *heh heh* Heh. Like his insides are millstones, grinding too fast, smashing the flow of air into uneven pieces. He needs to slow them by thinking quiet, serene things. But his thoughts aren't serene. His thoughts are full wild and buckish, running like:

An earl?

His dad not really his dad, brothers not really brothers.

A put-to-death father and a sham father.

Two dead childbirth mothers not remembered.

An earl?

It can't be real. It's like a ballad. Like he's been picked up and put into a ballad.

It's this idea, strangely, that calms him. The millstones slow, at last.

He's a hero, living in a neat ballad with a beginning and a middle and – no doubt – a meet end to come.

And Little John played at a yeoman
A boy raised on the farm
He went by the name of John Collan
So to come him to no harm

Though Johnny Collan was his name
'Twas Edward he went by first
And Lambert he shortly after became
To escape the old king's curse

Riding along he thinks of his dad
No Christmas with his brothers
The two mothers that he never had
never smelled the rosemary in her hair...

No.

The ballad flies out of his head, the millstones crash together, and he, the earl, has to jump from his horse and be sick by the side of the road.

2

Sim, writes Lambert. *I may have been.*
Sis. You may have been
Sint. They may have been.

May I be free of Latin grammar, is what he would write, but can't, because he doesn't know enough Latin, and so won't be free of it for some time.

Lambert's sitting by the window of Maister Richard's house. It's an unhomely-feeling place with nothing on the white-limed walls, nothing in his own room but a rough chest and a less comfortable bed than he had at the farm. Slotted in beside its neighbours, the house is long and thin, with a solar on the upper floor for his and Maister Richard's bedchambers. Downstairs there's a room for eating in, and a rear garden with a kitchen at the other end.

They live on St John the Baptist Street, which leads on to Gropecunt Lane. Their landlord, a pot-shaped man with a pink face, said that the lane is where the innocent young demosels of the city congregate in their considerable splendour. Well, there and in the maidens' chamber of Bocardo prison.

Nearly everything of what the landlord says seems to have an extra, humorous meaning that Lambert can never understand.

Prison? said Lambert.

Sometimes it's necessary to put young ladies in confinement for a spell, said the landlord. By all accounts they enjoy it. They even make their captors gifts of money as they leave, out of gratitude.

I don't see how they'd find confinement so enjoyable, said Lambert, with a shrewish side-look at Maister Richard. I find it—

Hup! Back off to your study, now, said Maister Richard. Nobody cares about your findings.

Then later, he said Lambert had better remember how to keep secrets, because secrets and heads go together. If one rolls away from you, so does the other.

Got it?

Gropecunt Lane and its mysterious inhabitants aren't visible from the window. Lambert can only see the houses opposite: Headington stone, like their own, facing him blankly. The window glass had attracted him at first, greenish and wavering in its tiny panes, like caged water. But he can't see through it properly. Shapes move in the street, never becoming quite human.

We're none of your *business*, say the shapes.

It's February now, and he sits in the cold, narrow garden of the house for so long, and so still, that goldfinches and robins come to sing in the old pear tree above his head. He saves up pieces of bread for them, but they won't hop into his hand. Then he gets wroth and flings the crusts at them and they fly away, making high alarm calls. Then tears come to his eyes. It's Maister Richard that he has a maugre against, not the birds, and now he's lost the chance of their friendship.

The answer is no, say the birds. *Stop trying.*

The answer to everything here is usually: no. Whenever Lambert has a question, Maister Richard either says no or isn't telling.

For example:

Will I see my dad – Will Collan and his sons – again?

– No.

What happens to me when my education is complete?

—Don't ask me.

Does that nobleman want me to be king?
  —Maybe.

Why would I become king when we have a king, and he has a son?
  —We don't talk about these things.

How long will I live here with you?
  —We must pray it doesn't take long.

How long is long?
  —As long as it takes.

The nobleman in the drab hat left them before they got to Oxford.
Maister Richard and Lambert passed alone through the North gate,
Lambert staring up at the great round towers, the wide bridge over
the stinking moat, the portcullis (he knows this word now, he didn't
then, it was just another fright, these teeth hanging over his head),
the vaulted tunnel – a sudden loudness under the stone, the crowd
bunched and pulsing, people crowding his horse.
  The horse was a lot calmer than Lambert was.
  Then the city enveloped them. The gabled and beamed buildings
Lambert knew – though not so many storeys, and not leaning so
far over their own foundations, over him, like a warning. The paved
streets he didn't know. Nor the sewage running in the gutters. Nor,
when he finally looked up, the—
  The *what*?
  He gaped upwards, nearly fell off the horse. Above him so many
things he couldn't name: gargoyles, grotesqueries of centaurs and
mermen and monsters, crenellations, buttressed towers, triple-ga-
bled pinnacles. Decorated spires, tiny spires on spires, like dendritic
ice crystals on glass, repeating out of sight. Why was everything so
pointed? *Should* anything be so pointed? So tall? The spires jabbing
at God Himself— *Don't!* he wanted to cry. If an angel came down
to deliver a message it could burst on the spikes.

For a moment Lambert was on top of a spire, looking down at himself, a tiny mote of hay dust. Then back in his own body, the body coming to the door of a house, stumbling in, falling up the stairs.

It didn't know stairs.

The first morning of his stay the house was silent. Maister Richard's door, opposite his own, was shut. Lambert went – carefully – down the stairs and into the hall. The fire was lit but he couldn't find the lighter of it. He sat down at the table, which had fresh linen on it. A short man with the appearance of a servant came in, smiled at him, and handed him a cup of water.

Hello, Lambert said.

The man nodded and turned away to attend to the fire.

I'm John, he said. I mean, I'm Lambert.

The man didn't turn around, so he repeated it, confused. The man, ignoring him, finished with the fire and walked toward the rear door.

Hey! Lambert said. Are you japing with me?

The man left, walking back up the garden and into the kitchen.

What's wrong with *him*? Lambert said.

He said it to himself but Maister Richard answered. He'd come down the stairs, apparently at practised speed.

He's a deaf mute, you muddy divot. He can't hear you and he can't answer.

Can he write?

No. That's the whole point. We're here on privy business. Not a word of it leaves the house.

Another question:

Can I go out to play?

—No.

Lambert still has a maugre about that one. Not the biggest of his maugres, but a small and bitter one, like an angry rat. The window, miraculously, had manifested some children. A group of five wobbly shapes running by, shouting about playing jacks in the derelict house at the end of the street.

Lambert forgot the rules about going out. He'd only been in Oxford for a couple of weeks, so rules weren't uppermost in his brain-pan. Lambert was too new a creature; it was easy to slip back into being John. So he ran down the stairs, and collided with Maister Richard at the bottom.

Where are you going?

Outside to play with those children. Can I?

It's '*May I?*' And you *may* not.

Why?

You're not here to play with town ruffians. You have a bigger purpose.

Oh, yes, Lambert said. My purpose is to be an earl. Maybe a king. Well then, I *command* you to let me play with those— argh!

Maister Richard gave him a cuff that made his vision fill with sparkles. He stumbled back. Shock and outrage overflowed him.

What the fuck? he cried. You can't do that!

Even kings have masters, Maister Richard said. And *your* master says: for as long as you're here, you keep your nose low. And no large language.

I won't be able to keep my head down if you knock it off! Lambert shouted.

At that Maister Richard laughed and made as if to hit him again. Lambert leaped back – the goat had taught him the art of the quick dodge, not that he'd admit that – and Maister Richard missed.

You hop like a little frog, he said. So hop off back to your books. And no going out without me. Got that, your grace?

Yes, said Lambert.

He went upstairs making gargoyle faces, stretching his cheek skin in monstrous grimaces, thinking about how Maister Richard was out most afternoons, and that if Lambert saw the children again there'd be nothing to stop him leaving the house – maybe even running away with them; their parents saying, *one more, why not*; and having friends again, and games every day. And if Lambert's disappearance would work Maister Richard wrack, then so much the better; if it meant Maister Richard's head got chopped off and rolled away: good. It was no more than he deserved.

3

Lambert wasn't sure if he'd remember to answer to the name Lambert, but he does, every time. What kind of soul does he have, that can tip itself out of a John Collan cup into a Lambert Simons cup without spilling a drop? The idea inquiets him.

But then there's nobody else here except the deaf mute, so when Maister Richard speaks, of course Lambert answers.

But then if someone shouted from outside, *John Collan*, he'd jump up. (*John Collan! We're sorry! Come back home!*)

Lambert can't think about John Collan. Nor his friends playing football; Emma Mylton at her sewing; his father at his work; the dairy maids making cheese; the labourers travailing in the fields; his brothers teaching him letters; Sir Nicholas reading his *Marco Polo*. Jennott with a loaf on her head – Jennott in Southampton, maybe right now throwing a pot at her new love.

He has an agreement, with himself, not to think about all that. What does thinking achieve, except to bring dole and black wroth, make him weep at the loss, make him furious at the unfairness, at his life until now being a sleight – a jape! To make him cry over the loss of his sham dad even as he feels so angry he never wants to see Will Collan again, make him long to be John even as he scorns John as a lie.

It's so *stupid*.

So when the thoughts come, he stands on his own threshold and says: You are forbid.

Though he doesn't throw away the purse Will Collan gave him, with the ship and the arrowhead inside. Maybe one day he'll see his former father again. And he can either throw the pouch at his face, with a *Fuck you, for your doubleness*, or show the pouch; make Will cry from great guilt and say, *I'm wonderly sorry, I love you as if you really were my son* – maybe cry himself, lay his own head down on Will Collan's shoulder, and forgive.

He hasn't decided.

But he bides the day.

And the thing is, this is the thing, *hoc est:* he loves the reading. He doesn't enjoy learning Latin, but he wants to read Suetonius and Ovid. And he loves the spiced buns that the deaf mute sometimes brings him, and the deaf mute's gentle smile – the sole gentleness of Oxford. And he loves history. Today they're studying Geoffrey of Monmouth's *History* and Lambert learned about Britain's first king, Brutus of Troy, who beskift all the giants from England, and then went to France and slaughtered *that* hideous race, every last one of them—

'What?' asked Maister Richard. 'Your mouth is ajar, as if about to form a no-doubt-stupid question.'

'It's just,' says Lambert. 'The French are still… *here.*'

'Clearly some of them escaped with their low cunning.'

'The knaves! What about the giants? Did any of them escape?'

'No, thank Saint Honestus. And we chased the sea monsters from our shores. If you want wizards and monsters and giants you must sail overseas.'

'Yes?'

'No! Don't look so overjoyed. You *don't* want those things. Nobody does. And you'll never go to those lands. Lord Christ in heaven, help this boy to be less dull-witted.'

But Lambert isn't listening.

He's making a plan.

He won't run away with the town children. That's a childish idea. Better to stay, and study until he's learned everything – and also eat as many spiced buns he can – and *then* run away.

He could go to Jennott in Southampton. She'd look after him until he's old enough to become England's Marco Polo. Then he'll sail the world, see the monsters and giants, and come home with divers treasures. Some for Jennott, some for himself, some to maybe buy back his former family.

He doesn't want to be Edward, Earl of Warwick. There's already an Edward, Earl of Warwick, one who was raised with the name.

Nobody ever talks about how doleful it will be for that boy to lose his whole life. Maybe it's not a true life, but it feels true to him.

Let the poor fucker keep it.

Maister Richard often goes out in the evenings to the Golden Cross. When he gets back he smells of wine, his cheeks wax rosy, and he's more inclined to answer questions.

He tells Lambert that on Christmas Day the Tudor pretender to the throne, Breton Henry, swore an oath to marry the dead king's daughter Elizabeth of York, and all the exiled English nobles pledged their allegiance to him.

'Is Henry close in line for the throne?' Lambert asks.

'Ha. King Henry V's widow had ado with a former page and bore a couple of sons she later got legitimised. It was one of those unbastardised nobodies who fathered Henry Tudor. If my boot trod in some manure from the royal stable it would have more claim to the throne than that half-Welsh, half-Breton crown sniffer.'

'But he could invade and *make* himself king?'

'Maybe… if his treacherous Breton allies don't sell him to Richard first. The continent is a spiders' nest. If he bides there too long, they'll wrap him up like a parcel and send it over.'

Maister Richard's struggling to get his boot off. When he finally unwrasts it with a yank, he nearly pitches off his chair. Lambert's encouraged to see it.

'Why hasn't King Richard killed me?' he presses. 'I mean, the me he thinks I am. You said the official Earl of Warwick was safe in a castle and that Richard put him there. Why did he murder his nephews, the two princes, to then be a friend to his other nephew?'

'Richard's under no peril from an Earl of Warwick,' Maister Richard says. He raises a hand to his mouth, to cover an escaping blast of alcohol. 'The two princes were ahead of him in succession. But as the eldest brother of the late king, he's ahead of you. As is his little son. And right now so is your cousin John de la Pole, Earl of Lincoln, because *you're* banned from the right of succession, under the terms of the attainder King Edward put on your father the Duke of Clarence for his treachery – oh, no need to look so adread. Attainders are overturned all the time.'

The attainder isn't what inquiets Lambert.

'Clarence was really so evil?'

57

'Yes, it grieves me sore to say, your true father was a marvellous knave and then he lost his wits. Obviously we all pray that you'll be different. Though that's an interesting question, isn't it? What's in the blood, and what's in the *mud*. Your inheritance is madness, your learning is peasantry. But once we've scrubbed all the dung off we'll see what you really are.'

'But what then?' Lambert asks. 'If I can't be a king, why bring me here?'

'You really don't know anything, do you?' Maister Richard marvels. 'Nobody loves Richard. His reign is wrackful and shaky. Henry will probably kill him. Then he'll have to kill Richard's son, Lincoln, and the Earl of Warwick. He can't have stray York heirs around; nobody would accept him over them, little Breton nobody that he is. Anyway, the people will make a great mourn for the dead supposed-Earl of Warwick, as they do the two princes. And that's when we bring you out: the true boy. Kill the wretch Henry. Make you king.'

'But King Richard could defeat his enemies?'

'Maybe. But certain people have decided to provide for the eventuality that he... doesn't.'

Death got King Richard onto the throne – and now they want Lambert to hop from dead man to dead man, like stepping stones, to take his place.

'I'm a provision?'

'Don't be offended,' says Maister Richard. 'A provision's better than a peasant.'

Lambert isn't offended. He's hopeful.

He prays that night for King Richard the grimly boar, King Richard the prince-killer.

'Keep our king long on the throne, so I don't have to do it, may it please you God, Holy Father, amen.'

And God listens. Lambert thinks he does, anyway. God seems to work mostly through the landlord these days.

Without the landlord, and his: *Oh, you worship at Merton? I've never seen you there?* Lambert wouldn't be sitting in this church; a place far beyond his ideas of a church: his neck straining as his eyes move over the towering stained-glass windows of glowing blue and yellow and red, the vaulted ceiling high, high above.

'She lusted after her lovers,' says the priest, 'whose genitals were like those of donkeys and whose emission was like that of horses.'

What? Lambert is startled onto earth.

'With us again, are you?' murmurs Maister Richard. 'Of course it would be the farmyard creatures that catch your ear.'

The landlord hails them outside. He, like the rest of the congregation, is talking about the former queen, Elizabeth Woodville, who had taken to sanctuary at Westminster Abbey with her daughters after her husband King Edward died, and from there had been negotiating the marriage of her daughter Elizabeth of York to the Tudor, Breton Henry. But has now come out of sanctuary, and accepted Richard's rule.

God's workings! thinks Lambert. Praise him, and his blessed emissary the landlord.

The landlord is shaking his head over Elizabeth Woodville.

'You'd think she'd be sore wroth over Richard murdering her sons,' he says, 'but she's in the pottage herself. Still, though. If my brother-in-law killed *my* children – not that I have any, my wife's barren. But you take my point. Ah, women are light-minded, aright. They change with every cock in the morning, and we love them for it. Eh, Maister? The *cock* rising in the morning…'

'Yes. Very funny,' says Maister Richard. But he looks distroubled.

Afterwards Lambert asks, hopefully, 'If the Princess Elizabeth won't marry Breton Henry after all, will Henry give up on invading and stay in Brittany? What will be done with the two of us?'

'By Saint Lawrence, enough questions!' Maister Richard says. 'You're like a buzzing fly. You don't need to know.'

So: Maister Richard doesn't know.

Spring comes. The patch of grass in their garden is greening up, studded with dandelions. There's a little blossom on the twisted-up tree, fluttering in a chill grey wind.

Lambert begs Maister Richard to take him to the market, and – miracle of God – Maister Richard agrees. They walk, dodging carts, into a great press of bakers, butchers, poulterers; reeking rows of stockfish and herrings and Winchelsea fish; woollen drapers and glovers; sellers of hogs outside St Mary's; sellers of timber and coals and brooms and earthenware; tanners; sellers of beans and eggs and peas and milk and butter and cheese. Squawkings and shoutings and grunting and yelping and, above it all:

'Oyez, oyez, oyez!'

A bell clangs.

'What's that?' Lambert asks.

'You haven't heard a town crier before?' Maister Richard says, smirking.

'...traitor Henry Tudor late calling himself Earl of Richmond... against Richard our Sovereign Lord... drawers of treasonous images will be exiled from the city and excommunicated. Plotters of treason will be executed. Supporters of Henry Tudor will be hanged, drawn and quartered. ... recommended to visit the Swindlestock, for the best wines in the city...'

'What's a treasonous image?' asks Lambert of Maister Richard.

But there is no Maister Richard; the crowd has shoved in and Lambert has been transported sidewise. In the priest's place is a man who proves himself an improvement on Maister Richard by smiling kindly at Lambert, and addressing himself to the question.

'Well, it's anything painted on the walls or doors or whathaveit, against the king. Like how twenty years ago they excommunintated those students for drawing gallows on King Edward's royal arms. A lot here misliked him. This isn't a Yorkist town. Not that *I'm* against the Yorks. I personally don't give a gnat's shit. Richard came here last summer and reduced the fee farm, which is better than his brother ever did. Which, I say—'

But now Maister Richard comes, bows to the man, takes hold of Lambert and walks him quickly away.

'Why did you do that?' Lambert cries. 'He was wonderly full of good learnings. Why can't I talk to people?'

'I thought the rules on talking to people were obvious,' Maister Richard says. 'But if you really are this slim-witted, I'll lay them out. No. Talking. Or. Else.'

'But you let me talk to the landlord. And *you* talk to strangers.'

'Those are false equivalences,' says Maister Richard.

Which is the end of it, because Lambert doesn't know what a false equivalence is.

On the walk back he notices abandoned buildings and empty plots; the crumbling city walls, the ivy-leaved toadflax taking hold in the stone. The landlord said that Oxford used to trade in wool, but now the only successful industries are those that keep the university fed with books and beer and so on. The only building work is the expansion of the university's colleges and halls: a noise that only quiets on Sunday, an ever-present stone dust that coats their windows white.

Knowledge is the new power.

Lambert *wants* that power. But right now Maister Richard has it all, and he leaves no scraps.

In his own world, Maister Richard is the best of men. Handsome, learned, gentil. He takes a long time choosing clothes. He never met a mirror he didn't like. He is an admittedly goodly-enough-looking man, though his face is narrow and his eyes are too close together, like his head's been pinched in sidewise. In terms of intelligence, Maister Richard hasn't ever found anyone he couldn't place below him in some way. Aside from the nobleman in the drab hat. But Maister Richard doesn't talk about him.

Lambert doesn't know enough yet to argue with Maister Richard. His life hasn't prepared him for it. At the farm nobody debated. His dad did things. Jennott threw things. The goat knocked him down.

But – unlike with Gaspard – here Lambert fancies his chances. He'll study, and study, and one day he will acquire enough learning to humble and defeat the priest.

It's only later that Lambert thinks to ask: 'Why was the crier making that proclamation?'

'King Richard is frightened. His only son is lateward dead,' says Maister Richard. He squeezes his thumb and fingers together like a crab claw. 'His line has been pinched off.'

Lambert prays to God again for better fortune for King Richard – thinking as he prays about all the other people who will be praying, maybe at this same moment, for Henry's victory.

How does God choose who to listen to? Or does He do what He was going to do anyway? In which case – Lambert hesitates to think it, but here comes the thought anyway:

… *why pray?*

Instead:

'Dear God, please, if it isn't forbidden to ask, what exactly do You *want*?'

4

Unfortunately, the rest of 1484 passes without Lambert working out what God's up to. In June Brittany agrees a truce with King Richard, as part of which Brittany promises to stop supporting Henry Tudor and his invasion plans. Henry, full knowing the peril he's in, pretends to go out hunting, then escapes from Brittany to France. There he is welcomed by the new boy-king Charles VIII, who promises him help invading England.

Is this God's will? Lambert thinks, terrified.

But then Christmas comes, the former queen Elizabeth Woodville and her daughters are honoured guests at King Richard's court, and Maister Richard says, frowning, 'In no wise will Edward's daughter Elizabeth of York marry Breton Henry now. Richard will send her off to a continental prince.'

This must be God's will, Lambert thinks, and his heart lightens – until he remembers there has been good news before, waxes overwrought, and cries out, 'It's just good news after bad, after good, round and round.'

'Why, you're right,' Maister Richard says, looking comforted. 'By the Saints, maybe you're becoming a wise boy at last. And full worship to me, 'tis my work that has done it.'

The new year arrives, and Maister Richard announces that as Lambert has mastered simple Latin composition, they'll be moving on to Horace, which comes next in the curriculum. This isn't true. Horace is just his favourite poet. Maister Richard sees himself as a newfangled Horace: a writer passed over by Fortune in favour of vulgar merchants and peasants-on-the-rise. 'There's no meed in this world for sensitive men of minds,' he claims. 'What a fell state of things, when great scholars and poets go without land and money. Hence how I find myself here, tutoring *you*.'

'You were at university, weren't you?' Lambert asks. 'Why didn't you show your writings to the famous scholars?'

Maister Richard looks down then. An expression of intense dole comes into his face. He says something about old dotards being scared of original thinkers, but it's so quiet Lambert can hardly hear it.

Lambert feels sorry for Maister Richard then. He looks smaller, and less dislikeable.

'You could write satire, like Horace,' he says.

'I *should*,' Maister Richard says, waxing brighter. 'That would rattle the ancient skeletons of the establishment. By God, I'd poke my fingers up all their fundaments!'

Lambert, caught up in the sudden good cheer, exclaims, 'Maybe I could write a Horatian satire too!'

Maister Richard laughs. 'Asking *you* to write something Horatian would be like expecting a weasel to dance a rondelet,' he says. (Lambert, who has been reading at night about rhetorical devices, recognises this one as *diasyrmus*: the ridiculous simile. He feels a small triumph.) 'And who would you even write about?' Maister Richard continues.

Lambert hasn't thought about that. He casts about now for an idea. 'Well, if a finger ought to be stuck up someone's arse, why not King Richard's?'

He's thinking of the poem that was posted on a church door in York last summer, and more recently, in Oxford and other towns:

The cat the rat and Lovell our dog
Are ruling all England under a hog

'You cheese-headed doorpost,' says Maister Richard. '*Think*. Who did Horace satirise? Disgusting old women, jumped-up freedmen, light-minded mistresses. He couldn't satirise his betters: it would have been the death of him.'

'But that's not fair!' Lambert says.

'Not fair? You think people should criticise someone set above them by birth, sex and nobility? By God Himself? It's for the wise noblemen to criticise the low people. And those people ought to reflect on their ill-demeaning, and be grateful for the learnings.'

'What if a nobleman is sinful and a peasant is good?'

'Those equal to or above the nobleman must be the ones to deal with him.'

'So!' cries Lambert. 'I can write what I want, because I'm noble by birth.'

'Not yet, you're not. Until history takes your part, you're just an unknown lusk with a sore head.'

'Sore head?'

But of course: the book catches him on the side of the pate.

'That's for getting ahead of yourself,' says Maister Richard.

Lambert feels the wroth of injustice roaring up in him. Wickedness! Knavery! This is not how books are meant to conquer!

He let Maister Richard outwit him, that was the problem. Next time he'll leave no opening in his arguments, and Maister Richard will be too cowed and ashamed to so much as lift his hand.

But that's next time. This time, he has to finish his study, then let Maister Richard take close hold of him and teach him dance steps, the weasel learning its rondelet.

'Two steps, two steps – no, not that way, you plodding country cowpat!'

Later that day, Lambert is trying to study – ignoring the dole that's drawn in, dark and close – when the deaf mute comes in. Lambert raises his hand in welcome, but his face won't lift itself properly, or make a convincing smile, and the deaf mute looks concerned. He comes over and puts a spiced bun on the table. Then he touches Lambert's shoulder – so quickly, and so hesitatingly that Lambert only realises what's happened when the hand is gone.

'Thank you,' Lambert says, bowing. He feels churlish now to be sitting here so heavy when the deaf mute has far worse mischance to be dealing with. He wonders if he can do something good for him.

He gestures to the books on the table and tries to mime the suggestion of teaching the deaf mute to read. The man looks confused.

Lambert writes a few letters, as a demonstration. The deaf mute smiles approvingly and nods. Lambert holds the quill out to the deaf mute – and now the man looks startled, taking a step back.

'What *are* you doing?' Maister Richard says, coming into the room. 'Writing lessons? By Christ, do I really have to explain this to you? He hasn't got time for that: and if he did, what do you think you'd achieve? His value is in his silence. You'll teach him straight out of a job and he'll end up a beggar. You arrogant boy! You should think of someone beyond yourself.'

Lambert feels a moment of wroth, but then: shame.

It's true, it was his own sadness that moved him. He wanted to teach the deaf mute to read so that he, Lambert, could have a friend.

5

It's spring.

Oyez, oyez, oyez!

King Richard's beloved wife, the Queen Anne, is dead! Seers say Henry Tudor's murder expected before Rogation day!

Townsfolk:

rumoured poisoned by Richard, rumoured got out of the way so Richard could marry his niece, the beautiful Elizabeth of York, lateward promised to Breton Henry. The poor Queen Anne! The poor York girl! No, she's a wily girl, just like her Woodville mother, fucking her way up to the mountain top – though she should watch out, *circa regna tonat* and all that, and there's a lot of thunder around these days.

Oyez, oyez, oyez!

King Richard has stated before the Lords and London City Councillors that he in no wise purposes to marry his niece! Anyone spreading such slanders will be imprisoned! King Richard pursuing a marriage with the sainted Joana, sister of the Portuguese King Alfonso! Elizabeth of York to marry King Alfonso's nephew and heir! Seers give Henry Tudor less than a week!

Townsfolk:

oho, he denies this, so why didn't he publicly deny killing the princes, then? Because he smothered them in their beds, the poor little lads. And where's all our money going? He's no different from his brother. We're being pressed like cider apples to pay for his campaigns, and he hasn't even managed to kill Breton Henry. So he sent that York harlot away to a Northern castle, so what? He can visit her there to play at couple their navels. No, no, she's a victim of his evil. No, a whore. We haven't decided on that one. Come back to us.

Oyez, oyez, oyez!
   Regard, townsfolk, this letter from the king!

Be warned, you divers seditious and evil persons in London and elsewhere within our realm, who enforce themselves daily to sow seeds of noise and dislander against our person, to abuse the multitude of our subjects and avert their minds from us, some by setting up bills, some by spreading false rumours, some by messages and sending forth of lies, some by bold and presumptuous open speech and communication.
   The king did not kill his wife!

Townsfolk:
   Well, he would say that, wouldn't he?

'Did Richard really murder his wife?' Lambert asks.
   'He's a murderer aright, but he didn't murder her,' Maister Richard says. 'The noise from above is that she was distroubled in her health. Anyway, he had no reason to kill her. He can't marry your cousin Elizabeth of York, the common people would tear him apart. He's not so stupid. I wish he were. Right now everybody mislikes him, but nobody cares enough to beskift him… by Saint Isidor! This is wonderly bad for us. Henry Tudor's been pulling his pizzle so long in France that the French King has lost interest. If Henry can't get private loans to fund his invasion, that's it for us. No King Henry to overthrow. It's a disaster. If Richard has no more children, he'll pass the throne to your cousin Lincoln – or even your double, the supposed Earl of Warwick. And nobody will require you then.'

Lambert is overjoyed. His plan to:
1. Finish his learning
2. Humble and make a mock out of Maister Richard
3. Go to Jennott at Southampton
4. Set sail for adventure
is exactly on track.

Maister Richard is in a warly mood though, so he hides his smile.

At night he keeps on with his reading, sitting in bed with a candle and a stolen bun, a book propped in front of him on the bolster, accruing greasy fingermarks. Feeling not quite happiness. Happiness seems like something that fell behind him before he realised he had it.

But the books do what they can. They distract him from his memories; keep him from womanish tears; graciously pour their good learnings into his brain-pan – and when they're done, he'll get on a cart and go, and be happy again.

Summer in Oxford is ripe, and rancid. The breeze that rolls around the surrounding hills doesn't stir the city. Every smell sits still, occupying its own parcel of air. The blood of the shambles, the climbing roses and herbs in the gardens, bakery yeast, hot leather. They avoid Fish Street after noon, and the streets without covered gutters. Sewer-odour and manure claim St John the Baptist Street. To escape it, Lambert sits in the small shade in the garden, under the pearless tree. Purple foxgloves poke up, bees buzzing inside them. The walls shut out some of the town noise. If he closes his eyes it feels almost like ~~home~~ the farm owned by Will Collan.

Don't think of that.

He opens his eyes. Maister Richard is standing in front of him.

'Breton Henry is landed,' he says.

Really?

But the town crier says: yes, really. Arrived at Milford Haven, with hired mercenaries, recruiting the Welsh as he goes.

Maister Richard says, 'About time.' Then he does a dance, his thin calves flashing. One! Two! Hey! Ho! 'I'm going to be rich!'

Lambert can't dance. He feels too sick.

'If Henry wins, it won't be long before I quit here for London, where I'll be known at last! I will be taken into the hearts of the people, and my family will be wonderly proud to own me, and my writings will bring me large fame,' Maister Richard says. There are tears in his eyes.

'Where will *I* go?'

'To Europe, of course.'

'Europe? Why? Where?'

'Burgundy. You have an aunt there. One of the York sisters.'

'Is she kind?'

'She's a duchess. I don't know that kind or not kind is of any significance.'

Breton Henry and King Richard are marching to battle. Maister Richard goes into town every day to hear the latest happenings.

It's too hot to get too excitable, seems to be Oxford's view on the matter.

And who the fuck is Henry Tudor anyway?

War rolls into Leicestershire, two counties up, makes a brief noise, then disappears. What was the noise? The wind didn't carry it. The hooves, the cannons, the whistling arrows, the trumpets and the swords swapping off heads. Lambert imagines it as the sound of the deaf mute's clanking tin bucket, multiplied thousandfold.

The news comes:

King Richard has been killed at the Battle of Bosworth Field by a halberd to the head, slicing through the helmet and the brain-pan; his body stripped naked, tied, slung over a horse, stabbed again in the back and buttocks, then carried off to be displayed at the Franciscan Friary.

Later, Maister Richard has more detail, from the man who brings him his money.

He says that Henry's stepfather Lord Stanley stayed away from the fight until it was clear Henry was the victor. After which, his troops thrang in, killing the fleeing and defeated men.

That Richard shouted, 'This day I will die as a king or win!' and charged into the press, toward Henry. Not seeing the marsh, which took his horse. Fighting on regardless. While Henry stayed back behind the lines, dismounting from his horse and hiding behind his men so nobody could see him.

'A battle won on holding off and hiding,' says Maister Richard. 'They should knight the bog.'

Henry's men go over the battlefield looking for corpse-treasure. They find Richard's crown in some bog mud and blood, and carry it off to be cleaned up and put on the head of King Henry Tudor.

Lambert is in a panic. He didn't want any of this. And yet his destiny is approaching, one death at a time. First Richard was killed. Now Lambert will be expected to kill Henry. Can he imagine that? No: his brain won't stretch itself around it. But he's sore adread anyway.

He thinks about his real father and mother, the Duke and Duchess of Clarence (dead); King Richard his uncle (dead); Richard's son his cousin (dead); King Edward his uncle (dead); the two princes his cousins (dead). He can't imagine any of them, either. But he can't help but notice they're all dead. As with fairies, their world seems to run on a lot of gold and a lot of peril.

Maybe Lambert can't go back to the farm, but he can't enter the land of the fairies or he'll never get out alive.

What can he do?

Praying didn't work. And God's wishes are inscrutable. Does he want Lambert to kill Henry? Surely not. Not more killing. No. What God probably wants is for Lambert to run away. Like Lot, or Moses. Yes! Running away is exactly what Lambert wants too.

Blessed be God!

The only problem is that Lambert needs money to pay for his passage out of Oxford, and he doesn't know where Maister Richard keeps it.

He creeps downstairs late one night, hoping to collect enough pewterware to sell then slip out – but there's a sound by the door; a moving shape in the darkness. The deaf mute, on a mattress roll. Lambert stops still. The deaf mute gets up and smiles at him, questioningly. Then he looks comprehending. He puts his fingers to his lips and goes to the table, where something is wrapped in cloth. He picks it up and offers it to Lambert.

It's a spiced bun.

Which Lambert has to accept, with thanks, and take back up the stairs with him, to bed.

6

At the start of September, King Henry VII arrives in London, welcomed by trumpets. His hand is kissed by officials; in St Paul's Cathedral he gives thanks for his victory. There are pageants and celebrations in the streets – the like of which haven't been seen for a full two years, Maister Richard says sarcastically.

When Elizabeth of York arrives in London, summoned from the Northern castle where she and her cousin the Earl of Warwick had been put for safekeeping, there's no state welcome, and no celebrations.

Lambert asks, 'Does Henry have a maugre against her because she was overfriendly to dead King Richard?'

Maister Richard says, 'More likely, Henry doesn't want it said that it's through the old king's daughter alone he has the right to rule.'

People say it, though.

High and low, they say it everywhere.

Lambert hears in town what happened to King Richard's favoured nobles. Ratcliffe was killed on the field. Catesby was executed after the battle. Nobody knows where Lovell is. Henry's confiscated the estates that made Lord Lovell one of the richest and most puissant men in England, but he can't lay hands on their former owner. The criers noise large reward money for his capture.

Lambert thinks of the poem that satirised the four men who ruled all England. Now the hog is dead, the cat is dead, the rat is dead, the dog is lost.

Not that Lovell was ever a dog. He was named for the wolf of his heraldic arms. Lambert imagines a wolf moving alone across England, at leisurely speed, impossible for hounds to catch.

It moves him; his thoughts follow the wolf at night: below the moon, over hills, in and out of trees, along rivers…

To freedom.

Lambert wonders if he can use his new learning to convince everyone that his life would be better spent as an unknown lusk, and not an earl. He opens the debate with a question for Maister Richard:

'Am I supposed to take the crown from Henry by violent means?'

'Oh, no, I'm sure he'll hand it over full apologetic,' Maister Richard says, smirking. 'Don't be an ass.'

Lambert allows himself a moment to imagine an ass treading on Maister Richard's narrow head. Then he says, 'But to take it by force is civil war. And Geoffrey of Monmouth's *History* said God punished the Britons with plague and famine after King Arthur died, because of their habit of warring amongst themselves – and Horace also despises civil wars, and says, "shame on our scars, our crimes".'

'Horace meant the previous war,' says Maister Richard, looking irritated. 'That was what set things wrong, the murder of Julius Caesar. He didn't mean Augustus' war, which was necessary to put things right. The last but one war was the wrong cause. The most recent was the right war. Got that?'

Lambert doesn't get it. Confused, he loses his original point.

'So it's the person who wins the last war that's right?'

'Yes, and this will be you because God has chosen you.'

'Did He choose Henry?'

'May He forgive you for thinking it! God would never choose such a knave.'

'But doesn't God choose everything?'

'No! We men have free will. Isn't that enough questions?'

'Why does God choose some kings and not others? Why wouldn't he make sure we only have good kings? How can we have free will but God also chooses kings?'

'By the saints, I don't know what to do with you!' exclaims Maister Richard. 'You're questioning God now? Are you telling Him he's made mistakes? *Committed crimes*? Are you calling on God to face trial? Is that it: heresy? Or are you just stupid? Well, which is it? Stupidity or heresy?'

'Uh… stupidity?'

'That's a shame. Stupid people don't get *Le Morte d'Arthur*.'

The tales of King Arthur – knights, sorcerers, quests, beautiful demosels, heroic battles, giants, jousts, beautiful demosels – have lateward been printed. The book is in high demand. Lambert has been begging for a copy for weeks.

'Heresy then,' he says quickly.

Maister Richard laughs. 'Heretics get burned.'

Lambert, outdone, makes a grimly face behind Maister Richard's back. He imagines Maister Richard being burned. But no – he mislikes the thought: it's too cruel. Something gentler then, like putting Maister Richard into a barrel and rolling him into the sea.

Yes. That's fitting.

It's a warm September day, and they're out on a walk. Maybe the deaf mute has told Maister Richard, with gestures, that Lambert was creeping about at night, because Lambert is never alone now. When Maister Richard goes out at night, the deaf mute is by the door. When Maister Richard goes out in the day he takes Lambert with him, close by his side.

At least Lambert gets to walk. He enjoys being under the sky, waiting now beside Maister Richard at the pie shop; shutting his eyes briefly, listening to horses' hooves thudding, dogs barking, the shouts of market stall holders and food sellers, children playing football, men playing pike-staff, people playing tennis on illegal courts, masons striking stone, people laughing, animals on Slaying Lane bellowing and shrieking, carts clonking. And a voice:

'Richard!'

Maister Richard looks suddenly panicked. He doesn't look to see where the voice came from. He throws his money down, snatches the pies, takes a fierce hold of Lambert's arm and pulls him down the street, shoving past ladies and old folk, hieing in the direction of their house.

'Ow,' Lambert cries. 'My arm! Why are we going so fast?'

Maister Richard doesn't answer. He rushes on. Lambert, stumbling on the uneven ground, looks behind them. There's a lady coming in their direction, nearly as fast as they're travelling. Her eyes are hard on Maister Richard's back, full of wrothful intent. Lambert catches fright at her expression.

'She's after us!' he squeaks.

They run around a corner and then another, leaving the woman behind. They're on an unfamiliar, empty street. Lambert, reeling his breath back in, realises it's Gropecunt Lane.

He's delighted. He looks around for the famous maidens of the lane, wondering if they might offer him and Maister Richard sanctuary; give him wine and cakes, let him listen to their sweet singing. But everywhere is deserted, the buildings divided into motionless light and dark blocks by the flat midday sun.

'Come on,' Maister Richard says, towing him on.

'Who *was* that?' Lambert asks, as they reach St John the Baptist Street and their own door. 'Was she coming to kill us?'

'What?' Maister Richard says. He's out of breath, but he manages a little laugh. 'No, Lambert. Just me.'

Then he starts, and makes a squawking noise.

'Bella!' he says. 'What, er… what cheer?'

The lady emerges from a group of friars, pushing through them. She's young and thin and full of unknown maugre.

'What cheer?' she says. '*What cheer?* A family, is it? This is your son? You have a wife in there too? So this is why I couldn't come to your house?'

'Go inside,' Maister Richard says to Lambert.

'You lying, dishonourable knave,' the woman continues, her volume rising.

Lambert, now that his life isn't in danger, is inclined to tarry and hear what other fell words the lady has to say about Maister Richard, but a shove to his back sends him inside, and Maister Richard closes the door behind him.

Later, Maister Richard explains that the lady, Bella, who is in fact a housekeeper, is going to be at their house sometimes, and Lambert is to stay out of her way.

'What about the deaf mute?' he asks, worried. 'Where will he go?'

'The deaf mute will bide with us. Bella is an… additional help. It's important that the people who pay me know that's all it is. And she doesn't know the truth about you. Like the landlord, she believes that I am a chaplain currently without a living, supported by a modest stipend from my family. And that you are my illegitimate child, come from Reading, taken on by me after the death of your mother, out of my own tender charity.'

'But she said you were a lying knave,' Lambert says. 'Why would she work for you?'

Maister Richard shifts. He looks inquiet. 'Bella didn't know that I had a child as my ward. She was, uh, distroubled at the idea.'

'Because of having to do more housework?'

'Yes.'

Lambert smiles, remembering it. 'You were sore chidden,' he says.

Looking forward, privily, to more chidings to come. Anything that puts Maister Richard at a disadvantage is a joy to Lambert.

7

Maister Richard's instructions when it comes to Bella are not illuminating. In fact, he darkens the matter, and from the darkness comes mislike.

Firstly, Bella isn't a housekeeper of any sort that Lambert understands. She only comes in the evenings, and quits them in the morning. And she doesn't do any work.

Secondly, it's impossible to stay out of her way. The house is not big. It's only a day before Lambert encounters her, leaning on the table in her shift in the lemon-grey light of the morning, her coarse brown hair down round her shoulders, eating a piece of chicken. He bows and greets her. She doesn't answer.

'Are you a deaf mute now too?' he asks. 'Is it usual for town housekeepers not to wear anything on their heads? May I have some chicken?'

Bella blinks at him. She has a pretty face and large, wide-spaced eyes. The eyes are not friendly.

'I see what he means about mannerless,' she says, to a point beyond Lambert. He turns around, but there's nobody there. She continues, speaking again over his head: 'A motherless hedge-egg, presuming to mock *my* position!'

Maister Richard comes quickly down the stairs then, and takes Lambert upstairs.

'I told you to leave Bella alone,' he says.

'But she's in the way of the food,' Lambert says, sensing opportunity. 'I just wanted some chicken.'

'You stay up here until I've said goodbye to Bella,' Maister Richard says.

'She's leaving? Why isn't she dressed? What sort of housekeeper *is* she?'

'The priest's sort. Now stop asking questions, I need to go down and sort this out before I have to buy her a present.'

'So can I—?'

'Yes. Devil take you, let me go smooth this and then you can have your chicken.'

Lambert's writing a Horatian ode: mostly because Maister Richard said it was beyond him. He writes it hudder mudder, then leaves it out by mistake, and comes downstairs to see it suspended between the thumb and finger of Maister Richard.

'What,' says Maister Richard, 'is *this*? A flaxen-haired goddess on a *milking stool*? You've compared a dairy farmer to Jupiter? And what on earth is "Gaspard the noble foe"?'

Lambert, alive with shame – and in danger of shameful tears – jumps up to try to wrast the paper from Maister Richard.

'But poetry is meant to glorify—'

'Not to glorify *peasants*, you donkey! It's against the natural order! As Geoffrey of Monmouth says: easier for a kite to be made to act like a sparrowhawk than for a wise man to be fashioned from a peasant. And *you've* fashioned them into gods!'

He throws the poem into the fire.

Jennott, Will, Tom and Oliver – the peasants – collapse into soot.

Lambert's own anger flares, drying up his tears. He says, 'But Horace *wasn't* a noble. He says himself, he's of *the blood of poor parents*. And Suetonius says Horace's father was a freedman. Horace was born low.'

Maister Richard blinks. His eyes become very small.

'Suetonius?' he says. 'You've been doing extra reading, have you? Well, you probably translated it wrong.'

'Show me then, where I got it wrong,' Lambert says. He hears his own cool tone, and is passing impressed with it. 'Go on. We'll see who the donkey is.'

There is a silence. They stare at each other. *You* are the donkey! thinks Lambert, exultant. I am the wise man!

I win!

Then Maister Richard says, 'Well! I don't have time to quarrel with a child in a tantrum.' He picks up his hat, performs a leisurely, artificial-looking stretch. 'I'm meeting Bella at the Fleur de Luce. You may continue your studies alone, as seems to be your pleasure. Oh,' he adds, from the doorway, with a smile, 'I almost forgot to tell you. I couldn't lay hands on the *Morte d'Arthur*. But I'll get you more Latin grammar instead, by way of apology.'

This is when Lambert realises: knowledge may be power, but *power* is power. And he has none of it.

The people with power have only used it to work him wrack. Will Collan had power, and he lied, and sent Lambert away. The nobleman of the drab hat had power, and he left Lambert imprisoned in Oxford with Maister Richard. Now Maister Richard – a dullard, a fathead – has power over him. It's unfair; it's unjust. When Lambert runs away, he hopes they all run around sore adread, looking for him, to make him do things, make him be Lambert Simons or Edward, Earl of Warwick – but they'll never find him because he'll be gone.

Gone!

On account of Bella and Lambert having got off on an evil foot – through no fault of Lambert's – when she sits opposite him at dinner, she doesn't look at him. Actually, no: when Lambert's not looking at her, she looks, and looks long. He tests her by glancing up suddenly, catching her eyes sliding off him. Then for as long as his head is up, her gaze moves freely over everything but him. It's as if there's a gap in the scene, and Lambert sits neatly in that gap, invisible, like a mouse in a crack in the wall.

He squeaks, and she jumps.

'Richard!' she says. 'He's *squealing* at me.'

'It was a squeak,' Lambert says. He squeaks again.

'Well, don't,' says Maister Richard. 'Or you leave the table.'

There are lamb and mint pies from the cookshop on the table, and wine. (Bella doesn't cook, and she doesn't like to have the deaf mute cook, or even be around him: she says he's ghoul-like, he must have done something bad to be punished this way by God. So Maister

Richard gets dinner from the cookshop.) Lambert lays off squeaking. But he's still wroth about the loss of the *Morte*, so he adds a 'Sorry, Daddy', is rewarded with a furious look from Maister Richard, and is full delighted with himself.

'It's funny how your son looks nothing like you,' Bella says to Maister Richard.

Lambert finds her tone strange.

'He's the sib of his mother, God rest her,' says Maister Richard.

'Mother looked like an angel,' says Lambert. 'That's why my face is fairer than Daddy's. And my hair is thick, where his is thin.'

'That's enough about her, and you,' Maister Richard says, eyes a-slit.

Lambert eats his pie with satisfaction. He's thinking about power again. And how things have shifted, a little, since Bella got here.

8

In autumn the sweating sickness comes to Oxford. The noise is that Henry's mercenaries brought it with them from France, and now there's hardly anyone left in London. Lambert stays at home. Maister Richard goes out with cloth wrapped around his face, and burns herbs. The air is thick with rosemary smoke, lavender smoke. Henry's Coronation is delayed.

The landlord and his wife catch it, and his wife dies. The land-lord survives, and becomes a subdued man. His humorousness is all sweated away. He says he thought he would die too; his limbs all aching, his head battered by demons, his body trembling. He thought in his fever that he might go to hell; his first act when he could walk was to seek out the pardoner, but the pardoner was dead.

The official Edward, Earl of Warwick had been sent to live with King Henry's mother Margaret Beaufort after King Richard's defeat. But people had started wearing his badge conspicuously, and there was talk of his being the true York heir. It wasn't long before he was put into the Tower of London, for security.

'Praise be to heaven,' says Maister Richard. 'This is a good thing for us.'

'Will he be alone there?' Lambert asks. 'What will he do? Will he have friends?'

'The ghosts of your cousin princes will keep him company,' Maister Richard says, merrily. 'Before long he'll probably join them.'

Henry is crowned in October.

Townsfolk:

God save the king! Or not, who cares? It's a good excuse for a party though, isn't it? God save the party! We dance in the streets and sing and some of us take it too far, as usual. There's a drawing of Henry on a wall, holding his own cock.

Nobody to hold it for him aright.

Why won't he marry poor Elizabeth of York? God's bones, what a miserable cunt he is.

Here we go: oyez, oyez, treasonous drawings of the king will be punished. Yeah, yeah, we know.

They hauled off an out-of-town butcher, Cox, for painting a York rose.

What about the little Earl of Warwick, stuck in the tower? What if Henry kills him privily, the way Richard killed his cousins the princes?

That lad Warwick is the rightful king.

He is aright, he's got the claim. But I'm fucked if I'm going to war over it.

On Sunday the priest at Merton tells the worshippers about a priest who sees a vision of his dead mother in hell tormented by toads suckling at her breasts; snakes biting her sinful lips.

'How do they know that story?' Lambert asks Maister Richard. 'That happened to a priest Sir Nicholas knew.'

'Sir Peasant,' says Maister Richard. 'And it didn't. This is how exempla work. They aren't written by the priests. There are books of them. This story is from Bromyard or Anglicus.'

'Exempla?'

'Stories warning of the evil consequences of sin.'

Lambert doesn't hear any more exempla, because they stop going to Mass. The congregation at Merton have always alarmed Maister Richard with their '*What cheer?*'s and '*New here?*'s. Then, last week, someone didn't say anything, but sat in the pew behind and watched them for much too long.

God will forgive me, Maister Richard said. Henry's spies are lateward everywhere. Church is important, but not dying is more important.

'Are there any exempla about people looking… at things they shouldn't?' Lambert asks Maister Richard.

'What?' he says. 'I don't know. Why?'

'Never mind.'

Two nights ago Lambert looked at something he shouldn't.

He was curious about the sounds coming from Maister Richard's chamber. So he stood outside with his eye to the gap between the door and the frame, and he saw Bella on her hands and knees, Maister Richard behind, gripping her reddened buttocks; the priest's own bottom – flat and somehow mournful-looking – jolting back and forth.

Maister Richard was asking: how big?

And Bella said: oh, it's so big, it's shockingly big, I think it might tear me in half. (Making yelps and cries, to illustrate the point. At which Maister Richard's bottom picked up speed, and Lambert thought this was slightly *overmuch*, because he'd seen Maister Richard dressing and the priest has a very little penis, compared to some Lambert saw back in the village – where he also picked up from Jennott that if there's one thing a woman doesn't like it's a teeny peeper.)

Lambert knew that he shouldn't be watching. But he didn't move. The glimpses of the place between Bella's thighs held him there – a sight beyond his previous imaginings: dark, wet hair, livid pink, folded lobes – until he became aware of his own shameful condition; the consciousness of sin bore down him, and he ran back to his own bed, clutching his hose-front.

God doesn't strike Lambert down immediately.

His punishment is more obscure, maybe more fitting. God arranges it so that one evening Lambert, running suddenly upstairs to his room, nearly collides full-body with Bella, who is herself hieing *out* of Lambert's room and toward Maister Richard's.

Bella looks alarmed. 'I was looking for Richard,' she says. Though they both know that Maister Richard had gone out ten minutes ago to get wine. Later, Lambert notices that the papers on his desk – his scholarly readings and writings – are disturbed and out of order.

His first feeling is fright. Could Bella have looked under his mattress? Where lies an exemplum of Lambert's own writing, about a boy who spied to satisfy his lusts, and ended up in a hell in which demons plucked out his eyes and toasted them on the fire. But he doesn't think she'd have had time to discover it.

Thought the second: why *would* Bella search Lambert's room?

Did she see him looking at her, that night – and decided to look back? In which case, full worship to her for coming up with the perfect revenge. Curiosity stings him head to toe, like a thousand nettles.

He puts hairs and crumbs on his piles of paper in the days after – and on several occasions finds them disturbed. At dinner he watches her, inquiet, but here all is as usual: she refuses to so much as look at him.

But then a strange day comes, in which Bella not only looks at Lambert, but *speaks*.

It happens at dinner. Lambert's saying something about his arrival in the city, when she interrupts.

'What? *Which* gate did you pass through?'

'The North,' Lambert says.

'He's muddled,' says Maister Richard. Messaging forcefully to Lambert with his eyes. 'It was the South gate.'

Lambert doesn't understand what's going on. But he sees an opportunity to work Maister Richard wrack.

'I'm sure it was not,' he says.

'Did you see the bridge hermits on the Grandpont?' Bella asks him.

'Did I? Hmmm… no, I don't think so.'

Bella says to Maister Richard, 'If his mother lived in Reading, *why* would you arrive from the North?'

Maister Richard looks wonderly distroubled now. Lambert relents. 'I think I do remember hermits,' he says. But Bella is looking at Lambert, again, with a calculating expression that alarms him too.

'You speak gentil,' she says. (This is down to lessons from Maister Richard: *Butter, you clod, not buh-urrr.*) 'But when you forget, your accent is westerly, not Readingish.'

'My… mother came from there,' he says. 'She didn't always live in Reading.'

'Hmm,' says Bella. Then she changes the subject. Maister Richard gives him a look of gratitude, and extra stewed pears.

Yes, Lambert thinks, the power in the house has moved around – is moveable still. Despitous as she is, he could almost welcome Bella's arrival.

The landlord stops by on rent day. He tells them he married a new wife yesterday. He says it's a shame he can't get into St Bartholomew's chapel, they've got the comb of Edward Confessor in there, curer of headaches, and he's got a shit of a hangover. Plus some fuck-ing students smashed one of his windows. Students! They're devils aright. The other day some of them got fined for baptising a cat. The landlord says the townspeople used to riot against the scholars, but this only worked themselves wrack. The last massacre was over a hundred years ago and the mayor and aldermen are still paying the university apology money every year.

'A woman's fit of rage gets her new gloves,' Maister Richard observes. 'A man's gets him fined. How come men lose money on both sides?'

He and the landlord laugh. Bella's lips become small, return to their usual shape, then turn up into a smile.

'I'd put all those wretched students into Bocardo jail,' says the landlord.

'Bocardo is a strange word,' Lambert says.

'A bocardo is a type of syllogism,' says Maister Richard. 'A difficult one. Like the prison is hard to get out of.'

'What's a syllogism?'

'All kings are of noble birth. You become a king. You are of noble birth,' Maister Richard says. He laughs to himself, in a surrounding silence.

Lambert feels embarrassed for him. Bella and the landlord don't understand his jape; Lambert gets it, but doesn't find it funny. It occurs to him that Maister Richard, among adults, is not quite the figure of sophistication he's led Lambert to believe.

'Did you hear the story of the Powderham Pretender?' the landlord says. 'John of Powderham. Only had one ear. Got himself imprisoned in the Bocardo for claiming to be Edward II. He said that when he was a tiny princeling, he was playing outside and a sow bit his ear off. The servant who had charge of him was adread that she'd be hung for it, so she swapped him with a carter's baby. Thus, the king was a carter and a carter was a king. John offered to fight for the throne in single combat.'

'Did they fight?' Lambert asks.

'No. He confessed to inventing the story. Said the devil in the form of his pet cat had led him down a bad path. The cat didn't make a good defence of himself and was found guilty along with John. They hanged them both – oh, look now to the boy, he is ill.'

Lambert's vision is all glitter. A burning liquid swims up from his stomach, pressing against his throat. *Hanged them both*. His heart pulses oddly.

'Too much cake,' Maister Richard says, at which Bella looks at him sharply, because there hasn't been any cake. 'Come on, Lambert.'

Lambert finds himself travelling up the stairs, half pushed, half carried.

When they're out of hearing range, Maister Richard says, 'You've got to be sturdier. It's important. You can't quail at innocent stories. You're not defective, are you? You weren't truly kicked by a cow?'

'I was knocked down by a goat.'

'Maybe that's it. Lie down for a little while. Come back whole of your wits.'

9

King Henry is crowned at the end of October. The beautiful
Elizabeth of York is not at the ceremony. The nobles would have
liked to see her, but have to look instead on the new king's mother,
Margaret Beaufort, weeping copiously – as if she had the tender
heart of a woman, which all present knew she did not.

(Did she cry, when she waved her guest the young Earl of Warwick
off to the tower?)

The hudder mudder man who pays Maister Richard also brings
him tidings. He tells him that at the Coronation they took care to
say that the king *rules most rightfully over the English people, and that not
so much by right of blood as of conquest and victory in warfare*, because of
course Henry can't admit he's a usurper nobody, and that his putting
a baby in King Edward's daughter will be his only legitimacy –
though how he'll do *that* Maister Richard doesn't know, because it's
not likely she'll get any pleasure from that miserable stockfish, and
without pleasure she won't release her female seed.

Henry repeals Richard's Act that declared Elizabeth of York and
her siblings illegitimate, and orders every last copy of it destroyed.
Struck from history, *forever out of remembrance*.

In other Acts, Henry backdates his reign to before the Battle of
Bosworth, making anyone who fought for Richard a traitor and
their lands forfeit to the Crown. He gives his mother back all the
lands that were taken from her by Richard. He restores to Elizabeth
Woodville her title of dowager queen – but not her lands.

Townsfolk:

He doesn't have the blood of the Yorks, but he has their avarice aright.

'That new king's raising the fee farm,' says the landlord. 'The tight-fisted cunt.'

Maister Richard asked the man who pays him when it would come time to hand Lambert over. He's told Bella that Lambert will be leaving soon for an apprenticeship, after which the two of them can live alone together like two stupid doves.

The man said: not just yet. But he gave Maister Richard extra money for Christmas. So for now Lambert is delighted with the *not just yet*, and Maister Richard is delighted with his money, and Lambert watches Maister Richard, trying to work out where he's hiding it.

Yuletide comes to Oxford, and the gutters ice over. The sky is white and flat as frozen milk.

Last Christmas Lambert and Maister Richard went to Mass in a freezing blue-black fog and ate a scanty feast prepared by the deaf mute. Then Lambert went to bed early and wrapped his face in a blanket, to think about Christmases in the village – the mumming, the revels, the costumes – and let his sadness out unheard. (He thinks he can allow himself a cry, once a year, at Christmas. As a present to himself. It doesn't make him a weeper.)

Christmas this year is better. The landlord's new wife, who has become friendly with Bella, invites them over to their house on the other side of town, past the twirlgate in the city walls, next to Perilous Hall. A Lollard den, says the landlord. Oriel men rioted in the 1410s for Wycliffe.

'Lollards!' Lambert says. 'Are they still there?' He's thinking of his great-grandfather then remembers that man was no ancestor of his.

'Oh, no. Those days are gone.'

They eat goose and drink wine. Maister Richard becomes red and prolix, Bella almost lively. Lambert wins three pennies – his means to escape! – from the landlord at cards. They eat sweet bread, brought by Maister Richard, who also bought mead and biscuits, and a silver brooch for Bella.

Maister Richard's whole demeaning has changed. He's suddenly expansive. He says *Blessed be God!* a lot, and has a new habit of patting his tummy complacently, as if he's just drunk off some wine, which he usually has.

The bread is delicious. It has imported Spanish raisins in it.

'I've never eaten a raisin,' Lambert says. He wraps some of the bread up, to take home to the deaf mute. Nobody else has given the man any gifts. Bella has all but banned him from the main house, on account of his 'lurkings and lookings' – which is ironic because Lambert is the one who's peeped at her quoniam.

'The fruits of Italy are savourly beyond belief,' the landlord says. 'You should try an orange.'

The landlord once went on a pilgrimage ('with a right rascally band') and travelled all through Southern Europe, where he saw 'all sorts', including a lion. Though there were leopards in Oxford once, he adds. Caged ones, at Woodstock Palace.

Lambert feels melancholic at that. Giants, Lollards, leopards. The maidens of Gropecunt Lane. Everything interesting is gone.

After dinner everyone becomes wonderly cupshotten. The landlord does a backwards roll and breaks a stool. Maister Richard is given the dare of aping Bella, and flounces around the room in one of the landlord's wife's shifts, lifting his skirts and making noises of bumbulation, everyone crying of laughing – even, unexpectedly, Bella herself.

When they get home Maister Richard says he's as unfitted for stairs as Lambert on his first day in Oxford, lies down on the rushes in front of the dying fire, and goes to sleep.

Lambert and Bella look at each other.

'No stairs in Reading?' she says.

Lambert doesn't answer her. He doesn't like her look, and his head is full of wine. He goes up to his room and lies on his bed, the drink inside him slopping gently from side to side, like he's carrying a bucket of water. He tries to keep very still, so nothing will spill out.

A little later, with sleep beyond his reach, he hears small papery noises coming from Maister Richard's room. He goes quietly to the door. Through the crack he can see Bella, going through a pile of

Maister Richard's letters and books. She picks each one up, looks it over, and then takes care to put it back in its former position.

Hmm, Lambert thinks to himself. In gladness, that Bella wasn't doing him, Lambert, some personal evil. He doesn't know what she *is* doing. He doesn't care overmuch. Women are – by nature – nose-pokers, rummagers, peerers. Maister Richard says so. And if Maister Richard knows that, he must know not to write down his secrets and leave them on his desk. So: no need for any hue and cry. Lambert's got his own hudder mudder plans to think of. There are three pennies in his pouch. Enough to get a carter to take him South.

Maister Richard observes that lateward Lambert has seemed jumpy and distractable – too much yellow bile – and takes him to the bull baiting at Carfax to get his blood up. Melted frost drips on them from the stone grotesques of the city as they walk, dodging puddles and piles of half-frozen horseshit.

'Less clumsy these days,' Maister Richard says approvingly. 'The baby donkey is turning into a human.'

Lambert hears Jennott, then.

The foal, she says. *Not a baby donkey. You ignorant, wine-drinking, mirror-peering, gold-rubbing town rat.*

Lambert's so glad to hear her.

He realises now why his dad didn't marry Jennott. She'd never have let Maister Richard and the nobleman in the drab hat – rich as he was, puissant as he was – take John away. She'd have made a fray upon him first. A nobleman in a drab hat is still a man, and a man can be hit with a pan.

'I may place a few pennies on the one-eared dog,' Maister Richard is saying. 'He looks like a—'

Bang, a pot takes him down, he falls in the street.

No, he doesn't.

Jennott isn't here.

The yellow bile rises.

Lambert isn't excited about the bull baiting. They'd had it in the village, and so he'd thought the priest would disdain it, not throng in like this, with his red face agape, like he and not the bull has had a noseful of pepper. Early on a dog is thrown and doesn't spring up;

lies shrieking with its back broken, until the owner steps in and clubs it.

'And a penny for you to bet, if you like,' says Maister Richard, newly generous.

Lambert pretends to bet his penny, but puts it into his purse instead. The action gives him a feeling of sudden means. When Maister Richard is distracted, he lets himself pass back through the crowd when it next presses forward, the people squeezing in from the sides carrying him outwards into the uncrowded fringe.

He'd meant to get some clothes and books from the house before he left, but this might be his only chance to leave. He has to seize it. He backs toward the nearest alley.

Maister Richard comes out of the crowd then, looking panicked; sees Lambert, and hies toward him. Lambert considers running, but they're too close.

It turns out Maister Richard isn't alarmed at Lambert's escape. He thinks Lambert has seen what he saw: a man in the crowd, following them.

'That was goodly work, slipping away,' he says, hurrying Lambert down a nearby alley.

'Who are you afraid of?' Lambert asks.

'Henry has a lot of spies,' Maister Richard says. 'This is his great puissance. He learned it from the French, no doubt. They love doubleness. Since he took the throne, divers York supporters – our friends – have gone missing. If the wrong people are caught and tortured, you and I are lost. We might already be lost. That man in the crowd might know you exist, a York heir, and he might have others with him.'

'What would they do?' Lambert asks. His voice emerges strangely, like a crow crawk.

'Kill you quietly,' Maister Richard says. 'So that nobody ever hears of your existence.'

King Henry finally weds Elizabeth of York at the end of January, after being petitioned to do so by an impatient parliament. ('So much for Amor,' says Bella.) There is much pomp and nobley. Feasts, dances and tournaments. Celebrations for everyone, high and low.

Not for Maister Richard. He mislikes the wedding, but his foremost worry is that the man who gives him his money hasn't come to meet him. This is a particular problem because Maister Richard, in expectation of a coming windfall, has spent the last of the Christmas money on a new purse and some rumney wine.

King Henry claims the legendary King Cadwaladr as his ancestor, in accordance with Cadwaladr's prophecy (reported by Geoffrey of Monmouth) that a Welsh king would restore this ancient royal line and rule over all Britain.

And now here he is: Henry.

He has Cadwaladr's red dragon added to his standard.

Just to make things clear.

Sometimes Lambert feels like a shadow. An absence. Officially, he isn't here. He's not in this house, he's not on the farm, he's not in the Tower. He isn't Lambert, or John, nor Edward, Earl of Warwick, not yet.

And what is the province of shadows? Behind doors. And who can blame a shadow for silently overhearing? As Maister Richard and Bella hiss at each other:

'You're making a fool of me, Richard! Cozening me with brooches and measly pieces of silk. And now you can't even afford them! The mayor himself helped me over a horse dung yesterday and told me I was the fairest creature in Oxford. I could be marrying mayors, not watching my best years slide by in this midden.'

'It's temporary, my leman, my love, he'll be off to an apprenticeship soon… no, I can't say when exactly. But then I'll resign the priesthood, and we'll be married. I'll have gold then. Just like I told you.'

'You tell me nothing. Why did you have money at Christmas and none now? Where are his other kin? Where are yours? I never heard of a father having to raise their own mishap. There's something you're not telling me. I know you didn't get him from Reading. Why are you lying? Where are you getting this gold? If you don't tell me the truth, I'm leaving. Go find another woman to live on lies and give worship to your miserable pizzle.'

The next morning Bella isn't in the house, and Maister Richard is pacing the hall in a fury.

'Where the fuck is that money? Where are the tidings I was promised?' he shouts. Lambert's never seen him so wroth. Or using the word *fuck*. Lambert's missed *fuck*. It reminds him of Jennott.

Could this be a good time for a question? Rage, like drink, makes people unpredictable. They might say something they wouldn't otherwise. Or they might hit you.

It's worth a gamble.

'Maybe they've forgotten about us,' he says. 'We could just... go back to where we came from?'

But the bid was misjudged: Lambert can feel it even before Maister Richard swings round.

'You halfwit shithat,' he shouts. 'Get out of here. I've no stomach for your ignorance today.' He kicks out at the table. 'Argh! Fuck! To hell with fucking all of it.'

Then, unexpectedly, he sits down at the table and cries.

'Sorry,' he says.

He's never apologised for anything before. Lambert doesn't want to speak, in case the enchantment is broken. So he abides in silence.

'I was promised a house in London and a thousand pounds for a year's service,' Maister Richard says. His elbows are in a puddle of spilled ale but he doesn't notice. He looks up at Lambert. 'We have both been abused. It was a fell day that we took you from that stinking farm. Well, let your heart be lightened: maybe you'll end your days there. Oh, no, I remember now. It was going East that sparkled your eye.' He gives a strange laugh, both bitter and gentle, and more disturbing than his wroth. He says, 'I can promise you now, you'll never go East. Don't look dismayed: you'll thank me later for that honesty. Hope is the most insidious curse of man. Look at me. I was hopeful once.

'And now I have no money and Bella, faithless jade that she is, is leaving me.'

'Do you *want* her, if she's a faithless jade?'

Maister Richard waves his hand. 'That's reason talking. Reason has nothing to do with this. My heart is my master, and right now it's doleful beyond measure. There are some things women do, Lambert, that put a spell on you.'

'Sorcery?' Lambert asks.

'It's sorcery aright. It was an evil day that Bella preyed on *me*: coming over in the Golden Cross; showing her breast-tops, all smiles. Remember the exemplum of the priest who sacrificed his benefice for his leman, but she cast him off, because she couldn't profit from him anymore? Bella will desert me for any man that can keep her in silk. What she really wants is someone to marry her – oh, then she'd have a roof over her head for life! By Saint Julia, she'd be in a trull house or begging on the streets if it weren't for her wicked enchantments. If it weren't for her clicket gate. It takes money to open it; I wonder who she'll be opening it for next? Some rich fool who can't tell a well-used path when he treads one. God help him.'

He folds his arms into the puddle, lays his head on them, and groans.

Lambert, for the first time, feels sorry for Maister Richard. He moves over, uncertainly, and pats his shoulder.

Maybe without Bella and her evil enchantments, Maister Richard will be a kinder, wiser man. That would be a good ending. And Lambert won't have to face Bella's questions: infinitely more inquieting than her silent mislike. And it seems likely that Maister Richard's York masters *have* forgotten him. Which means Lambert will be free, and Maister Richard can go back to being whatever he was before now – and also repent his sins, and make things right for his soul.

Nobody will die.

Everybody will go to heaven.

'There, there,' Lambert says to Maister Richard. 'Everything will be well. I know it.'

The next morning, Lambert wakes up to the sound of Bella singing, and Maister Richard standing in his doorway.

'I know this isn't wise,' Maister Richard says. 'But I couldn't be without her.'

Lambert doesn't understand.

'I told her,' Maister Richard explains. 'And you mustn't tell anyone that I did. Or it's death for both of us.'

'Fine,' Lambert says.

He's not as irous about their secret being shared as he is at the prospect of more Bella. But downstairs, she startles Lambert by smiling at him, and saying, 'What cheer?'

Which is congenial.

Bella also has a lot of questions. More than Lambert has thought of. And Maister Richard can't throw a book at her and tell her to shut up. He listens with interest as she asks, 'How old is Lambert? He looks twelve.'

'He is twelve.'

'But the Earl of Warwick is ten. Why's he older than the other Earl?'

'They told me he was born earlier but his father the Duke of Clarence hid the birth. They sent Lambert here away, but it took a year to lay hands on another child as a substitute. Something went awry, I think. Obviously Clarence thought he'd overlive his brother King Edward, and be here to explain it.'

'Where did they find the substitute boy? Was he the son of the farmer that raised Lambert?'

'I think not. They were a dark-headed family.'

'So what's this Duchess of Burgundy waiting for?' Bella asks. 'Why doesn't she send for her nephew? Why has the money stopped? Are they waiting for Henry to kill the Earl of Warwick in the tower? That poor boy. I don't see why he has to die.'

Lambert feels more friendly toward her, then.

'I'm sure nobody will kill him, my leman,' says Maister Richard, patting her hand. 'They'll probably just announce the unfortunate child is a fraud, and release him from captivity, so he'll be in a much better position and wonderly grateful, I'm sure.'

'This duchess must have plenty of people helping her in England,' Bella says. 'Who are they? Who was the man who went with you to take Lambert from the farm?'

But Maister Richard shakes his head. 'Don't ever mention him. It's peril to know him. I wish *I* didn't know him.'

'I can keep secrets. I know you think I'm just a jangling woman, but I wouldn't even tell my priest.'

'A priest is the worst person to tell! By Saint Eloy, they'll sell the information for a penny to pay a harlot. Remember it's your own life that's in the balance too, since you forced me to talk.'

'Forced you? I was tired of being treated like an idiot. I knew you were lying.'

'You aren't an idiot, my darling,' Maister Richard says. 'But these are weighty matters. Not for women's minds. We will speak no more on them.'

Bella doesn't reply to this. Her eyes move to Lambert and rest on him, heavy in unknowability. His heart, which had felt so much warmer just now, falls small and still like a mouse.

'Not a low hedge-egg,' she says. 'A little imposter. A secret earl, right here among us.'

11

Lambert has reached the last of his books. No more are coming. They can't afford them. But he's delighted to find, in the last pages of his Macrobius, two unexpected poems, added by some unknown scholar of Greek.

The first, according to the scholar's notes, is a pattern poem by Simmias of Rhodes, copied from the famous *Greek Anthology* and translated into Latin. The poem is about Eros and the words form the shape of a pair of wings.

'Like Cupid's wings!' Lambert says to Maister Richard. 'Isn't it clever? I never saw a poem like this!'

'A diverting trick for small children, no doubt,' Maister Richard says. And now Lambert wants to wrast the book back out of his hands, but it's too late. Maister Richard is reading the second poem, a translated fragment of a priamel by Sappho:

Some say an army of horsemen, or footsoldiers, or a fleet of ships is the fairest thing upon the black earth. I say it is what one loves.

Lambert thinks it's beautiful. One day, when he finds a lady of his own, probably in the East, he will say these words to her.

'Not of the best quality,' Maister Richard says. 'But being a woman, Sappho couldn't help being second-rate. That's why so little of her work survived. If she weren't a tribade we wouldn't even know her name. She's only famous because she ate pie instead of sausage.'

Lambert has no idea what he's talking about.

'I think it's a wonderly fair poem,' Bella says.

Maister Richard, looking at her lovingly, says; 'Oh, certainly a meet poem for a lovely innocent demosel,' before returning to his previous activity, looking at himself in his knife.

'If this money ever comes, I think I'll buy a plum colour cloak,' he says.

Lambert makes a grimly face: eyes thrown up, mouth twisted, teeth bared. Then he catches himself and looks at Bella. Bella is also making a grotesque face. She sees Lambert see her. They both start laughing. Maister Richard puts the knife down, startled.

'What's the jape?' he says.

'Nothing,' says Bella.

'Hmm,' Maister Richard says. He looks between the two of them – Bella to Lambert and Lambert to Bella – as if suspecting a new ordering of things, and misliking it.

Lambert's fairly astonied by it himself.

February comes. The city is cold; the trees are still sticks. The money is running out. Maister Richard talks no more of cloaks. Melancholy has paled his face. His eyes are red around the rims.

'I'm full crazed in the body,' he says. 'I think this foul air and cheap bread is killing me.'

'It's an ague,' Bella says. 'Just don't bathe and you'll be fine.'

'We shall see,' Maister Richard says, irously. 'Imagine, if I avoided a murdering but got put in the earth by a cold.'

When the day comes, Maister Richard goes to meet his money man, making his usual great fuss of cloaking himself, covering his face and taking convoluted routes across the city. But the man doesn't come.

Now he and Bella are upstairs in his chamber, arguing. Lambert the shadow is listening at the door.

'I left my family for you,' Bella says. It sounds as if she's crying. 'I left them on false promises, and now I have nowhere to go back to. What am I facing, life as a tavern whore or in the London stews?'

Lambert is taken aback by her tone of desperation. He supposes this must be the enchantment and trickery Maister Richard was talking about. It's very convincing: Bella sounds truly pitiable.

'Forget this money carrier,' she says. 'You said it yourself, he's a nothing man. Who pays *him*? Who is that nobleman you won't speak the name of?'

'By Christ! Stop with that! Why do you keep on with it?'

'Don't chop at *me*! I was only thinking you could go directly to him, whoever he is.'

'My body might make it through his door but my head wouldn't,' says Maister Richard.

'Well, that little cuckoo earl may as well be your bastard. You're saddled with him now. What are you going to do?'

What indeed? Lambert presses closer to the door frame.

'I have an obligation to the boy,' Maister Richard says. 'Maybe I could get him a position as an apprentice clerk. Though that's costly. Perhaps find him a place in a great house. In the kitchen or something. He does love biscuits...'

Lambert almost loses all governance of himself in his longing to rush in. But he waits, and says to Maister Richard later: 'Take me to Southampton. Please. I have people there.'

Maister Richard stares at him for a moment. Then he lifts his hands.

'Fine,' he says. 'But in exchange for this favour for you, I need a favour in return. Those pennies you won from the landlord at cards. We're out of money. Will you loan them to me? Only for a short while, until we can get to my family. My people are in London, and though they won't want to see me, they won't see me starve.'

'You can keep them,' Lambert says. 'In exchange for getting me to Southampton.'

'On my oath,' Maister Richard says.

In the morning Lambert goes down to the hall, singing a little song of celebration. Blessed be God! Holy be His name! He's imagining Jennott's face when he arrives at her door in Southampton. He doesn't know what door she lives behind, but he can ask around.

The deaf mute is mopping up the table. The shutters and windows are open and the melodic sound of the blackbirds in the garden rills above the clanking of the tin bucket; cold sunlight streams in. The deaf mute gives Lambert a smile and a salute. Lambert feels a great tenderness for him.

'I'm leaving here soon,' he says. 'I'm sorry we never talked, and that I couldn't teach you to write. Also I'm sorry you can't hear any of this. Uh. I'm going to stop talking now. It's probably wonderly annoying to be talked to when you can't hear.'

The deaf mute smiles again, and ducks his head.

Maister Richard comes in then.

'Lambert, have you seen my bundle of papers?' he asks. 'They were on—'

The door opens, without a knock.

Two men come in.

Lambert doesn't recognise them. They are averagely sized. Unremarkable visages. One has a fat belly, the other is thinner. There doesn't seem to be anything unusual about them as they walk through the door, hardly giving Maister Richard time to stand out of the way.

'What cheer, Simons?' one says. 'We're here for the boy.'

'This is… not… I was not told,' Maister Richard says, waxing pale, then red. 'Why – why would—'

Lambert stands astonied. His hope of going to Southampton is snapped like a chicken neck. The force of an earl-shaped future arrives with a crash, knocking the wits out of him.

Maister Richard is yattering something about no warning, no tidings. But his words fall off. Lambert realises why the priest is agitated. Bella is supposed to arrive here soon with her things, ready to leave town tomorrow. And Maister Richard's not supposed to have a Bella. But then, Bella's often late. But today she might not be. Lambert can see these thoughts chasing each other round and round on the priest's face, until he brasts out: 'Go up and get your things, Lambert!' Jabbing at Lambert's shoulders. 'Hie now, hie! Don't keep these good men waiting. They'll be wanting to leave right anon.'

'We have your money,' one man says. He puts a sizable purse down on the table. It makes a loud noise. 'And extra, for the inconvenience and whatnot.'

In any other time Lambert would have been interested to watch the love of gold collide with the fear of death in Maister Richard's face but he's sore frightened himself, so he runs upstairs to pack.

It doesn't take long. In a blind kind of tempest he puts his clothes in a bag. His own purse with the whittled ship and fairy arrowhead is already around his neck, below his doublet. Maister Richard's print book of *The Canterbury Tales* is on a table. He'd always refused to lend it to Lambert, but relented the other day. Lambert hasn't read it yet. But when he goes downstairs and hands it back to Maister Richard, the priest says, 'Keep it. With my blessings.'

Maister Richard looks less distroubled now. Bella is nowhere in sight. And the gold has done its work. For the first time he has the saintly countenance of a man of God.

'Thank you,' Lambert says. Through his state of demolishment, unexpected soft feelings emerge for Maister Richard, whom he'll never see again. He's relieved that Maister Richard won't get in trouble. He considers an embrace; bows instead.

'Come on then,' says the fat-bellied man to Lambert. Then, to Maister Richard: 'Now tell us, did you speak about this to anyone?'

Maister Richard is looking nerve-strung again. 'Nothing, I swear I'd cut my own tongue off before I betrayed these dealings.'

Oh, quiet, Lambert wants to say. He's just noticed the deaf mute come in; it seems rude to be talking about missing tongues.

The front door bangs and everyone looks up.

'What cheer!' calls Bella.

'Who the fuck is *that*?' says Fat Belly.

Maister Richard puts his hand over his face, desperately. 'Gentlemen, don't worry, she knows nothing, she's a common woman I pay to visit me, it's been two years, you can't expect me to have been chaste, surely? But I told her nothing, nothing at all.'

Bella, entering the room, looks startled, then comprehending. 'You have guests?' she says to Maister Richard. 'I have come at the wrong hour.' She takes a step back, toward the door. 'I shall leave you, good sirs,' she says.

'She knows nothing,' the priest mouths to Fat Belly, who is looking at him with head cocked.

The deaf mute says: 'She knows everything.'

12

Lambert is in the empty chapel of New College. The men escorting him are stopping there so they can meet someone. Fat Belly has gone to find him, and Thinner bides with Lambert. Thinner is holding the bag of money. There are a few dark spots on it, which the two men tutted over before they left.

Make it look like a lovers' fight, they said to the deaf mute. *Then raise a hue and cry.*

Lambert can hardly see; his eyes are constantly producing tears, a steady drip. The stained glass is blurred; the extent of the great ceiling arches are beyond him. Eventually the towering reredos comes into focus, the gold-painted saints in their ultramarine niches like stars in heaven. But the saints glare back as if they're about to clatter down onto him, like the boys from his village when they shouted *pile on*, and all threw themselves onto whatever wretch was on the ground. Except the weight of these saints will send Lambert through the marble-tiled floor, through the earth, into hell.

Not caring what Thinner thinks, he puts his face in his hands and folds his body down to his knees. His fingers press against his eyelids until red sparks fly.

He wants to say something, to make mourn, call out to God, *I'm sorry, I'm sorry*, but he can't do that either, for fear that God will ask:
Why?
And he will have to say:
Because two people are dead.
And God will reply:
Because of whom?

Fat Belly comes back and speaks to Thinner quietly. 'Sore grieved,' says Thinner. They both approach Lambert, looking close and solicitous.

'Hello, lad,' says Fat Belly. 'We know you're right heavy about us killing that priest and his whore. Well, there's no need to be. They were planning to sell you to the usurper King Henry, who would drown you like a kitten. Greedy swine that they were.'

Lambert is astonied. Then memories come to him. Bella's curiosity. Maister Richard's fear of her sorcery.

'Bella was a spy?'

'A spy? Oh, a full villainous spy, yes. She'd turned the priest to her own side.'

'By enchantment?'

'That's exactly right,' says Fat Belly, looking sorrowful.

Many feelings come over Lambert then. The first is a great relief that he isn't a murderer once-removed, that nobody was killed for him, that hell isn't waiting. But then he understands what happened: that Maister Richard and Bella, whom he'd never loved exactly, but had believed and trusted and sometimes felt tenderly toward, and certainly would never, ever have killed – that these two people were in full purpose to kill him. They were never going to take him to Southampton. They were going to murder him for money.

But then he's angry at himself. Stupid Lambert, his mind stuck in his old village where nobody would dream of killing a child. What a clod. What a daffish dumb-pate. In the world he lives in now, children are killed all the time.

And he didn't get it, and gave his enemies his escape money.

Grief and wroth, the dark pair, so well penned until now, brast out from his heart, flow through him. Chaotic things come to his mind: a memory of lying under a tree at the farm, Will Collan reciting a ballad, Bella making a comical face, Maister Richard giving him *The Canterbury Tales*, smiling.

The grief says: All of these things were tricks, and nobody in the world has any love in their heart for you.

The anger says. *They* tricked you. *They* hid you from love's sight.

He tells himself: well then, Justice has been done, on earth as it is in heaven.

He just didn't expect justice to be so—

—don't think of it.

'Well, now that's all explained with no further questions,' Fat Belly says, 'Bishop Stillington wants to see you.'

A small heap of fabric Lambert takes to be Bishop Stillington enters the nave now. The figure is *so* small, and so slow, that Lambert wonders if a jape is being played on him and they've dressed up a child or an ape. But as the bishop emerges into the light Lambert can see a face half lost in white-downed wrinkles. It's the bishop who is the victim of a jape: old age.

Lambert comes forward, unwillingly, to bow. He's adread that the man, already so frosted and slow and labouring, will creak to a halt as he approaches and just

no

don't think the word

die

Tears come to his eyes again; he wipes them quickly.

'At last,' the bishop says. 'My lord. My dear, dear boy.'

White and tremulous as he is, he's richly dressed. His clothes are embroidered, shining, trimmed with fur. On his hat there's a ruby. Lambert's never seen a ruby. It looks dark in one moment, and then the bishop shifts and slow lights move in its depths, red as roses.

Stillington is in front of Lambert now but he moves in close, closer, far too close. Lambert feels thin breath on his forehead.

'Yes, you look just like him, God rest his soul.'

'The... Duke of Clarence?'

'Why, of course,' the bishop says. He sits down, sinking into his stiff gown. 'Ah, you look strook. Are you trembling? Your father was a brave boy. Maybe too brave. I wonder if you have his temper. He was, it's true, warly and buckish. But so fair. And so well-beloved. I helped him many times, out of all sorts of trouble. I went to prison for him. Am only lately freed. Oh, yes. He did like to get into trouble. The roguish dear boy! But his death, in that cursed wine barrel... that was villainous work.'

He stops speaking. His gaze moves off to somewhere in the distance. Fat Belly and Thinner exchange their own looks. Lambert thinks of his father, the Duke of Clarence, dead in a cask, steeped purple. He feels sick.

'Now you are to be king. Lucky that I am still alive, to bring it about, yes, your father's will is still alive in me. He told me his secret, to be kept until the death of his brother, King Edward. I kept it, God witnessed it. And now his dreams will be reborn in you. His dreams and mine. My dearest wish…'

His gaze has left again.

Lambert's feeling dizzy. The smell of incense, the old man's translucent skin, rivered with veins, the bag of money with its dark blood-spots, the lateward—

—don't think of it.

Fat Belly steps forward. 'Time we got on,' he says, gently.

The bishop sits unhearing, as if he's slipped underwater. Thinner indicates the door with his head, and the three of them quietly leave the church.

Simnel

I

They cross Quaking Bridge as they leave Oxford, the partly frozen stream visible between the wobbling planks. On the other side, a cart and horse are acquired from a man wedged deep in a bundle of cloak. Fat Belly and Thinner pay him for the transport then barter for the cloak, which Thinner starts wrapping around himself, before Fat Belly says, 'Give the cloak to the boy, you shithead. He's blue.'

'They wanted him delivered fresh,' says Thinner. But he takes the cloak off and passes it to Lambert. 'If it please your grace,' he says.

'Oi,' Fat Belly says. 'None of that.'

'Who's going to hear me?'

Lambert pulls the coarse, horse-smelling cloak tightly around himself. The men argue on. He watches the empty road roll by, the mud's hard, glittering ridges.

His tears are gone now. It makes sense, he can only have so many in him. He feels dry and light, like chaff. He wishes a wind would come and take him off, away from all the people who know him as an earl, with an earl's destiny.

'We need to be in the right habit, namewise,' Fat Belly is saying. 'I'm Miles. You're Jenkin. Now, we can't call *you* the Earl of Warwick yet,' he says to Lambert. 'And you'd best leave Lambert behind in Oxford.'

Leave Lambert behind in Oxford.

Yes.

It was Lambert, back in Oxford, who had a bad thing happen to him; who heard things through his hands, and saw things at the edge of his vision, as he stumbled from the house.

'What was the priest Richard's last name?' Thinner is saying. 'Symond? Simnel?'

'Simnel's the Lenten cake, you turd.'

'Ha! Let's call him that. What do you think, Simnel?'

'I like it well enough,' Simnel says.

Goodbye to Lambert! Sad, shocked, shamed Lambert. Miserable, twisted-up Lambert.

Goodbye forever.

They stop at an inn for the night. It's warm and dim when they enter; the smell of smoke, wet wool and beer surrounds them. The place is empty aside from an old man tipped almost into his beer, who jerks upright as they approach, and reveals himself to be the innkeeper.

'Not many people pass this way now,' he says by way of apology. 'The new road…'

'We like the old road,' says Jenkin. 'Good and quiet.'

At night Simnel is woken by someone shaking him. Miles' face floats above him like a battered moon. He shuts his eyes, hoping it will go away, but it carries on breathing beer on his face and saying something about a meeting. He opens his eyes. It's dark. There's a real moon hovering in a crack of the shutters, lead-white, and a noise of horses and voices.

'Get up, lad, and get dressed,' says Miles.

Simnel sits up and peers through the shutters to see people below, removing caparisons from horses. The caparisons are more beautiful than the clothes of any human Simnel has met.

'Who's that?' he asks.

'Earl of Lincoln. And you've got a meeting to attend.'

'A meeting with whom?'

'With the Earl of Lincoln, who else?'

Simnel wonders, as they cross the dark corridor, if he's going to his death. He doesn't trust Miles and Jenkin. He's had enough of trusting people who seem good. And Miles and Jenkin aren't even pretending to be good. They might decide to run away with their stained bag of money. Or sell him to Henry themselves. His fear rises the closer they get to the final door, until, by the time Miles knocks and it opens, Simnel's lost the power of motion and has to be propelled inwards by his shoulders, into a glare of light so blinding he wonders if he's made his murder unnecessary by dying of fright, and is now in heaven.

The divine light turns, after a moment, into a large fire and a multitude of candles. So many candles. Simnel's never been somewhere so bright at night. There's a young man rising to his feet in front of him. Simnel's never seen such deep colours on a man's hose, his doublet, his cloak – never saw a glitter so bold as the gold brooch on the black velvet cap; the jewelled rings on his fingers. This must be what it's like being rich, part of his brain says. Everything is brighter.

The rest of his brain seems to have gone away somewhere.

Please come back and help me, he begs it.

'The Earl of Warwick,' says Miles, formally, from behind him.

Who? This is the Earl of Lincoln, isn't it? Then he realises, he, Simnel, is the Earl of Warwick.

Behind him Miles exits. The door is shut and latched.

Edward Plantagenet, Earl of Warwick, is alone with John de la Pole, Earl of Lincoln.

They're *cousins*, he remembers. Lincoln is the son of the Earl of Warwick's aunt. Yes. His brain is back, blessed be God.

Lincoln looks in his middle twenties, thin, with brownish-red hair and a passing beautiful countenance. A kind smile. Simnel's not sure what he expected one of the highest men in the land to look like. But not this. A young man with a fair, smiling face – and so much puissance, a marvellously vast amount of nobility and history and money compressed into a single body – now folded at an angle, performing an elegant bow.

To *him*!

A small, astonied titter escapes his clamped mouth. He remembers, almost too late, his own bow.

'Welcome, your grace,' says Lincoln. 'By Saint Mary, I can hardly believe I'm meeting you at last!'

(Your grace? Why is Lincoln calling him that? And what does *he* call Lincoln? *Your lordship*, is what he would have said on the farm, if someone of this stature had come to visit, which they wouldn't. But the Earl of Warwick wouldn't say that. What would he say? What?)

'Thank you, your lordship,' Simnel says.

The lordship matter was upmost in his minds, that was the problem.

'I know that's wrong,' he says. 'Sorry. I've never been anyone's grace before.'

'The confusion is my fault,' Lincoln says. His expression, when Simnel finally drives his eyes up to meet it, is of unexpectedly gentle concern. 'I called you "your grace" because you're our rightful king.'

He's smiling.

'My lord,' Simnel says. 'That's what I should have said.'

'Oh, you can call me John,' says Lincoln. 'Or Lincoln, or whatever you want.'

Can Simnel say, I used to be called John? Maybe it would be a friendly thing between them. Or it would just sound stupid. Yes, passing stupid. Find something else to say.

'I used to be called John,' he says.

'An excellent name,' Lincoln says. 'I've always enjoyed it.'

'Would you… uh, maybe you should call me Simnel?' he says. 'Then we're in the right habit. Of disguise. Miles says it's important to be in the habit.'

Simnel doesn't give a fuck about the habit. He just needs the feeling of overwhelming terror to drop to a tolerable level, and *your grace* is not helping.

'Miles…' says John. 'Oh, the man who brought you. I can call you Simnel for now, if you like.'

'I'm sorry,' Simnel says. 'It's just you're the first great noble I've met. Besides maybe the nobleman in the drab hat.'

'I'm the first… Wait,' Lincoln says. 'How long have you known who you are?'

'About two years.'

'By God, this thing's at sixes and sevens,' Lincoln says. He shakes his head. 'You should never have been left so long. I imagine it was on account of your father's death, then King Edward's death, then King Richard, all following so hard on each other.'

There's a broken bit of air, before *King Richard*.

'You fought for King Richard,' Simnel remembers. 'He wanted you to be his heir, after his son died.'

Lincoln's head droops.

'I did,' he says. 'I kept faith in him. I was in the North and I believed what he told me: that the dowager queen Elizabeth Woodville had married King Edward bigamously, that her family were trying to kill Richard, that it was Buckingham who murdered our cousins the young princes. I never liked the Woodvilles or Buckingham, so I believed him. Richard said he was going to end the avarice and corruption. I thought he was good. But… none of them were good.'

Simnel's own eyes fill with tears. Lincoln has trusted bad people, as Simnel has. He has suffered the same betrayals. His spirit reaches tenderly toward his cousin – though his arm does not. The thought of putting his hand on such fine fabric, presuming to pat it, is too frightening.

'So you understand now what I have to atone for,' Lincoln says. 'I have to make things right again. That ill-blooded clerk Henry sits on the throne at least in part because I fought for Richard and not Edward's murdered sons. And every day Henry insults our family. His spite is endless.'

'But he's just married your – our – cousin, Elizabeth of York. What will happen to her if he, uh, has to give up the throne? Because of being dead?'

'She won't be queen anymore, which will upset her mother. But being married to Henry is an over-large price to pay for being queen. He doesn't treat her kindly. He suspects everyone of scheming against him, and he sees her kin as a particular peril. Of course he's right about both things. Did you see the wretched poem he had Giovanni de' Gigli compose for the wedding? I don't know Elizabeth well, but I know she never said:

'"*Oh, my beloved! My hope, my only bliss!*
Why then defer my joy? Fairest of kings,
Whence your delay to light our bridal torch?
O, my illustrious spouse, give o'er delay,
Your sad Elizabeth entreats."'

'By God! It makes me exceeding wroth. He humiliated a York princess by making her wait, then commemorated his insult in verse.'

'*Bad* verse,' Simnel says.

113

'Oh, the augmentation is wonderly bad. There are no Chaucers at Henry's court.'

'I have *The Canterbury Tales*,' Simnel says. (Trying not to think of the circumstances of the gift.) 'I haven't read it yet.'

'You have excellent taste. Did you know Geoffrey Chaucer is my great-great-grandfather? Which makes him distant blood to you also. Do you like to write yourself?'

'I love to write.'

Simnel's heart had been open until he was sent to Oxford. There, it was given a kick that slammed it shut. Now the door is swinging outwards again, and light is coming in.

'May I ask something?' he asks.

'Anything.'

'Is there large danger in this? If we try to defeat Henry? Could we... die?'

'Of course,' Lincoln says. 'But good men need to be brave and fight for goodness. Or the wicked will rule us forever.'

Simnel thinks of Maister Richard and Bella, of Henry, who was going to kill him. The wicked. For the first time he imagines himself as an earl without dread: a gentil earl fighting beside his gentil cousin Lincoln, in service of goodness. Simnel asked God to tell him what God wanted. Maybe this is his answer.

But—

'You have the look of another question,' Lincoln says.

'I don't know if I can,' Simnel says.

'I will never forgive you if you don't,' Lincoln says.

'Alright. Why isn't it... *you?* Who should be king.'

'Because Richard made me his heir. Heir to a man monstrous in the eyes of God?'

'But it's not just that. Isn't the Earl of Warwick – uh, me – still under the attainder that King Edward put on the Duke of Clarence? I mean, my father Clarence. I'm barred from the throne. Aren't I?'

'Oh, I see what you mean,' says Lincoln. 'Your father was an... unlovable man aright, but it was Edward's queen who talked him into attainting your whole line, out of fell cruelty. But that will be overturned. These things are easily done from king to king. Richard should have done it, but he was worried you'd be a threat to his own son, who was alive then.'

'But why overturn anything? Why not be king? I would gladly serve you! And you're the York heir right now. And you're older than me. You don't have to explain about being swapped. Everyone knows you.'

'Everyone knows *me* as Richard's loyal pet,' says Lincoln. 'Not even a cat or a rat or a dog. I was only his little mouse.'

'But I don't know how to be a king!'

'You'll learn,' Lincoln says.

He says it firmly. He looks like he could even become, for the first time, stern. But Simnel has a vision of the future in his reach, in which he is the Earl of Warwick and travels the world and brings back a captured dragon for his beloved king. *A gift for you, my cousin!*

'But *you* don't need to learn!' he says.

'Stop,' Lincoln says.

He doesn't sound stern or even angry. It's worse than that. It's like the walls have fallen down in the room and the night has come in black and cold and extending in all directions: wide, tall, deep. That is the sadness of Lincoln.

'God doesn't want that for me,' he says. 'I'm… not fit.'

'I'm sorry,' Simnel says, quickly.

Lincoln, head downturned, appears sunk in something unfathomable, and doesn't hear him. Simnel, adread, looks around the room, as if somebody else might manifest themself and help him cheer Lincoln up. Nobody appears.

'I didn't mean to cause you dole,' he says. 'Please. I'll learn to be a king. We'll beskift Henry and make everything right again.'

Lincoln takes a long breath. He looks up with a painful smile.

'I want that wonderly much,' he says. 'My heart longs for it. God has cursed me for my sins, cousin. But now I think we might save my soul, along with England. Praise be to Him, in His infinite generosity, for giving us this new hope.'

'Amen,' says Simnel.

Lincoln is smiling in earnest now. 'By His grace, I'm passing glad we've met! I can admit it to you now, my cousin: I was worried. I met the false Earl of Warwick several times, during Richard's reign. He was not wise, and a little shrewish. I thought he might be growing the same as Clarence. I even thought maybe there was no hope for the Yorks. That our blood was corrupted. When I heard about you, I wondered: Will he be another Clarence, too? Gone even more awry, after so many years untended? But now I meet you and it's... it's as if blood counts for less than circumstance! As if it were *doings* that turned the Yorks bad. Here you are, not a misshapen rose from the palace garden, but a rose that has grown unseen in the woods, pure and good!'

What to say to that?

But no need to think of anything; Lincoln seizes his hand: he wants them to pray together, for the salvation of England.

Simnel looks at him, privily, as they pray. Lincoln's eyes are closed: his mouth, speaking, retains a faint smile, his thanks to God are full of joy and relief. He looks like a man facing the gates of heaven. And Simnel is joyed to see it– until he remembers that it's him, Simnel, who has just volunteered to get them both through.

Lincoln and his liveried men and horses disappeared in the early dawn hours; Simnel heard hooves and that was the end of it. He won't see his cousin again soon: Lincoln can't flee England yet.

Henry has no especial maugre against me, Lincoln had said. His eye is fixed hardest on the dowager queen and her son from her first marriage, the Marquess of Dorset – but Henry isn't dullwitted, he watches too. So Lincoln goes about hudder mudder, having meetings on the road, raising money and men, along with others who privily support the Yorks – even some close to Henry – but then that's no marvel: the nearer anyone is to Henry, the less they like him.

Now Simnel is back in the company of Miles and Jenkin, on the road to Dover, which is long and ice-cobbled. Their arses are sore from jouncing against the bare wood of the cart. Lincoln seems a long way away, part of the strange night and not the cold day. Simnel wishes he was back in that room with his cousin, lit up by candles – lit up, for just a moment, by the idea of being the Earl of Warwick. Maybe even by being king. He could believe it because Lincoln, who was so noble, believed it so strongly. Simnel himself lacks that power of belief.

Like everything else, he supposes he'll learn.

2

A labourer named Bill who'd once worked the harvest in John Collan's village had come from the Devon coast. Bill said that people who see the sea for the first time always act the same. They stand astonied. They wonder at the size. They wonder at the waves. If it's blue they wonder at the blue. But it's mostly grey.

And here's Simnel now, looking out: knowing how usual his awe is – but feeling it anyway. He wonders at the size, the waves. He wonders at Bill's failure to mention how the sea seems more alive than the land; the way it quivers, as if it's breathing. And the ships on it! Tall as houses, with great sails, improbably balancing on the contorted waterscape.

Behind him is Dover harbour, the smell of fish, the hammering at ships being built on the shore, the voices on the busy dock behind him, the shouting oyster sellers. Walking back through the town, somewhere, are Miles and Jenkin. They left him at the dock. It wasn't an emotional parting.

'Bye then, lad, said Miles.

Jenkin raised a hand.

'Bye, said Simnel. Thank you for saving— But they were gone.

A priest named something Simnel can't remember is waiting to accompany him to Burgundy. The priest is grimacing at the thought of the crossing. He says, 'I mislike boats. A very rocking, sickening kind of travel. I have to keep below decks and read scripture beside a pail.'

At sea, Simnel's stomach is strangely well. On the boat his sense of dread at his own incoming destiny lifts away like the seagulls flittering in the white skies – though often on deck it's more violent than that, like the wind is pulling his skin off his bones, rubbing salt into him, the way Jennott used to scour a pot with sand.

He'd planned to read *The Canterbury Tales*. But *The Canterbury Tales* is gone: it blew overboard as soon as he brought it above deck, and all the sailors laughed at him.

The sailors are Flanders men. They don't know exactly who Simnel is, but they know he's travelling under York protection. The protection covers his person only. It doesn't save him from being laughed at.

'Don't worry, my little friend Seemnel,' says one sailor. 'There are plenty of other things to do on a boat. We need someone to count the waves. Come back and tell us when you know how many there are.'

Simnel likes the sailors. They remind him of his friends from the village. With them, he remembers what it's like to be John Collan. A wild feeling rushes through him.

'Why don't *you* count my arse cheeks?' he cries. He aims them at the man. '*Un*! *Deux*! *Et une grande merde pour vous!*'

This goes down very well.

'The little fucker's a mathematician!' shout the sailors, and carry him around on their shoulders.

Simnel asks his new best friends the sailors to tell him stories, just as the pilgrims did in *The Canterbury Tales*. (The poor priest is still thundering below decks.) When they're on land, he purposes to write all the stories into a book. The idea is wonderly well received. The sailors are going to tell him their best *fabliaux*.

What is a *fabliau*? A funny story. Like the one about the priest who catches a bishop in bed with his mistress, consecrating her cunt in Latin, and so the bishop has to allow the priest to live with his own mistress. Or the sharp-witted lady who not only talks her husband into disbelieving the evidence of her affair with a knightly lover, but convinces him he's mad and must go on pilgrimage for a cure. Or the wily blacksmith who tests his wife by telling her how big their new servant's pizzle is, then catches her trying to fuck the servant, and beats her black and blue. Or the goodly husband and wife, Constant and Ysabiau, who, when three local men try to coerce Ysabiau into having ado with them, get their own revenge when Constant rapes all three of their wives. Or the—

'Hey, Simnel! Where are you going?'

'Simnel? Are you going to write your book?'

'Tired?!'

'Tired, my arsehole.'

'His mouth is puckered like an arsehole. Too pious for merry stories.'

'Nah, he's shamming – he's off to pull his pillicock below decks.'

'*Au revoir*, Simnel!'

'Don't wear it out, Simnel!'

Simnel's joy at being John again, briefly, has left him. He sits with the priest retching softly into his pail. With his own familiar dread. He can't say if it's the *fabliaux*, or the heavy memory of Oxford, or his promise to Lincoln, that distroubles his heart most. Maybe it's nothing in the past at all. Maybe the land ahead is what scares him: his aunt, the Duchess of Burgundy. Or fear of the identity he's sailing into, a future as excruciatingly bright as the sun on the horizon.

Maybe all of it.

What can he do? Nothing yet but wait, as he's carried into whatever's next.

Edward

'Or if the winged son of Maia
imitates the shape of a young man on earth,
allowing himself to be called
Caesar's avenger' –

Book 1, Ode 2,
Horace

I

Edward Plantagenet, Earl of Warwick, is in his bedroom – not alone, because he's never alone: the attendants are always with him. They sleep in his room, the chorus of their breathing audible beyond the red velvet bed curtains, rowing in and out, drawing along the hours of the night.

He's used to sharing a room. But these aren't his brothers from the farm. They're gentlemen, here to serve him – though he doesn't see how gentlemen can be his servants. He broke an etiquette rule almost immediately, standing when one of them got up, at which they all looked startled and then one older man said, My lord, please, it's not right for you to stand for us.

Sorry, he said.

You mustn't apologise to us.

He's terrified of them. The number of ways of inquieting them. When he started dressing himself the first morning (fur-trimmed damask gown, fine white linen shirt, velvet cap, soft scarlet hose, Venetian gold buttons), they were distressed, and he had to let them do it. He was adread when they brought him a basin of fragrant water to wash in – but it was alright: he's allowed to wash himself.

Two nights he's been here.

He's sitting at a table now, an illuminated manuscript of *Les Visions du Chevalier Tondal* before him. He's too tired to read it. He hasn't been sleeping well – not with all the gentlemen breathing; his own body swallowed by the eiderdown bed, the excess of satin cushions, each one embroidered with the York rose.

His own body. Is that even true? It feels strange to him, encased in such heavy splendour. The body of Edward, Earl of Warwick.

Stealthily he moves his fingers over his collar. He's only touched fur once before: a kitten on the farm that died before his dad could drown it. He caresses the collar as if it were the kitten, back from heaven, though he can't imagine a heaven more exalted than this.

He'd arrived in Mechelen, Flanders late at night. The dimly visible grey stone palace of his aunt was simpler in style than the churches of Oxford, but then, inside, a hundred times more magnificent. Gilded, frescoed, enormous. The floors are covered not in rushes but ornately patterned tiles, and the sound of his own footsteps, each one shivering through the great empty spaces, rising up to the high ceiling, was passing strange. He looked, fascinated, at the tiles as he walked, whereupon the patterns converged like ripples and made him stumble, and the men escorting him rushed in horror to steady him.

He was washed, dressed and taken immediately to Margaret's own study. The room was lined in purple silk. The Flemish tapestries and paintings on the walls were too dark to see in the candlelight. But his aunt the duchess blazed with such majesty that he fell into shock. She seemed far above him, in her yards of skirt, shining dark green with divers flowers, like a woman sitting atop a hill. The jewels at her neck flashed. There was food, but it was too beautiful to understand, let alone eat, so he didn't.

She spoke to him and he answered, in a daze. He's got no memory of what he said.

One thing he's grateful for: Margaret isn't as affectionate as Lincoln. She isn't unfriendly, but she isn't a hand-seizer or an embracer. Blessed be God. What would he do if she made to embrace him?

Cower, cringe, shrink into his fine clothes; turn into a beetle, wriggling on his back, until one of her men takes pity on him and throws him into the fire.

There should be a book to help people like Edward, who are faced with too much splendour. It could give useful advice, better than anything he could come up with, which is:

Hide in the garderobe.

The garderobe is one of the only places he can be alone. He's seen other people say 'leave us' to their attendant nobles, but he doesn't feel able to say that yet, and even if he did and they quit the room, he'd know they were standing outside, waiting to come back in.

So he sits in here. Though the despitously cold February wind surges up through the wooden seat-hole to snap at his bum. And sometimes when he stands to piss, the sight of the height, through the same hole, makes him dizzy. And at first the garderobe presented its own overwhelm; its walls painted with flowers and vines, a bowl of lamb's wool for wiping, and a basin of water for handwashing. He didn't know what to do with the wool at first; he thought someone must've left it in there by mistake, and he brought it out to find its owner.

Oh, no, my lord! said his gentlemen. It's for the fundament.

He waxes red, remembering it.

And then, when he tried to go to the garderobe at night:

My lord? Where are you going?'

He was presented with an item that he didn't understand; it was more beautiful than anything he'd seen before arriving in Mechelen – though not as beautiful as most things in Mechelen, which should have been a clue. At the farm this pot would have been given a proud position in the hall, with guests directed to admire it.

Here, he's told he's to shit in it.

A guide: that's what's needed. Yes. He's heard the library here is one of the finest in the world, containing almost a thousand books. There has to be something there for a person learning to be a prince.

Edward and his aunt are dining tonight in Margaret's own chambers. We are quiet today, she said. Only ten people. (She didn't mean the servants, of which there are twenty.) Edward's sitting beside her, trying to watch what the people around him are doing. He's been in peril of error once already; he was taking out his own knife and spoon when he realised that knives and spoons were already on the table, glinting on the white cloth. They must be gifts. He hid his own cutlery in his sleeve, and it's been jabbing him ever since.

The table is laid with wine, beer, trenchours not of bread but silver, plates of elaborate assemblages that smell like food but don't look like food; an ornate silver ship, the size of a small dog. This is sitting just to Margaret's left. Edward, to her right, isn't sure if he's meant to address the matter of the ship. Is it a gift? A surprise? He watches it carefully, in case it suddenly plays a tune, or opens up to reveal a mouse dressed as a sailor.

Anything is possible.

The food was waiting for them when Margaret and her guests entered, as one gentleman brought her an ewer of water, bowed, and offered it for her to wash her hands; as another gentleman arrived with a towel, bowed, and carefully dried the hands. Another gentleman-servant then showed her to her chair, accompanied by two assistants. Once she'd sat down, the same man showed Edward to his place, alone on her right, and then the rest of the guests, according to some unguessable order.

Still nobody around him reaches for the plates. Instead, two new men enter. Their hands are formally washed by another man with an ewer. The two men then walk the length of the table, moving from from dish to dish, taking delicately cut slivers of each and tasting them. Then they leave. Another man comes in, and begins to speak a grace in Latin. It takes several minutes. The man bows, and leaves.

And then, finally, Margaret reaches out and takes some of the nearest dish.

God be thanked! Edward copies her exactly. The food – lark pie – is beautifully flavoured and completely cold. He remembers eating freshly baked bread at the farm, stealing pieces off the meat cooking above the fire. Will he ever burn his tongue on anything again?

'You must be wondering about the suddenness of your arrival here,' Margaret says.

He hasn't been wondering. He tries, obediently, to wonder. *Why is my arrival so sudden?*

'Yes, I was indeed wondering,' he says honestly.

'It's because of the Viscount Lovell.'

Edward's heard this name before. Lovell the dog, one of the richest and most powerful men in England under King Richard the hog. And now, presumably, not.

'I thought Lord Lovell disappeared?'

'From sight but not from existence,' Margaret says. 'Lovell is a very valuable loyalist to our house. And a full formidable man.'

'A master of hidings and disguisings,' says one of the courtiers.

'He certainly has money hidden here, there and widewhere,' says Margaret. Edward always finds her tone hard to read, but now he detects: approval.

'And so proud and noble a man, he refused to submit to the disgusting rule of the usurper Henry!' says someone else.

'I considered that a mistake and counselled him to submit,' Margaret says.

'Very wise advice aright,' says the same courtier.

Margaret says, 'Your cousin Lincoln, the most honourable of men, has been able to keep his maugre against Henry hidden, and yet Lovell, the master artist of dissembling, has found it impossible. Why do you think that is?'

She speaks to Edward like he's a man. An intelligent, learned, grown man. It's very gentil of her but he can't help but long for someone to hit him on the ear and say: *keep quiet, you little turd,* so he can quietly focus on what people are doing with the silver ship. He's worked out that it's a salt dish, but he keeps missing the moment when they take their salt.

Margaret is more human at this proximity, though not completely. She's tall; taller than a lot of men. She wears the high cone-shaped hennin the women wear here, a shimmering translucent fabric draped off it, black velvet lappets around her face, intensifying the light on her pale skin. She is forty but she isn't very wrinkled. But then she doesn't seem to laugh or frown. Her face is hardly used.

She's not beautiful. There's nothing awry or misshapen about her eyes or nose or small mouth. It's the composition that's just not beautiful – yet it seems like there's a higher type of power in that, as if her face is saying: I don't need to please you.

You ought to be thinking of how to please *me.*

Edward wishes he knew what answer would please her. Her manner has gone back to its previous calm unreadability.

'Maybe it's because of their situations?' he says. 'Or maybe… their characters?'

'So your answer is that you don't know?'

127

'...Yes?'

'Good,' she says. 'It's better not to pretend you understand, when you don't. Nobody will tell you anything if they think you already know it.'

'Right.'

'Of course, that's only true of one's allies. For your enemies, your ignorance is an axe with which they can cut off your head. And knowing who is an ally and who is an enemy is one of the greatest puzzles of all.'

She sips her soup serenely, and adds, 'One which few men ever manage to solve.'

'Very well said, my lady,' says a courtier.

Margaret, ignoring this, continues, 'Lovell is a puissant man. Some men of this kind are like wolfhounds – Lincoln, for example – and some are like leopards. The hound hunts with others, and is successful by collaboration. The leopard conceals itself and strikes alone. A hound will submit to its keeper, but a leopard can never have a master. So Lovell will not obey the usurper Henry. And he won't obey me.'

'Pride is a detestable thing aright,' says a lady in blue velvet, with a hennin headdress so tall she has to move her neck with great care She rotates her face slowly toward Margaret now. 'I have always said that Lovell is overproud. I—'

'Lovell's pride could be the means to triumph,' Margaret says. The lady, waxing red, turns silent. Edward feels sorry for the courtiers. He can see they all want so much to agree with Margaret, but her expression is so hard to read, and her opinions arrive so obliquely, that they're misfiring their own opinions hab and nab and everywhere.

Margaret proceeds as usual, stately, with no sign of noticing the distroubled souls in her wake. She continues.

'And now Lovell, acting alone, purposes to start an insurrection in the North of England in your name, intercept Henry on his progress, and kill him. I don't like the idea. But...' She takes a sip of wine and inclines her head; gracious. 'It may work. We hope for the best.'

'This is what *I* have always said,' says a man a few places down. A chaplain, or maybe a bishop. It's hard to tell. He looks like a king. The woman in blue velvet turns stiffly to give him an irous look. But Margaret, the impervious umpire, seems not to hear him, so Edward isn't sure if a point has even been won.

'I hear you're reading *Tondal*, my lord,' the churchman continues, addressing Edward.

'I am,' he says.

'*Tondal*, is it?' says the woman in blue velvet. 'The journey to hell! I know it well. I often think of the men and women all filled with barbed snakes, writhing inside them, then brasting out, from all the body parts, tearing as they go, gnawing and thrashing and lashing their way through the tormented flesh of the wailing sinners. That's the punishment reserved for the men and women of God, is it not? The ones who break their vows of chastity to indulge in carnal pleasures.'

The churchman shifts in his seat inquietly.

'It is so,' he says. 'Amen.'

There's a piece of meat caught in Edward's throat; he signals for the beer, confidently, as he's seen others do, wipes his lips politely, as he's seen others do, and takes a deep drink.

Margaret's eyebrows rise up.

'I pray you ware, nephew,' she says. 'A long drink before the meat course cools the stomach fires overmuch.'

'Oh. Indeed,' he says. 'I'll be careful.'

He doesn't say: perhaps if the pottage were hot the stomach fires would be less vulnerable.

Edward manages to get through the rest of the meal without too many mistakes, but each mistake is like a barbed snake, forcing its painful way out. There's the snake that emerges when he takes the roasted meat before the boiled, the snake that's loosed when he doesn't eat enough cheese – and puts himself, as Margaret observes, in peril of not sealing up the stomach and thusly allowing the vapours of the fruit course to rise straight into his brain. A snake for the moment he gathers up his new spoon and knife to take back to his chambers; realises nobody else is doing likewise, and drops them with a clatter.

A snake for not knowing that at the end of the meal he should be the first to stand and bow to Margaret, then lead the way for the other guests to line up in order of status at the end of the chamber, to hear another grace.

A snake for having the hiccups during grace.

He limps back to his room, slowly, bleeding from many places.

Margaret came to this country from England many years ago, to be married to the Duke of Burgundy, Charles the Bold. Charles had such an exquisitely refined sense of etiquette that he once stood in the pouring rain with the Holy Roman Emperor for half an hour, each with his hat in his hand, rather than accept precedence over the other.

Charles is dead now, as is his only child, Mary of Burgundy. A horse did them evil in both cases: Charles pitched into a group of enemy soldiers; Mary into a ditch, and the horse after.

'I'm sorry,' Edward says to Margaret. (Hesitantly, as he says everything here.) 'Your daughter—'

'Mary wasn't my daughter,' Margaret says. 'She was the duke's daughter from his second marriage. He also has two illegitimate children.' (Margaret prizes accuracy.) 'I never became pregnant. We had ado with one another, when we saw each other – perhaps one full year out of seven, but consorting several times on each visit.' (Margaret prizes detail.) 'And I visited shrines to improve the condition of my womb, which the leeches said was aslant or otherwise crazed.' (Margaret prizes demystification.) 'But God wished it that nothing would grow there. And I was doleful, but later understood why this was His will, because in truth another child could never have been her equal and I would have loved it less than I loved her.' (Margaret prizes honesty.)

'Oh,' says Edward.

'Though I do love my step-grandson, Philip, nearly as much. May God watch over him in his time of ill health.'

Philip the Fair is Mary of Burgundy's son with Maximilian, King of the Romans. He's heir to the Dukedom of Burgundy, currently under Maximilian's guardianship. But Maximilian is at war in one of his many territories and has left the guardianship to Margaret. Edward hasn't met Philip yet: the kid is in bed with a cold, has been for the past week.

Edward can see that Margaret's worried. Doctors bring her news of Philip every morning and afternoon. She looks softer as she listens; then the doctors leave, and the softness is gone.

'I pray he's whole of his sickness soon,' Edward says.

'Thank you,' she says. She sighs. 'So many of us are dead.'

Does she mean the Yorks or the Burgundians? She could mean either. So many of all of them are dead.

When Mary and Maximilian's son Philip the Fair was born, the French King Louis XI, the Universal Spider, spread the rumour that the child was actually a girl, not a boy.

On the day of Philip's baptism, Margaret stopped the royal party on the steps of the church, took off the baby's gown, and held him up naked to the populace.

That's an end to that, she said.

How does Edward feel about being Edward, Earl of Warwick? Now that he really can't get out of it, not with his promise to Lincoln – and also the fact of being in a fortress in a foreign land.

He isn't sure. He can't feel his own feelings. He isn't sure if they've fled somewhere or if they're here, talking, but he can't hear them. He listens for the voices of pain, joy, dole, excitement, wroth, mirth. No sound.

He thinks it happened when he entered the palace gates, as if whatever condition a person was in when they crossed over would be their condition here forever. And his condition was: shock. He was struck astonied when he arrived; he went to bed in the same wise, and when he woke up he was still shocked.

Now the shock has set. Inert and cold, like a moulded jelly. Edward travels around the palace in this new, pressed form; lies unmoving in bed; wakes up in the same shape, every morning – like he wasn't asleep but dead. Like he's too scared even to move in the night.

He prays that it will pass. He tries not to commit any sins, anything that might tempt God to prolong this limbo-like condition. And he keeps doing what he needs to do.

Watching. Learning. Keeping from mistakes. Waiting for it all to seem less… large.

Edward asks his new tutor, François de Busleyden, if there's anything in the library that would help him learn to be a good king.

'What you're looking for is called a mirror,' says de Busleyden. 'And I commend your wisdom. The ill-favoured realm of England will be much benefited by an educated ruler, one who can banish ignorance and poverty and terrible ale – like your story of King Arthur, but real.'

Edward is taken aback. He says, 'But Arthur *is* real.'

There is a brief pause.

'Ah, yes. English is not my first language, my lord. The suggestion that your King Arthur is a fictional character was my own error of phrasing, as sometimes happens when men are as rough about the tongue as I. No, no, don't be polite, I can barely even speak, I gibber like an ape. To save my blushes, let me leave immediately and find you these books.'

But the mirrors are no help.

Gerard of Wales' *De principis instructione* is all about morality: how to rule with not only magnificence but moderation – for example, only branding people or cutting off their hands after a second offence – and has nothing at all about, say, salt ships. And Hoccleve's *Regement of Princes* seems more concerned with Hoccleve's own precarious finances than actually advising the prince, or else Hoccleve's advising the prince to give him some money.

'Are there any mirrors for children?' Edward asks de Busleyden.

'No, my lord. Children here read courtesy books, much as the English do. Providing instruction on basic matters of manners and so on.'

'Courtesy books? Are there any in the library?'

'No, my lord. These books are not literature. They are practical things.'

'Are there any in the palace? I, uh, I've been trying to remember one I knew when I was young. It's a... silly curiosity I have.'

'Silly? This is *sehnsucht*!' says de Busleyden. 'I know it deeply, yes... blown as I have been so far from my birth-town Arlon, I feel the painful sweetness of the lost home, *ja*, the memory of drinking Maitrank by the Knippchen with my darling Christina...'

Edward doesn't like the idea of *sehnsucht*. It sounds dangerous. If he were to spend his time running his fingers over the little ship whittled by his brother; remembering the rosemary-smelling hair of his mother-that-was, or Jennott cursing at the churn ... it could shake his pressed spirit loose – and not in a good way.

Not in a way that helps him become a king.

De Busleyden doesn't notice Edward's expression. With tears standing in his eyes, he says he'll get Edward every courtesy book in the palace, until he finds the one that reunites him with the part of himself that he left in another place, years ago, and which doubtless waits for him still.

3

Caxton's *Book of Courtesy for Little Children* says:

> *'Put not thy mete in to the salt*
> *In to thy Seler that thy salt halte*
> *But lay it on thy trenchoure*
> *To fore the and that is thy honoure'.*

Praise God for one thing: now Edward can eat salt.

But mostly the courtesy books aren't helpful. Maybe he should write one: a book for children who used to be peasants but are now princes.

> *No-one wants to hear of making cheese.*
> *Talk of ploughing makes nobles ill at ease.*
> *If they give you a marchpane subtlety*
> *They are to eat, not to keep privily*
> *~~Don't cry out when you see an orange~~*
> *Don't let sight of an orange make you cry out*
> *Don't let the commode lid hit your towte—*

—but who else would ever need it?

Philip the Fair is heal of his sickness and joins Lambert in the court-yard for sword practice.

Philip is, as named, a beautiful boy, with thick shoulder-length dark blond hair and a small rosy pout. He excels at archery, tennis, hunting and dancing. He has an ear for music and gentil conversation. He's eight, four years younger than Edward, but is better than him in all disciplines.

Unexpectedly, Edward finds he doesn't hate him.

Philip beats him at swordplay. Then Philip teaches Edward the same sequence of moves.

But now I'll know how to beat you, Edward said.

Yes, exactly! said Philip.

They looked at each other, neither understanding.

Philip is pleased to have Edward here. He was only three years old when his mother died and he was taken hostage by an alliance of Flemish cities, who announced their right to rule on his behalf. His father Maximilian, who never said no to a war, promptly waged one on the cities. It lasted for three years. Maximilian won, and Philip was given back to a man he didn't recognise. He's lived in Mechelen since then, under Margaret's care. A happy ending. Except for his mother still being dead, and Maximilian leaving immediately for another campaign.

Edward's day is now divided into the slices of Philip's day. Mass at seven a.m. in the magnificent chapel, then breakfast in Philip's rooms, then study, then desports in the afternoon in miniature suits of armour. Before dinner they can do as they like. Philip thinks they should allow themselves an hour of play and then an hour of reading, so they know they are improving their minds while also keeping their humours in balance and loneliness at bay.

'You feel in peril of loneliness?' asks Edward.

'Do you not?' says Philip.

Edward isn't sure how to answer. It's like asking a man who has been eaten by a bear if he's frightened by bears.

He has no enemies and no friends here. He has the sense that palace life consists of many revolving spheres, like celestial bodies, each containing a number of people. Some spheres are separate, some intersect. He exists in his own sphere, with his retinue of gentlemen servants. Margaret in another sphere, with her ladies of honour, chaplains, almoner and confessors. But then she also commands a sphere of councillors and officials. Then there are spheres of servants, courtiers, guards – spheres on spheres, as mysterious to him as the planets of the sky.

Really Edward is in a sphere of one, within the larger circle of his retinue. The flawless, smiling gentilesse of the men frightens him, and holds him at bay. They politely switch to English when Edward comes into ear, but their laughter doesn't make the crossover. He feels like a cat running into a garden, making all the birds fall still.

Do cats feel in peril of loneliness?

He doesn't approach anyone beyond his spheres. There are knights on guard, and at first Edward wanted to ask them about their chivalric quests, battles, and all the fair demosels they've rescued, but they only seem to stand at attention, or escort Margaret – and he worries that asking them about adventures might cause them dole.

He'd been looking, at first, for the servants. Not to talk to. He's not *that* stupid. But he wanted to see them – wondering if they would *see* him too, with a look of surprised recognition. He spent his first couple of days wondering where they were: the low people. Then – after an incident in which he bowed to a footman, thinking his resplendent livery was the dress of some envoy from an exotic land – he understood. The formal, elegant people moving quickly and silently through the palace are the maids; valets; falconers. They're nothing like the people from his village. And none of them look at him.

Is he lonely?

The true answer is: loneliness implies that the person expects not to be lonely. And Edward's gone beyond loneliness.

He doesn't say that to Philip. He isn't sure if anyone says things like that. Instead they play at stones-in the-fountain, until the clock strikes and Philip says it's time to go to the library.

Edward wants to read *Le Morte d'Arthur*. But each time he asks for it, somebody else is reading it. Last time it was the Baron of somewhere. This time it's the Bishop of something.

'Bad luck,' says Philip. 'You should just command them to give you the book.'

'Oh, no, it's alright,' Edward says, alarmed. 'I don't want to do any commanding this afternoon. I… er… did a lot of commanding earlier. I'll abide until the bishop's finished.'

'You can read about Alexander the Great with me,' Philip says. 'My father says Jehan Wauquelin's history was wonderly inspiring to him. And it's inspiring me, too, I'm sure it is. It's hard to know, isn't it, how inspired you are?'

'Maybe the inspiration struck so deep, into your bones, that you can't perceive it,' Edward says, to chase off the little shadows moving over Philip's face, and is surprised when – easy as that – it works.

'Truly? Thank you, Edward. I'm right glad you're here. You've lighted my heart by a pound.'

Is Edward's own heart lighter? As he and Philip throw pebbles at the noses of the warly-looking merpeople of the fountain, one flies wide toward a stained-glass window. Fear flies at Edward: at the same speed, but much larger. The windows astonied him when he arrived; he thought stained glass was only for Saints, but here it has ducal emblems, which do make sense, Margaret seeming like a kind of saint herself, the saint of good governance—

—and now he's about to break one.

The stone reaches the window and bounces off it with a small, distant clink.

They look at each other, and then they start laughing in surprise and relief – and Edward has a distinct feeling of *feeling*, of an old kind of happiness stirring again.

4

The jellied quality of Edward's early days at Mechelen slowly warms, melts away. He learns the routines of the bedchamber, the dinner table. He is triumphant admiral of the salt ship. He's still timid around Margaret. But with Philip he's full merry. He looks forward to sword practice, to their reading – even if Philip just wants to read Alexander over and over.

'This is my favourite part,' Philip says, 'When Porus the King of the Indians challenges Alexander to single combat and they are both full of dread – but because the duel will spare their men from dying, they subdue their fears. And Edward... I'm sore frightened when I think of battle, while my father has never been scared of anything, and I always used to worry I was an unfitting son for him, but since I read that, I feel better.'

'Hmm,' says Edward, not listening. He's reading the part where Wauquelin says that historical accounts differ on how Porus met his end. Whether it was there on the field or much later. Wauquelin says it's up to the reader to make their own judgement.

Up to the *reader*?

Edward is astonied. How can a reader judge history? It's like a reader judging God. History is what happened. Nothing can change it. But some dead historians have lied, or guessed, and now nobody knows what's true.

The fragility of the past horrifies him.

He doesn't say *fuck* here, not anymore. But sometimes he thinks it, privily.

What. The. Fuck.

Only the account of Alexander's journey into the sky in a cage drawn by griffons and his encounters with six-handed men and other marvellous beings of the East, cheer Edward up. On these, at least, the sources agree.

Could he go…?

No, he cannot. He has to go back to England and beskift Henry and take the throne and make everything right again. He'd promised Lincoln he would.

He got a letter from Lincoln yesterday. His retinue brought it to him. They were in a high state of excitement. Edward had been so astonied by the splendour of Lincoln, his grace, his polite demeaning – and then he got to Mechelen and everybody was beautifully dressed and graceful and polite. A whole court of Lincolns, in which the original might perhaps go unnoticed. But his men explain that, even to Belgians, Lincoln is impressive. So gentil! He's like a European, hardly Angle-ish at all. His posture is just sublime. His command of language: exceptional. His swordsmanship is a technical marvel. And of course the ladies are, how do you say, *hot* for him.

Edward feels a redoubling of his pride at being the cousin of such a man. Next time he sees Lincoln, he'll ask him to show some swordwork.

And maybe ask him about ladies: how to get oneself in the orbit of a lady, what should be said to a lady once face to face, and other things like that.

Lincoln's letter was, like Lincoln himself, amusing and melancholy.

The usurper Henry Tudor and his mother's faces are as pinched closed as their purses, he writes. *Conversing with them would make you long for the comparatively merry talk of a Spanish Inquisitor. Henry's planning to begin Holy Week by washing the feet of twenty-nine beggarmen. Everyone pities these men, who would undoubtedly rather be given some money, but Henry would rather wash a thousand feet than part with one penny.*

We pray Lovell's rebellion in the North succeeds. I have evil dreams at night, in which God visits me and tells me that I'll never be able to undo my mistakes, my past support for the child murderer Richard, because I'm not a good enough man. My cousin, I meet men who talk about God so much, or so pompously, and when I hear them I think they must be like me, hiding their fears.

I wish I had the certainty of a man like Lovell. He's so sure of the holiness of his mission that he never even speaks of God at all.

When did women come into Edward's likings? he wonders. In this particular *way* of liking them? At court his head is tugged up by the rustle of a skirt. When they read Wauquelin he lingers on a picture of naked ladies – little breasts sitting high on long, pearlike bodies, peeled white – and the stories of Queen Candace of Meroë.

There's one girl he likes most. She has red-brown hair and is often blushing. She seems like the sort of maiden priests say God likes best: shy, sweet, silent.

But then there's Queen Candace.

It's complicated.

Queen Candace isn't a young girl. Nor is she shy. She's puissant and beautiful and rules an Ethiop land. She outwits Alexander and then laughs at his anger. See how it only takes one woman to unman you, she tells him. You should have remembered there's always someone more powerful than you!

But she spares his life. And Alexander notices her breasts. And both of them lie awake that night, stung into wakefulness by… *images.*

What these images are, Wauquelin *leaves to the imagination of readers with like experience.*

A turd on you, Wauquelin! Edward thinks. How about throwing a scrap or two to readers with no experience?

When the book is finished Philip cries, 'Let's begin it again!'

'No, I'm tired of Wauquelin,' Edward says. 'He leaves out much of *great* importance.'

The problem with the nobility is it's hard to tell when you've hurt their feelings. Philip, for example. Edward gets back from the library with a different book about Alexander, greets Philip, and sits down. After a few minutes of reading it begins to creep on him that Philip didn't greet him back. He looks up. He perceives the changes in Philip, almost too tiny to mark. A different position of the shoulders. A small frown, down-slant, bouncing gently off the floor.

'What?' he says.

'Nothing.'

Edward isn't sure what to do with *nothing.* He wishes Philip would just express whatever maugre he's got in a healthy way: a running kick to Edward's back, a pinch, a wrist-burn.

'Tell me, dear Philip,' he says instead, cajolingly.

It turns out Philip's hurt about what Edward said about his book. He thought it was full of good and wise learnings. His father had told him to read it. Was his father wrong?

Edward knows the answer to this one.

'By all the Saints, no!' he says. 'I spoke ill. I spoke wrong. Content your minds of that.'

Philip doesn't look cheered. He sighs. Then he says, 'He hasn't written. I wonder if letters are reaching the palace.'

'Hmm,' Edward says. 'Where is he now?'

'He's retaking French territories. He had them, then lost them again, so he has to go and get them back. And after he does that, he has to go to Germany to be crowned King of the Romans. He can't be Holy Roman Emperor until my grandfather dies. My grandfather is the oldest man I've ever heard of. Everyone calls him *Erzschlafmütze*, the Arch Sleepyhead. I think he gave my father the title to say sorry for not being dead yet. Anyway, I don't expect I'll see my father for a while. I hope he doesn't die in a horse misfortune first.'

Edward's thoughts go to his own family-that-was. He never considered before that his former father or brothers might die. Nobody could write to tell him.

Don't, his inwit says. Don't think of it.

'My father would be passing impressed with you,' Philip says. 'You're going into battle to take back a country that's been stolen from you.' He looks doleful. 'It's going to be so long before I'm old enough to do anything like that.'

'Hmm,' says Edward.

'What was *your* father like? Is it true you never met him?'

'I never did,' Edward says. 'But it doesn't seem as if people had any love for him. Sometimes I wish I'd met him, and sometimes I'm glad I don't have to.'

Philip sighs.

'I know what you mean,' he says.

As for Edward's history.

Margaret tells him about his father, the Duke of Clarence. The story is starting to sound familiar.

Ah, Clarence.

That's what people usually said. And:

So well-favoured as a boy
Such a shame.

Clarence had started so promisingly. He was handsome, orgulous, the brother of King Edward – who gave him grants, titles, lands, anything to keep him merry. Clarence was charming company when he was merry. But he longed for puissance, and he was sore wroth at anything someone else had been given and not him.

Not that this was a long list.

When his younger brother Richard was given the Yorkshire lordship of Richmond, Clarence raised a commotion, and it was regranted to him instead. By the time Clarence was seventeen, people were laughing at him for having his sword carried full cere-moniously in front of him by an attendant, betokening his position as second-in-line to the throne.

Clarence rode in Margaret's procession to escort her when she left England for Burgundy. He took his sister's hands and cradled them, and said with tears in his eyes that he would miss her grievously. She warned him about his finances: he was spending beyond even a king's means. And she urged him to stop the performance with the sword.

Did he listen?

Does anyone ever listen?

Clarence betrayed Edward by marrying the then Earl of Warwick's daughter Isabel Neville ('Your mother, Edward') instead of the match the king wanted for him. Then he joined the Earl of Warwick in a rebellion against Edward. The two of them spread rumours that Clarence's mother once had an affair with an archer and Edward was the bastard result, and that Edward and Elizabeth Woodville's marriage was invalid because she was a widow. Nobody listened. So they gave up on whisperings, and issued a proclamation that the Woodvilles were corrupting and controlling the king. They defeated Edward in battle, executed a few Woodvilles, arrested Elizabeth Woodville's mother for sorcery, and took Edward prisoner. But they didn't have enough support, and had to let him go. A queasy truce was agreed.

Next Clarence and Warwick offered to help put down a rebellion in the Midlands. Edward found out later that they'd organised the whole thing. Clarence and Warwick were declared traitors. They went to France, where they allied with their former enemies in the Wars of the Roses: the defeated Lancasters. They invaded England and forced Edward to flee to Burgundy. His queen, Elizabeth Woodville, had to take sanctuary in Westminster Abbey.

Clarence was now full witting that things hadn't unfolded well.

At all.

He'd thought he was going to be king. But the Lancasters weren't going to give him that, nor any new titles. And they wanted the great estate of Tutbury – once theirs, now Clarence's – back.

And so Clarence reconsidered. Always at home with hudder mudder and false counsel, he now showed a loyal face to Warwick – but secretly, via Margaret and their other sister Elizabeth, he reconciled with his brother the king.

'And you all forgave him?' Edward asks. 'After everything he'd done?'

'Of course,' Margaret says. 'He was our brother. Also, we needed his wiles.'

So Clarence set spies, and raised an army. He played the same tricks on Warwick that he once played on Edward. He gave Warwick counsel so false it cost Warwick a battle. He delayed the march of Warwick's men, then took his own troops to join Edward's forces.

The brothers – Clarence, Edward, and Richard (who'd remained loyal to Edward) – were reunited. Clarence fell on his knees and Edward lifted him, kissed him, forgave him. Warwick was killed at the Battle of Barnet. The Lancaster king, Henry IV, was killed by Richard. The Lancaster heir was killed by Clarence as he fled the field at Tewkesbury. Justice was done and the sun in splendour shone on England once more.

Margaret stops talking. A moment of time stretches, darkens. Edward understands. Her three dead brothers are here.

He wishes the story were over, so they would all go away.

But she sighs, and says she'll continue it another day.

5

The next time Edward's with Margaret, sitting in the pink evening, listening to her stories, he senses Clarence in the room. His face is hardly visible, but dissatisfaction and wroth spread out from him. Eddies of wine colour the air around him; dark clouds chase each other around his head.

Edward looks around. None of Margaret's ladies seem to notice. Her jester seems heavy, but then he always seems heavy. Edward once asked his retinue if jesters were meant to be like this, somehow draining the life of the room, but they said no, the man turned doleful because Margaret didn't laugh at any of his jokes.

Edward sees something of himself in the fool – always trying to guess at what's required, always failing – and he avoids the man. His sadness feels contaminating.

'I'll tell you more about Clarence,' Margaret says now.

Edward wishes he could say, I don't want to hear any more. But that's not how things are between him and Margaret. She leads the conversation. Edward, awed and small, creeps along behind.

'Are you in healthy spirit, nephew?' Margaret says. 'You look blanched. It seems to me that your gut is waxing cold. Make sure you take extra spices after dinners. Now, we were talking of the perfidy of your father. Which rose up again, not twelve months after he was restored to favour...'

King Edward's second reign was a joyous one. The country was rich: even his own prodigious spending couldn't exhaust it. He was happy. Everyone was happy.

Not Clarence. He had a baby son now ('You, Edward') born – officially, anyway – in 1475. But

he was furious because his brother Richard had married Anne Neville, the sister of Clarence's wife Isabel. Clarence had tried to prevent the wedding by concealing the girl in London, disguised as a cook-maid. He always loved a trick. But Richard had found her and married her and now Clarence had to split the enormous Neville inheritance with his brother.

At the end of 1476, Isabel Neville died after a difficult childbirth. Her baby son died shortly after. A month later, Clarence purposed to marry Margaret's stepdaughter, Mary of Burgundy. He didn't have anybody's approval in this, and Edward refused it. A tempest arose in Clarence then, and he quit the court

Not long after that, Clarence had three former servants of his wife's tried and executed with such disworship to proper law that it was – plainly – murder. He said they'd poisoned Isabel and her baby. One of the servants had been lateward employed by the Woodvilles, and Clarence noised that it was the queen, Elizabeth Woodville, who ordered the poisoning.

Margaret wrote to Clarence, then, to tell him to stop attacking his brother. There wasn't even any strategy behind his doings now – unless he wanted to get himself beheaded. She wondered if he'd lost his wits.

He never replied.

It ended quickly after that. King Edward had three men arrested for treason and witchcraft. One of the accused was Clarence's man, Burdet. He was hanged, drawn and quartered. The king then announced that Clarence's trial of his former servants would be subject to a judicial review.

Clarence had been warned, but he didn't stop. He'd lost the mastery of himself. He brast into the king's council chamber, disordered in his minds, crying and shouting: that Burdet and the others were innocent, that the queen was a sorceress, that she'd had his family killed.

He was arrested, put in the Tower, and charged with treason. One of the accusations against him was that he'd purposed to secretly send his infant heir ('You, Edward') out of the country, exchanging him for a stranger's child. The men who confessed to being part of this plot lied, to save themselves, and said that this plot hadn't succeeded. King Edward believed them.

Margaret had stopped writing to Clarence by now, as had her mother and sister. Why write to a madman? Why write to a dead man?

Richard busied himself drawing up a list of Clarence's lands and offices, to request the choicest after his brother's death.

Clarence was convicted of high treason and executed ten days later – in private, at the request of his mother. It was noised that he was drowned in a butt of Malmsey, at his own request.

King Edward was sore grieved by Clarence's death. Of course Clarence had to die. He was like a hound that had fits of biting. But you can also mourn the loss of the high-spirited pup you remember. Even the king's attainder of his brother was filled with emotion. Pain, outrage. Why, King Edward seems to ask, would Clarence demean in such wise, when the King, of tender youth unto now of late, has ever loved and cherished him, as tenderly, and as kinderly, as any creature might his natural Brother.

How?

But Clarence never answered.

'We none of us ever knew what possessed him,' says Margaret. 'He was secretive until the end. We didn't even know that he'd succeeded in exchanging you, until that ancient lizard Stillington told us. You were very nearly left to a life and death on an Oxfordshire farm.'

Before he got here, Edward would have longed for that ending. To live a regular and peaceful life; untroubled; unvisited by Clarence's ghost.

But.

He likes being here near Margaret – half-dead of awe, yes, but on the other hand, sipping hippocras from a cup made of glass: the first time he's seen such a thing. Eating dried figs in honey from a gold bowl. Admiring the enormous tapestries, the Van Eyck and Van der Weyden paintings on the silk-hung walls; luminous-skinned Belgians, no brush strokes to be seen. Admiring (more privily) the richly clad backs of two of her ladies, playing chess nearby. Enjoying the proximity of these near-divine persons: Margaret, Philip, Lincoln.

Wondering if maybe he can be one of them.

'What was my mother Isabel like?' he asks.

'I hardly knew her. A silly girl, by all accounts.'

'What would you do if you didn't become king?' Edward asks Philip.

'Emperor,' Philip says.

'Right. If you weren't emperor.'

'What do you mean?' Philip asks. 'Are you japing with me? I don't always understand japes. I'm too young maybe.'

'No jape. What I mean is: are there any heirs who decide *not* to be king?'

'By heaven, no,' says Philip. He looks alarmed. 'Holy God exalts us to the throne. It's heresy to refuse His will.'

This is the difference between Philip, growing up knowing his divine right to rule, and Edward, growing up in the shadow of a goat.

'Well, when I'm king I'll visit you,' he says to Philip.

'Yes!' says Philip. 'We will have treaties against the French and our children will marry each other to seal our accord and ensure the success of our lineage. Do you want to throw nut shells at the courtiers? There's a balcony I found; if we lie down they can't see where they're coming from, it's so funny.'

'What if I *don't* become king?' Edward asks Philip. 'What if their plans don't work?'

'You mean, if you die in battle?' Philip says.

Edward's about to say no, and then he realises: those are his options.

1. Become king.

2. Die in battle.

Faced with being king, he tries to prepare for it. He remembers his promise to Lincoln to set everything right.

What will he start with? Margaret's dowry, maybe. It had been agreed between England and Burgundy before her marriage, but her brother Edward never paid it. This wasn't a surprise to Margaret. The king found his own promises uncomfortable. Like the clothes of his youth, they fitted over-tight.

It's unjust! Edward said. I'll pay it, on England's part.

You are a noble boy aright, she said. Spoken in the temperate, rational way she said everything. Her manner is: *whether you like it or not, this is the unadorned truth.*

It made him feel that he *could* be a noble boy.

I won't let you down, he said, full of feeling – and she laid her hand, briefly, on his.

There is also the matter of the trading agreements revoked by Henry, said Margaret. Those must not be forgotten.

You are a noble boy.

The words float Edward back to his chambers. The people he passes smile at him as they bow. He realises its because *he's* smiling. His stomach isn't clenched; his humours are in balance, his inquietness lifts away.

He feels, for a moment, truly like Edward, Earl of Warwick. The boy that is wanted, needed, expected. It feels good.

But more needs to be done to become Edward. Manners alone aren't enough. He needs gentilesse. He needs to study knightly heroes. Consume and somehow embody Alexander's ambition, Arthur's puissance, Maximilian's bravery, Philip's confidence, Lincoln's nobility of soul. To show these things to a beautiful lady. Possess her heart. See her in her nightgown.

He thinks *Le Morte d'Arthur* ought to help, but it's still not to be had.

'It's wonderly popular,' de Busleyden says.

'Is there else anything I can read that's *like* the *Morte*?' Edward asks.

'Chivalric adventures? I used to like reading Marie de France's *Lais*, in my youth.'

'Do they also have great kings and brave knights? And queens? Fair queens who know things. Who have experience.'

'Experience, my lord?'

'I mean – wisdom.'

'I don't know about *wise*,' de Busleyden says. 'Beautiful, yes. And oftentimes wicked or faithless.'

'Oh, yes, that's fine too.'

But the *lais* are a mistake. It is in the *lais* that he meets Sir Gowther. A person Edward wishes he could forget.

But he *sticks*.

Sir Gowther is born of a duchess and a wicked fairy, who tricked her into swiving him by disguising himself as her husband. Sir Gowther is a cursed child who tears off his mother's nipple when at suck, and kills his nurses. As an adult his favourite pastimes are rape, murder, and burning nuns to death. But, later on, Sir Gowther is right sorry about his naughty doings. He does penance, saves the Princess of Germany from an evil Sultan, and God forgives him. Later, as Emperor of the Holy Roman Empire, he builds a convent in which nuns can pray for the souls of the unfortunate nuns he torched in his younger years. After Sir Gowther dies, many miracles are seen around his tomb, owing to his great holiness.

This all leaves Edward sore inquiet. The idea of *blood* has been sitting heavy on him awhile now.

Maybe this is what his father's ghost wanted. To show Edward who he really is: the son of a wrothful murderer and a silly girl. Edward would rather be haunted by Will Collan, who would never have hanged anybody.

But then: Will was a liar. Edward's the son of a liar, raised by a liar. Is he destined for dishonesty? How can he be a king who sets things right, if he's dishonest?

And now what is this story?

Is it a sign?

Don't worry, Edward, a heinous father will produce a heinous son, but your evil can't last forever, and in the end you'll become a saint, no matter how many nuns you burn.

Is this… comfort?

6

The quiet demosel is crossing a courtyard filled with orderly topiary, bright green in the sunlight. She's accompanied by the older woman who usually has charge of her. Like all the noblewomen, they are an intimidating sight: floating over the ground in their wide skirts, like ships; the veils streaming from their tall hennins.

An impulse gets hold of Edward. He puts himself directly in their path. The two women are forced into a ceremonious stop. They curtsey. He bows.

The two women look at him curiously.

'Fine weather, isn't it?' he says.

'Indeed, my lord,' says the older woman.

The younger waxes pink, the colour crossing the neat bridge of her nose. There's a short silence. Edward knows he's about to turn red too.

Don't blush, he commands himself.

His face, misunderstanding, gives forth its best, brightest glow.

He bows again, and moves around their skirts, and they all pass on.

Fine weather, isn't it?

Fuck's sake.

Edward tries to write a *lai* of his own, a brighter one, about the Duke of Clarence hiding his baby son, to reclaim him when the war was won. Something like that. The boy is taken to a new land, where he meets a mute maiden of great gentilesse, but his own voice flees before he can make address.

The maiden waits; she gazes at the boy. Her eyes ask him to say something wise, noble and beautiful.

And the boy—

—finds he has a lot of study to do. And many reasons to hurry on by, when they pass in the halls and courtyards.

And, when the boy is alone, he thinks of Queen Candace of Meroë, smiling at him, approving of his chivalry, his good-meaning, his poetry, the confident way he deals with a salt ship. Looking down at him from her Amazonian height, bidding him come to her chamber that night.

Lie down, she says. Listen, obey.

Well done, she says, I'm so pleased with you.

(Lying beside her in her solid gold bed, gazing like Alexander at the curve of her breast.)

You did so, so well.

Edward asks Margaret if he can attend one of her council meetings. It seems like the best way to learn how to rule. The goodliness of his decision is confirmed when Margaret inclines her head and smiles.

'I'm glad you asked,' she says. 'This interest augurs well for your kingship. But you must forgive the smallness of the council chamber. It is not meet, not meet at all.'

The council chamber is one of the largest rooms Edward has ever been inside. He could stand in the marble fireplaces. One of the tapestries could blanket his whole retinue.

'This is a *small* room?' he says.

'You must forgive it, my nephew. We're rebuilding the entire palace,' Margaret says. 'There was no ducal palace when I arrived here, so we bought eight houses and combined them, which has resulted in a labyrinthine confusion. I've heard from your retinue that you are quite incapable of getting about, and keep taking embarrassing wrong turns.'

'Oh,' Edward says. He didn't realise this would be reported to her.

'Humiliation for you, nephew, is humiliation for us.' She lays her hand to her chest. 'The palace is inexusable. Hence, we are reshaping it, and also adding a tennis court, and improving the baths, which are not of the best standard.'

'But the baths are magnificent!' Edward says.

'Look, his eyes are shining,' says Margaret's jester. 'He must mean the *town* baths.'

There's a short silence.

'My jester is referring to the number of whores that frequent the public baths,' Margaret says. 'His humorous pretence is that it is these women who enliven you.'

The jester sighs.

'My lady, may I suggest that we have the meeting without the presence of the fool?' says Margaret's chancellor.

'Excellent idea,' Margaret says.

The jester leaves, looking even more disconsolate.

Philip, who'd followed Edward to the council, says now, 'We need a shooting gallery in the new palace.'

Everyone looks at Margaret.

'Another excellent idea,' she says.

Someone writes the instruction down.

'And let's have mirthful devices, like at Hesdin, with monkey-shaped automata and statues that squirt you with water and floors that drop you into piles of feathers!' says Philip.

'What?' Edward says, astonied. 'This is a real place?'

'Hesdin is one of my castles. Built by the Count of Artois.'

'A strange man,' says Margaret.

Edward's trying to imagine her falling into a pile of feathers. It's not possible. There are some things the brain cannot conjure, and this is one of them.

'And all of this was made so long ago, we must be able to exceed it in magnificence,' says Philip. 'My mother had a pet giraffe. We could have a giraffe automaton!'

'A giraffe! Is the giraffe still here?' Edward asks, hopefully.

'It's dead,' says Margaret. 'Which was a relief, because it became doleful following the death of Mary, and reminded us all of our own dole. Also, it ate too much grain.'

'An automaton giraffe wouldn't eat anything at all,' says Philip.

'These sapient ideas are being given the fullest consideration, my dear grandson,' Margaret says, and Philip smiles and claps his hands. A councillor starts writing. Margaret shakes her head at him. The councillor crosses the writing out.

'Now, on to business,' she says. 'Firstly, van Royan has been useful to me lateward. Have him sent a goodly charger as a gift. But Dullaert has disappointed me. He is wonderly slow at his duties. Please beskift him.'

'You're killing him?' asks Philip. 'How will you do it?'

Margaret looks surprised. 'I'm not Caligula,' she says. 'I mean, remove him from his position. Philip, we need to talk later. About attaining the right... sensibility. Now, finances.'

'These renovations would be more affordable if you raised the tax again in Voorne,' says one councillor.

'They were lowered after the floods of 1485,' Margaret says to Edward. 'No. Give them a few months longer.'

'I was about to say,' the Bishop of Tournai says quickly, 'the suggestion of raising taxes so soon is a fell one. You are as kind as a saint, my lady. Blessed are you in God's eyes.'

'Kindness?' Margaret says. 'I don't see how kindness comes into it. People are not like dogs who will endure beatings and no food. They are like cats. They will withdraw their hearts from us and look for new owners. This is simply sensible governance.' She sighs. 'Edward, a ruler shouldn't be a saint *or* a Caligula. They should be exactly atwixt the two. You must ignore what you have heard today. The feelings of men oversway their minds at times; they are much knocked about by their humours.'

'I apologise,' says the bishop. 'I became overwrought.'

Afterwards Philip says, 'By the Saints, that was wonderly boring! But we're getting an automaton giraffe!'

Heavy tidings: Lovell's plan has failed.

He and his friend Humphrey Stafford had raised a thousand-strong army of Northern men to ambush Henry during his progress of the North. But their rebel allies surrendered to Henry on the promise of a pardon. Lovell then launched a bold ambush on Henry in York, which failed, and he had to flee. Several of his supporters were hanged on the spot. Humphrey Stafford was dragged out of sanctuary, in breach of all decency, by Henry's men, and is now to face trial.

'Poor Stafford!' Edward cries.

'These things happen,' says Margaret.

'Was the rebellion in *my* name?' Edward asks. 'Or in the name of… the other earl?'

'There's only one name,' Margaret says. 'Though two boys in possession of it is… a muddy story. It's not easy to explain the exchange without Clarence alive – and so late in your life. If Lovell's plan had worked, we wouldn't have had to explain. We could have proclaimed publicly that we were crowning the Earl of Warwick. No need to go into the details.'

'But it didn't work.'

'No. It did not.'

For a blink of time, Edward had started to think that he might become king without a war, without any trouble at all. Now dying in battle is back on the cards.

After Edward's council experience, he decides to try his hand at strategy. A little king-making. Or, more honestly, unmaking himself as king. He knows Lincoln doesn't want to be king either, but Edward has faith in Margaret's power to compel any man, even Lincoln.

He starts wonderly subtly, with a gambit he's spent most of the night preparing.

'My lady aunt,' he begins. 'You've wisely advised me in the virtues of kingship. It strikes me that my cousin Lincoln embodies all of these virtues.'

'Yes, he's an exceptional gentleman,' Margaret says. 'God has blessed me in giving me such a nephew.'

'A perfect king for England, perhaps?' Edward says. 'This is a new thought that has just this moment occurred to me. I wonder where it came from. Maybe God Himself put the thought in my brain-pan.'

'Certainly He did not,' Margaret says. 'Or He would have put Lincoln first in blood. I find your words strange, nephew, and your manner of saying them – with an up-and-down flitting eye – not meet for an earl.'

Her frown presses him small and flat, like a trodden-on beetle. Meet for a beetle – and this is Edward, in spite of all his learnings. A beetle in gold buttons, with a darting eye.

'But do the people even *want* the earl – me – to be king?' he asks. (Trying not to sound plaintive. He senses Margaret would mislike plaintive.) 'They didn't rise up with Lovell.'

'Oh, I understand your minds now,' Margaret says, with a nod. He feels relieved. 'There were riots in London in your name. Be content: people like the Yorks. But also they don't care overmuch who sits behind the palace gates. And they're lazy. And they fear death. Nobody loved my brother Richard, but they wouldn't have risen up against him. Likewise with Henry. If they aren't starving, they don't care who feeds them. What gets them hot is greed or anger. Lovell didn't appeal enough to the nobles' greed. Henry hasn't made them very angry. And he may never. He isn't going to charge any of the rioters, because he knows his position is weak. He's not a stupid king, unfortunately. See how he gives the Church great sums of money. Piety buttresses his shaky position.'

She shakes her head. Her tone is moderate as always, but Edward can tell she's annoyed.

'Lovell doesn't think this way. That is the problem. He didn't build support for his rebellion. He loves strategy, but he isn't interested in what happens in people's hearts. This is how young princes end up dead. Not that I'm saying Lovell was involved in that. I mean it as a general wisdom.'

7

Edward has found out he can walk in the courtyard alone, without anybody becoming astonied or distressed. He does it often. He's here today, bowing to the people he passes, enjoying the chill spring sunshine boxed within the red-and-white-striped brick walls.

On the other side of the gardens, standing by the arcade, are three young Belgian nobles and some young ladies. Ah, these men. Talking to women! Edward marvels at their courage. And their courtly manner! Each man in the same posture; a single leg extended in front of them, the upper body reclining backwards from hips to shoulders. None of them is at right angles to the ground. Their chins are tucked in, to emphasise the swanlike length of their necks. Their hands make dancelike movements, no doubt adding to their charming conversation.

He circles, orbiting closer and closer, wondering if they'll notice and make him good cheer. By his final circuit, the ladies have moved off.

He hears one of the men say, in French, 'You see what I mean. Look at Morgan le Fay. She spends the entire story trying to raise evil commotions against Arthur. And then at the end she comes to help him. But it's too late and he's dead. This is exactly – exactly! – like Jeanette.'

He sounds so urbanely weary.

One of the others notices Edward staring and says in Dutch, 'Hey, it's the English prince.' The Dutch words are near enough sib to English that Edward can understand him. The tone isn't unfriendly, so Edward stops and bows. They all tilt forward in three vastly more elegant bows and introduce themselves: lords, all – but Edward must call them Olivier, Jean and Antoine.

'Were you talking about *Le Morte d'Arthur*?' Edward asks.

'*Mais naturellement.* We three have something of a name around here for being literary types,' Antoine says. 'Do *you* like to read, my lord?'

'I lateward read *Alexander*. But I started to mislike it. It's supposed to be history, but all the historians are writing different things, and calling the others liars.'

'Ah,' says Olivier. 'But that squibbling and lying *is* history! And none of it worth a shit. Listen, all these historians, they're all paid by kings. What do you think your King Richard's historian wrote about Richard killing little princes? That's right. Nothing! History's corrupt. Like everything else.'

'Truth,' says Jean, laying a hand to his heart and nodding pensily.

'Truth?' cries Olivier. 'The truth, my friends, is *dead*.'

Admiration sweeps over Edward. Is his mouth open? He quickly closes it.

'But it's good for you,' Olivier says to Edward. 'You are to be king! You'll employ your own historians.'

'No,' Edward says boldly. 'I'm going to be like Julius Caesar, and write my own history. And I'll do it honestly. I'll do it *right*.'

'Full worship to you,' says Olivier. 'Horace says it is poetry that confers immortality. And you will be writing the terms of your own eternal life.'

Edward's heart feels large and light. Here he is, conversing with the most sophisticated of gentlemen, saying things they nod at, accepted as if he's their own kind.

'It's wonderly good to talk about such things, poetry and history,' he exclaims. Then adds, hopeful, 'And ladies, maybe? Do you talk much of them?'

They all laugh. Not despitously. He's looking between them, alert to signs that they're scorning him or japing him, but the atmosphere remains friendly.

'If you want to talk ladies, my lord, come and desport with us again sometime,' Antoine says. 'Though the talk might be a little shocking for some…'

'No! I want to,' he says. Was this overhasty? Too puplike? He tips his chin down; he shrugs. 'Mayhap I will.'

When Edward first arrived in Mechelen he was adread that Margaret would weigh him, assay him, pronounce judgement. Then, when that didn't happen, he felt relieved and comforted. Now he realises it's been happening all the time, that in every conversation he is being gently, yet firmly, tested. Her stories always have a purpose. And follow-up questions.

'I've been meaning to warn you about greed,' Margaret says now. 'Do you know why the Yorks lost the throne?'

'Uh… greed?' Edward says.

'Exactly. And those around them were just the same: Buckingham, Warwick… so many other dead men I've known.'

'Is it only men?'

'By heaven, no. The dowager queen would have exceeded them all if she were able. But then my other sisters-in-law, the Neville women, were just as bad in a different way. They never said no to anything. They let Richard and Clarence have their own living mother declared dead, so they could take possession of all her lands. Greed turns quickly to wicked doings.'

'Is that why Richard killed my cousins the two princes?'

'Well, Richard told *me* that Buckingham killed them – but neither man publicly accused the other of the crime, even when they went to war, and so I think it was the doing of both. I don't believe Richard purposed murder from the start. His mistake was that he never looked far enough ahead. He killed the princes' protectors and thought his work was done; he killed the council members and thought it done. Eventually he realised he'd never be done until the heirs were dead. So. What do you think the lesson is?'

'It's a great sin to kill people?'

'And very impractical. Every person you kill has someone to avenge them.'

'Lincoln hates King Richard for what he did,' Edward says. 'Do you hate him now, too?'

'I don't intermeddle in what I can't change,' Margaret says. 'It was done; it was not well done, but what would be gained by taking up a maugre against my brother? To let my country fall to the French because of a fine point of feeling? It was Richard who sent us six thousand archers. More than my brother Edward ever did.'

Summer has arrived in Mechelen; the air that comes up through the hole in the garderobe is all gentleness. It makes sinning in here easier.

Not that Edward can blame the weather. Margaret's chaplain is also partly at fault.

One of his men had brought him the *Morte d'Arthur*, but the chaplain was alarmed that a boy his age was reading such devil-bait.

Give it to me, the chaplain said. Now, I'll find you something more meet.

So Edward ended up with de Lille's *De Planctu Naturae*, in which Nature warns man to stop being so wicked.

But why did de Lille have to make Nature so formidable, so beautiful, so promising below-gown? How is Edward meant to master his own wickedness?

As soon as the pleasure flows out – mouth clamped over a finishing groan in the garderobe – the shame flows in.

But maybe it's forgivable, Edward thinks, at this age? Alain de Lille said people shouldn't masturbate but have legitimate, divinely sanctioned ado – and it's not as if Edward's old enough for that. But the very second he's allowed to – and this is a solemn promise to God – he'll have lawful sex all the time, and never lay hands on himself again.

Lincoln writes, to report that Lovell is in hiding in Suffolk following his failed coup attempt.

God looks after Lovell, Lincoln says. *He got him to safety while Henry's men were hunting him widewhere. Therefore we cannot take Lovell's previous failure as a sign of God's ill will.*

But Edward can tell Lincoln isn't convinced. He knows because he was wondering it too.

Sometimes Philip and Lincoln remind Edward of each other, they are both so noble, and so loving – the only people who offer love to Edward, and Edward is so grateful for any amount of love; like water dripping down a cell wall, he presses his mouth to it, desperate.

But they are also very different. Philip is sure of his rights in God. He and God are one. Lincoln wants to believe that he and God want the same thing – that he's finally guessed it, God's will – but Edward can see he's frightened too; worried he's not good enough.

It would be wonderly sweet to *know*, the way Philip knows. But Edward feels more of a shared spirit with Lincoln. Does Edward *know* God wants him on the throne? No. Which might mean God doesn't want that at all, and Edward's going to end up stabbed a hundred times and slung across a horse naked, like dead King Richard.

Margaret says Lovell will come to Mechelen once the ports are no longer so closely watched. She isn't worried.

'Of course we wanted his success,' she says, 'but we also planned for the other eventuality.'

'If he'd been… killed?' Edward asks.

She lifts her hands. 'A wheel comes off the cart, you replace the wheel.'

'But we grieve over the wheel?' Edward says. 'Don't we?'

'Of course,' Margaret says. A tiny frown, before she continues. 'Lovell enjoys this too much. We

politick because we have to: Lovell politicks for the love of it. Why is he still in England? He could have sailed here weeks ago. But he likes the peril. It inquiets me that a man like this is so central to our purposes.'

'An important wheel,' Edward says sagely. Then he remembers Margaret telling him not to pretend to understand when he doesn't, so he says, 'But… why?'

'Lovell is my connection to the secret Yorkists of England,' Margaret says. 'He knows every thread of the web. And some of these people are passing powerful. One of Lovell's very close friends is as near as kin to Henry. I won't say his name, not yet.' She glances up at the room, where her ladies talk and play games and eat dates. 'Even here in Mechelen. Like any perilous secret, it should be spoken as little as possible.'

Edward asks his new friends how to talk to ladies.

Olivier laughs. 'My dear friend. You don't *talk* to women,' he says. 'Haven't you read the *Roman de la Rose?* Not the first part. Nobody bothers with that. I mean the part written by Jean de Meun, about the eternal quest for the rosebud, which all men long to pluck, but are barred by various unfair obstacles.'

'Is the rosebud… love?'

They all laugh now.

'A rosebud is a cunt,' says Antoine. 'Rosebuds and roses: virgin cunts and deflowered cunts.'

'I expect you haven't seen one yet,' Olivier suggests. 'The look is very similar.'

Edward thinks of Bella. There was *something* roseate – but no, he doesn't like the feel of that memory. He'd rather not think of her at all.

'Have you seen very many?' he asks Olivier.

'I've had so many they call me the gardener,' says Olivier.

Edward wonders what Jennott would say about being a rosebud.

'Do women like the book?' he asks.

'Oh, some dried-up old grucchers who don't stand a chance of getting tumbled love to complain about it,' says Olivier. 'Like Christine de Pizan. Her writings will suck the juice right out of your plums.'

'And not in a good way,' says Antoine.

'The *Roman* shows how false, faithless and gold-hungry women are,' Jean says. 'That's why they don't like it.'

'By the Saints!' Edward says, alarmed. 'So, should we not avoid them? Is it dangerous to be near them?'

'Oh, no. Just don't let them get the reins. Don't tell them your secrets: they'll tell the world. Don't trust them: they'll cheat on you. Don't give them gifts: they'll bankrupt you. They want to be the rulers: nothing satisfies them but stealing the puissance of the man. A true devoté of de Meun knows how to fool *them* first. To pluck the rose without getting caught in the thorns.'

Edward nods. But he feels inquiet. This kind of activity with rosebuds is undoubtedly a sin. And the *Visions of Tondal* was explicit on the consequences of *that*. Edward's worried that his sophisticated new friends are on course to spend the afterlife with barbed snakes going into and out of all their entrances. That he, Edward, might get in some kind of trouble by association.

That day, for once, he isn't tempted by the garderobe.

The next morning he and Philip are training outside with their small swords, clinking and clanking in their small suits of armour, the sunlight on metal making them both sweat. Philip lunges; Edward dodges, lands on his back on the gravel in a great clatter, breaking the air of the courtyard into fragments.

'Good work!' says their instructor. 'Excellent *stichschlac*!'

'Want to play at *quilles* after this?' Edward says as Philip helps him up.

'That would be wonderly merry!' Philip says. 'But don't you want to be with your new friends? I was large glad in my heart that you found such goodly company… so sophisticated and literary, just like you.'

'Oh, no. They're not much like me,' Edward says.

'You are overmodest. I don't expect you to play games with me when you could be talking about poetry and theology and human-ism and divers other clever things. You're thirteen. I know I can't keep up. I'm much rejoiced to be overpassed for such fine friends.'

He clasps his hands with a creak of metal, and gazes tenderly at Edward through his grille.

'*You* are the finest of all friends,' Edward says, ashamed. 'And I'd rather play with you.'

'Pray forgive me,' says their instructor 'Do you two know Liechtenauer better than I? Is there a technique I'm unaware of? That of standing around blavering like a brace of demosels? No? Well then. Get back to practice, because God knows, if you ever see real battle, such pitiable *albersleibens* as yours will get you cut into tiny pieces.'

8

News from the English court blows over the Channel.
Elizabeth of York is pregnant!
Or fat!
But probably pregnant!

'What does this mean?' Edward asks Margaret. 'If Henry has an heir?'

'Babies do not necessarily halse fast to the womb,' Margaret says. 'Infants do not necessarily live to be children. Children do not necessarily live to be adults.'

'So we should pray for it to die?' Philip asks.

'No, Philip. That's a grievous sin.'

'Alright,' says Philip. 'No praying for death. Should we pray for anything?'

'Always,' Margaret says. 'We pray that it's a girl.'

Edward hasn't given up on the *Morte d'Arthur*. (Would a knight give up on his quest for the Grail? No, he would not.) He just needs to read it hudder mudder, without being seen by the chaplain. Who is a holy man, but perhaps over-churchy: a sheltered cleric who doesn't understand what worldly, newfangled men ought to read.

So he bides two weeks, then sends one of his noblemen-servants to privily look into the whereabouts of the *Morte*.

'Sorry, my lord,' says his man. 'I asked for it for myself, as you told me, but was informed the chaplain has it. And he sent word he'd not be soon done.'

A notable thing happens.

Edward and Philip are with Margaret in her chambers, after dinner, the women around them playing with a little white lapdog, the silk-lined room rosy in the light of the pink and gold sunset over the city outside. He looks up, to see his aunt looking at him – and then she smiles.

A smile! He wishes he could inhabit this moment forever: a moment in which he is worthy, necessary, lovable. All these things could be meant by this smile.

He smiles back.

'It's time for us to commence our campaign, my dear nephew,' Margaret says. 'I have been speaking to the Lord Deputy of Ireland. In one week, you'll sail to Dublin.'

Edward wants to say: *no*.

He knew in his minds that this day would come. But his body didn't comprehend it, and now it blanches; his heart dips low, like a flame in a gust of cold air.

'How exciting!' Philip says.

Everyone is looking at Edward now. As if a grand speech is in order.

'Thank you, my lady aunt,' he says. 'I, uh, look forward to restoring England and Mechelen's friendship, and glorifying your reign therewith.'

'Not my lady grandmother's reign,' says Philip.

Edward is confused. 'Not…?'

'I am in my minority,' Philip explains, 'and my father the King of the Romans is regent in my stead. Obviously he's away a lot, so it seems as if my grandmother makes all the decisions, and people jape that they wouldn't know my father from the King of Finland – but my father's still the ruler. It's *his* reign, on *my* behalf. My grandmother just does all the money and political things. But ladies can't rule on their own.'

Margaret's ladies look up from their game with the dog. The dog, following their eyes, gazes confusedly at Margaret, head cocked.

Margaret herself looks at Philip for a short while. Her expression – as always – hard to know.

'That's exactly right,' she says, and pats his hand.

Edward understands how dullheaded it was of him to try to convince Margaret into letting him stay. He'd been trying to put his own ideas into her head, but her brain-pan is too formed, too formidably hard.

He thinks now of Philip. So ready to believe that Edward loves *Alexander* as much as he does, or that he's getting an automaton giraffe.

He says sadly to Philip, 'If I go to battle now, I won't be able to fight. They won't let me. But if I can stay here longer, and train with you, then I can go into battle properly, like your father would, and have that honour he enjoys.'

(Thinking privily that by the time he's grown, Lovell or someone else will no doubt have dealt with Henry. Kings don't last long. Maybe whoever deposes Henry won't need Edward anymore.)

'You are wonderly brave,' says Philip, looking admiring. 'But my grandmother has decided—'

'I thought she was your proxy only?' Edward says. 'The Lady Margaret doesn't make *your* decisions, does she?'

'By God, that's right,' Philip cries. 'Do you know what I'll do? I'll tell her you must stay longer!'

'I bow to your great wisdom,' Edward says, triumphant.

Philip comes back a little later.

'I spoke to my grandmother,' he says. 'She explained everything to me. We can't wait, Edward, because of the *money*. England owes us all this money. Also there are trade agreements, which need to be restored. And we need the money because my father's campaigning is so expensive. Then there's the renovation of the palace.'

Edward, dismayed, says – in more of a crow-crawk than he intended – 'Money is more important than honour?'

Philip looks confused. 'Money is honour,' he says. 'You can't have honour without money. But don't make dole, Edward! When you're king you'll have divers opportunities for battle. If you're lucky, people will try to invade or overthrow you, or you'll go to war in France, and – oh! – you can charge in, rashing and lashing, and vanquish everyone in magnificent style. Or you'll die bravely fighting, and you'll be in all the songs, the most noble king, for evermo.'

A king wouldn't be trying not to cry, Edward reminds himself. A king would comfort himself with reason.

And reason does have its consolations. If he becomes king, he can have Margaret and Philip to visit. Anyone he likes. The shy demosel. He could invite Jennott! His brothers – even Will Collan, if he says sorry. They'll all come to his palace, sleep in gold beds, play at games on the velvety lawns, eat roast swan for dinner.

Reason says: yes, all of that.

So long as you don't die in battle.

The feast day of Mechelen's patron saint, St Rombout, falls just before Edward's departure. It's his first public event. Margaret has decided that it's time for visibility; for his presence to be noised among the people. God bless Edward, Earl of Warwick, the saviour of Engeland!

The saviour can barely move for gold braid; he feels his body sweating under his rich clothes. The air outside his window is loud. People have gathered to see the sacrament, the bones of St Rombout travelling down the streets in a silver casket. Miracles are expected. In the press men and women and children pack in shoulder to shoulder, cheering, singing, shoving a little, quarrelling, falling down and being picked back up again.

Edward watches them waiting for the parade until he's summoned to Margaret's balcony, from where the royal family take their own turn at being watched. Soon this jolly townswoman drinking from a bottle, her large breasts dazzling white in the July sunshine, will be casting her eyes over *him*.

He hopes she likes gold braid.

Will she cheer?

Or will she shout, *What the fuck is this? He is no prince, you're all crazed, Engeland is doomed.*

But no.

'Nobody would ever shout wicked things at us,' Philip says. He looks astonied at the suggestion. 'I don't know how it's done in your country, Edward, but that's definitely not allowed here.'

No shouting of wicked things. Instead: dances, singing, showers of flower petals, a parade like a single giant animal, of divers colours, quaking, flashing, roaring with trumpets, pipes, trombones, stretching all the way to the unfinished cathedral tower in the main square, all the way inside his skull, stamping round and round as if to brast the walls. Edward looks at Philip beside him for reassurance, that people don't lose hold of their wits at these things.

Philip has his hand over his mouth, politely pressing back a yawn. He sees Edward looking at him.

'Not too much longer now,' he mouths.

That night there's a banquet. The great hall is filled with people. Oil torches light the frescoed walls; musicians do battle with the squawk and rumble of hundreds of voices. Edward sits with Margaret and Philip on a raised stage, with a larded boar's head in front of him that keeps trying to catch his eye.

After the feast is over, tumblers and jugglers and knife dancers and acrobats arrive, and a wilder merriment breaks out. Edward watches astonied. Margaret is in one of the quieter gatherings, talking with her bishops and officials, sipping her cup of digestive spices. She doesn't seem to have noticed the drunk courtiers directly behind her playing a game of smacking each other's bottom and squealing. The rules of the game are a mystery.

'Latewards, I grant you, France has not been much of a threat,' she says. 'The dauphin's sister is wrapped up tight in internal rebellions. But they will be working us wrack again soon. And the usurper Henry is too close to them. Ah, my nephew, welcome.'

'My lady aunt, my lords,' he says. He bows to the gentlemen. The wine he's drunk – more than he realised – nearly carries him body over head onto the floor.

'The councillors here are worried that the usurper Henry Tudor will hear of your presence here today.'

'I think it is a risk,' one says. 'We know he has spies in every state, including in Mechelen.'

'Untrue!' says another. 'Our great Mechelen is impregnable—'

'What I like to say about Henry Tudor is this,' says another. 'He has a hundred ears and one mouth. His ears hear all. And his mouth says—'

'—the extent of his resources is overstated, by fearful types—'

'It's a play on the old saying: you have two ears and one mouth—'

'He pays so little his spies are all double, selling tidings to enemies to afford their bread—'

'The point being, my lady, that he's going to hear—'

'—*I* considered it rather witty—'

Margaret raises a hand.

The men stop talking.

Edward looks at the hand. It's a normal-seeming hand, small and white. It doesn't look so different from his own. What has Edward's hand done today? Picked his nose, washed, pulled his pintle (may God forgive him), scratched his armpit, grabbed at food. He wonders if it will ever have such power.

'I mean for the usurper Tudor to hear about this,' Margaret says. 'I don't want him to sleep easy. And I want him to waste his efforts paying spies to watch Mechelen, and not Ireland, where we will keep my nephew full privily.'

'Brilliant, my lady!'

'Magnificently cunning!'

A toast then, to the esteemed Lady Margaret – and one to her nephew, who the councillors can tell immediately is as wise as he is gracious. His reign will be long, and will usher in a new Anglo-Burgundian accord. The countries are sib, after all: they both love wool, they both hate the French, their blood beats with the same pulse.

'To Engeland's saviour,' they say, raising their cups.

Edward tries to copy Margaret's look of regal puissance. An important discovery: the more wine he drinks, the more puissant he feels. And the less inquiet about the future. Yes, wine is really excellent, and should be more readily available at all times. As king he will mandate it.

The saviour of Engeland!

He drinks deep.

After more wine, he's realised drinking can't make him more confident or clever. It's merely brings out what's *already there*. Buried treasure. The wine somehow fills up his brain-pan, and all the fascinating and erudite things hiding within it spill over. His heart feels large and loving. His vision is hazy. He sways, joyfully earlish, from group to group, and every group is full pleased to see him.

He talks to de Busleyden about bull baiting as a metaphor; he tells a bishop that he thinks everyone will be travelling the seas in diving bells within ten years, at most. He invents a device to get hairs off the ears of old people. There's some wine on his hose, suddenly. How did that happen? Never mind it.

Over his shoulder Edward sees the quiet demosel, with her usual chaperone. Filled with vinous boldness, he excuses himself to greet her. She smiles shyly. The smile fills him with courage. He smiles back and – God be thanked for such a miracle – says something that's not stupid.

Edward will be much missed, she says. She herself will be quitting the court in a few weeks; she's betrothed to a nobleman from Germany. Edward wishes her good fortune. She thanks him. There is a small silence. He bows. She curtseys, and departs.

Well, he thinks. He spoke to a young lady! That's something. Maybe he'll talk to another. He's on his way toward a small blonde demosel when he sees Olivier appear from the side, and put his hand on her sleeve. Edward stops to watch. He feels worried for the young lady. She may not know she's a rosebud. Olivier moves his hands a lot, shows his teeth in a broad smile, talks, talks, talks. He's in the middle of talking when the girl pivots and walks away. She joins another group of noblewomen. She says something to them, and the women laugh.

Edward follows Olivier back to Jean and Antoine.

'I realised something,' he says to them.

He thinks de Meun might have been mistaken in his maugre against women. Because the women Edward knows aren't like de Meun's women. They aren't even like each other. They're as divers as men. Jennott was different from the Widow Mylton, who was different from Bella, who was different from Margaret of Burgundy.

'Maybe there are hundreds of kinds of women,' he concludes. 'And Jean de Meun had the misfortune to encounter only one variety. The *French* variety.'

Olivier has been frowning throughout. Now he says, 'Well, my lord, I am *wonderly* grateful for these learnings. With all your experience of Amor, I'm certain to benefit from your advice.'

Jean and Antoine look surprised. Then they start laughing.

Edward feels wroth rising. It comes on quickly, his wine-mingled blood jumping into his face. He was trying to be kind, and this laughter is not kind.

'What do you say, then: that women are weak and faithless, that men should be over them?'

'Obviously,' Olivier says, rolling his eyes.

'All women?'

'They're all daughters of Eve aren't they? They're as light-minded and greedy as she was.'

Edward looks over Olivier's shoulder and widens his eyes. Then he bows, and says, 'My lady aunt.'

Olivier doesn't jump. He goes still. Edward knows Margaret mislikes hangings, but Olivier doesn't look as if he knows this. He turns slowly, his face as colourless as if he's been bled – and then he realises Edward was japing him.

Now the laughter turns on Olivier. Edward feels the power in the room shift with it, he can sense it with his body, a current in the air, like a changeable wind. He feels a new kind of delight. Olivier's choleric expression only increases it.

'Oh, dear, Olivier, your hose is bepissed,' he says.

A village-ish joke, but it goes down just as well here. Louder laughter, more laughter – and he wants more still. He's about to expand on his theme when Jean and Antoine point behind him.

'Come on! You can't do the same jape twice,' he says. By the time he's said it, Margaret is at his side. She's frowning. The others bow, and hie themselves off.

'What is this Clarence-like demeaning I see, nephew?' she asks. 'Do you want a sword brought, so you can have it carried before you?'

'I'm sorry,' Edward says. 'I didn't mean to—'

'Power isn't a pleasure. Power is a duty,' she says. 'It is not to be revelled in.'

Her jester appears beside her. 'Time for the drunken nephew to be put in his cot,' he says, and plays a little fartlike blast on his flute.

Margaret gives this serious consideration. 'The fool is right. You are overdrunk. It's not meet. Go to bed; I'll have my chaplain bring you a relic to help your health – and you must pray God your bowels escape the morning afterclaps.'

The next day de Busleyden brings Edward Boethius's *Consolation of Philosophy*.

'Low spirits, a lack of sleep, following an excess of merriness. What you need is the *Consolation*.'

'He can't read with a headache!' says one of Edward's noble-men-servants. 'Don't the Engelish cure their hangovers by drinking wine in which an eel has been suffocated?'

'No, that's for *before* you start drinking,' says another. 'Too late for that. He needs his stones washed in vinegar to carry away the poison.'

'Thank you, my lords,' says Edward. 'I'll take the book.'

'It passes belief that your Engelish tutor didn't *start* with this,' de Busleyden says. 'Horace! God help us! You ought to have been studying the search for wisdom above glory and material pleasures. Your tutor should have been banished.'

'He was put to death.'

De Busleyden laughs. 'Very meet.'

Edward picks up the volume. It's not illuminated, but it's heavy. His arms tremble. He thinks of Maister Richard; his last sight of him, on the floor. He only just manages to drop the book and turn away before a surge of vomit brasts out of him, over him, over the chair and the rug.

'By Saint Barbara! See! *That's* what books do,' says a nobleman-servant to de Busleyden. 'Fetch the vinegar!'

Before Edward leaves, Margaret calls him to a meeting in her state rooms, where she sits on a chair of black velvet, with her officials around her. She tells him that while he's in Ireland she'll be raising an army of men, for the invasion. Then she gives him some papers to sign, for the restoration of favourable trade terms to Burgundy and the repayment of her dowry. Also the cost of the army.

When this is done she lays her hand on his. That small, powerful hand! He wonders if any of its puissance is travelling into his own body. But all his body feels is a pulse of misery and dread, at leaving Margaret and Philip and his new friends here; maybe to die, which is terrifying; maybe to be a king, which is more so.

'I know you'll restore our family to greatness, nephew,' she says. 'You have a sound nature. Now, I have a parting gift for you,' she says, gesturing to a book on the table. 'I heard you'd asked for it. It's heathenish and uncivilised, but I know it's the sort of thing people enjoy.'

It's *Le Morte d'Arthur*.

'I'm passing doleful about you leaving,' Philip says to Edward. 'You're my best friend.'

Edward is warmed by this. Also surprised. Are they best friends? But then: who else is there?

'Do you wonder if we're each other's best friend because we don't have any other friends?' he says.

Philip looks puzzled. 'You'll *never* have any other friends,' he says. 'Friends have to be equal and alike. Look at us. We're both born kings but we're also still children. Do you know anyone else in the same condition?'

'That's a good point.'

'And do you think anyone can be your true friend when you're a king, except another king?'

'Probably not.'

'Exactly,' says Philip. 'Which is why it's a passing great tragedy that kings never *do* make friends with other kings. They always end up warring and scheming. But not us. We'll be the first kings to be friends. And all the kings that come after will follow our example.'

The Pale

'So anyone who stirs her tongue in lying, she makes her tongue into a cradle for the devil's child, and rocks it eagerly, like its nurse' —

Ancrene Wisse,
Anonymous

Edward arrives in Ireland at dawn though the sky doesn't admit it, being full dark, sending down a hard rain that beats at the heads of the horses, bangs loudly on the leather roof of the whirlicole.

The men escorting him are talking around and over him in Gaelic. They aren't unfriendly – they'd made him great welcome, and told him proudly that he was travelling in one of the only carriages in Ireland, a wonderly fine machine, luxuriously appointed with cushions – but Edward was shy, and shamefully teary, because of having to leave Mechelen, so early in the journey he'd pretended to fall asleep. Then he stuck to the pretence even though the rough road was jolting him up and down on his cushion like a sack of grain, and the rain was deafening, and the men must have been laughing at him, with his eyes still clamped closed.

It's still raining when the carriage stops at Maynooth. The seat of the Earls of Kildare. The castle itself is an enormous pink shape, obscured by violent sheets of water. Edward looks up and the rain crashes into his eyes. But he's also started to cry a little bit, and so the rain is a good thing, it hides the tears.

God has been kind to send rain, he thinks.

God is still with him.

He's borne off through the arched entranceway, with much shouting.

'This way, my lord!'

'Mind the puddle – oh, down he goes.'

'He's drowning!'

'We can't drown the hope of England!'

Hands pull him up, draw him along. Blinded, Edward hardly registers the cessation of the rain, or the change of scene, the men drawing back from around him.

'You naughty knaves,' says a tall man; a dark figure only, in front of a wall of flames. 'Be careful with my prince.'

Edward rubs the water out of his eye sockets. He's in a cathedral-sized hall, less ornate than those of Mechelen, less gilded – but rich still, hung with tapestries, windows glass-mullioned, with a wagon-sized fire at the far end. The dark man-shape sharpens into the Earl of Kildare. The Great Earl. Gerald Fitzgerald. He's a handsome man, with imposing shoulders, blue eyes, red cheeks, dark red hair. He bows.

'I pray forgiveness for this despitous downpour, my lord. We none of us can fathom it. Ireland is a hot and dry country usually.'

The men laugh. Edward laughs too, without knowing exactly what the jape is.

'By Saint Boniface, he's the exact sib of the Duke of Clarence,' Kildare says, staring at Edward with a force that feels physical: like he's being poked in the face, his mouth opened, his teeth checked. 'The very crop and root of him.'

'Did you know him?' Edward asks.

'Oh, passing well! An excellent boozing companion – though somewhat maltempered, if he thought he wasn't getting due worship. But I bore him much love. It was he who made me Lord Deputy. When your father was put to death, King Edward – though more likely his Woodville queen – unseated me.'

'But you're… Lord Deputy now?'

'My unseating couldn't endure long. King Edward replaced me with an Englishman. But we wouldn't have it. Ah, that was a japeful year. The Lord Chancellor of Ireland, Lord Portlester – my dear wife's father – refused to allow the Englishman the use of the Great Seal, then the acting Constable of Dublin Castle – my friend Brother Keating – now *he's* a lively lad, we've had to pay him out of a couple of murders and he's technically excommunicated – Brother Keating barred the Englishman from the castle—' He has to break off here for laughing. 'In the end the English replacement fucked off back to England, and I had my Lord Deputyship back. Anyway. We were talking of your father. He's sore missed by me – by all us Irish. Not a man, woman and child of us would not say that we've been blessed by God in having his son tread our ground.'

Edward isn't sure what to say to this, but his speaking doesn't seem to be necessary. He smiles and drips onto the floor and Kildare continues.

'The men will show you to your room and get you out of these bepissed items. And bring wine. You must be sore parched. Then once you're reclothed you'll meet my family. Be warned, this is a house full of women of all ages and dispositions ranging from saintly – in the form of my wife – to as demonic as the devil himself. Praise God I have a baby boy now, the next Gerald – I can tell you, I thought my cock was cursed these lateward years; I thought I'd have to visit a sorcerer to remediate it.

'That's a jape: we don't resort to black magic here. You thought I was serious though, didn't you? You milky purselip. Let me tell you, Ireland is more gentil than England. Our wine is better than that in Henry's cellars. And we don't murder child-princes. Or so you'd hope, eh? Only japing, content your heart, I'm just an Irishman of no large wit. Now, lads, take our revered guest to his room, and make him right welcome.'

Edward's room is upstairs, at the opposite end of the keep to the solar containing the chambers of Kildare and his family. The walls are painted in a design of green and gold; the bed is curtained in deep green wool; there are fresh rushes on the floor and a fire in the hearth, smelling strangely earthy.

His wet clothes are taken away; his silk and velvet clothes are unpacked from their trunks by servants, brought to him by other servants, drawn and tied and buttoned onto his body by yet more servants. He used to dread this procedure, but now it reassures him. He touches his gold buttons gently.

The saviour of Engeland!

Outside the rain has stopped. From the window in the garder-obe he looks out over a landscape on which the sun has broken, swathes of light lying over hills, trees and fields. Tiny sheep move in the distance, tiny carts crawl along the road. A tiny man stands by the stream, bends down, splashes his face, then stretches his arms.

The gesture reminds Edward of Will Collan, his father that was. It immediately stings his heart, like an arrow shot from his old life.

But every farmer stretches this way; every working man splashes his face the same way. Will Collan is gone. His fatherhood was leased, and the contract is over. Whatever Will Collan's doing now, he's not thinking of Edward.

Forward! That's the only direction now. And he won't tackle it at a limp, feet hobbled by the past, but stride with great boldness: proud, gentil, kingly.

Gerald Fitzgerald takes Edward around the castle, which he says is every part as lavish and beautiful as any castle in England – observe the gold and silver plate, the silk-upholstered chairs, the tapestries of unicorns and castles, hunters chasing stags, Greek goddesses with their paps out. He hails servants in Gaelic as he goes. The pink exterior was created by mixing oxblood – buckets and buckets of it – with the limewash. Has Edward ever seen anything like it? No, he has not. Kildare also has castles in Portlester and Kildare, manors in Maynooth and Leixlip, and a Dublin residence, Thomas Court – but enough boasting. His lady wife is approaching. Edward will agree that there is no more beautiful or learned woman on the surface of the earth.

'Alison FitzEustace Fitzgerald,' Kildare says. 'Lady of Kildare. Rose of the hills, I call her.'

'He's full of this sort of blaver,' says Alison.

'That creature behind her is a poet. She's mad for the poets, we've several of them trailing about the courtyards. I think she must be fucking them because sure their poetry is passing awful—'

'Gerald—'

'I'm japing with you, my Lord Edward. She's not after fucking any poets.'

'He's japing about the poems too, I'm sure,' says the poet. 'Most agree they're very well turned verse—' But Kildare is on the move again;

'Is that my girls I hear?' he shouts. 'Ah, they are come. Well, nearly all – Margaret is no longer here. She's lateward married Piers Butler, of the Ormonds. House of our enemies. But Margaret, like her mother, is beautiful and stout in her wits and so she's got the rule of

the Ormond boy already. The second in age is Joan, she's fourteen –
where's Joan?'

'Shall I fetch her?' says a lady in waiting.

'Ah, no, a turd for her. You'll meet her some other time, my lord,
to your great woe. Now, this radiant heliotrope is Eleanor, she's thirteen, your age, then we have the orgulous Eilis, at a mighty ten years
old, then shy Alice, who is six—'

'Seven! Stupid Da!'

'Sorry, kitten, there are grievous many of you to follow. And finally:
Eustacia, four years old, a full warly savage. Where's my son Gerald?'

'With the nurse. I'll fetch him,' Alison says.

'Nay, no need to disturb the tiny earl,' Kildare says. 'He is neither
so beautiful nor so charming as you. He created the most wonderly
bum-storm the last time I dared approach him. He's easier to celebrate when he's not around. And celebrate we do. We have an heir,
at last. Do you know, my wife told me this morning I'm to find a
mistress. She's had enough of heir-making, she said. She won't be
able to stay away from me for long though.'

'Eurgh, *Da*,' says Alice, and runs away. Eustacia follows her, whooping, '*Crom a Boo!*'

'The Fitzgerald war cry,' Gerald says proudly.

'Shall we show our guest around the castle?' says Eilis.

'No, I've done that, and he'll be wanting to rest now. You'll have
to lock him in the cellar another day.'

'We were going to lock you in the cellar,' Eilis says to Edward.

'Not for long,' says Eleanor.

'There's all sorts of wine and food in the cellar so you'd have a
better time in there then out here. You don't mind that we were
going to lock you up, do you? We do it to everyone. You have to
make us a promise and if it's a good enough promise you get released.'

'What kind of promise?' Edward asks. Eleanor has red hair and
bitten-on lips that look pink and crumpled. Her skin glows like
warm milk. He can't think of anything he wouldn't promise her. His
possessions, his service, his life.

'We wanted you to grant us a monkey. Did you tell him about the
monkeys, Da?'

Kildare explains that the family crest features a jackanapes, which
is on account of a fire a hundred and fifty years ago that would have

taken the life of the baby heir, were it not for a pet ape that brast out of its chains and carried the boy to the safety of a tower.

'We want a monkey but we've not been allowed one,' says Eilis. 'Don't you think we should be granted one, your majesty?'

'He's not king yet,' Kildare says, 'so he'll not be granting anything. You've got a wanton ape, anyway.' He picks up Eustacia, who is back and hanging off his leg, and inverts her. She squeals and essays to bite his calf. 'Ah, not really, you're a goodly gentil lady, aren't you, Stacia? Well, maybe not. Listen. That pet ape was taking the baby off to eat, I tell you, not to save it. They're fell creatures. Speaking of. Tell your sister Joan to show herself at dinner or I'll—'

'You'll what?' asks Eleanor.

'I don't know,' Kildare says. 'Ah —' waving to a figure outside the window ' – the messenger is back from my brother. As for your sister, I have no idea how to manage her. Do some threating for me, girls, would you?'

He walks away in one direction, Alison and the poet in another, followed by the lady in waiting and Eilis. Eleanor quits the room via a different doorway, leading to Edward knows not where. Eustacia and he are left in the hall. 'Watch me,' she says, and does a forward turnover on the ground, ending rolled inside the layers of her dress. The bundle of fabric struggles, then goes still. A few moments pass.

'Do you… want me to help unwrap you?' Edward asks.

'No, thank you,' the roll says.

'I'm going to go, then. If you're sure you don't need me.'

'I don't,' the roll says. 'Farewell.'

'Goodbye.'

So here he is. Fallen through the cracks of the day, alone in his room with the *Morte d'Arthur*. The sun comes wavy through the glass, lighting up the page.

Edward thought the *Morte* would tell of Christian adventurings. But the noble King Pelles has just got his court sorceress to enchant Lancelot into believing that Pelles' daughter Elaine is Lancelot's beloved Queen Guinevere, so Lancelot will have ado with Elaine and fulfil a prophecy that says Lancelot and Elaine will father Galahad.

When he finds out, Lancelot waxes wonderly wroth, but he forgives Elaine, who promptly enchants him into swiving her again.

Nobody asks Elaine if it's necessary to trick Lancelot into having ado with her so many times. But then having ado seems to be a favourite preoccupation of the knights and ladies, no matter whether they're virgin, married, neither.

Edward wonders if Margaret had read any of this before she gave him the book.

Praise God that she can't have – but then if she had, he wouldn't be in this situation of stubborn, ungovernable *erectness*, his pintle refusing to lower its head, pushing at the hose – with dinner approaching, too, and his name – oh, God – his name being called on the stairs, to hie him to the great hall.

There are about half the number of people eating dinner here at Maynooth as there were at Mechelen, but somehow it's twice as noisy. The clamour claps around the high beams of the roof like a great flock of gulls. Each trestle table seems to be competing with the next to talk louder; the soldiers at the doorways are shouting jokes at each other; even the conversation at the high table under the canopy is more meet for sailors than for little ladies, with which Edward is surrounded.

'Eleanor stabbed me with her knife,' Eilis cries.

'Eilis was wiping her fingers on my kirtle.'

'Joan just whispered a bad word.'

'By Saint Brigid, I did not,' Joan says calmly, a few seats down. 'May God have mercy on you for telling lies.'

Joan has very white skin, small shoulders, and high black eyebrows. Also blue eyes – the same blue as the rest of her family, so he doesn't know why they seem so strikingly sharp. So much so that it's hard to meet them.

He realises, pensily, that he's learned to bow and dance and read Latin, but nobody taught him how to behave around young ladies. Maybe he'll find a book here on the subject.

'Do you have a library?' he asks Lady Kildare.

'Oh, yes,' she says, smiling.

'He thinks we can't read,' Gerald Fitzgerald says.

'Oh, no,' says Edward, 'I didn't mean—'

'Well, you'd have been right. Most of these pigstick Irish nobles can't read. But I have an excellent library, in the upper floor of the keep. You can help yourself. There are books in English, French, Latin and Gaelic. Virgil, Juvenal, Boethius. Romances. Ranulf Higden, Gerald of Wales. And some books with pictures of stark belly-naked ladies in, such as we all enjoy.'

'There he is,' Joan says. 'Ireland's foremost man of letters.'

'Oh, how now! Who is this to chop at me?' her father cries. 'The whisperer of bad words at table?'

'It began with C,' says Eilis.

'Thank you, Eilis, we don't need to hear it,' Lady Kildare says.

'And on the matter of your absence earlier, Madam Joan,' Gerald continues. 'You were supposed to be meeting our royal guest. He was sore grieved that you showed him such disworship.'

'Was he?' says Joan. Edward can feel her looking at him. But he has the wine, praise God, and he holds it to his lips until the moment is past.

'He said it was a spear to his heart. The hope of England, and you caused him grievous dole. Where were you? Reading? In the stables? Under a tree? I should have told you we were meeting under a tree, then maybe you'd have come to the hall.' Kildare has raised his voice, but it's obvious that Joan amuses him. 'I know what. You can make amends by showing the Earl of Warwick the library.'

'It would be an honour,' Joan says, with a dip of her head.

Edward is inquiet now. He's reminded of Eos, the Greek goddess, wishing for her human lover Tithonus to have eternal life, but forgetting to ask for eternal youth so that Tithonus ended up as a shrivelled little cricket. Edward has wished for books of guidance, and for beautiful demosels – and now he has both, but in full wrong order, and how will he end up?

Answer:

In the end the Lady Joan and her father both forget that a show-ing of the library was ever purposed, and while Edward would rather go alone, it might be seen as disworship to his hosts, and so he finds himself without books or girl.

2

Mass is held in the family chapel, a prebend of St Patrick's Cathedral in Dublin. The family sit in a high balcony, with the servants below. The prebendary, Maister James Burke, is a short barrel-bellied man with pleading eyes. Today he's urging them all not to question God's will. It's the fashion among nobles, he says, to say things like: 'Why should we pay for Eve's mistake? We don't know Eve! Why should that silly girl's foolish demeaning, so long ago, spoil our pleasaunce?'

'Heh. I hadn't heard that,' says Eleanor to Edward, low. 'It strikes me as a fair question. I'm sure there'll be a clever answer.'

'And then some of these nobles – sick as they are, from imbibing the poisonous air of heretical questionings, but thinking themselves still devout, still wise – seek to get answers from their chaplains and bishops. They think that this is the correct course. But it is a perilous course! They are on the road to fiery hell!'

'Cock's bones,' Eleanor says. 'I always guess these ones wrong.'

'And what will happen to you once you are in hell? All stuffed and overflowing with your questions for God, like a rat swollen with maggots? Well, Satan will have these questions! You'll be stripped naked and tied over a barrel, and the questions will be poked out of you by the demons. There'll be a queue of demons behind you, each one carrying a club, or a peppered parsnip, or divers other devices, and each one they'll thrust up your fundament, and all the while you'll cry out, "I repent, I repent," but it will be too late.'

'I don't understand how that gets the questions out,' Alice says, on Edward's other side. 'Can we ask?'

'Didn't you hear? Asking questions is the road to hell,' says Eleanor.

'A much-used and well-worn road,' says Joan, further down the pew. 'And not the only one, by the sounds of it.'

'Yes, poor Maister James, 'tis a fair wide path by now,' says Kildare, turning around in his seat, and they both laugh.

After Mass, Edward goes looking for Kildare, who has disappeared, to ask if there is any sword-training. He wanders through the courtyards outside, ends up making a full circuit of the castle in the shadow of the great curtain walls, under a grey sky speared with thin shafts of sunlight. In a neglected corner he walks paths overgrown with cow parsley and nettles, skimmed over by bees; picks strawberries, tumbles into a memory of eating strawberries on the farm.

Sehnsucht.

Nein danke.

He thinks he sees Joan in the distance, sitting under a yew with a book. But when he reaches the spot he arrives at a patch of flattened grass, and no girl anywhere.

Edward can't walk beyond the walls.

For now, his presence here is a secret. Edward's supposed to be in Mechelen, and as Lord Deputy, Kildare's supposed to be the servant of that small-eyed cunt King Henry. Even though, he says, a ninety-year-old man has a stronger grip on his own pizzle than Henry does on Ireland.

Kildare explains that Ireland is mostly under the rule of the Gaelic kings. Only the Pale – a small bite of Ireland – is under the control of the English, with the English of Ireland supposedly of a piece with the English of England. Maybe a couple of hundred years ago that was the case. Not any more. The Palesmen were of Norman seed, but they couldn't resist the fine manly men and fair womanly women of Ireland. They got into the Irish habit – despite the statutes that still stand, forbidding them to intermarry with the Gaelic, ally with them, even worship with them. Palesmen aren't allowed to use Irish names and law and dress and tongue, are not meant to play at horlings or coiting but lancing and archery. Fuck like English; fight like English.

The only statute of any worth is the one forbidding Irish poets to visit English territories, Kildare said. Not that my wife abides by that one.

Do you abide by the rest? Edward asked.

By Jesus, no, said Kildare.

(More Irish than the Irish, is what they noise of Kildare.

More king than the king.)

Still, they have to observe caution. It won't do for Henry to know what they're about before they're about it, and send over ships. And the Fitzgeralds have enemies here, in the shape of the Butlers – fell shrews, right hated by all. Sir James Butler has a maugre against the York kings. He picked the Lancastrian side in the great wars, the doddard. The Fitzgeralds took the York side and were mostly merry under them. Richard III, God rest him – sure he may have killed a few people he shouldn't, but he was so good as to look the other way as Kildare established his own standing army.

Now the Butlers think that the House of York's rose is plucked, and they're sticking loathsome close to King Henry, tucked up cosy and warm in his arse cleft. If they hear Kildare is tending a new York sprig here, they'll be at Henry's ear with their despitous tellings, hoping to make Sir James the next Lord Deputy.

The very idea.

A week after the Feast of Saint Peter and Paul, the news reaches them that Humphrey Stafford, the man who helped Lovell start a rebellion, was executed. Kildare's steward, Maurice FitzMaurice FitzGerald, brings them the tidings. Maurice is a Geraldine cousin, from a distant branch that even Kildare can't puzzle out.

'The younger Stafford brother was pardoned, along with other supporters of the rebellion,' says Maurice. 'But Humphrey, as an example, was hanged, drawn and quartered. And his tarred head spiked upon London Bridge. He'll watch over the Thames for the summer, the poor fucker.'

Edward feels shaky when he hears this. He tries to send up a prayer: *Dear God, please.*

Please what?

Please take Humphrey Stafford into Your divine grace?

Please don't do this to me?

''Tis a shame, now, about the elder Stafford,' says Kildare.

'The English are a strange race,' says Maurice. 'All this fucking around with intestines and tar. We had a thief's body tarred and put up once. It looked very striking, everyone admired it, but we had dead crows and magpies all over the place for weeks after. My surmise is that the tar wasn't agreeable to their birdly humours. Do birds have humours?'

'I don't know,' Kildare says. 'But I grant you, tar is not in a bird's natural diet.'

'A burning makes good spectacle,' says Maurice. 'The peasants find it very cheering in the winter months.'

'Ah, now, I'm a beheading man,' says Kildare. 'I've a soft heart in that way. But I follow the Brehon laws. No need to be killing people when they can pay restitution. Listen, on the subject of death sentences, are you still courting Joan?'

'I fear she's not in favour of me,' Maurice says.

'She's not in favour of anyone on God's earth,' Kildare says. 'But she doesn't seem to have any particular maugre toward you. I take that as encouraging. This demeaning is a symptom of her tender age. She's undomesticated, and childish in her minds. Says she won't have babies, or submit to a husband's rule. Her elder sister said something very like. But they leave these thoughts behind once they're grown.'

'God be praised that these things are not a woman's choice,' says Maurice.

'Good lad. A stout husband is what she needs. Not *too* stout. I don't want to hear any stories like the ones told by the St Lawrence daughter, run back to her family scarred and misaligned.'

'By Saint Augustine, you will not,' says Maurice. 'I will supply her with songbirds and sweet presents, and only ever remonstrate with her open-handed.'

'Good lad.'

When Maurice has quit them, Kildare says to Edward:

'Now, these are men's conversings. Joan has no witting of them yet, and won't until the time comes. She's contrary, and she'll try to escape the halter. So it's carrots and running free for now, and no word of anything else.'

186

Edward's wandering past the yew – as he sometimes does by chance, on his afternoon roamings – when he's accosted by Joan herself.

'My Lord Edward,' she says, and curtseys. She's wearing a dark green kirtle, shiny as a holly leaf. He hasn't seen her quite so close, or quite so frontwards, yet. It's a lot to suddenly address. As he bows pieces of her come to his eye at random; a gold brooch, a small shod toe under her skirt, her tender-looking lower lip – no—

—a mistake to focus on her lip. All kinds of thoughts related to the *Morte* and Queen Candace and an inquieting dream he had last night have come into his brain-pan—

Look at something else, suggests a voice. Edward himself seems to have divided into parts: a part that has lost its wits, and a friendly yet firm advisory part, which is talking to him now.

Her eyes, perhaps?

Yes. He stares fixedly into her eyes.

Now speak.

'I sometimes walk this way quite by chance,' he says.

There's a moment of silence. She looks at him with interest. Not enchantment exactly, or delight. But not loathing or scorn either. Just... interest.

'Right,' she says. 'It's a lovely spot. I have to confess to you, my lord, that I am not here by chance at all. In fact, I thought you might be here because I see you pass by every afternoon around the same time.'

'Not *every* afternoon—'

'And I waylaid you here because I wanted to ask you something.'

She steps in closer to him, so near he could count every eyelash – maybe feel her breath on his face, commingling with his own, if the wind were blowing toward him, which it is not.

'You're aware of my being affianced to Maurice, I know,' she says.

The reminder lands on him like cold pottage.

'I am not witting of any such,' he says awkwardly, thinking he may as well follow her father's wishes, even though the ground seems to have shifted and he doesn't know who knows what and where he stands in all of this.

'Ah, don't worry,' she says. 'Maurice and I have been secretly in love with each other for months. We always purposed to marry, but my da likes to have things be *his* idea. He wants to surprise me with the news, then accept my gratitude for having chosen so well for me.'

'Oh!' Edward says.

How many parts of him are there now? A confused part, still, and a relieved part, and a disappointed part – and the guiding voice seems to have gone. He says, 'Well. I'm, uh, in great gladness for you both.'

'Thank you,' she says, bowing her head. 'And this brings me to my request. Lateward, Maurice and I have been in the habit of sending each other little love notes – fixed with the family seal, so that nobody will suspect my dear one of possessing anything other than official letters. It gives us much delight. So far we've only managed to pass each other these notes hand to hand, brushing by each other in the corridors and so on. But I thought it would be mirthful if I could contrive it so one of my love letters ended up in his bag – so when he was alone, he might discover it and be overcome with surprise and joy at the ingenuity of me, his love. It's a passing good jape, isn't it?'

'Passing good, my lady,' agrees Edward.

She claps her hands. 'Joan, I beg you. And so what I was hoping – because he mustn't suspect anything of me – is that *you* would talk to him after Mass tomorrow, before he goes out on business of my father's, and slip the note into his bag, among his papers? I think it could be done very naturally – if you were cunning. Do you think you could be so cunning?'

'Do I think…?! I am wonderly cunning, I promise you! I won't fail you.'

'Then I'm right glad I asked,' she says, and she gazes gratefully at him for so long with her blue eyes that he gets confused and walks away without the note, and has to be called back to take it.

3

The next afternoon Edward comes back from sword-training with Kildare's men – thinking he's getting better at it, or certainly his armour is less full of mud and gravel than it was yesterday – to find the keep full of even louder shouting than usual.

'How?'

'With my fucking seal!'

'We put him in a cell, my lord.'

'He read it?'

'Of course he fucking read it!'

'Who read what, Da?'

'Sir James Butler, that's fucking who. And none of your business. Someone get the girls out of here, fuck's sake.'

'Where was it?'

'In with the papers relating to Margaret's inheritance and rights.'

Edward rounds the corner as the girls, their nurse and two ladies in waiting all rush past him. Eustacia is sobbing. He hesitates on the threshold, not knowing his place. Kildare, Lady Kildare, several men and the prebendary are in the entrance hall, talking furiously. Nobody notices Edward.

'Maurice came straight to me after,' Kildare says, 'throwing himself on my mercy: he'd never seen this letter before in his life. Sir James opening it was the first he knew of it, on his oath.'

Edward takes a step back. He's panicked. It must be the love letter. Read, so far as he can make out, by Sir James Butler and not Maurice. But he can't understand why Kildare is so angry. His face is a livid red, extending down his neck; his eyes are unearthly bright.

'What exactly was in the document?' Lady Kildare asks.

'Nothing!' shouts Kildare. 'Some personal matters of finance and law. Nothing that is criminal, but, in some eyes, might be misthought of as such. In the king's eyes. By the body of Christ! A curse on him! That turd Butler will be writing to Henry as we speak.'

'Maybe Maurice is telling the truth,' a man says. 'Why would he give Sir James evidence of your wrongdoings?'

Gerald grips the man by the shoulder.

'*No wrongdoings.*'

'Forgive me, Lord, I meant to say, your *seeming* wrongdoings. But, uh, why would he give Sir James the document and then come back here and tell you what he'd done?'

'Fearganainm was right next to him,' someone else says. 'It must have been that he meant to hand the note over hudder mudder, but mistook it for something else, and then realised his mistake, and knew that Fearganainm had seen it.'

Edward retreats back out of the doorway, his body weak with horror at his part in these nightmarish unfoldings. What has he done? What has Joan done? Surely not Joan. It must be a mistake. He remembers her eyes, like windows open onto blue sky.

'Enough! I don't give a turd for the whys and withals,' Kildare cries. 'I'm neck-deep in the midden now and it's the fault of that fucking Maurice. The letter was in his bag. Now it's in the possession of that despitous shrew Butler. I call that treachery.'

'In hell,' Maister James says, 'there is a special fruit that grows and is used to punish traitors, by way of their bottom holes.'

There's a moment of silence. Then someone says:

'Isn't that radishes?'

'I heard mullets.'

'That was the ancient Romans. That's what they did to adulterers. The spines were meant to be wonderly painful.'

'This is none of these,' says Maister James. 'It's a bulbous kind of turnip that grows only in hell. The shape of a very large man's part. Thrust in and out repeatedly.'

'Well, this is earth,' Kildare says. He rubs his face. He sounds calmer now. 'I don't see any hell-turnips. And we're not going to invade the man with any other foodstuffs. You may leave us, Sir Priest, thank you.'

Maister James exits.

Edward lets his body collapse against the wall with relief.

'We'll just take his head off,' says Kildare. 'Go now, Donal. Do it fast and privily and get the men to bury the body. Alison, write to his family, tell them he caught a fever and we gave him a Mass with full honours.'

'My lord, are you sure?'

'Am I not loud enough? Am I speaking in tongues?' Kildare roars. 'I said: *I want his fucking head.*'

Edward can't find any strength in his legs. He manages to prise himself off the wall, get down the steps and sit in the mud with his back against the warm pink side of the keep. Men come out of the door and walk past him. Nobody is japing now; their expressions are dark.

When he lifts his head he sees, in the distance, Joan sitting under the yew. He runs over. She looks up, shading her eyes from the sun, and smiles.

'It's a lovely afternoon,' she says. 'Want to join me? Why are you so dirty?'

'Please, Joan,' he says. He's out of breath. 'Maurice. Please tell me you didn't...'

She makes a doleful face.

'Oh, but I *did*,' she says.

'Why?'

She puts her head on one side. 'You're fair newborn in wit, aren't you?' she says. 'I didn't want to marry Maurice. Obviously.'

'What? But you *knew* you were going to marry him! Why would you do this wicked thing now?'

'First of all, I didn't know I was going to marry him until you told me. Secondly, I'm not here to be chidden by a muddy boy. So, if it please you...'

She indicates the route he should take back to the castle.

'They're going to kill him!'

'Good. By the time my da recovers his wits there'll be no chance of amends.'

He is astonied. His words stick in his chest.

'*Wickedness*,' he croaks.

'My lord,' she says, sharp now. 'Don't look at me like that. This is a lesson you should have learned already, and though it comes late, I have taught it to you. You ought to be grateful.'

'Lesson?'

'Yes: not to trust other people.'

He finds his hurt and horror have gone, all transmuted into wroth. The last time he was angry with a girl was back in the village, when the miller's daughter stole his fairy arrowhead. He wanted to hit her but Jennott warned him off hitting a woman.

It's not fair, she said. We're weaker.

John's gaze went to the iron pot she'd clanked his brother's head with earlier.

Women in general, Jennott said. *I'm* not weaker. None of those village pullets have Saxon blood.

'You heinous sorceress,' he says to Joan. She looks surprised, then amused. 'Now I don't feel sorry for Maurice. Having his head taken off seems like a better ending than being married to you. You're a loathly serpent. I should tell your father what you did.'

'Oh, please,' she says. 'Then you'd have to tell him what *you* did. You need to think before you open your little chick's beak and cheep. Hey, that's a second lesson at no cost. And here's a third: try losing your virginity, so all the blood won't rush out of your brainpan next time a female asks you to do something.'

Edward goes to Kildare.

He knows he could be imperilling himself, and Joan too, but what else can he do? Let a man die? He's halfway out with the whole thing – after a fashion: trying to suggest that false counsel had been had, and tricks had been played, he doesn't know by whom – when Kildare holds up his hand.

'You're a fine lad, destined for a fair spot in heaven,' he says. 'But I know this was Joan's doings. Did I not warn you to be ware of her? Maybe I forgot. I'll tell you now: she's good-looking, but she's a perilous beast. You know the worst thing about this matter is that Maurice was actually purposing to marry her. Now I'll have to dupe someone else into taking her off my hands. It can't be anyone local because they've all heard word of her evil disposition.'

'So you won't be beheading Maurice?'

'It's already done. He's loyal, and I did it with full heavy heart – God knows my regret – but he's embarrassed us. Running around confessing to everyone that he gave my enemies the means to ruin me. That such means exist. Cock's bones! Maurice should have kept his mouth shut.'

Edward quits Kildare and goes outside again. He doesn't know what to do with himself. He walks from place to place, without making any difference to anything.

He finds himself by the postern gate next to the East Tower as two of Kildare's soldiers walk by. Their broadswords are sheathed but there's blood on their clothing, a spray like the spatter thrown up by cartwheels.

The sight reminds him of Maister Richard and Bella. The last time he saw them – or didn't, because he couldn't look. It makes him feel strange and disordered in the heart to think of them now.

The voice of his inwit says: *Then don't think of them.*

To the list of people he won't be thinking of, he adds one more: Joan. He'll never, by God, talk to her, look at her, even so much as *think* the name Joan, ever again.

Joan is apparently forgiven by dinner. She appears with the rest of her sisters, the very model of seemly demeaning, her gaze pointed down at her small pale hands. Kildare also appears light of heart. He pinches Eustacia's cheeks and says he's sorry he was a grimly boar, but his wroth is all passed and she must forgive her daffish da. He tells Lady Kildare quietly that there were enough inaccuracies in the document (which, they are to remember, was itself wholly made of lies) for Butler to realise that making such demonstrably false accusations to King Henry would be to his own disfavour.

'Could have fortuned very well for me, in fact,' Kildare says. 'Almost a shame Butler was not inclined to intermeddle. By my life, this is a savourly dish. How do you find it, my Lord Edward? Did you ever eat roe this tender in England? No? I thought not. We will hunt tomorrow, and find us another even better.'

'This was sent by the Bishop of Meath,' Lady Kildare tells Edward. 'In honour of your arrival. John Payne is a goodly gentil man, and a great supporter of the House of York.'

'A great supporter of local women,' Joan says, audibly.

Kildare laughs. 'It isn't as if they can support him, not the weight of that fat belly. They have to go uppermost.'

'Uppermost of what?' asks Alice.

'By Saint Mary,' Lady Kildare says. 'Would you save it for later?'

'Humble apologies,' Kildare says. 'I am rightly chid. Will you forgive me?'

'Always,' she says, and they smile at each other.

Sometimes, Edward wonders not whether God is really watching earth – no, *not* that, it's heresy – but that *maybe*, if it is not sin to wonder it, *maybe* he isn't watching over all people and all places equally?

By way of explaining how Kildare executes a man without trial in the morning, but by dinner is wearing silks, dining on the finest venison, his wife's lovely hand resting approvingly on his, his perniciously beautiful daughter entertaining him with disworshipful japes, all full mirthful, all in sight of God.

By way of explaining the *Morte*, all those Christian ladies and knights having large ado with each other, with no thought of whose husband or wife they are with, and bastards everywhere – and at no time does their author Thomas Malory come forward, as he's supposed to, to condemn the wicked deeds of those times and warn his readers not to fall into like sin. No! Malory's as silent as God. And yet he lives, and is famous, and his book is not banned but printed widewhere.

What does it *mean*?

Could it—

Surely not that Edward could *do this too*?

Be like the *Morte*'s Sir Bors, who had unmarried sex but was allowed to find the Grail?

Be like the Bishop of Meath, and lie under a woman?

Surely not?

He wants to ask a priest, but he doesn't want to go to Maister James and hear about what items might be put up him in hell, so he has to wonder on, part excited, part afraid. Hoping – as he brings himself off in the garderobe – that God isn't watching.

4

Two of Kildare's great allies come to visit. Thomas Plunket is Chief Justice of the Common Pleas, a thin man with a dark, jabbing gaze. Rowland FitzEustace is Baron of Portlester and father of Lady Kildare. He's nearly sixty and looks like a cliff collapse: a great height, fallen partly in. But his shoulders are still wide; his grey hair abundant.

Portlester has brought the news that Elizabeth Woodville, the dowager queen, has been retired against her will from court, on account of annoying every last man, woman and child near to death.

'She's gone to Cheyneygates, at Westminster,' Portlester says. 'And much mislikes her lot. She'll be casting about for new friends, I'd stake my beard on it.'

'Now, don't be pledging that fine white brush on yon whore,' Kildare says.

'She'd never come to *us*,' Plunket says.

'She came around to Richard and he killed both her young sons.'

'Even if she did, what gifts could she bring?' Plunket says. 'She has no more allies. Her son Dorset is an asset, yes, for five minutes, until he switches sides. He's as slippery as a strumpet's slot. And King Henry has so many spies in Dorset's house they overnumber his staff; his bed goes unmade and his food is burned.'

'I'm a man for policy,' Kildare says. 'But the day I ally with that despitous Woodville viper is the day I run naked through Dublin with my balls swinging free.'

'Again,' says Portlester, and they all laugh.

'Have you met the dowager queen?' Edward asks Kildare.

'No. She didn't like our kin because we were friends of your father Clarence. My uncle, the Earl of Desmond, the most handsome man in Ireland, was murdered by her pet John Tiptoft, when Tiptoft was Lord Deputy.'

'His nickname in England was the Butcher,' says Plunket.

'Disordinate fond of cutting off heads and doing strange things to corpses, segmenting them and rearranging them and what have you.'

'What? Is Tiptoft still alive?'

'No, the Lancastrians killed him,' says Portlester. 'Our great enemy, the Earl of Warwick-that-was, did us a favour there.'

'Warwick's dead now, too, of course.' Kildare says. 'That's the thing with revenge. You can chase after it, but if you sit and wait it's not long before Lady Fortune does the work for you.'

'But it's more satisfying to do it yourself,' says Plunket.

'By Jesus, yes,' says Kildare, a dreamy look in his eye. 'No thrill in the world like it.'

There's an especially grand banquet that night, with Portlester and Plunket joining Edward and the Kildares at the head table, and acrobats entertaining them after dinner. Afterwards, Kildare says,

'Joan will tell us a story from *The Táin*. She's not so gracious as her sisters, or so melodious in her speech, but she has the best memory for the book.'

Edward looks, much against his will, at Joan. She looks straight back at him, one eyebrow up.

'We might as well listen to the crows on the roof,' says Alice.

'As the most gracious sister, I won't pass remark,' Eleanor replies. 'But Alice is right.'

'Tell us about the army of boys,' Kildare says.

Joan nods, her eyebrows full meek now, and begins. Edward doesn't want to listen, but he's taken up by the story of Cú Chulainn, the ancient hero, and how Cú Chulainn's boy army of Ulster was slaughtered by the army of Connacht. When Cú Chulainn hears what happened, his body writhes and turns in its own skin, and he transmutes into a hideous monster. One eye is sucked into his head, the other falls out, his lungs and liver disgorge into his mouth, his lower jaw overtakes the upper, his hair stands on end like spears. In this form he tears through the Connacht camp, piling up six bodies for every dead Ulster lad, until he's made a wall of the corpses, limed with blood.

'Beautiful,' says Kildare, applauding. 'Wonderly well told.'

'Shall I tell now of the many lovers of Cú Chulainn's greatest enemy, the warrior queen Medb?' Joan says.

There is a brief silence. Plunket looks at Joan with his strange, sharp stare, sharper than before. Portlester's mouth twitches into a smile, then quickly restraightens. Kildare and his wife look at each other.

'Another time,' says Kildare.

'Plunket's wife is a great beauty and a well-known cock-chaser,' Eleanor whispers to Edward. 'He loathes talk of it.'

'A misfortune for your unwitting sister,' Edward murmurs back, full solemn – though innerly delighted at the idea of Joan talking herself into trouble at last.

'Oh, no, Joan's witting,' Eleanor says. 'She loves to salt a wound. And Da only encourages her.'

Edward sits back, despairing. Lord Christ, save me from this father and daughter, he prays in his heart. Let me get out of here whole of minds and body, and never come back, amen.

The next body in Joan's own wall is Maister James. Edward had no idea he was gone until a new prebendary rides in through the gate, on an expensive-looking horse.

'What happened?' he asks Eleanor.

'Oh, this is Joan's work. Maister James annoyed her, I'm not sure how. She paid a tavern wench to say she was pregnant with Maister James's child and demand that he marry her. So he fled in the middle of the night.'

'Like anyone would believe he was playing at Adam and Eve with the village women,' says Alice. 'He couldn't tell a quoniam from a quail.'

'Sure he's mad for his own cask-hole.'

'Your sister!' Edward says. 'Will she get away with this, too? How are the rest of you even sib to her? I know you like japing, but your hearts are full of kindness. So kind that I expect you'll tell me hers is the same.'

'Christ, no, she's full awful.'

'And she'll get away with it,' adds Alice. 'Now and evermore.'

'Better to just accept it,' Eleanor says. 'I mean it, Edward. If you set yourself against her, you could be next.'

Edward's walking around the castle grounds, avoiding the yew, face turned up to the sun, catching a scent of rosemary from the herb garden, the burbling of the nesting blackbirds, a snippet of some female song from the servants' quarters, when his lovely afternoon turns abruptly unlovely. Joan appears.

She drops him a curtsey. She's wearing a charming smile. She reminds him of a magpie: jaunty, white skin, black hair, cocked head, her eye turning, assessing.

He saw a magpie kill a nest of baby fieldmice once, leisurely, picking them out one by one.

What is Edward in her story, but a baby mouse?

'What do you want?' he says, bowing as rudely as he can.

'My lord,' she says. 'Are you enjoying this fine Irish weather? I was listening to the chirping of the little birds, myself, and my heart was wonderly lighted in contemplation of the divers beauties of nature.'

'Ballocks,' Edward says.

'Sir!'

'This is some new treachery,' he says. 'If you're purposing my destruction, go ahead, but do it somewhere else.'

'Ah,' she says. 'You're still holding a maugre against me after the jape I played on Maurice.'

'Jape! By God. And whatever you did to poor Maister James. What will happen to him now?'

'Probably getting sodomised in a bathhouse by a gang of ruffians,' she says. 'If he has his way.'

Edward tries to step around her. She moves to one side and blocks him. They repeat the dance on the other side.

'Edward,' she says. 'Can I call you Edward?'

'No.'

'Listen, Maurice was a heinous shrew. He seduced servant women and hanged villagers without proper trial. And you must have noticed his foul breath. I couldn't marry him.'

'So you repaid evil with evil?'

'With justice.'

'Justice? Where was the trial? You're not a judge. You're just a scheming girl.'

'Judith was a scheming girl. She tricked Holofernes into trusting her, and then she took his head off and saved her people and we revere her for it.'

Edward recognises one of Maister Richard's favourite rhetorical devices: biblical allusion. Well, well. Joan's not the only one with an understanding of techniques. Maybe he'll astonie her with some pate-scratchers of his own.

'I'm sure you're right,' he says. 'I won't mention that Judith was saving her people and you're only benefiting yourself.'

'Apophasis?' says Joan. 'What is this, a nursery debate?'

The ire rises in Edward, feet to brain-pan. The pan hisses and boils over. 'Here's some elegant rhetoric for you,' he snaps. 'Go fuck yourself.'

He pushes past her; she catches his arm. Her face changes. She looks suddenly pleading.

'Edward, please.'

He hadn't expected this. He finds himself stuck to the ground, his arm stalled by his side, as if all the life has been drawn out of his body by the pressure of her hand. *Sorcery*, is what he would say, if he could speak.

'I see we are on a road of ill will and suspicion,' she says, 'and I admit that part of that is my fault. But Edward, please, I'm here to make amends. I am right sorry. On my life and that of Our Lord! I pray you, believe me.'

Her mouth trembles.

'Alright,' he says. 'You can let go of me. Stop looking like that.'

She takes her hand off his arm, but she doesn't take her eyes off him. Their blueness really is wonderly bright. He knows he can't trust her, but her eyes speak of heaven and bugle flowers and butterflies, goodly things, and he finds himself losing his sense not of why he shouldn't trust her, but why it even matters. Trust, trust: if you repeat the word often enough, its edges dissolve, all its sense flows out.

'I didn't waylay you to argue,' she says, gently. 'I want to propose a fair exchange. In which we help each other. I want you to teach me Latin.'

'You don't know it?'

'No woman in Ireland does, Edward. Right now in Padua, Cassandra Fedele is making Latin speeches before academics and corresponding with famous humanists on matters of philosophy. Did Cassandra's father say that firstly he couldn't be arsed to find her a Latin tutor? Secondly that it was a waste of time as it wouldn't attract any husbands? That, thridenly, she was over-clever already?'

Edward can actually understand the third point. Giving Joan more learnings would be like England sending cannon and archers as a gift to the French.

'Maister James knew Latin but he said my female brain wouldn't be able to comprehend it,' she continues.

'Is *that* why you beskift him?'

'I?' she says. 'Alright, yes. Though I fear the new prebendary might actually be worse than Maister James. The signs bode ill. My sisters are going to be sore wroth.'

'If I refuse to teach you, are you going to work me wrack?'

'No! You can say no. But listen. If you teach me Latin, I'll teach you how to survive. As things stand, you're fucked. I mean, you've got as much chance of getting through your rebellion as a puppy in a bull ring. I can tell you secrets. Who would sell you out to Henry for an English manor. Who would arrange a hunting accident for you, if you weren't a full obedient pet king. Are you intrigued?'

'If I thought you'd tell me the truth, maybe,' he says. 'As things stand: no.'

She puts her head on one side, corvine-like. 'Look at you, already growing in guile!' she says. 'Well then. If you have no softness or pity for me, and you want to treat with me like a merchant at the assizes, think of it this way. You have nothing to lose by teaching me. You know you can't trust me, so I can't trick you. And if you're my tutor, you know I won't work you wrack, because I'd lose my Latin lessons. You can think of it as insurance, on your own hide. So. What do you say?'

Later, Edward tries to understand why he said yes.

It wasn't a yes. It was an absence of a no, was what it was. A failure to think of a good enough no in time.

Yes, then.

He prays he won't regret it.

5

Sir William the new prebendary's first sermon is about women going abroad and looking at things. He's noticed the Fitzgerald girls seem to travel freely about the land with their ladies. In their innocence they don't realise the peril they are placing themselves in. They might well say, 'Oh, I simply went out, and looked upon the people. How could that be any danger?'

Sir William sees the women in the church looking at each other now. This is how it begins. From looking to talking, and from talking straight to hell. Wise indeed the woman who sits quiet, in great fear for her soul, knowing that one wrong turn of her gaze could drag her into deep sin. Wise the girl who keeps her eyes lowered.

Dinah, Jacob's daughter, went out and looked at the women of Shechem. And by her looking, she exposed herself to looks. And what happened to her? Shechem saw her, and took her maidenhead by force, and then she became a whore and the city burned down and all the men died. Because of her light looking.

This is why women must not go wandering abroad, looking foolishly at whatever they like. They must keep themselves privily within the home, though they are not even full safe there, no, and Sir William will next tell them about the dangers that wait for them in the home.

'Thanks for that Joan, you turd,' Alice says on the way out of the chapel.

'We're none of us speaking to you,' Eleanor says. 'And Edward shouldn't either, if he wants to stand on the side of goodness and honour.'

'Can't Joan just beskift the new priest?' Edward says. 'Not kill him. No killing, Joan. But get him sent away?'

'It's hard. He's a St Lawrence. Related to the Baron of Howth,' Joan says. 'Da likes him because he gets blavering and accidentally tells Da all the Howth business.'

Little Eustacia takes her thumb out of her mouth, where it had hidden itself during the sermon, and says, 'He's a cunt.'

'He wanted to be an anchorite,' Joan says. 'His family talked him into priesthood. He's as mad as a midden rat. Look, I'm right sorry, girls. I might have fucked this one. I'll sort it out.'

'Well, we're not talking to you until you do. Or you either, Edward, if you're going to make an alliance with the enemy.'

'It's not a war!' Edward says, to which nobody replies, and fairly so, because it's a stupid thing to say.

The other girls walk away. He's left with Joan. Who says, 'I didn't ask you to do that, so don't be expecting any soft thankings from me,' and then walks away in the other direction.

He's alone in the cloister. A fine rain is coming down, drifting through the arches, velveting his face.

How it's turned out like this, he doesn't know. It happened too quickly, that was the problem.

He prays, again, that he won't regret it.

Joan and her lady, Grania, come to Edward's room for the Latin lesson. He isn't expecting them. He'd been reading the *Morte* for the second time, and is at the part where four women have taken Lancelot prisoner and are trying to get him to kiss them.

'Are you meant to be in here?' he asks.

Joan pushes past him. Grania follows, with a look at Edward that says, *Tell me about it.*

'Da knows,' Joan says. 'And doesn't care. Anyway, grimly Grania here will make sure no raping occurs.'

'Me?' Edward says. 'Rape *you*?'

'I call that wonderly rude,' Joan says. 'Am I not as ravishable as the next demosel?'

'That is not what I meant—'

'Never mind,' Joan says. 'I accept the insult meekly and without complaint. See how courteous I can be? Let's get the lesson started.'

'Fine.'

'Thank you.'

After she leaves, he realises that she's stolen the *Morte*.

'Give it back,' Edward says.

'What?'

'You know what. Maybe I'll tell your father you have it. I wonder if Sir William will judge the *Morte* a danger in the home? Especially to virgins.'

'Oh, the *Morte*. I've only borrowed it. Don't wax wroth. I'll give you something better in the meantime. Have you heard of the work of Apuleius? *The Golden Ass*, in English. Now you may not want it, because it's wonderly wicked. Being a virgin myself, I blushed when I read of Lucius and his mistress Photis doing things I hesitate to name. Not that you're interested in that. Believe me, Grania, the gentil earl is like a stone in that regard. Very… hard. I imagine he'll be reading this purely for moral instruction. So, is the exchange acceptable to you, my lord? Good. No need to be talking to any priests or fathers.'

'What now?' Joan says.

She's sitting under the yew, even though it's an overcast day. It occurs to him that yews are poisonous, every part of them.

'You know what now,' he says. '*The Golden Ass*. It has an interesting beginning aright, but then he turns into an ass and now he's just been beaten and abused for most of the book. Even though he deserves it for never heeding any advice and making the same stupid mistakes over and over.'

'An interesting observation,' she says. 'Have you not got to book ten yet?'

'No.'

'I thought not, or you wouldn't be here complaining. Be patient. In book ten the wheel of fortune turns. Lucius is rewarded with great worship. And he even swives a woman of passing prodigious appetite, the doing of which is described in large detail.'

'Alright,' Edward says. 'I'll give it a chance. How do you like the *Morte*?'

'I'd like it more if I could read it in peace.'

He leaves her in peace. As he returns to his room he passes the other Fitzgerald sisters, playing bowls. He waves. Eustacia waves back and Eilis swats her hand out of the air. Then they all turn away.

I've chosen poorly, he thinks.

He reads the rest of *The Golden Ass* before dinner. After dinner he finds Joan playing cards with Grania and a couple of other women. Their faces are gold in the light of the oil lamps. They all look as grimly as if they're going into battle. There must be money on it.

She ignores his approach, so he has to lean over her shoulder while she's sitting and say, 'Fuck you, Joan.'

She laughs so much she almost chokes on her wine.

He says, 'You're a chamberpot full of lies.'

'Now, now,' she says, one finger lifted. 'I told no falsehoods. I said Lucius swives a woman.'

'You didn't say he was still in the form of an ass!'

'I don't know why you're so wroth,' she says, round-eyed. 'I didn't think you were reading the book for *bawdy* reasons.'

'Give me back the *Morte*.'

'You're distracting me,' she says, waving her hand at him. 'I'm fair set to win this round.'

'I don't understand you,' he says. 'I know you want to learn Latin. But you must perceive that if you keep tormenting me, and discomposing all my humours, I'll have to stop teaching you. And maybe even take sick and die. Why do you do it?'

She ignores him.

'I think it's that you can't stop yourself,' he continues. 'You're like the scorpion that asks its friend the turtle to carry it across the river, but stings the turtle when they're halfway over. Do you know that one?'

Now she looks at him, grudgingly. 'No.'

'It's an Eastern fable. The turtle isn't injured. Its hard shell protects it. It asks the scorpion what devil made it act so despitously, when it can't hurt anyone but itself. The scorpion says it simply can't resist its own urge to sting. And so the turtle drowns the scorpion in the river.'

Joan stares at him. He realises he's seeing something rare – possibly never seen before, and maybe nevermore. She doesn't know what to say.

'Aha! The round goes to me,' says Grania, spreading out her cards. 'And the money.'

'A fart on your head,' snaps Joan. Turning to Edward: 'And a shit on yours. You interrupted me. Maybe I'm a scorpion, but you're a jackanapes.'

'An ape teaching you Latin.'

'An educated ape,' she says. 'But still a stinking one.'

This angers him. It reminds him of Maister Richard, mocking Lambert for smelling of donkey dung or goose shit.

He does the only thing he can think of to do, which is pull his lips back, jump up and down, and shout: 'Whooo, whoo, whoo!'

The women jump, astonied, then they start to giggle.

'What are you doing? That's not an ape!' Joan has to shout over him. 'Apes don't make that sound, you ignorant churl.'

'Whoo whoo whoo,' Edward yells, hopping. 'Whoo whoo whoo.'

She pushes her chair back with a rude gesture, and walks out of the hall. The women all laugh.

'Fair play to the young prince,' says Grania to her neighbour. 'It wasn't cunning, or even clever. It might be said it was unmeet and shaming to his dignity. But he did get the best of her.'

And Edward's satisfied with that.

6

News from England:

The queen's baby persists in existing.

'Tenacious little fucker,' says Kildare. 'Still, what are the chances of a male heir first time? It took me seven assays. And I'm ten times the man Henry is. So by those maths he'll need to sire sixty whelps before he scores a boy.'

The king and queen move to Winchester at the end of August, so the baby can be born there, among the ghosts of Camelot.

The round table is still at Winchester. Imagine it! The great table of King Arthur, and around it brave Lancelot, good Sir Bors, questionable Gawain...

'The table's a sham,' Plunket says. 'A Norman knock-up-job. And Winchester's a midden-hole. Half of it's derelict; the castle's a leaking wreck. The queen's been installed at St Swithun's priory for the voiding of the heir, for fear of catching damp in the lungs. It's all so they can noise large about the infant being the second coming of King Arthur, who never existed in the first place.'

'What?' says Edward.

'Don't look so stricken, my lord,' says Plunket. 'Did you not know? Arthur's just an invention of your doddypoll historian Geoffrey of Monmouth.'

'An *invention*?'

'The boy's not an innocent, is he?' Plunket says to Kildare. 'You don't purpose to put a defective king on the throne of England, do you? I'm japing, my lord. But seriously, this Arthur stuff is vittles for peasants and babies, not learned men.'

'We have no universities here,' Joan says to Edward, 'so I'm not sure what he means by learned men. To be a judge in Ireland all you need is enough words to say: how much, and enough numbers to count a bribe.'

'Your fair daughter fancies herself a satirist,' Plunket says to Kildare.

'She's drawn a passing good picture of you though,' Kildare says, chuckling.

'So Arthur did live?' Edward asks Joan.

'Of course he did,' she says.

Plunket drops her an offensive bow. 'With all due worship to your doubtless considerable learning, my lady, Arthur isn't mentioned in any ancient histories of the continent. He exists only in the pages of romances read by simple maidens, which I suppose is how you discovered him, and in your tender youth and credulity, took him for truth.'

'Oh, sure, 'tis wonderly strange that none of the nations defeated by Arthur – including our own – recorded their humiliations in their histories,' Joan says.

'When I was on the continent, their great scholars laughed to think that any history could be credited as anything other than politic fiction,' Edward says.

'Have *you* ever been to the continent, my lord?' Joan asks Plunket.

Plunket waxes red and silent at that, and Kildare, who has been laughing along like a man at a cock fight, says, 'Now, children, you know well Plunket's choleric. If you keep goading you'll dry him right up and we'll have to steam him. You'll have sport enough later. The Bishop of Meath and Bad Brother Keating are dining with us. If you're meek and good today, Joan, I'll sit you next to Brother Keating so you can study how to increase in wickedness. But if you're disobedient, I'll put you next to the bishop and you'll be answering questions about how you've grown and if any bold lads have ever stolen a kiss from your shy lips, and so on, all night. Understood? Right, beskift yourselves.'

'Don't think I'm your defender now,' says Joan to Edward, on the way out. 'I just don't like to hear lies about King Arthur.'

'I didn't think anything, so don't vaunt yourself,' Edward says. 'Who is Brother Keating? Why would you want to sit next to someone so bad?'

'Ah, Edward,' Joan says, more gently. 'Sometimes I forget you don't know any women. I tell you what, I'll teach you how to understand the female brain before you leave here, so you can get a ride in England. If you don't die in battle first.'

She walks off laughing to herself.

'I want that in writing,' Edward shouts after her.

Eleanor comes to Edward and says:

'We held a sister council and we were thinking we ought to talk to you again. You've looked full repentant, and much cast down of late. And we have kind hearts.'

'I'm passing glad to hear it! I—'

She holds up her hand. 'You misperceive me. We hadn't decided on the date of the rapprochement. We need to hold another council first.'

'Oh.'

'I'm sure it will be soon,' she says comfortingly. 'Abide a little longer. We'll let you know.'

At the banquet that night Joan is next to Keating. Keating is at least forty-five and has grey hair but his eye is quick and his nature hot, which is probably the devil in him. Joan seems to be laughing overmuch. Surely nobody is that funny. Nor does Edward understand how a man named Bad Brother Keating, who tried to kill a Justice while the man was on pilgrimage; who was thrown out of his own order; who took the man sent to replace him prisoner, until the man died of a 'cold'; who got excommunicated and ignored it and continued as prior; who said the Pope could 'stick his eye up his arse, and his finger after'. How a man like *this* can not only be seated at dinner, but seated next to young ladies.

Edward looks up, wondering where God is looking right now. Not at Keating, surely. He prays that God's eye won't fall on Joan. While she's definitely a wicked girl, the idea of her in hell is an unpleasant one. Maybe he, Edward, can teach her honesty and piety, along with the Latin. Or at least talk her out of any more murders.

After the feast they all go out onto the lawns of the inner court-yard to play bowls. The red sun glows just above the curtain wall; pink leaches from it across the sky, deepening the rose colour of the castle, its plaster warm – like something living – when Edward puts his palm against it. The people running to and fro across the grass have lost their sharpness in the low light. The Fitzgerald girls seem to float like angels. Joan's face looks almost gentle.

Later that evening she comes to sit beside him.

'Want a strategy lesson?' she says. 'I did promise.'

'Thanks, but I don't want to hear your kind of strategy,' he says. 'All I need is honour.'

'You also need wisdom, or you'll be honourably dead.'

He's offended. 'You should know that the most educated and sapi-ent nobles of Mechelen considered me to be passing wise. And they laughed at my japes, too. There was one about a purse of steel, a jape with words—'

'Tell me it.'

He does, and she sighs. 'Lesson one. Those people couldn't show you their true minds because you outranked them. They were shamming.'

'Well, I'm wonderly glad I don't have any of that here,' he says, irously. 'Fine. Teach me some strategy.'

'If I were you, the most useful thing to know would be exactly who I was.'

'What?'

'I mean, who are you? Are you the true Earl of Warwick or...'

'Of course I am! What else would I be?'

'Oh,' she says. 'You truly believe it. That's interesting.'

Edward, agitated, demands, 'Why wouldn't I believe it?'

'You have to admit, it's very convenient for Margaret of Burgundy and Lovell and my father to have an Earl of Warwick,' she says. 'How did they say they found you?'

'Bishop Stillington said—'

'Him? He'll lie for gold. King Richard paid him to say your cousins the two princes were bastards. But then, on the other hand, I don't believe the Yorkists just stumbled on a random blond peasant child in the Oxfordshire countryside who looks exactly like Clarence. And Clarence *did* try to swap his son. King Edward said he failed, but King Edward was a liar too, and wouldn't want it noised that there was a York heir on the loose. But then, you're the wrong age.'

'They said it took longer than they meant to get a replacement for me,' Edward says. He's flustered; he can feel the deep red of his face.

'Or maybe it was Clarence's supposed first child, Margaret Plantagenet, that they swapped you with,' Joan says, speculatively. 'Maybe you were even a twin of hers. Though more often I've heard it rumoured that you're a bastard of Clarence's — or even of your Aunt Margaret's. Heh. I guess the jury's out.'

'There's no jury!' Edward cries, wroth. 'It's not a case. I'm the Earl of Warwick. I won't sit here while you slander me! A bastard? You just want to injure me. I'm going to talk to the adults. Who conduct themselves with right worship.'

They look over to where Kildare is essaying to do a headstand, the other men helping by catching his waving legs.

'Truly you're bound for gentil company,' says Joan, curtseying. 'Farewell, your grace, farewell.'

Edward can't sleep that night. He lights a candle and tries to write his own *Morte* tale. It's mostly the same as the story of Sir Tor, the son of a cowherd who turns out to be of noble blood, at which point everyone says they knew Sir Tor wasn't a cowherd because he was fair and brave and wise and much *more* than his cowherd family.

After that, Edward struggles. He means to send his knight, Sir Edtor, on a quest for the Grail, or give him a giant to kill. But he keeps writing down dark paths. One in which Sir Edtor falls in love with a beautiful demosel, but it turns out he was a cowherd after all, and Arthur rules that his head must be swapped off for faiting, and tricking a noble lady into cleping him.

Another in which Merlin reveals he'd meant to switch the son of a cowherd with the son of a king, but lost sight of whose baby was whose. Nobody knows how to resolve the confusion, and so, to be safe, Arthur settles the matter by swapping off both men's heads.

Edward gives up and goes to bed.

It's Joan's fault. She ruins everything, and now she's ruined the *Morte*.

Kildare announces the next morning that he's had word of Lovell. The man's safe with some allies – not to be named, they're Tudor men – and means to get to Mechelen as soon as the coast quietens.

'God protect him,' says the Bishop of Meath, crossing himself.

'God? Lovell's got a different master,' says Kildare.

'You mislike Lovell?' Keating says.

Sir William is frowning at Keating. Edward had heard him complaining earlier about excommunicated knaves, which was hard to hear – being his own thought, but coming out of Sir William's mouth.

'I like him well enough,' Kildare says. 'Which is to say, enough to let him make war while I sit at home. Liking Lovell... is that something that's done? Do men *like* Lovell? Better say we admire him. He ought to be dead ten times over. He's still alive.'

'It's good fortune to be on the side of a man that can't die,' says Plunket.

'Except it's everyone around him who dies instead,' Joan says, joining them. 'Look at yon Humphrey Stafford.'

'Sure Lovell's made a bargain with the devil,' says Kildare.

'Keating would know,' Sir William says, turning to him. 'How is the devil these days?'

'Ballocks-deep in your mammy,' says Keating.

To which Joan, predictably, laughs.

That afternoon Joan doesn't come to Edward's room for the Latin lesson. Her lady Grania arrives instead. She's holding the *Morte*.

'Joan can't come today,' Grania says.

'Why? And how has she finished the *Morte* already?' Edward asks.

'She hasn't finished it. But she's been confined to her room for a few days, with her books taken away, so that she might repent her wanton demeaning in laughing at Sir William. She tried to hide this one, but I found it and told her father it was yours, so here it is.'

Edward takes it, inquieted.

'You betrayed her?' he says.

'What? I thought you wanted it back? And I didn't think *you* had any love for Joan. I thought you'd be pleased.'

Edward's saddened to think of Joan shut up without anything to do. Though she undoubtedly deserves it. Still. It seems overhard. Then a new worry occurs to him.

'Does she know you were the one who gave up the book to the earl?'

Grania pulls a droll expression. 'You must think I've no more sense than a cheese wheel,' she says. 'She has no idea I tell her father all her tricks. By Saint Dorothy! If she found out, she'd take off my ears and feed them to the crows.'

She laughs for some time at the thought. Then she looks stern.

'Don't *you* think of telling her.'

'By God, I've no desire to,' Edward says. 'I've met the earl, his daughters, nobles, servants. As far as I can see, you're all mad as weasels in a bucket. I'm not imperiling myself by intermeddling in any of your doings.'

'Good,' she says, and quits him.

Later that afternoon Joan's sisters come to him. They've embroidered him a sampler. It shows Edward as a king on the throne. The proportions are off and he's as wide as a house, with a head the size of an apple, but the trouble they've gone to brings tears into his eyes.

'We want to welcome you back into our graces,' says Eleanor. 'Given Joan's arrest and imprisonment, we consider that justice has been served, and we're lifting the attainder on your head and that of your descendants. You are pardoned.'

Eustacia, overcome, brasts out in tears, and wipes her face on the sampler.

'You're not still wroth about Sir William?' Edward asks.

'We heard him telling Da that we were right seemly maidens, and Joan was the one who needed to be under watch, so it seems we're safe. Praise God!'

'Amen,' says Edward.

He doesn't feel good. He feels as if there's a fish in his stomach, cold and heavy. Like it's dying, and every now and again, like now, it gives a sad twitch.

I'm not intermeddling, he tells the fish.

The fish lies still.

You know what will happen if I do, he continues. Grania will hate me, and Kildare will work me wrack, and his daughters will attaint me again, and at the end of it all Joan will say, *I didn't ask for your aid, you dullwitted midden beetle.* That's what you'd have me do?

That's what it would have him do.

So here he is, in Joan's room, having lied to the guard to gain admittance, which he'll have to atone for later. And he's not even sure if he's done the right thing because – looking around – this is the first girl's bedchamber he's ever been in, and it's much more *personal*-feeling in here than he expected, with tapestries of nymphs on the walls, roses painted on the plaster, a faint smell of lavender coming from the direction of the disordered bed. It's like a garden in heaven. With one ill-natured angel standing in the middle of it, saying, 'What the hell are you doing in here?'

He holds out the *Morte*.

'You hadn't finished this, so I brought it back to you. I don't know why it was given back to me. I don't know anything at all, about anything, and if any of this turns out ill, it can all be explained as a matter of my own misperception.'

'Lord Christ,' she says, with a scornful face, but she takes the book. 'Thank you.'

'I was thinking about what you said about King Arthur,' he says. 'Do you really believe he lived? Or were you just japing Plunket?'

'Of course he lived,' Joan says. She looks melancholic, suddenly. 'When he died, all the magic of these isles went with him. The sorcerers and enchantresses and dragons and giants.'

'There are still giants and enchanters and dragons in the East,' Edward says. 'That's where I want to go. Though I do need to be king. But maybe I can leave my council in charge for a year, and I'll fund ships and a great delegation of brave men, and we'll journey to see the race of men with one foot and the people of Meroë and divers other wonders.'

'A turd for you,' she says. 'I'll only ever make one journey, to the house of my husband, and there I'll stay.'

'I'm sorry—' he says.

'Ah, don't make dole. I said it to put you out of ease. You were starting with this back and forthish friendly conversation, and I didn't like it. You'd better go, anyway, or someone will notice you're here.'

'I lied to the guard to get in. I don't know if he's trustworthy.'

'Oh, don't worry about Feargus. He's already brought me some Latin books in exchange for ten seconds of looking at one of my breasts. He won't tell anyone. And as you can see, I'm the mistress of the room now. They thought it would be a punishment. Ha! No more women. No snoring, sniffing, slandering, squawking, sweating, or shamming.'

'What about spying?' he says.

'What do you mean?'

He wonders how he's going to save both her and Grania from each other's maugre. And himself. It would be pleasant if he wasn't torn limb-meal. He probably will be. But he has to warn her.

'I've heard of gentlemen setting spies among their own daughters' ladies,' he says. 'The daughters would never know who it was, and in fact they shouldn't waste their time trying to find out. But they should be ware.'

Was that cunning? He repeats it back to himself. Yes, it was. Very well done. He doesn't see why Joan should look first mirthful, and then mocking.

'Uh *huh*,' she says. 'Well, thank you for the advice. It's wonderly wise. Gramercy, kind sir, and so on.'

She opens the door.

'Wait, did you really show Feargus—'

The door closes.

7

On St Eustace's Day Joan is released from her punishment and the Queen of England gives birth to a small but healthy prince.

'On St Eustace's Day!' Kildare says. 'Our dearest Saint. Sometimes I wonder what God's about. I cannot believe He means to mock us, confuse us, turn us upsodown. But sometimes I wonder.'

'What does this mean for us?' Edward says. Lateward he's been feeling much more like the saviour of Engeland, and is alarmed at the threat to his future reign.

'Your aunt in Burgundy won't abandon this war,' Kildare says. 'And Ireland is behind you. That baby is nothing royal. It won't stop us, you can be right assured of that.'

The son of King Henry and Queen Elizabeth is named Arthur. What else? King Arthur was born from the union of a red king and a white queen, so Merlin said, and Henry thought the words wonderly meet. The birth of the New Arthur is noised all over England. Proclamations are nailed to doors. Criers cry it. Bonfires are lit on the streets.

'The English will celebrate any old shite,' says Kildare.

The christening is held at Winchester Cathedral. Lincoln attends, still acting the part of a Tudor loyalist. It weighs heavy on him, he says, in a letter to Edward. Edward worries about Lincoln. He remembers how Lincoln held his hands so tightly. He hopes Lincoln escapes soon. Hopes he's getting enough sleep.

To celebrate the New Arthur's birth, King Henry's pet poet, Bernard André, composes a poem of one hundred verses – which Edward has to take on faith, as he can only get through ten of them.

'"Come celebrate the child's birth, O Muses," reads Kildare, '"and the noble offspring born of illustrious royalty. To celebrate the festal day, wreathe your hair with a comely flower, O English, and crown your brows with garlands—" By God, this dull word-turtle is worse than *your* poetasters, Alison.'

Joan writes her own version, which starts 'Come celebrate the cock's girth, O Muses', and everyone says it's passing mirthful. The prospect of her verses falling into Sir William's hands doesn't seem to concern her.

'I have a premonition that he'll be gone before Hallowmas,' she says.

The next day Joan doesn't come to Edward's room for her Latin lesson. She isn't under the yew tree, or any other tree. She isn't in the great hall, the library, her room, her sisters' rooms, the cellar, the kitchens, the barracks, the gardens or the cloisters.

He comes to a stop outside the chapel.

Surely not...?

But there she is inside, on her knees, head bowed, beside the altar. The stained-glass window has coloured her nose red, her forehead yellow and her chin blue. She's so still he's almost adread to approach, in case this isn't Joan, but some wicked thing in her shape.

He goes as far into the nave as he dares, and asks, 'What are you about?'

'Look,' she says, standing up. The colours slide off her face and down her gown. She's holding a bottle. 'Whiskey. Hid behind the altar.'

'What's whiskey?'

'An Irish Aqua Vitae.'

'But that's just medicine.'

'Then why does he hide it here? Why do his hands tremble over the sacrament? Why do we leave Confession with our heads whirling from the vapours?'

He accompanies her back out into the daylight, which is grey and discomposed. The wind chases them along the cloisters.

'Are you going to do something heinous to Sir William?' Edward asks. 'Joan? You can't tell your father about the bottle. He'll know you've been spying.'

'I won't say anything to him, and God forgive you for such ill thoughts,' Joan says. She's hurrying away. Over her shoulder she says, 'And no word to anyone that you saw me here.'

The Queen of England is ill, says Portlester to Kildare. She's been ill since the birth of the New Arthur.

'Let's hope it's a fever that takes the baby too, and not some woman's thing that carries off her alone,' says Kildare.

'Amen,' says Portlester.

A wished-for death comes two days later. Not to the Queen of England or her child, but to Sir William.

Everyone knows the news by morning. The prebendary lost all his wits and went creeping about the castle in his smock and slippers, speaking in tongues. He managed to come out with enough English to convince the guards to let him into Kildare's room, where the earl was abed with his wife, and then Sir William shrieked that the room was full of demons, and laid hands on Lady Kildare, crying that she was a siren and an abominable succubus – and right anon Kildare seized the priest and threw him out of the window.

'The devil must have got inside the prebendary somehow,' says Fearganainm, Kildare's steward.

'I suppose there'll be no getting the devil to pay for that glass,' Kildare says. 'Shit! Send word to his family. No, I'll go myself. These heavy tidings need an explanation. I suppose the St Lawrences won't be friends to us in the coming war now. Fuck it all. By God, I won't have another overpious prebendary. There are too many fair women in this castle. It's a death sentence for a man who refuses to bring himself off or visit a local jade. The pressure reaches their brain and overturns it. That's science aright. You may as well keep a gunpowder barrel by a fire.'

Alice starts crying uncontrollably.

'What's bringing off? Do the men know they have to?' she gets out, through brasts of tears. 'What about the guards? What about the cooks? If the cooks explode, what will we eat?'

'What about Grandda?' wails Eustacia.

The younger girls are taken out of the hall by Joan. Edward hears her murmuring comforting words to them.

Her kindness makes him suspicious. He finds Eleanor and Eilis later and asks them if this was Joan's doing.

'How?' Eilis says. 'She can't make men lose their wits. She doesn't know enchantment.'

Edward tries to think of what he knows about witches. In Mechelen, an inquisitor named Kramer kept writing, seeking an audience with Maximilian. He'd been on the hunt for a patron after being thrown out of Innsbruck for being annoying. The Burgundian nobles said he was writing a treatise about witches having orgies and eating children and consorting with the devil in the form of a black cat – tail lifted, that they might kiss its sooty anus.

Poor man, his wits have hopped away like frogs, someone said.

Good people that they were, they couldn't imagine anyone being so wicked as to enter into a pact with the devil.

They hadn't met Joan.

Edward goes to her.

'I know you did this,' he says. 'I won't noise it anywhere. I just want to know *how* you did it. Please tell me it's not some perilous magic.'

Joan smiles. 'Why, when you look so entertainingly adread?'

'If you don't tell me, no more Latin.'

Up go her brows then.

'I see you're becoming less tender-hearted,' she says. 'Fine. It was me. Not magic. A kind of mushroom that grows in sheep pastures. I ate some when I was young and was crazed in my wits for a full day. Then I was whole again, as if nothing had happened. No leech or book mentions them. I steeped some in his whiskey. But I was perhaps… overhandy with the dosing. It's been a while since I last did it. I forgot the quantities.'

'Since you last did it?!'

'Oh, that was years ago. An aggravating lady of my mother's. I dosed her every few days, just a small amount, so she brast out in fits of laughter and saw things in the soup. They put her in a convent in the end.' She laughs.

'This isn't funny! Sir William's dead! You're killing people!'

'If people stop annoying me then people won't get killed,' she says. 'What did Theognis say?

A man's heart shrinks, when disaster strikes, but when he gets revenge it grows again.'

'By the saints, you're exactly like your father,' Edward says.

It's a spear to her, he can tell as soon as it's thrown. He thinks of his own father, the mad duke; of the murderer Sir Gowther and his evil fairy father. And now he wants her to prove him wrong, laugh at the thought of wickedness being passed down through the blood.

But she says nothing. She just looks, briefly, pained. And then the expression snaps away, like she's closed a book.

To try to ease his inquiet, Edward walks around the courtyard. Devil take Joan! Ruthless eyes, glistening eyes, malicious mouth, soft pink mouth, soft skin, soft breast, evil heart, evil heart. She should be grimly-looking, like a giant insect, and then all men would know her. She wouldn't be able to cause so much dole if she looked like a centipede.

He turns a corner, and sees Joan's lady Grania talking privily to Kildare in the gardens.

Now he's alarmed. He doesn't think the earl would kill his own daughter, but he could marry her to a churl, or put her in a nunnery.

He goes back to Joan.

'Did anyone see you with those mushrooms?' he asks. 'Like Grania? She's always with you.'

Joan looks confused. Then she laughs.

'Oh, I perceive what you're getting at.'

'No, you don't,' Edward says, alarmed. 'Or if you do, please don't murder Grania.'

'Content your minds. Grania is my dear friend. I told her to give you the *Morte* back. To see what you were made of.'

'But she said she passes word of you to your father—'

'Only the words I put in her mouth. She betrays me in small ways so the bigger doings go by. Everyone knows her as my enemy, so they come hudder mudder to her when they hate me, and then I know who hates me.'

'Right.'

'You know, wonderly many people come to her,' Joan muses. 'Anyway, I want your oath that you'll repeat none of this, or you know I'll kill you in your bed, and say it was by the hand of an agent of King Henry.'

'I could kill *you* in your bed,' he says, but his heart isn't in it.

'Grania sleeps at the foot of my bed and she keeps her knife by her all night. She's like a Cerberus. She stands between me and the bad things of the night. Like owls.'

'You're frightened of owls?'

'Of course. They bring ill luck.'

'They can't get into the keep. That's not a rational dread. You should be more afraid of ghosts.'

'Ghosts!' she says. 'They only want our prayers, to get them out of purgatory. Is that what you're scared of? Ghosts?'

'I'm not so suet-headed as to tell *you* what I'm scared of,' he says.

Things Edward is scared of

Acting like John Collan by mistake.

Turning out like his father Clarence.

Dying in the coming war.

Not dying, but not being a good king, failing to set things right, disappointing Lincoln and Margaret and Philip, dying without the love of his people, being taken to hell.

8

The problem with being the saviour of Engeland is that after a banquet Edward can't play at shovelboard or cards with the Fitzgerald girls, or dance to the fiddle music with the young men and women, but has to stand with Kildare and his noble guests – tonight: Portlester, Plunket and the Baron of Slane, James Fleming – and nod as Fleming, a large man in black velvet, like a great mole, says how passing lazy peasants have got these days.

'No danger of mine revolting, as they did in England,' he says. 'My tenants couldn't even be bothered to swing an axe onto my neck.'

'They've no inwit,' says Plunket. 'Not like us. It's like Gower said, they're closer to animals. A peasant couldn't be a poet. Their thinking can't reach the abstract realms. They only think of ploughing, or swiving, or what's in their pottage.'

(A memory of the farm: Emma Mylton's pottage, stuffed with chervil, carrot and rabbit, the fragrant scents rising off it.)

'Or how they can avoid work,' says Fleming.

'I hope so,' says Portlester. 'I'd greatly mislike being torn to scraps by villagers.'

'No chance. They're ware of what happened to the English Lollards. A donkey kicks, you beat it with a stick, and the donkey learns peace,' Kildare says. 'And unlike donkeys, humans can watch another human get beaten and learn the same lesson.'

'It's just a shame the clods can't *read* their lessons,' Fleming says. 'Those dull-witted English peasants rose up under the name of Piers Plowman. They didn't realise Langland's book was telling them to get on with their work, and not to fancy themselves capable of self-governance.'

'Pray God that fancy is full dead and buried,' says Portlester.

'Weren't you raised a peasant, my lord?' Plunket says, indicating Edward. 'You ought to have some idea of what goes on in their brain-pans.'

Edward, as seems meet, pretends not to hear or understand.

'I think I'm wanted at shovelboard,' he says, bowing, and quits them.

Joan comes to him for her Latin lesson with Grania, who, once the door is closed, takes out a cake, unwraps it, and puts her feet up.

'Ah, I'm glad to drop the doubleness,' she says.

Joan has gone over to Edward's open books and is looking at them with her magpie head-tilt.

'Piers Plowman's wife is called Work Well in Time,' she says. 'And his son is called Suffer Thine Sovereigns To Have Their Will And Judge Them Not Or You'll Pay Dearly For God's Word Is Final.'

'Imagine calling him in for dinner,' says Grania.

'Why are you reading this?' Joan asks. 'And *Vox Clamantis*. Really? I wouldn't have thought you'd love Gower.'

Edward doesn't. His misliking of Gower is passionate, but also painful, and confusing. He thinks of Will Collan; Will's Lollard grandfather. He hasn't seen these men in a book before. And now here they are, as farm animals that have forgotten their natures, sluggish, greedy, envious, murderous. His father-that-was is an ass coveting a jewelled saddle, his great-grandfather-that-was is a blood-crazed boar. What if Edward were Will Collan's son and not a duke's? How would Gower write him: as a beshitten donkey, braying for a crown?

Joan mislikes Gower too, but not for the same reasons.

'The problem with Gower,' says Joan, 'is that he's a humourless cunt.'

'I'm done reading him, and Langland too,' Edward says.

Joan is looking at him closely. It makes him uncomfortable.

'They're neither of them near in greatness to Chaucer,' she says. 'You know Gower and Chaucer used to be friends? Until Chaucer made a mock of him. It's interesting that Chaucer never mentioned the peasant revolts. Isn't that strange? I think he had sympathies with them.'

Edward feels lighter, hearing this.

'What was your peasant name?' Joan asks him.

She asks gently enough, but he can't say it. So he says: 'Lambert Simnel.'

'Like the cake?' She laughs. 'We should call you Simnel cake.'

'Because I'm sweet?'

Joan looks at Grania's cake, now a ruin of crumbs.

She says, 'Sure.'

October comes. It rains for a full week. Every trace of broken glass and Sir William is rinsed from the courtyard by the time the new prebendary arrives. Sir Patrick Walsh is a mirthful man with a bald top and a sanguine countenance. He likes lying flat on his back under trees and prays they all try it, as a cure for any sickness. He declares he has no use for money. He sends his pay to his former mistress, a 'fine stout lady', who lives in Dublin. His almoner is instructed to be generous with the people who beg at the castle gates.

'See,' Joan says to Edward and her sisters. 'Isn't this merry now? You ought to give thanks to me.'

News comes to Kildare from England, from his Yorkist friends at court. King Henry has heard about Edward's appearance in Mechelen. He's put his spies to work, on the following business:

Find out the plans of the faiter Earl of Warwick.

Do not noise it that there is a faiter earl.

Find out the traitors in our royal household.

Do not let any man hear that we have traitors in our household.

Stop the talk of him among the people.

Do not let the people know that there is talk of him to stop.

Kill the pretender.

Do not let it be known that there was a pretender to kill.

9

Joan and Edward are lying under an oak tree, wrapped in fur cloaks, because the ground is cold, looking up through the gold leaves.

'How do we know if it's working?' Joan says. 'I don't *feel* in better health.'

'It's only been a few moments,' Edward says. He admires the way the bright yellow leaves twitch and flutter, against a sky the bold blue of Joan's eyes.

What?

—No.

The sky and Joan's eyes have nothing to do with each other.

Please God, pluck such thoughts out of my head, thank you, amen.

'I looked at your pile of books,' Joan says. '*The Temple of Glass, The House of Fame*. More dream visions? Are you going to write one of your own?'

'I'm not going to write one.'

'You say that, but you have a look of wanting to.'

'You know my looks so well?'

Edward's never told her about his plan to be a poet king who immortalises his own reign. He has a feeling she might not receive the idea with the solemnity it deserves.

'I don't want to write anything right now,' he says.

'Read with me then,' she says. 'Let's find some obscene Roman verse. How about Juvenal? Plunket said Juvenal despises well-read women who quote poetry at dinner, as if they're men. I think it would be a good jape to collect Juvenal quotes to recite to Plunket over dinner.'

'Fine. Anything but Horace.'

'Why not?'

'He was the favourite of a tutor I misliked.'

'Oh, I know, the Oxford one. What happened – did he follow the model of the ancients and their boys? Wasn't he a priest? Classic. First it's Holy Communion, then it's communion with your hole.'

'What? No!'

'What then, hand business? One of my cousins tricked me into doing that when I was young. He said he had a newborn kitten and asked me to stroke it.'

'*What*? Maister Richard did nothing like that! And your cousin did you a great wrong! Wait. He tricked *you*?'

'Well. Not really,' Joan says. 'I knew what he was about. Then he had to bribe me to not tell anybody. I've still got the silver. Later I was somewhat despoiled by one of our music tutors. He even tried to have my maidenhead by force. But I stabbed him in the ballocks with my embroidery scissors.'

'A meet punishment for a monstrous sin,' Edward says. He wants to offer more than this but isn't sure how. His hand moves abortively in the direction of hers. Moves back again. He looks at her face, leaf-patterned. She's looking at the sky, with a small smile, as if reminiscing over something pleasant.

'It happens to most women at some time,' she says. 'And fair boys. Servants have it the worst. At least my maidenhead has a value, in the heir trade. You can't rape the goose that lays the golden eggs. By Saint Wilgefortis, I learned a lot from those early doings. When I first saw a pintle I thought there was something ailing it. Like when I broke my finger and it was inflamed. And afterwards, the pintle just... crumpled, and was so small and ashamed of itself. I think this is why men are such shrews, because privily they're pained, and they're ashamed.'

'All men?' he says.

'Most men are villains.'

'Lincoln is kind and full gentil,' he says.

'Lincoln is crazed in his courage.'

'What?'

'Didn't you know? My da told me. Lincoln's a knight who can't fight. And he has no heirs, so probably he can't swive either. He isn't a whole man.'

Can this be true? No. Edward ignores it.

'Do you think *I'm* a villain?' he asks.

'Not right now. But how do I know what you'll become? Especially if they ever do get a crown on your pate.'

'I won't change,' he says, and she laughs.

'Have you changed before?' she asks.

'Yes,' answers John Collan, Lambert, Edward.

'But you believe you'll never change again?'

'I take the point. But I didn't change for the worse. And I never will.'

She sighs. 'I believe you mean that. But it'll only work you wrack. You're too soft and unwary. It's a shame that priest *didn't* despoil you. A difficult early life is good fortune. To be like the fish born in boiling water. When it's caught and put in the pot, it can't be cooked.'

'But the Bible teaches us there's no virtue in maugre or vengeance,' Edward says. 'God would have us be meek and soft.'

'Sure, and that's all very well, in heaven. And you'll get there wonderly fast, too. What are you going to do on the English battlefield? Offer King Henry your neck?'

'That's different. War is different.'

'It's all a war,' she says.

Edward, Grania and Joan are eating oranges; given to Grania by the new prebendary Sir Patrick, who got them shipped from Spain. Sir Patrick is in love with Grania. He bought her an embroidered pair of gloves last week. Meanwhile his own fur cloak is patchy and his hat goes jewel-less. He says he'd rather see beautiful things enhancing a fair lady; there's no point augmenting a fat hedgepig such as himself.

'This must be what the sun tastes like,' Joan says, her fierce eyes closed for the moment. 'Not in the morning, but when it's ripe in the afternoon.'

'It's a shame that when you do turn Sir Patrick down these gifts will stop,' Edward says to Grania.

'Turn him down?' says Grania.

Edward waxes red.

'Edward's a virgin, remember,' says Joan. 'And somewhat God-happy.'

227

'You're a virgin yourself,' says Grania.

'But not in the same way,' says Joan.

'No,' Grania concedes.

Edward asks her, 'Aren't you afraid of hell?'

Joan laughs. 'If the harlot in the *Gesta Romanorum* can get into heaven without even doing penance, on contrition alone, I think Grania has a fair chance. She's our own Mary Magdalene.'

She smiles at Grania. Not just a smile, Edward realises: this is a look of love, a warmth suffusing her face. She looks suddenly tender and young.

He doesn't know why the sight should pain him.

(He does.)

'Live merry, repent later,' says Grania, used to looks such as this from Joan, calmly eating her orange.

Edward started teaching Joan to read Ovid, because Edward wanted to read Ovid. But he's not enjoying it. It seems like all the Romans were either sodomising boys or insulting women, or both.

'I can imagine the French women Jean de Meun knew were faithless and greedy and lying,' he says. 'But surely not all Roman woman. It's Roman men that are all awful. I'm stomach-sick of them.'

'Roman poets,' Joan says. 'Not Roman men.'

'What do you mean?'

'It's like a syllogism,' she says. 'All the Roman poets hated women. But not all Roman men were poets. Writing is for those who are *without*. Those who can live, live. Those who can't, write. Men who aren't wanted by women say women are shrews or strumpets. Men who are happy with their women don't write poetry.'

'But *we* write,' Edward says.

'And hap one day, when all our desires are met, we'll stop.'

Plunket, of course, loves Ovid, and Jean de Meun. He started jangling on at dinner about them. To which Joan said that Ovid was the more worthy of the two woman-haters, because at least Ovid openly admitted he was being cuckolded.

Really it's women's fault, she said. They should know that if they turn a man down the result will be an outpouring of bad poetry. Whoever rejected Jean de Meun owes us all an apology. She should have unlatched her clicket gate for the good of literature.

Plunket, looking wonderly wroth, said between closed teeth that Joan did not know Jean de Meun and had no business jangling on things she had no witting of.

When a husband is being cuckolded, *everyone* knows, said Joan.

Everyone laughed.

Plunket did not laugh.

'You should be ware of Plunket,' Edward says to Joan. 'I don't mean you should kill him. Just leave him be. He could work you wrack.'

'Ah, he's part of a rebellion against the King of England,' Joan says. 'He'll be dead soon. You all will.'

IO

In November it snows. Feathery flakes pour from the white sky, so thick Edward can't see the chapel from his window, the stripped black limbs of the trees. When it settles he runs around the court-yard with the Fitzgerald girls, throwing snowballs. Joan lands a hard snowball on Edward's nose. He pushes her into a snowdrift in the crook of the castle wall. All her sisters throw themselves in after her, shrieking.

He's so happy.

Edward says to Joan, 'I've been reading Christine de Pizan's writings…'

Leaving a pause, here, to see her reaction. Her face doesn't move.

'—I found them full of many goodly learnings. For example, she said Jean de Meun was nothing more than a frequenter of harlots, who then claims that all women are of the same kind.'

Not even an eyebrow raised.

'And she says that though there are passing many books stuffed with tales of evil women, it would be different if women had more power to compose books, and could tell of men's sins.'

Joan sighs.

'And furthermore—'

She holds up her hand.

'I've read it. I know what you're going to say. That men work each other more wrack than any woman ever did. That no land or kingdom has been lost through the great misdeeds of women. Was that it?'

'Something sib.'

'Well, I say men and women are both stupid and both cruel. Women just don't have the power to work any real wrack. Ovid was right that it's a war – and men have won, because they're stronger. So women lie and steal and cheat, to win some small liberty from the occupiers. Except most women don't even do that! And the kind of woman who kills her husband is sadly rare. They're as cowardly as pigeons.'

'*Sadly?*'

'I think it's the womb that's at fault,' Joan muses. 'Once a woman gets pregnant, the womb steals the vital courage and drinks the brain strength, to feed the child. The poor woman never recovers. Think on it. Who do you know that has the force and wit of a man?'

'My Aunt Margaret. A woman I knew called Jennott.'

'Does either of them have children?'

'No. Margaret said she could not. But Margaret's step-daughter Mary of Burgundy had a child and she ruled very well.'

'Ruled? Not rules?'

'She's dead now.'

'Because her body couldn't sustain both maternal force and *mascula* force,' says Joan. 'I imagine she collapsed in on herself like a windfall apple.'

'Her horse stumbled and landed on her during a hunt.'

'Did anyone see that happen?'

'What? I don't know.'

'They probably came along after, found her all crushed in and thought it was the horse's work. But it was beyond doubt an implosion from within. The true test will be my own sister Margaret. She was powerful in her will and her wisdom when she left. She'll be pregnant soon and we'll see how long that lasts.'

'I don't expect *you* to understand this, wicked as you are,' Edward says, annoyed, 'but have you considered that women aren't as warly as men not because of their wombs, but because of their kind hearts? They don't want to raise any affray, in case their children are harmed. While men take their sons into battle. In Pizan's *Epistre*, Cupid says that woman's nature is mild, loving, hesitant, sweet, humble, charitable, modest, forgiving. See? Women have better hearts.'

'Better?' Joan says. 'This is a list of shameful weakness. Whether it's a woman's heart or her womb that makes her pitiful, the result is the same. They'll never overcome their oppression. If women were worth anything they'd throw their boy babies into the sea, and kill all the men in their beds.'

Please God, remove from me this unnatural longing, I will begin my Advent fast early, I will drink water instead of wine, I will renounce custard, I will pray morning, afternoon and night on my knees, thank you God our father, amen.

Advent is over and Christmas is come: brightly and noisily, the moment Mass is over and they all come out of chapel into the cold dawn and Kildare plays a blast on a trumpet.

Pears poached in wine, dancing, plum pudding made with Spanish figs, companies of players from Dublin, wine, honeyed hams, card games, roast swan, wine, a whole cooked boar's head brought in on Christmas Day accompanied by dancers wearing animal masks, singing in Gaelic. A twelve-day holiday and a goodly feast for the village farmers. Disguisings. Wine. Cakes. Blind man's bluff. Wine. Hazelnuts. Dates in spiced cream. Pipers. Marzipan. Wine.

On New Year's Day, the Feast of Fools, Sir Patrick holds Mass wearing a woman's red gown, much gaping and strained, and a headdress of holly. He's painted his eyebrows with charcoal and has red lips and cheeks.

'Queen Medb will give you your sermon today,' he says, to applause.

'Isn't that your kirtle, Grania?' asks Joan. 'I'm not sure you ever wore it so well.'

'He's got me a velvet one to replace it,' says Grania.

After the Eucharist, Sir Medb announces that as today is the day of gift-giving and also the day of tricks and turnabouts, all the nobles of the castle should go into the village and bring the peasants goodly gifts. And not only that: they must offer to perform a service for the household, washing pots, feeding animals, stirring their pottage.

'I'll stir *your* pottage, you fine wench,' Kildare says to Sir Medb, trying to catch hold of his skirts. Sir Medb smacks him about the pate.

'You'll not get a taste of this stew,' he cries.

'That's enough church for today,' says Joan, leading the way out. 'Grania, let's go to the cellar and get a wineskin as our gift. If we can get our peasants drunk enough, they won't care whether we've travailed or no.'

Edward walks into the village with Eleanor. He's looking forward to the work. He's been an earl for months now, but he's still not wholly at ease in his new form. His heart is suddenly light at the thought of being in a place where he can feel *usual*. In no danger of wrongness. He knows it's not his home village, but the thatched cottages he's seen from the castle walls, the distant honks of geese and shouts of men – he knows these.

But when they arrive at their allotted house they get little worship from its owner, a widow who speaks only in Gaelic. Her face is scored like a chopping block with wrinkles, lines cross-hatched on lines. At the sight of Edward and Eleanor the lines multiply like cracks on ice.

They take their gifts – a black pudding and bacon – into the low house. Eleanor had also brought some blue ribbon, lateward given to her by Lady Kildare, which she thought would be a pretty present for a woman on her own, mayhap looking to remarry. The widow takes the ribbons with a look of confusion and offence.

Edward's trying not to feel dismayed. It's only that the house is *so* small, and so dark – was it always so dark, in his old home? – and the green wood she's burning on the hearth spreads an evil damp odour about the room. When they go outside to milk the widow's cow, the frosty air doesn't quell the smell of the midden heap, the hot mule piss steaming in the mud.

'So, how do we do it?' Eleanor says.

Edward realises he doesn't know how to milk a cow. The dairy maids never allowed him anywhere near them. But he shams an air of authority, grasps the teat and – after a long time, with the cow shifting and making long lows of resentment – manages to direct a goodly amount of milk into the pail.

'God be praised,' whispers Eleanor. 'Let's get out of here right anon.'

Once they've reached the bridge over the frozen stream, they start laughing.

'What are *you* thinking of?' Eleanor says.

'When that cow let go a blast and made you jump.'

'I was imagining that lady wearing the blue ribbons in her bonnet. That was a poor gift, wasn't it? I thought she'd be younger.'

'Why?'

'I don't know. I didn't know someone could *be* so old.'

They're laughing again when they're hailed by Joan and Grania, coming up the lane. They're clearly drunk. They went to the household of a father and two merry lads, who just wanted Joan and Grania to dance with them, which they did, and then they all drank perry and told bawdy jokes.

'We should do this every week,' Joan says. 'How was your day? Did you get large worship for your peasanting skill, Edward?'

'The lady said something as I left that I didn't understand,' he says.

'The widow said he was lucky to have a fair countenance,' Eleanor says, 'because a more useless dandelion puff she'd not seen in all her life.'

Joan and Grania fall about laughing again.

'And then a cow farted on us,' says Eleanor. 'Let's go back to the castle.'

'Amen,' says Edward.

He hides the sadness he feels at how wrong he felt; how alien and unfitting he was in this village. Nobody notices his inquiet. Is that his problem? Is he so good at hiding the unwanted parts of himself, that they sicken and die? He tried to find John Collan today, a boy bricked up like an anchorite, but when he knocked through the wall, a skeleton fell out.

May God rest his soul.

On Twelfth Night there's pageantry in the great hall, recitations of Gaelic poetry, a troupe of dancers. Hundreds of candles light their forms on the walls, already patterned with the umbras of holly and ivy wreaths. It looks like a forest of teeth and claws, flickering.

Edward is handed a slice of fruit cake. He takes a bite, makes his jaws chew. His heart is heavy. It's not a new weight, it's a heaviness that's always with him, like his own shadow. Most of the time he forgets it's there – and why? Because he's only been looking at Joan. But now the end of Christmas is coming, the shadow comes creeping out, and says: This year you'll leave here, march upon King Henry and all his men, and kill them or die yourself.

Evil tidings to the most powerful.

A cry goes up across the hall. Kildare's father-in-law Portlester has discovered a small dried bean in his cake. He's crowned the Lord of Misrule with a copper cooking pot, and begins making laws. Parents have to bow to their children, or else get their nose blacked with a coal. Men have to address women as 'my lord'. Women will address men as 'my lady'. Wooden swords are to be given to the women. In addition, any lady can ask a kiss from any gentleman, and no gentleman can say no. Little Eustacia follows Edward around, asking him for kisses then hitting him with her sword.

'That's love aright,' says Kildare.

'We sisters have been talking,' Eleanor says to Edward, with a flush on her pale neck. 'We debated whether to tell you this or no. But we're worried, and decided it was better to warn you. We know you've fallen in love with Joan. No need to be alarmed! None of the men have noticed. But we have. And if we have, Joan has. And if she has, there's no ending to the travails and woe she might devise for you. You know we love her. But she's got a devilish heart. She's always been our da's favourite, and he lets her do anything she wants. So it's not her fault. And she's full kind sometimes. But mostly she's guileful, irous and vengeful. She might try to seduce you for some wicked purpose.'

Edward's wine goes down sideways; he coughs, sputters, manages to say:

'She'd try to seduce me?'

The Lord of Misrule's reign ends at midnight. When the hour turns Edward feels a dull, heavy impact, like he's been falling out of a window for hours and his body has just hit the earth.

He didn't know until that moment that he'd been in suspense.

The merry-making continues. The dancing waxes wild, women spinning, young men leaping like hares. Lady Kildare trips over her kirtle. Kildare picks her up and kisses her. With standing drops in his eyes, he makes a speech about how much he loves her, and his beautiful girls, and his baby boy. The fiddles and pipes and tabors go faster and faster. A young cousin sprains an ankle and is carried off. Eventually, people go to their beds or fall asleep where they are, heads down on the tables; in the window-niches of the hall; in corners, covered in ecstatic dogs. Eustacia, previously thought lost, is discovered under the high table curled up with a wolfhound, and growls when the nursemaid tries to extract her.

Edward is drunk, but not tired. His heart is running fast. The blood races through his body. He tells the servants and guards not to mind him, wraps himself in a bearskin from one of the dancers' costumes, and goes outside.

It's a clear night, shockingly cold, and the stars glitter like sugar crystals. The sky is perfectly black. Beyond the few lighted windows of the castle buildings and the torches at the gates, almost nothing is visible. The frozen ground is as vague as fog; he can hardly see where his feet are. Only a soft crunching sound gives away their continued existence.

There's another noise of crunching behind him. He doesn't realise it's Joan at first, she's so swaddled in furs. A pale cloud issues from the area usually occupied by her face.

'What cheer?' Joan says.

'You're awake,' he says.

'Nothing escapes *you*,' she says, but without much scorn. Her voice is more deliberate than usual, like her tongue is feeling over the words. She's drunk too, then.

An owl hoots above them.

'I hate owls,' Joan says.

'I know.'

'Oh, you know all! So you know why I'm out here?'

'I... don't.'

Even this close to her, which is closer than usual, he can hardly make out her features. She pushes the furs back and now he can see her white teeth; the pupils of her eyes. Black and white. Her expression is beyond him.

'Guess,' she says.

Her fingers reach inside the bearskin, brush the front of his hose. He has to stop the involuntary sound that rises in his throat.

Guileful, irous and vengeful, is what comes into his head.

'Pray God—' he says.

She laughs. 'He's not here to save you.'

And that's when it is.

Right then, invisible in the darkness, so who could even say it happened.

His first kiss.

II

The remembering of Joan's kiss troubles him, arouses him, troubles him. It was a sin, he knows it.

Even though she laid her hands on him first.

He masturbates, imagining what could have happened if they hadn't thought they heard a guard, and run back to their rooms.

He worries that he's turning into his father Clarence: impulsive; uncontrolled; ultimately un-alive.

He prays to God, but he can't say sorry because he's not sorry; he wants it to happen again.

But God saves him, whether he likes it or not.

At the Epiphany feast Joan ignores him. Grania winks at him. Edward finds comfort in this. If Joan had gone to Grania and said, *I did the stupidest thing when I was cupshot, I'm sore ashamed* – surely Grania wouldn't feel that a wink was a meet gesture? But then Grania said she'd had ado with Sir Patrick while he was still wearing her dress. Which places the minds of Grania far beyond the comprehension of the likes of Edward.

The next day Joan comes to him with her Latin books as usual. Grania is behind her. She winks at Edward again.

'I can tell you're winking, you woodenpoll,' Joan says to her. 'You're inquieting Edward.' To him she says, 'Your face is too readable. It'll work you wrack if you can't master it.'

She and Grania sit down.

'Well, his face is all dole now,' Grania says. 'He's short of word from you, the poor boy.'

'I was getting to that,' Joan says. 'Edward, I'm not sorry about what happened, but we both know we must never do it again.'

'Oh,' says Edward.

It's little cheer to him that Joan looks exactly as uncomfortable as he feels.

'If it were discovered there would be evil commotions,' she continues. 'My da would marry me to some low chieftain with no books. Or put me in the nun house. Nobody would chastise *you*, but your heart is over-soft and I think my fate would weigh on it.'

What can he say?

He nods.

Grania cries out, 'Oh, it's a great pity! I wish you two could just marry.'

Why *can't* they? Edward almost says. Then he remembers: he's either the next King of England or a peasant pretender, and neither one of these marries the daughter of the Lord Deputy of Ireland.

'God forgive you, Grania,' Joan snaps. 'It's difficult enough to talk in front of you without these womanish outbursts.'

'Sure, I suppose this is the last we'll see of *your* female weakness,' Grania says.

'Christ, yes. I've fully beskift it,' says Joan.

A few days after Epiphany they get a letter from England and one from Mechelen.

Kildare says, 'Tidings from your cousin Lincoln. The usurper Henry knows what we're about. Lincoln's under close watch these days. In the meantime he sends you his deep and abiding love, said Christmas passed pensily under the misbegotten king, but he trusts next year will be such a one to fill his heart with marvellous gladness, and so on. He went on at some length. By Jesus, I never thought one man could contain so many emotions.'

Letter the second:

Lovell has arrived at Margaret's court after a long and perilous journey involving time spent in disguise as a blacksmith and a sailor.

('He's mad for the disguisings,' says Kildare.) A few days after Lovell's arrival, a servant sent by the Yorkist Abbot Sant reached Mechelen, carrying gold for Lincoln. Other men are busy in England, collecting more donations from loyalists. The money is flowing now, a tide; it will carry Henry out.

'By Jesus, these tidings overlight my heart,' Kildare says. His eyes are filled with an almost indecent joy.

'It's happening, then,' Edward says. 'Henry can't stop it.'

Does Edward want this? He doesn't know. All he can think about is Joan.

'Oh, yes, my dear lad, the day draws near, marvellous near, and soon we will give Henry a breakfast the like of which he's never tasted.'

The next day Edward is in the stables after a deer hunt, feeding his favourite courser some apple, when Joan comes in and sends the stable boys out. She's visibly hot from the hunt and small strands of her black hair are stuck to her neck.

'I don't know what's wrong with me,' she says, sounding annoyed. Then she kisses him. She presses herself close to his body and keeps her mouth on his and he feels the wroth in the kiss, an exasperation with it – even with him. Still, he doesn't want her to stop. He puts his hands on her slick neck, her slender back, the area of her arse – far distant beneath layers of cloth, but arousing anyway.

She steps back. Her mouth is red and shining.

'Let's see,' she says.

Her fingers have unlaced his hose and hooked his pintle out before he has time to object. (Would he have objected? No, he would not.) The chill air is a shock. Her touch is a shock. She wraps her hand around his penis, which has risen eagerly to meet it.

'Oh, dear,' she says. 'There's the problem.'

'What?'

'It's just too *big*, Edward. Truly I didn't think it would be. You don't seem like the type. But there it is.'

He remembers Jennott and the other women talking in the dairy, saying a large cock was a good thing. Now he finds out his own pintle is large on the same day he finds out it's not a good thing.

'That's bad?'

'God's bones, yes. The smaller the better. Ideally I wouldn't feel it at all.' She looks at it with narrowed eyes, apparently making calculations. 'No. Not possible. Far too streit.'

The news hasn't reached his pintle yet, its hopeful head bobbing blindly about in her hand. She lets it drop, and he wrangles it back into his hose. It takes a while.

'How did you do that so quickly?' he says. 'I thought you'd never...'

She holds up her hand, flutters the fingers. 'Sewing. Stealing. Cheating at cards.'

'Right.'

'I *am* sorry, Edward,' she says, on her way to the door. 'Let's not do this again, agreed? You should probably bide back there awhile. Don't let the stable boys see your frontside. I'll come for Latin later. Farewell.'

The Latin lesson is interrupted by Kildare, waving a letter around his head like he's under attack by wasps.

'From your aunt-in-law,' he says to Edward.

The dowager queen has written to say that if Margaret and her rebel forces march on Henry, she'll support them, and her son Dorset will too, if her daughter and grandson's lives are spared and the new king agrees to give her back all the privileges, titles and lands she once owned and is now owed.

'That whore is sucking two cocks at once,' Kildare says. 'And her son goes back and forth more often than a tennis ball. Now,' he says to Edward, 'it's time for a lesson in politics. What would you do?'

'Maybe she's genuinely sorry this time,' Edward wonders. Joan snorts. 'But then she lists all her lands and so forth at such length. One line on her kin, fifteen on her lands. So... I wouldn't ally with her. If it were my decision.'

'It *is* your decision,' says Joan.

'Now, now. Even if he were king, he's still in his minority,' says Kildare.

'Nobody asked *me*,' Joan says, 'but if they did, I'd be wondering whether the king had her write the letter to entrap you into giving away your invasion plans. Though I consider this unlikely. The dowa-ger queen is dispossessed and without worship; her daughter the queen has no power to restore it to her; Henry and his mother hate her. So I think she sees you as her best chance to get her position back. But she's treacherous. She'd only help you if your victory were certain. And she'd happily kick you into the midden if it suited her. So I say, send her letter back to England, place it in the hands of one of your spies among Henry's spies, and plunge *her* into a huge heap of shit. And panic Henry besides.'

'I've said it before, and I'll say it again,' Kildare says, ''tis pity you're not a man.'

As Joan foretold, King Henry panicked. It wasn't long after Candlemas, and the news of Edward was all over Europe by then, though nobody was sure where he *was*, to the point that the French Embassy asked Henry what he was going to do about the little York heir – look for him under the beds and tables? – and Henry lost his temper. So much as he could lose it: he was not a shouter, a flinger of cups, not even a user of oaths. So said Lincoln, who was there. But his hands went tight and white.

First, Henry took away all Elizabeth Woodville's property and banished her to Bermondsey Abbey, known for dampness and malign vapours, to live on a pension that would barely keep her in gloves. He didn't want word spreading that there was support for a pretender, so his men put it in noise of the nobles that this act was punishment for Elizabeth's earlier back-and-forth between Henry and wicked King Richard, offering her daughter to one then the other. But that was years ago. The nobles weren't buying it. Among themselves, Lincoln said, they speculated that Elizabeth Woodville was eagerly awaiting the arrival of her nephew the Earl of Warwick, the York heir, the flower of England – not the sham one in the Tower but the real one, who would soon come to save them all.

What next?

Henry produced a priest named Sir William Symonds, who confessed to a council of nobles, clergy and officials of London that he had trained the son of an Oxford organ-maker to pretend to be the Earl of Warwick, and had taken him to Ireland, and that Lovell was part of the plot.

But the priest *died*, Edward said. He was planning to betray us, and Lovell's men killed him.

Oh, Henry's men captured one of Lovell's men, Kildare said. They roasted his feet and he told them what he knew. In all this busyness this was inevitable. But no man knows more than his share, that's the beauty of it.

Edward said, Roasted his *feet*?

Yes, and now they've got themselves a sham priest to tell their story. Don't look so stricken. It's no problem to us. You're not in Oxford anymore.

What next?

Henry took his own Edward, Earl of Warwick out of the Tower and paraded him through London, like something between a May King and a dead king, to demonstrate that he had the real earl in his possession. The boy was installed at St Paul's, then Sheen, and nobles were brought to speak to him – most particularly the nobles who might be inclined to join the rebels. Of course Lincoln was one of these. He said the boy, once shrewish, seemed dazed after his spell in captivity, like a dormouse pulled out of a tree. The child was most confused at the idea that he was an imposter: he had only ever known himself as an earl. Lincoln pitied him then.

What next?

The exhibition lasted a couple of days, then Henry's Earl of Warwick was put back in the Tower. And Lincoln – by then waking several times a night thinking he could hear the hooves of the king's horses – made plans to quit England with full haste.

What next?

A nest of Yorkists in the Southern counties was discovered, and arrest writs made out, for the plotting of sedition and rebellion. The leaders of the group, John Beaumont and Henry Bodrugan, got away. A few others were captured but knew nothing of substance, so no harm done.

'What will happen to them?' Edward wants to know.

'What do you think?' says Joan.

'Get our men in England to noise that Henry is lying,' says Kildare, his eyes alive with blue light. 'Accuse him of doubleness, say his earl is a faiter. Put it in the hearing of the people that the true earl escaped from the Tower long ago, and they've put a doddypoll boy in his place.'

'But that's not what...' Edward begins.

'Don't worry, nobody can prove otherwise. I grant you, it's unfortunate that Henry didn't privily kill the official Earl of Warwick when he took the throne. Then he'd have no earl of his own to put up against you. But he's a canny fucker. Got his learnings from Richard's mistakes. Nobody likes a child-killer, that was the lesson there. Anyway. Only the queen, Elizabeth of York, and her family ever met Henry's Earl of Warwick. And nobody trusts them.'

'But why can't we tell the truth?'

'The truth is overlong and overcomplicated. This is a simple story that won't cause undue strain on the plebeian brain. If we have to explain that your father Clarence – never trustworthy, and now dead – sent you away hudder mudder and you've been mired on a farm for years, that confuses matters. Also, what sounds more mob-rousing to you? Evil King Henry keeps a sham earl captive for his fell schemes? Or: well-meaning King Henry believes in good faith that he has the true Earl of Warwick under his protection?'

'The first, but—'

'People don't like Henry,' Kildare says. 'All we need to do is give them something they do like.'

12

Joan starts working on writings of her own: she says she's doing a dream vision written by an executioner.

'You said dream visions were dead,' Edward says. 'You told me not to write one.'

'You did though, didn't you?' she says.

She must have looked through the papers hidden in the pages of his books. He's full red now. He tries to remember what he wrote. Something about a fair maiden with hair ebony black, descending over a marble-smooth back—

He winces.

'I saw you scribbling hudder mudder,' she says. 'And you denied you were writing anything, so I had to check you weren't writing something that might work either of us wrack. But the only harm done was to literature.'

Edward tries not to write any odes after that. But he can't help it: a few slip out. Then he burns them in the fire, thinking pensily about how Ovid treated women with great disworship and yet they longed to be immortalised in the great man's work, while he, Edward, has to hide all evidence of his own in case the tender flower of his longing finds them in one of her routine searches of his room, and makes a mock of him.

In early March King Henry demands the arrest of Bishop Stillington. He's in refuge at Oxford, but Kildare says the university will give him up without overmuch protest. Much as you'd give up a spider in your hair if someone asked you for it, thinks Edward. He mislikes the memory of the old man. He can't say what inquiets him more; the stories he's heard of Stillington's many, many evils, or his thin, thin skin, indented with rings, draped over the fingerbones like a damp veil. What's more frightening: the thought of evil, or the thought of death?

'They won't roast his feet, will they?' Edward asks. Loathly as Stillington is, the idea of his delicate papery body being deliberately damaged is upsetting.

Kildare misunderstands his meaning. 'Content your minds, they won't get any information out of him,' he says. 'The old worm has nothing left to tell. And besides, clergy can't be tortured. This is their usefulness.'

'He knows my history, and that of Henry's Earl of Warwick,' Edward says.

'History is written on wax,' Kildare says. 'Puissance is graven on stone.'

By the time the king's men arrived at his parents' estate, Lincoln was gone. After he departed from the king at Sheen, he went straight to the coast, and from there to Mechelen. He didn't go to his parents first, for fear of putting them in peril.

To Edward he writes, 'I'll see them soon enough, or else in heaven.'

'What will you do after I'm gone?' Edward says to Joan. 'Will you marry some Irish nobleman?'

He's trying to inquiet her, and maybe by doing so, provoke her to kiss him again, but she only laughs.

'Yes, a minor one, I pray. It's dangerous to rise too high. I'd like a sickly man, or an old one.'

'Like Keating?'

She seems to consider it. 'No. Too healthy. Too thin. Grania says overfed men are prone to internal rupturings during a roust. I think their hearts overpace their bodies. I'd ride that husband like a fat horse, apply the spurs, make him go faster and faster, until – bang!' She claps her hands together. Edward flinches.

'Couldn't you just jump out at him from behind a door or something?'

'Better to take him hunting. Like William the Conqueror. You know what happened to him?'

'A riding accident.'

'He *burst*.'

'I'm sure it was an accident on horseback.'

'It was on horseback. His belly was overflowing the saddle. It collided with the pommel and that was it. Bang! Then later, when they tried to fit him in his coffin, he was too big for it and he split open like a late plum. The smell was such that everyone had to flee the church.'

Edward feels he's losing his grip of the conversation.

'We were talking of marriage,' he says.

'*You* were.'

'I was thinking about how King Edward married Elizabeth Woodville privily, and even though everyone was wroth, they had to accept it.'

She looks at him, and for a moment a new expression overtakes her face, unexpected and delightful. Tenderness: the first true sight of it he's had – at least in his own direction. He wants to put his hand out, touch the radiant surface of her skin.

'You bog turtle,' she says, still with that tender look. 'You're only fourteen, and the boy you're replacing is twelve. They'll marry you off to a European princess long before you reach your majority. And if you ever manage to marry privily, do you think they'll let you live after you fucked everything up for them? You'll die, and your cousin Lincoln will sit on the throne.'

'Lincoln would never see me murdered!'

'No. *He* wouldn't. You haven't met Lovell yet, have you? By Saint Thomas, Lovell would kill you and make it look like an accident, and then Margaret and my da and the others would tell Lincoln he has to be king for the good of England, and Lincoln would be sore grieved, and pray over your body with full many tears – but he'd do it. For England. Lincoln is wonderly obedient.'

She takes his hand and puts it on her cheek. Her skin is exactly as soft as he imagined, like a kitten's fur, like Burgundian silk, like a velvety fig warmed in the sun.

'I'd advise you kiss me while you can,' she says.

'And then never again?'

'That's right.'

Every day tidings come to them of the bafflement and wroth of King Henry. At the end of March he went to Suffolk to visit Lincoln's parents, who denied having any witting whatsoever of their son's treachery. Henry had no proof of their doubleness, and their status meant it would be unwise to torture them.

He ordered the arrest of the Marquess of Dorset, Elizabeth Woodville's son, but again he had no proof against him – and, because Dorset was the queen's half-brother, Henry couldn't torture him either.

'I'm glad nobody is being tortured,' Edward says – but quietly, conscious that the Irish lords will mark him as a milksop.

Other English nobles slip off to Mechelen. Whenever Henry darts at one, another quits the country while his back is turned. That's what they crow about, here in Ireland. There is a feeling of things growing, an excitement and a queasiness that can't be separated from each other.

And then the day comes when Kildare says, 'Right, my lord! This summer you'll go to England, and get it back.'

April comes, a mixture of blue and grey and rain and sun. Wood anemones are flowering under the oaks; cuckoos calling. In the distance the oxen are dragging their ploughs across the thawed fields.

Soon Kildare's household will go to Dublin. They'll stay at the Abbey of St Thomas Court, which Kildare has the right of. Edward hasn't seen anything yet in Ireland that Kildare doesn't have the right of.

In Dublin they'll meet Lincoln, and Viscount Lovell, and all the other Yorkist nobles – at least, the ones who are in open support. And Margaret's general, Martin Swartz, and his troops.

Then they'll sail to war.

13

The Abbey of St Thomas Court is outside the Dublin walls, south of the Liffey: a fair, dressed-limestone palace adjoining the abbey itself, with cobbled courtyards and large traceried windows. Kildare's guards stand sentry outside.

Edward is brought inside without large worship, because the Yorkists have noised it among the people that he's to be coming from Mechelen along with Lincoln and Lovell. This is meant to keep him safer, and also so he can make an entrance with full nobley.

'It's all about the pomp, lad,' Kildare says. 'Nobody sees you now without a crown on that fair head of yours – and it'll be "your grace" then, too, if people are fond of their own heads.'

Edward looks out of the window over Dublin. There's a market going on on St James Street; the noise faintly reaches the abbey. Oxford comes into his memory. The last time he – Lambert – walked through the city on market day; nearly carried off his feet by the press, ears filled with sounds harsh and sweet, nose filled with smells savourly and stinking, eyes filled with people, people, nobody knowing who in the sight of God this boy was, just a silly lad holding his pastry and gazing at the tavern girls, this Lambert, this nobody.

The next time he sees people he'll be wearing a crown.

Why are all his memories arriving like this lately? Why can't they bring pleasure? Instead they're like the barbed snakes of Tondal; they hurt him as they pass through his body.

He wishes he'd asked to walk through Dublin, just once, as a nobody.

He wishes—

But what's this?

Noise, commotion, horses' hooves, shouts—

Lincoln is here!

Lincoln rides through the gate at pace. The sun blazes behind him; his horse prances and snorts. Edward, joyed out of measure, rushes outside, past the Fitzgeralds and their men, to welcome his cousin.

Is Lincoln thinner? He looks tired. But he cries out with gladness when he sees Edward, and embraces him.

'My lord and beloved cousin,' he says. 'By Saint Francis! You're three feet taller! And your shoulders are growing beyond all reason.'

'Oh! No. They're really nothing of significance,' Edward says, waxing shy.

'Nay, nay, I'm astonied you fit through the gates,' Lincoln says, squeezing the shoulders, then embracing him again.

'He's always had those shoulders,' says another man, behind Lincoln. 'But he's fitting them better than when I first saw him.'

'Heaven forgive me,' Lincoln says. 'In my joy I forgot to make introductions.'

'We've already met,' says the other man.

Who is the same man who came to the farm with Maister Richard, to take Edward away.

Who said, *Who am I? None of your concern.*

Lovell, thinks Edward.

Wearing a significantly better hat.

'My lord, this is Viscount Lovell,' says Lincoln. 'We've known each other for years, since he was under my parents' wardship as a boy. One of the finest knights any king could hope to have in his service.'

Lovell steps forward now, smiling, and bows. 'I didn't name myself before. Forgive me, my lord. It was expedience.'

'You've met?' Lincoln says, looking surprised.

'Not long after the death of King Edward,' Lovell says. 'Bishop Stillington told me that the true heir of Clarence was living on a farm. I thought the old villain had lost his grip of his wits at last. But it was true. Later I went to essay the boy myself, and here – ' he indicates Edward ' – is his father's son.'

'When Richard was on the throne...' Lincoln says. 'You didn't tell him?'

'Things had started going badly for Richard at that time. I thought it prudent to have… options.'

Lincoln is frowning. 'I didn't know that,' he says.

Kildare and his brother, who have stayed silent until now, look at each other. As usual, nobody meets eyes with Edward

Edward wonders what would have happened if things hadn't gone so badly that Richard ended up dead and stabbed in twenty places and slung naked over a horse. If he, Edward, had no longer been considered a useful option.

'Nobody knew it,' Lovell says.

'I know you mean naught but the best good,' Lincoln says to Lovell, 'but sometimes you are so close and secret that you almost seem – well. You needn't be so over-privy. I suppose it is your history of hiding and disguise.'

'I try to live by the saying of your aunt, the Lady Margaret,' Lovell says. '*Everyone knows what is meet for them to know.*'

'Amen to that,' Lincoln says. 'It is very wise. If any of our number fall into the wrong hands, God forbid, the men who know the least are the luckiest. Well, in some ways not, because their ignorance might not be believed and they'll probably be tortured for longer. But they will not face the shame of having betrayed their fellows. Truly, a noble end.'

He clasps his hands, looking as beatific as St Francis himself.

There's a great banquet that night, with Kildare and his brother, Lovell, Lincoln, Brother Keating, Lord Portlester, the Bishop of Meath, Plunket, General Martin Swartz, and several English Yorkists.

Edward is overloaded with noblemen. To his great good fortune, none of them asks much of him. *The very sib of his father!* they all say. That's all they have to say to him. They're all older men, they all know each other, their conversation is about things that happened years ago, before he was even born. They talk about the splendour of the Yorks: the revelries of King Edward, the gold and the tapestries; the tournaments; the humiliation of the French; the tall and fair king, resplendent in his youth, a velvet-covered six-footer, a serial tumbler of women from the finest demosels to the bawdiest wenches; the undeniable beauty of the despitous Elizabeth Woodville;

the endless battling between the three Plantagenet brothers, Edward, Richard, George – all dead now.

Edward's struck by that. How few of them, the Yorks, there are left. Outside the bounds of the talk, he sees its melancholy – though they are all drinking and japing – the longing for something lateward, a craning back into the past.

He feels something land on him. He doesn't want it, but it's too late now. The burden of being one of them, the one they've chosen as their last hope.

Lovell, too, sits apart from the rememberings. He doesn't talk about the past. No tears stand in his eyes. And yet there's no sense of his being a man of the corner, alone and disregarded. It's hard for Edward to work out, watching Lovell and Kildare, who has the most puissance. When either of them speaks, everyone listening turns to them immediately. When they both speak at once the group falls into disarray, not knowing who to align with.

Edward doesn't turn to Lovell. He doesn't enjoy the feeling of watching Lovell; having Lovell's eyes turn to him in response. Even Lovell's friendly smile of acknowledgement is a weight Edward doesn't know how to bear: a strange kind of cross, that he senses he mustn't stumble under.

Hard to believe that an army has arrived. Two thousand Swabian and Swiss *landsknechts* with pikes, two-handed swords and crossbows. Five thousand Gaelics; some of them gallowglasses with axes, but mostly kern with long knives and javelins. If it weren't for the reports Kildare and his brother receive daily, of the turbulent conditions in the temporary barracks, of street commotions and tavern fights, the chasing and swiving of local women, the occasional fatal fray with local men, Edward wouldn't credit the troops' existence.

Whatever happens, happens beyond the castle walls. And is nothing to worry about. Kildare says that the Dubliners are, on the whole, delighted to play host to the troops. Upend a harlot or an inn-keeper and they'd rain coins.

Edward wonders what these men think of him, the Earl of Warwick. If they aren't real to him, what is he to them? He must mean *something*, or else why are seven thousand men gathered for the sole purpose of making sure he, Edward, sits on a throne in England? They're ready to die for it. For a boy they don't know to live in a palace they'll never see.

'They're getting paid,' says Joan. 'They're all mercenaries. Didn't you know?'

Margaret has written him a letter. She and Philip are praying for him, and wish him the most glorious triumph in the coming war. She has sent him an illuminated psalter, containing many a good wisdom on which to focus his contemplation. She looks forward to meeting him again in England, in the palaces she frequented as a girl and remembers fondly. She has drawn up a bond for the money she spent on the ships to take his army from Belgium to Ireland to England, to be repaid when England is conquered.

Philip adds a note:

Most beloved friend (I hope you haven't forgotten me, and still remember our vow of friendship unto evermo!),

I trust you are in great happiness, with your coming triumph large in your heart!

There has been evil news here. Such as I weep to tell.

There are to be no automated giraffes at the new palace, for money reasons.

I know you will make great dole at this but do not! Remember, I am to be an emperor. And when I am, I'll build a great herd of mechanical giraffes, to the wonderment of every soul in Europe. I will send you one as a gift – and when it gallops through your halls, you will laugh and say, There! My dearest brother-king, Philip, is sending proof of his continued great love.

Anyway. I think of your visit here wonderly much. The day of throwing nut shells at people was one of the best of my life. I pray God we'll meet again soon, before we are too old and kinglike, for another nutshell-throwing.

Edward sees Lincoln sitting alone in a cloister, turning something over in his hands. He looks melancholy. Edward wonders if what Joan said is true: that Lincoln is broken in his courage. Whatever the cause of his doleful moods, he seems to attract women like September wasps. There are other goodly-looking, elegant men around the court, but none of them get followed about as much as Lincoln, who – preoccupied as he is – doesn't appear to notice. Even Lady Kildare has been seen bringing him poetry she thinks might inspire him to greater heights of spiritual contemplation.

It's wonderly annoying, Kildare observed. I stubbed my little toe this morning. I was sore doleful. Did any women offer to so much as play with my ballocks? No, they did not.

Edward isn't sure whether to walk over, but Lincoln looks up, sees him and smiles.

'I was thinking about my family,' he says. 'I hope to be there when you meet them.'

'Your wife?'

'Oh, no. My wife and I… it's not that we mislike each other. We don't know each other.'

'You didn't know her when you married her?'

Lincoln laughs. 'That's a privilege only the peasantry enjoy. I was married when Elizabeth Woodville was queen. She conquered by marriage. Her kin are seeded in all the highest houses of England. I ended up with a Woodville niece. It could have been worse. My wife's not a vicious woman. Her head's as empty as an eggshell, but she's pleasant enough.'

'It's your parents you're thinking of, then?'

'Yes. I know they'll be safe. They're wise. Though they've been suffering a little for my escape. Henry took my father with him on his Easter progress to Norwich, to keep him under watch. Henry's been washing poor men's feet and visiting shrines like Saint Edward himself. I imagine my father's full sick of it. He's got a twenty-year feud going with our neighbours, he'll be irous at having to abandon it for beggar-bathing.'

'Can you write to them?'

'No. Too dangerous for them. But their hearts abide with our cause.' He shows Edward his livery brooch, a delicate rose in white enamel, set in gold. 'My mother gave me this. It reminds me to make her proud of me. I thank God I am being given another chance at it.'

'I have something,' Edward says. He takes out the small purse of Will Collan's, striking now in its crude plainness. He shows Lincoln the fairy arrowhead and the ship his brother made.

'I don't know if I'm supposed to want them to be proud of me,' he says. 'I know they weren't my real kin.'

Lincoln presses Edward's hands.

'Were they good people?' he says.

Edward hesitates. He used to be wroth at Will Collan for lying to him. Now he sees his dad-that-was didn't have much choice. Some nobles, emissaries from the fairy kingdom, came to his farm and told him what to do. He was a peasant. How could he say no?

He nods.

'Well then,' says Lincoln. 'Why do we do anything, if not for good people? And God knows there are few enough of them where we're going.'

Edward manages to get away from the nostalgic nobles for long enough to play bowls with the Kildare girls in the gardens. Eustacia seizes his sleeve and tells him tearfully that she's written him a poem, but she forgot it.

'Praise God,' says Eilis.

'You look like a king already,' Eleanor tells him. She makes a strange face. Her nose goes red. Then she laughs.

'We had a bet that Eleanor couldn't say that with a right solemn countenance,' Joan says. 'And now she has to give me her green dress.'

'I *do* think you'll look like one soon,' Eleanor says.

'By Saint Leonard!' Joan says. 'Nobody looks like a king. Then they sit on the throne, and everyone says they are the most kingly king they've ever seen.'

'That's treason, isn't it?' Eleanor says to Edward. 'Maybe when you're king you could behead her?'

'It'll be the first thing I do,' he says. And Eleanor rolls her eyes, and Joan smiles mockingly, and Edward waxes red – because they all know he loves Joan: it's so glaringly, painfully known.

14

Lateward Edward hasn't seen so much of Joan. She doesn't suggest they read or write together. She doesn't come to him, and she's harder to find. She walks a lot with Grania.

In an unwise moment, Edward decides to copy his cousin Lincoln's air of distracted dole. When he's next with the Fitzgerald girls he sighs, and stares off at the horizon.

'Are you well?' Eleanor asks.

'He looks as if he has a cold,' says Eilis, moving away from him.

'He's aping Lincoln,' Joan says.

'Oh, yes!' cries Eleanor, and they all start laughing.

'It's a passing good Lincoln.'

'Like Lincoln with a cold.'

'Do someone else!'

Edward says, irous, 'I'm not doing impressions.'

But they ignore him, and shout, 'Do Lovell!'

'Lovell's already doing Lovell,' Joan says. 'And very masterfully.'

Why are you avoiding me? he wants to ask Joan. But he can't, he doesn't have the right of her. Still, the question doesn't go away. His heart drums it out: *Why? Why? Why?* He sits, now, in the sunny window with a book, open on the story of the Earl of Toulouse; hoping she might appear in the doorway, like she used to, and say: *What's this shit?*

Instead it's Lincoln who comes in, bowing politely and asking what it is Edward's poring over.

Edward shows him the page. The Earl of Toulouse has gone to war against Sir Dioclysian. The two sides clashing together; knights riding with shields and lances, men hacking with swords and axes as if crazed, great strokes smitten, rashing, lashing, spears and shields broken into splinters, chain-mail shredded, brain-pans split in two through their helmets, horses punctured, barons bubbling in their own blood. A lake of blood, soaking the field. And elsewhere, the wives who used to sleep full tranquil now sit and weep instead.

Lincoln takes a step back from the book, as if it's a biting animal.

'Oh,' he says, in a pinched voice, not exactly his own. 'Yes. I have read it, I believe, long ago. Strong reading matter. And no doubt relevant. Yes. For the coming battle.'

'Is it… like that?' Edward asks.

'Yes,' says Lincoln.

There's a long silence.

'Are you alright?' Edward asks. 'What is it?'

Lincoln doesn't say anything for another long while.

'I'm frightened that I'm not—' He hesitates. 'Not fit for battle. I suffered an attack of something, in my body, at Bosworth. I fell down insensible before I could strike one blow. Everyone thought I was dead until after it was over. I know they scorn me for it. But now I think: was it God acting that day? That God saw I was fighting for a sinful man, and he struck me down. And now that I'm fighting for a holy, noble king, God will be with us. And my honour, at last, will be restored.'

Edward's been trying not to pursue, question or harass Joan. But when he sees her and Grania in the courtyard, speaking with Lovell, his curiosity drives him over.

'We were just talking about you, my lord,' Lovell says, as if in answer to his privy thoughts. 'Did the wind carry it to you?'

'What was the talk?' Edward says.

'The Lady Joan was asking me what happened the day I met you, on that manure-beclagged farm in Oxfordshire. I told them how the nobility shone out from your form, even in peasant clothing, like God's own holy light.'

Edward has the distinct sense that he's being mocked.

'Like a changeling story,' says Grania. 'But in reverse, I suppose. As changelings are dark and wicked things, and Edward a fair prince.'

'You find them out in the same way,' Lovell says, smiling. 'By holding them over the fire.'

Joan laughs. Edward can tell it's not a true laugh. When he looks at her, he sees with alarm that she has a look he recognises. She had it with Maurice, Maister James, Sir William St Lawrence, Plunket. He doesn't know what she's about to do, and so he can't stop it.

'What will you do with Henry's Earl of Warwick?' she asks Lovell. 'The one in the Tower. He won't end up like the two princes, will he?'

'Oh, no, my lady,' Lovell says. He doesn't seem inquieted by the question. 'I'm sure he'll be fairly pensioned off with some manor or other. We are not in the business of killing young boys.'

'Not for the last couple of years, at least,' Joan says, smiling.

Lovell looks at her with waxing interest. Edward wishes he wouldn't. Grania, too, looks uneasy. There's a feeling of mounting peril in the air, close and greasy.

'You must have been sore grieved to find out that it was Richard, your dear friend, who commanded the princes' deaths,' Joan says. 'God rest their souls. But who exactly killed them? Did Richard oversee it himself? Or was it Buckingham? Or some other man?'

'I don't know how it happened,' Lovell says, shrugging. 'I only heard they were dead months later.'

'That must be hard,' says Joan. 'So unknowingly near to the crime, and now you must carry it heavy in your heart ever after.'

'I bear it as I can,' Lovell says, with a bow.

'And God bless you,' says Joan, closing her eyes and pressing her hand to her own breast.

Grania sends Edward a look of *?* with an undercurrent of, *that could have gone worse.*

Edward tries to reply with his own look, that says, *I also have no idea,* and, *yes, relief here too.*

The Coronation approaches, differently from before, like it's playing a game. Edward turns his back and it rushes forward. Then when he turns around again, it's nearly on him. He wants to be king, to save

England, to set everything right for his family, Lincoln and Margaret. He doesn't want to leave Joan. He doesn't want to die.

He weighs his wants like someone with the power to act on them, he thinks, sourly. When all he can do is lie in bed at night, forwallowing in powerlessness and frustration, thinking that he might well split open if he can't do *something*.

So he goes to Joan, and says, 'Why are you avoiding me?'

Joan sighs. She doesn't sham confusion at the question.

'Because it's hopeless,' she says. 'It's over. You know that. I could meet you at night and give you a handjob but that's all it will ever be, and it will only increase your dole.'

'I don't want a handjob,' he says (somewhat less than emphatic). 'I want you. I love you.'

'See,' she says. 'This is the problem.'

'Do you love—'

'Yes,' she snaps. 'I love you. I wish to God I didn't. Oh, no. Don't look at me like that!'

'Like what?'

'Like you're *glad*.'

But he is. He's gladder than he's ever been in his life.

Joan says they can spend more time together, but he isn't allowed to talk to her about love. Instead, she gives him the Caxton book of *Reynard the Fox*. She was supposed to teach him survival, but he never wanted to learn, and now he's going to be on his own without her and she's worried about him. So, Reynard is going to be his nursery education.

Edward hates Reynard. He thought Reynard would be like Robin Hood, but Reynard is not good, or kind. He's not even cunning: the other animals who fall prey to his sleights are just really, really stupid. And perhaps this is a fault in Edward's character, but he doesn't find any mirth in Reynard's rape of the wolf's wife, or the moment when Reynard tricks the king into giving him the skin torn off her paws.

'But don't you see?' Joan says. 'The wolf shouldn't have been so gullible.'

'I'm not sure that's the moral,' Edward says.

259

'*Moral*? Moral! This isn't Aesop!' She drums her hands on the book in frustration. 'By Saint Dorothy! You know what has a useful moral? Lydgate's *Churl and Bird*. The gentil bird outwits the peasant and he lets her out of her cage. The moral is that it's impossible to teach a peasant anything. *A churlish churl is always woebegone*.'

'Christ, Joan,' Grania says. 'You're being a marvellous shrew.'

'I don't care. This is important. This is what happens in real life, if you don't protect yourself. The she-wolf should have tricked Reynard, and killed him the first chance she got.'

'So she's supposed to be as wicked as he is?' Edward says.

'Cock's bones, you're slow. *More* wicked.' She takes his hands, urgently. 'I'm not japing with you, Edward. You need to wake up. You need to get yourself a courtly countenance. Courtly claws, courtly teeth.'

'That is true,' Grania says. 'You've got an excessively soft face. Like a new cheese.'

'Fine,' he says. 'I'll be… less soft.'

'Good,' Joan says. She gets up. 'Now I'm going to show you how to counterfeit handwriting. All you need is something written by the person, and some dried pig intestine, very thin and clear. After that I'll show you how to press seals and keys.'

'You can forge letters? Seals? Why didn't you tell me?' he asks. But he knows why. 'You didn't trust me.'

'I don't trust anyone,' Joan says. 'Except Grania.'

He's annoyed. He says, 'You know, in *real life*, birds die in their cages. Gentil or not.'

She gives him an unexpected smile.

'That's the spirit,' she says.

'Wonderfully unsoft,' Grania agrees.

One small relief, in a swarm of fears, is that Joan hasn't played any tricks on Lovell. Not that she leaves off mockery completely. One evening in the gardens the talk travels to Lovell's many disguisings, one of which got him past ten of Henry's men.

'He fools nobles and gentilhommes,' Joan says. 'But did he fool anyone when he came to your old village, Edward?'

He looks at her, inquiet. He's already told her that Lovell didn't fool anyone from his village. He mislikes that she's asking again now.

'No,' he says, reluctantly. 'The noise for days was of the nobleman in costume.'

Lovell, unexpectedly, laughs.

'I don't need wiles around low people,' he says. '*They* have no reason to behead me.'

'I fondly remember your English peasant Johanna Ferrour,' says Joan. 'She had the Archbishop of Canterbury beheaded, back in the riots.'

'Oh, now, I wouldn't disguise myself as a bishop and go out into a crowd,' Lovell says. 'Just as I wouldn't wear a brush tail and shake my hindparts at the hounds.'

And Joan, to Edward's relief, laughs.

Is Edward more relieved for her, or for Lovell? He can't say. But she lets Lovell go unmolested through the rest of their game of *jeu de mail* – though she can't resist scorning Plunket's French pronunciation, which makes *Lovell* laugh, while Plunket grinds his mallet so hard into the grass that it makes a pit, which everyone keeps tripping over.

Edward's council assembles: Kildare, his brother Sir Thomas Fitzgerald, Lincoln, Lovell, the Archbishop of Dublin, Plunket, Portlester. The council tells Edward what to do at the Coronation. The main thing he needs to remember is that he escaped from the Tower and Henry put a poor imitation earl in his place.

'Unfortunately your father was executed without letting anyone besides the dotard Stillington know his doings,' Lovell says. 'Which has made the truth of your existence seem somewhat… unbelievable.'

'But isn't lying a sin?' Edward asks. He looks at Lincoln, who holds his own eyes low, as if inquiet.

'Not when it's a lie to convince people of the truth,' the archbishop says. 'Or a lie for a larger good. In your case, both are true.'

'Would you say that the word "lie" is inappropriate in this case, Archbishop?' says Lovell. 'Possibly – as it is God's plan for Edward to sit the throne – blasphemous?'

'Oh, verily, verily,' says the archbishop. 'This is holy work we do.'

'There we have it,' Kildare says. 'The word "lie" must not be uttered. It's an insult to God.'

'I have another question,' Edward says. 'If I may.'

'You are our king,' Lincoln says. 'To answer your questions is our duty and joy.'

'Indeed,' says Lovell.

'How do we know exactly that God wants me to sit the throne?' Edward asks. He turns to the archbishop. 'Did he, uh, say something? Or was there a sign? Because… Henry is on the throne now, saying God is on *his* side. And Henry is *on* the throne. God hasn't struck him off it.'

'Every king is God's chosen king,' says Lovell. 'Until they aren't.'

'The Lord Lovell doesn't mean to sound so heretical,' the archbishop says. 'What he is saying is that *you* are the means by which Henry will be struck down. This is how God works. Through us. And in your triumph the people will be moved to greater reverence, seeing a usurper cast into hell and the truest, noblest men raised high.'

'Yes,' says Lovell. 'That's what I meant.'

Joan says, 'Here's a strategy lesson: be ware of Lovell. He's not evil, exactly. He's *practical*. That could be worse.'

Wooden-headed though Edward may be, he doesn't need Joan to tell him to be ware of Lovell. His *body* is ware of Lovell. It tenses up when he comes into the room. It knows that Lovell was both King Richard's trusted Lord Chamberlain and also paying for John Collan's education. That he was preparing for battle at Bosworth and planning his own escape from the field.

What are Lovell's two useful options now? Edward and Lincoln?

'I'm not completely naive,' Edward says. 'I know what he is. I'm ware.'

'That's not enough,' she says.

'Advise me then,' he says. 'You're so clever; you can get to the top of any situation. Tell me what to do.'

She sighs, and says, 'Clever people know when they can't win.'

Edward thinks about changelings. It seems to him that the farm, the world he left, was the realm of the humans. *This* is the kingdom of

262

the fairies. Where there is gold and silver and finery and dancing, but marvellous danger, and you're not allowed to leave.

More troops arrive each day to join them, sent by Kinsale, Drogheda, Trim. A fleet of ships is anchored off Merchant's Quay, ready to take them to England.

Edward remembers the lines of Sappho:

Some say an army of horsemen, or footsoldiers, or a fleet of ships is the fairest thing upon the black earth. I say it is what one loves.

Maister Richard said Sappho was second-rate, because his brain was too small and villainous to know beauty when he heard it. But Edward knows beauty.

He goes to Joan, and says, 'I know I'm not allowed to talk to you about love, but I want to say that I know that's why you're teaching me survival, and I want to offer you something, for the same reason.'

'For God's sake,' Joan says.

But she lets him recite the lines, and she smiles.

Almost every day there are feasts and celebrations, and men arriving to feast and celebrate. It's like Edward's already won the war. Sometimes, after a few cups of wine, he can nearly believe it.

The noblemen talk about two things: war matters and bawdy matters. They can switch between the two with a speed that astonies him. One minute Kildare has thrown a drinking cup across the room because he's sore wroth at the tidings from Waterford: whose fucking mayor, John Butler, says the Great Earl has been deceived by an organ-maker's son. The next minute, he's telling a *fabliau* about a peasant couple who are given three wishes, and first the wife wishes the husband covered in pintles, then the husband wishes the wife covered in cunts, then they have to wish themselves back to normal and all their wishes are used up.

One of the English nobles joins in, with a story about a peasant's wife who tricks her doltish husband into chewing a piece of shit.

'Classic peasants,' says another Englishman.

'Classic women,' says Plunket.

'Hold now,' Kildare says. 'We've no maugre against women here. I don't know what the English wenches are like but our Irish ladies are goddesses on earth. Wit you all well my ancestor Gerald the Poet's words: *Speak not ill of womankind. 'Tis no wisdom if you do*. He was a great lover, and greatly loved.'

Edward finds Joan and asks, 'If writers are just wretches who don't have what they most want, what about your ancestor Gerald the Poet, who wrote so nobly of their goodness?'

Joan says, 'He wrote that poem in prison. If he'd had some women around he'd have been quickly reminded how annoying they are.'

Edward says, 'By Saint Mary, do you have to make everything so dark?'

'All writers are wounded,' Joan says. 'They write to make their pain bearable.'

'I don't know why I debate with you,' Edward says, and she laughs.

A strange girl, he thinks. Not for the first time. A strange kind of love.

But he wouldn't be without it.

John Butler the Mayor of Waterford continues to be a nuisance and a shrew, refusing to give support, calling them *rude enemies, traitors and rebels*. A tempest blew up in Kildare then, and he had that messenger hung in Hoggin Green. Then he sent a herald to the mayor to say he'd get the same ending if he didn't serve their true King Edward VI right anon, and the mayor said to go ahead and try it, they'd be answered with the sword of true loyalty to the true King Henry VII.

Other nuisances: the Archbishop of Armagh, the Bishop of Clogher, the Archbishops of Tuam and Cashel and the Bishop of Ossory.

Kildare swears that he'll have them all hanged for treason.

Lincoln is alarmed at the idea:

'They're just men, my dear lord, they have no true witting of their crimes, they haven't seen the Lord Edward, his fair demeaning, his God-given nobility, but they will, and anon they'll repent, and we'll embrace them, and be restored to loving accord.'

'And another consideration,' says Lovell, when Lincoln has gone, 'is that hanging the villains now makes us look overhasty, and weak. Better to wait. Take their heads later, at your leisure.'

Kildare's younger brother Sir Thomas Fitzgerald joins Lincoln and Edward in the courtyard for some sword fighting. He's not yet thirty and is a merry fellow indeed, as Joan says, though sadly underfurnished, brain-wise. His sword hand is better educated. He knocks Edward down immediately, then again, until Edward has to retreat with a ringing ear, and watch Thomas and Lincoln fight. Lincoln moves like a darting swift, never erring. Thomas has to yield.

'By Jesus, I've never seen a better swordsman,' says Thomas. 'If I wasn't so pressed, I'd admire the spectacle like a cock fight. But it's not so fun, being the losing cock. Heh. We should get some cocks to watch *me*. That would be a jape.'

'I thought I was improving,' Edward says dolefully.

'You're very good for a boy, and a lateward starter,' says Lincoln.

'But the battle will be full of men who started early.'

Thomas laughs.

'He thinks he's on the front line,' he says.

'Oh, no, cousin,' Lincoln says. 'Did nobody explain? You won't be part of the battle. You'll stand back and bide the result. We'll make sure no wrack comes to you.'

'Why won't I be part of it? I'm fourteen now.'

'Kings don't often go to battle. Henry didn't even know when he'd won Bosworth – he was squinting at it from the next county over, and then he had to send a boy to enquire.'

'We'll cut the Englishmen into tiny pieces on your behalf,' Thomas says. 'Their loved ones will be all day putting them back together.'

'Have you been in a battle?' Edward asks him.

'Of course,' Thomas says. 'Sure there's always a battle on around here. Lots of kings. Lots of mortal enemies. Every fucker wants every other fucker's castle.'

'You've killed men?'

'Oh, marvellous many. It's not like hunting wild boars or bears. That can be perilous. Men die so easily it's near harder *not* to kill them. Your cousin Lord Lincoln here being an exception. There aren't many as good as him.'

Lincoln bows, but looks distroubled.

'What does it feel like to kill someone?' Edward asks Thomas.

'Oh, the first time is strange. I remember I was sore adread. But when it's done and you step back and some cunt is dead, and not you – ah, by Saint Sebastian, you feel wonderly alive! And after that it's no trouble at all.'

'Maybe Henry and I could fight in single combat, like Alexander and Porus,' Edward says. 'And nobody else would have to die.'

At which Thomas and Lincoln laugh until tears stand in their eyes.

Edward carries on with extra sword training, this time under the German general Martin Swartz. The son of a cobbler, apparently. Edward could say to Martin: Hey, I am also of peasant beginnings. How does it feel to you, being here, eating at table with the nobility, having risen so far?

But Martin is so tall and has a long scar on his forehead and a face like a portcullis. It isn't a face that says: *Ask me about my feelings.*

Edward certainly can't ask: Martin, if you found out you were an earl, do you think you might struggle to… *feel* like an earl?

Might think, unwillingly, about Joan's speculations.

Earl, peasant, bastard.

Might wonder what animal Gower would choose for him: peasant or noble, or – worse – an *unknown*, an uncertainty that is the most disgusting, abominable state of all.

15

Ascension Day comes, the 24th of May: the day on which Edward, Earl of Warwick will be transformed into Edward VI.

This is what they tell him.

At Christ Church Cathedral, Edward waits to feel transmuted. To perceive his earthly corpus being turned into something finer and brighter. He isn't sure in which moment it's meant to happen. He wishes he'd been able to find a book of learnings on the matter.

It doesn't happen during the Mass, or the singing of hymns, the blessings, the homily preached by the Bishop of Meath, as Edward stands before the congregation composed of the curious faces of nobles and bishops, adread that the weight of gold decorations on his body will topple him.

It doesn't come about during the speaking of the Royal Oath. Holy oil is smeared on him by the archbishop: nothing. He is handed spurs and a sword, then two sceptres, which he clutches awkwardly, trying not to clank them.

The crown is approaching: an open gold circlet taken off the head of the statue of the Blessed Virgin. *How meet*, he thinks, as it approaches him. (Another unworthy thought. No wonder he's not transforming. He tries to empty his brain-pan of trivia and sin as the crown descends.)

It sits lightly on him, fitting perfectly.

And then he is led to his throne—

—unchanged, nothing but the same boy as before – please God, why? – a trembling grip on the sceptres, a bilious sweat under his furs; so sore afraid, at the thought that everyone sees him; everyone can tell.

Nobody can tell. Kildare looks twice his usual size with triumph. Lincoln has a tear in his eye. Lovell nods with evident satisfaction. None of the applauding nobles seem to have any witting that something isn't right.

Edward's brought out into the street lined with crowds, into a great noise of stamping and whooping and screams of his name, and cries from the back of:

Show him!

Where is he?

Show the king!

A giant is found, or as close to one as Edward's ever seen, a nobleman named William D'Arcy, near to seven feet high. Edward VI is set on his shoulders. And through the streets they go, toward Dublin Castle, followed by the nobles and soldiers. On St James' Street D'Arcy stumbles in a hole in the cobbles, and Edward wonders if he'll be flung onto the ground – a shove from God, his fine cloak up over his head, arse-to-sky, his crown rolling under the horses' hooves. But he stays safely aloft. On Thomas Street the merchants roar. On Winetavern Street the girls throw flowers.

None of them can tell either.

Joan, he thinks.

Joan would know, but she isn't in view.

King Edward VI's first parliament is held in Dublin. He spends it playing bowls with the Fitzgerald girls – because he's a minor, and so it's Kildare who does the holding. Edward had wondered if he ought to watch, but Kildare didn't think it would be meet. Parliaments could be a rough business, he said, with riots and affray not unknown, and he didn't want to risk any wrack coming to the new king's (bruisable, pierceable, snappable) body at this turbulent stage of his kingship.

'Why turbulent?' Edward asked.

Kildare was evasive about that. Though afterwards he's forthcoming, and full of crowings. He'd attainted two inconvenient Butler enemies, William and Thomas, ordered their manses demolished and their lands and possessions seized, in the name of the king. He'd also declared the franchises and possessions of the City of Waterford forfeit. The stubborn wind-eggs of Waterford had refused to accept this, and Kildare looks forward to attacking the city and *making* them accept it, with his fist down their throats.

'God save the king!' he adds.

Word comes that when King Henry heard about the Coronation, he offered an unconditional pardon to any nobles who may have been initially misled into supporting the false and heinous pretender-king, but now – having realised their grievous mistake – hoped to return to their allegiance to their true king, Henry.

'He's frightened,' says Lovell, smiling. 'And now everyone can see his fright.'

Edward finds Joan and Grania, walking along the cloisters. Nobody else is in sight. Grania looks at him and withdraws behind a pillar.

'You look red, your grace,' Joan says. 'Are your humours disordered?'

'Only my heart,' he says. The words don't strike her with the force he'd hoped for.

'Oh,' she says mockingly. 'That. Well, you won't need it where you're going. It will sink you like a lead weight.'

'I don't want to go,' he says.

His sadness feels desperate, constricting. He catches her hand, uncurls it. Her palm is damp and hot. She lets him hold it, without pressing his hand in return.

'You used to kiss me,' he says. 'I wish you hadn't stopped. The memory of it pains me now.'

She looks struck. A whitening, surprise – and then: anger.

'You've answered yourself,' she says. 'A kiss lasts a second and then it's another memory. Why would we create more, just to hurt ourselves with later?'

There are tears standing in her eyes.

He's never seen her cry – and she clearly doesn't want him to, because she takes her hand back, forcefully, and walks away.

A herald named John Wrythe is sent to Ireland by Henry VII, to question Edward and prove him to be a sham.

'Do we let him interrogate the boy?' Lovell asks. 'His farm years might show under pressure.'

'Nay, the lad's a human library,' says Kildare. 'He's eaten up every learning he's been given like a chicken after grasshoppers. Let Wrythe have at him. It'll be great disworship to Henry when his man comes back to him with nothing.'

Which was so, and Wrythe was passing wroth when Edward knew his family bloodlines, and Latin, and French, and Greek, and what a silver ship was for on a table (not that he was asked). But then Henry noised that Edward was only able to answer correctly because he'd been schooled by the traitors.

So that was a waste of time. Kildare didn't give a shit, he said. It was the war that mattered, the fight. The fingering is over, he said, and now it's time to fuck. He seems to wax in brightness with every day, like a red moon, glowing with energy, embracing every-one, shouting, making toasts. Meanwhile Lincoln seems to recede; quieter, given to reading his psalter.

Lovell is the same as always. He says little, he watches much, he smiles every now and again – though what he means by his smiles, Edward never knows.

Edward's playing cards with Eleanor after dinner, the torch light flaring as he picks up the knave of hearts, enlivening the little man's red hose and evil expression. It feels like a bad omen, even before he looks up and sees Plunket and Kildare standing over them.

Kildare has on a countenance of baffled amusement. Plunket looks purposeful.

'You *can't* mean Joan,' Kildare is saying. 'Your grace; daughter dear: Plunket here is claiming he saw some misdoings in the cloister. He said by Joan and Edward, but that's a nonsense: Joan would make a pottage of the lad. He must have meant Eleanor. Now, Eleanor, you fell strumpet, what have you been up to? This boy king isn't for you.'

'By Saint Mary, I've done nothing!' Eleanor says, waxing dark red and dropping her cards.

'My lord, it was Joan I saw, holding his hand full tenderly,' Plunket says.

'Joan?' says Kildare. 'Tender? No.'

'I say yes,' Plunket insists.

Edward can't speak. He stares at Plunket in fear and hatred, like a cornered rat. The words to save himself and Joan will not come. They all look at him.

'What is this?' Kildare says. 'What say you, lad? Did Plunket mis-see? Or have you been enjoying too much of our Irish hospitality? Has anything more than a hand been held? Hey? Has my daughter Joan been hoisting her skirts for you?'

His laugh is exposing more teeth than usual.

'Of course he hasn't,' Eleanor says. 'Joan and Edward would never!'

'Is that aright?' Kildare says. 'I have never known you to tell a lie, Eleanor. You'd vouch for your sister's demeaning? Even though, God knows, she'd hang *you* from the nearest oak tree, if it got her an extra portion of pudding.'

'I'm with them all the time,' Eleanor says. 'I've seen no love of any kind between them. In truth, Joan talks of Edward as something like a chick, or a baby mouse. She's pleasant to him because he's the king. Sorry, your grace.'

'Well, that does make sense,' Kildare says. 'Unlike your ravings, Plunket.'

'But I saw—'

'Hand-holding? By Saint Verena! Hand-holding isn't worth a turd. You've done yourself a dishworship today, Plunket. Go to bed, and make a better show of yourself in the morning.'

Plunket, his face empurpled with wroth, waits until Kildare's gone before he takes his own leave. Saying to Edward as he does, 'Watch you don't end up like Abelard, when he loved the harlot Heloise. Except you won't lose your pintle to her kinsmen's knives, but to your leman's teeth.'

They're alone again. Eleanor picks her cards up off the floor. Then she looks at Edward pityingly.

'So you're in love with her still,' she says.

'No,' he says.

Her expression of pity deepens.

'You know she's betrothed,' Eleanor says. 'To an O'Carroll.'

Her words enter his body like a cold wind, cooling his heart and brain and stomach, slowing them, so he can only say: '... *What?*'

'It was all arranged about a month ago. Da said Joan'd been fucking about for too long and she was to accept the next engagement and not give him any trouble, or else go into a nunnery. He means it. And awful as she is, I can't let her be shut up.'

He stares at her.

'Huh,' Eleanor says. She has her head on one side, an echo of Joan herself. 'I just realised a thing. If she's holding your hand now, she must truthfully love you. Because she's in much more peril than you are.'

Grania comes to Edward later that night, breaking into his sleep with a hand over his mouth. He gets up and they move silently between the sleeping men on their rolls on the floor, past the sleeping guard, down the corridors toward Joan's chamber, Grania whispering as they go.

'Hie on now. God help me, I'm no longer able to stand the dole of that girl. This is your fault. She wouldn't make such mourn over her marriage if her heart wasn't occupied by you. The man they're purposing for her is a fine gentleman. A Gaelic lord, not a Palesman. The Gaelics are far better men. By Saint Ronyon, if I could go back and put a stop to your book meetings, I would. I couldn't foresee how anyone could fall in love over something so wonderly boring. Fucking teenagers. I should have known. Don't look stricken, now. I like you, Edward. But I mislike what you and she are doing, I much mislike it.'

'What *are* we doing?' he asks, but she doesn't reply.

They step over the sleeping guard ('A dose of aqua vitae,' says Grania) outside Joan's chamber, and into the dark room.

'Where...?' says Edward.

Grania points at the curtained bed.

He hesitates only a moment, then crawls inside.

Within the curtains it's warm and black. He can't see Joan, except as a shifting and rearranging of the blackness. Her hand takes his, picks it up; he feels her lips touch its back. His heart feels as if she's lifted it too, and pressed it to her own.

'I hear you know that I'm pledged to this O'Carroll cunt,' she says.

'Grania said he was a gentil—'

'I don't care what he is. If I have to marry him, I'll kill him. That was one of my early plans. Lateward I've been thinking of full many plans. They fly out of me like bees. I had a plan to kill my da. I had a plan to kill the nuns. I had a plan to poison everyone in the castle in the name of King Henry, then go to him and ask for reward.'

'... Everyone?'

'That was an old plan. The plan I have now is less murderful. I'm going to steal a bushel of treasure, get to the harbour in disguise, pay a boatman and go to England. I can't hide here in Ireland. But then I thought – maybe, if you're not over-wedded to the king idea, you might want to... come with me?'

There's a silence. He can't locate himself within it.

'Edward?' she whispers. For the first time she sounds unsure.

Edward? Edward isn't here. He's astonied; he can't think; his brain has stopped.

But his heart is full of love and relief.

'Yes,' he says.

Thank God, yes.

She lets her breath out, a small explosive noise, like something brasting free. Then they are kissing; she clings to him, close and fervent. He clasps her back in wonderment, his lips against her neck, his own breath dampening her skin. Her hair, loose, trails against his shoulder. Without her kirtle and overthings her body feels small and soft. He didn't know how he ever thought she was so hard and shiny, a magpie with a snapping beak and stiff feathers, when the truth is slender arms, a tender mouth, hot skin, a quick pulse in her throat, small, velvety breasts—

'That's enough!' says Grania, pulling open the curtain. 'I'm a gentlewoman, not a bawd. Back to your own room, your grace – hie now! – the night air will subside your... situation.'

16

What troubles Edward?

Not the prospect of not being king. Of not having gold, feasts, falcons, European princesses, pet lions.

He could throw it all into the air like torn paper and watch it flitter away.

His dishonesty, in secretly running away: this troubles him. He's been avoiding Confession and prayer. But whatever path he takes now is dishonest. The Yorkists say he has to lie for a good cause. They mean: taking the throne. But what if *not* taking the throne is a better cause; if the boy Henry is keeping in the Tower is the true earl?

What is he? Lovell must know, and Stillington. Joan says the rest of them are just guessing. Surely even Lovell wouldn't crown a peasant or a bastard just to take power? But... if he *would*, it's Edward's duty to run away. Think of scripture.

Proverbs: 'The servant who becomes king is a crime that makes the earth tremble.'

'But if I'm a peasant or a bastard, how can I marry you, a gentil-woman?' he says to Joan. 'To violate nature, decency, the divinely ordained—'

'Nothing in the scriptures forbids it,' she says. 'And I don't care. So: I'm happy, God's happy. Be happy.'

And yet…

It troubles Edward that he might never know what he is.

The thought of Lincoln, too, troubles him. Lincoln's hopes of redemption. Yesterday Lincoln quoted Homer to him: *Pallas leads him unhurt through the press, turning aside the violent spears.* He said: I pray for this for myself, cousin, if only to live long enough to see your triumph. But I need no more than that.

Joan says, 'He'll get his wish. Which is to die. You know he can't fight? Sometimes he can, but other times he turns strange and folds up like a baby vole before a fox.'

Edward remembers one of the few military strategy meetings he's attended, with Kildare and Martin Swartz and Lovell and Lincoln. They agreed Edward would stay back in the fight, behind the lines, from where he could be easily removed to safety, if it came to it, and Lincoln should stay with him.

I purpose to be in the charge, Lincoln said. This is his God's will.

Lovell and Kildare had an eye meeting then. If Edward had to guess at its meaning, it was something like: *fuck's sake.*

You're too valuable to die, Lovell told him. If a battle goes wrong we quit the field, live on and fight again. We have people across England who can harbour us and get us back to Flanders. And think of strategy, man. If Henry gets hold of you he'll wring out all our secrets.

I won't talk, Lincoln said.

Everyone says that, Lovell said. Everyone talks.

And I won't run, Lincoln said.

Then I'll drag you, said Lovell. He looked wroth then: controlled, but visible. Lincoln looked unperturbed. A disturbing light radiated from his countenance. Edward knows Joan is right: Lincoln's truest desire is for his own death.

'It's better that we knock their war over,' Joan says. 'Like pushing over a cart. We end it before it begins and everybody lives, whether they like it or not.'

'Lincoln will perhaps forgive me one day,' Edward says.

Joan looks at him with her head on one side. 'Sure,' she says.

'He'll have to be king if I'm not here,' Edward says. 'I still don't understand that. I thought he couldn't rule because of his condition. But kings don't even fight in battles.'

'He's got a condition which is more debilitating: honour,' says Joan.

Edward, struck, marvels, 'He's as pure as Galahad.'

She looks around to see who might be in sight, then touches his hand, quickly, tenderly, maybe sadly – though he doesn't know why sadness would come into it. 'You're still too honourable yourself,' she says. 'Maybe incurably so.'

'I mislike that they'll probably think I fled out of cowardice,' he says, sighing. 'I was full ready to fight.'

'Oh, do you feel cheated?' she asks. 'There won't be an army of horsemen, or footsoldiers, or a fleet of ships for you now.'

'Fuck all of them,' Edward says, and she laughs.

'I know you worry that your father's vices run in your blood,' Joan says. 'But what would your father do now? He'd invade, for greed and ambition. My father would do the same.' She smiles. 'But if we run away, we prove we're nothing sib to them, and we're free.'

Edward and Joan are on the sunlit lawn with Eustacia, playing a game in which she is a dog and they throw sticks for her, which she finds passing mirthful. The real dogs are sitting around watching, looking wronged. Each time Eustacia's out of earshot across the grass, barking wildly, Joan and Edward can talk freely.

'Grania will help us,' Joan says. 'She doesn't want to, but she will. She can drug the guards' ale. And I can send her to Dublin harbour with money to pay a boatman.'

Joan's plans are tightly constructed; no space between the bricks.

'But we need more money,' she says. 'We need to gather treasure by day, when nobody expects theft. The chests of dinner silver are in the cellar, but you can go down there on pretence of looking for wine or something. The cups and tableware that are only used at banquets, so nobody notices. I'll get to my father's gold. He has some hidden around the place in case of emergency.'

Edward thinks of the best tableware: the Ottoman stone cup garnished with silver, with a silver marmoset on the cover, the gilt salt with a dragon on it, the cup made of an ostrich egg, the gold spoon with a lion on it.

Marmosets, dragons, lions, ostriches.

If he doesn't do this, he'll die or be king and he'll never get to see any of them.

He'll never again see Joan, the most baffling and beautiful of all God's creatures.

What is the most beautiful thing? he thinks.

Sappho answers:

I say it is what one loves.

'After this is all over, you could write a *fabliau,*' Joan says. Lateward her blood is running high; she's unusually merry.

'A *fabliau* about what?'

'About a wily girl and a cunning boy, who tricked a whole castle's worth of people.'

'It's good. But *fabliaux* are usually wonderly… uh…'

'Bawdy?'

'Yes.'

'Oh, it'll end bawdy,' she says, and smiles.

17

The Wily Girl and The Cunning Boy

In olde Ireland green there dwelt a pair
of lovers, both of them young and fair
But the girl's father stood atwixt them and their joy
He planned to marry her off and crown the boy.
At night the two met in the secret dark,
'I have a scheme,' the girl said. 'If you only hark,
We'll go to England, where none know our faces
We'll live happily there in shadowy places
Or we'll roam the world, we'll travel East
The splendours of God's earth will be our feast.'
The clever lady Grania came to their aid
Her lord and master she merrily betrayed
Grania didn't try to change the girl's course
Only a fool steps in front of a galloping horse.
The girl told the boy, 'See that hawthorn tree?
There we hide the treasure we stole privily
And I'll meet you there two hours after midnight.
Dressed as servants we'll hie to Dublin harbour
And the happy ending for our ardour.'
The boy lies adread and forwallowing all that night
Tired, he rises at dawn's first light.
He goes to his door – but there stands a gallowglass
Not japing, or smiling: he won't let the boy pass—

'—what is happening?' Edward asks, 'why won't you let me out, what is happening?'

But the gallowglass guard won't answer.

He hears a far-off sound of screaming.

He's never heard her scream before, so he doesn't know if it's Joan—

what would her scream sound like?

Like that?

'Let me out,' he says, and now he's shouting, 'let me OUT!'

The guard won't move

'Sorry, your grace—'

But he won't move

Edward runs instead to the window

sees the guards carrying a woman's body away

quickly moving, stumbling, in the dawn light

the glass ripples

breaks under his hands

her face – he can't see

the ground wet from the rain the night before

her dress dragging through the puddles

her headdress is loose

her hair is blonde.

not Joan

Grania

Grania's dress, Grania's hair

no, he says

please no—

18

Edward can't see the Abbey Court gate from his window. He can only hear horses, men, cartwheels on cobbles. He paces the room, frantic. He shouts at his guard through the locked door. 'I am the king! Let me out! I'll fight you! Get me a sword! I demand you bring me a sword!' He kicks the walls, damaging the painted plaster. He throws an ewer at the window, breaking a pane. He shouts out of it: 'I am a prisoner here!'

Nobody answers.

After some time passes, he has no witting how long, he hears talking outside. The door is unlocked. He rushes to open it. The gallowglass and another of Kildare's guard are outside.

'My lord,' one says.

He feints sidewise, then runs under their arms and out into the corridor in his nightshirt. As fast as he can he hies toward Joan's room. He's aware of the men following him. Not running: walking. Their leisure makes him more frantic. He speeds up even as he realises they aren't trying to catch him, because it's too late for him to do anything.

The door of Joan's room is open; the bed curtains are open. She isn't inside. Now the men come and take his arms. They draw him, not unkindly, toward the great hall.

'Under armed escort, is it?' he shouts. Servants duck away from them, wide eyed. 'Fuck you, I'm looking for Kildare anyway. Bring me a sword!'

In this wise – raging, tearful, barefoot – he reaches Kildare, and shouts at him:

'What did you do, where is Joan?'

Kildare looks astonied.

'Gone back to Maynooth. With her mother and sisters.'

'You killed her!'

'What? Are you broken in your wits? I would never kill Joan.'

'No! You killed *Grania*.'

'Joan's lady? *You* know her? By God, why does everyone care so much about this woman all of a sudden?' Kildare sits down in his great chair then, and rubs his face. He looks inquiet. Then he says,

'You know, *you've* been at mischief, you're not in any position to be chiding me. You were going to rob me and run away with my daughter. A king! After everything we've done for you. This is a heavy ill, lad. A grievous ill.'

'Hang me for treason against myself then!' Edward shouts. He sits down. The tears are overcoming him. 'I don't care. I don't want to be the king of murderers. You murdered Grania.'

He gives in and sobs. He can feel Kildare looking at him, considering. The sense of the other man changing tack is near tangible.

'Look now,' Kildare says, in a fatherly manner. 'Do I feel dole about the death of Joan's woman? Yes, I do. And the doctor tells me now Joan is untouched. Perhaps the storm overtook me somewhat. But, by God, those women drove me into it. Lying! Planning to rob me! Plotting to abduct the King of England! It's the highest treason, lad. It can't stand. Joan is a child but her lady is a grown woman. She paid a grown woman's penalty. I perhaps would that it weren't – that it didn't – but I was wroth.'

'What did you do?'

'I ran her through with my sword. We'll hold a Mass for her, and noise that she slipped on the stairs.'

'Does Joan know?'

'She was there. I regret that she saw it. She made mourn beyond all measure.' His eyes move past Edward, and now he looks distressed. Edward can't bear to think what sights he's seeing. 'I sent her away because she was crazed in her wits; she was not able to master herself.'

Kildare fixes his eyes on Edward. He looks almost pleading. 'It was a kindness,' he says.

The Abbey Court is changed after that morning.

At Mass Sir Patrick's eyes and nose are red. Edward remembers him japing in Grania's dress. Now his voice trembles as he reads his sermon. The servants are whispering, when they think they can't be seen. Kildare has lost his mirthfulness. At dinner he teases his beard with his fingers, frowning, and forgets to make a toast. It's Lincoln who reminds him. Lincoln has no idea of anything, and is almost intolerably merry.

'Two days until we sail!' he says. 'In two short days we attain our holy destiny, vanquish the usurper and rejoice in the sweetness of God's glory!'

'*Crom a Boo!*' everyone shouts. 'God save the king!'

Few people know the truth of what happened. They think Grania fell down the stairs and the Fitzgerald girls were taken home for fear of the sickness the mercenaries had brought to the city.

Lovell knows. Of course. He comes to talk to Edward. If he's wroth he doesn't show it. He sits down, lays his hands on his knees, and sighs.

Then he speaks.

He says:

'It was Plunket who undid you. He's had some maugre against your leman since before I arrived. He set people to watch you; he got the story out of the boatman. Don't worry, we had the boatman killed. Nobody else knows of this.'

He says:

'Oh, I see a flame in your eyes. Well, forget it. Plunket has gone back to his own manse. Did you think I'd tell you while he was still here? With you looking so warly?'

He says:

'It's this wrothful countenance of yours that makes me afraid, Edward, that you are not sorry.'

He says:

'I don't understand. Why do things in such a boistous way? Why not marry a princess, let the Fitzgerald maiden marry her Gaelic lord, then bring the pair of them to England on some spurious appointment so you can have ado with her later?'

He says:

'So, what do you want? We are not hostage keepers. We can take you back to the farm where I found you, if you wish. We can ask the Collan man there if he'll take on another man's child again, with no payment this time. You have no skills for farming, but maybe he will teach you, out of goodness.'

He says:

'This was grave sin, lad. I know Grania was beloved by you. But she broke God's laws, and the laws of her country. Do you think she could escape justice, as the two of you have? Kildare would say she is a grown woman and is responsible for *your* sin, but I see it differently. You two are the ones with the puissance. Grania was your servant. She did only what you asked her to do. Who bears responsibility for her fate? I can't say. Only God can say.'

He says:

'Penance must be done each day, and God must be begged for His forgiveness. You should pray for Grania's poor soul now, because I can tell you it's in mortal peril. I won't talk now of what might await *you* in hell. I hope that with a return to right doings, that will be avoided.'

He says:

'I'm adread to think of how your cousin Lincoln would feel if he heard about this. I'm picturing his expression. Are you? He had put his heart's faith in you. England has put her heart's faith in you. You purposed to break all these hearts, because yours had been struck by Cupid. Is this the king you want to be? Putting passing pleasure above the good of his people, the wishes of God?'

He says:

'I can see by your face that you are sorry. It lightens me to see it, by God. This was a goodly lesson for you, and fortune was on your side in preventing tragedy. Our Lord has saved you, in His large and mysterious mercy.'

He says:

'Will you give me your oath now, that nothing like this will happen again? That you will be honest and true? Yes?'

He says:

'We will none of us speak of this again.'

The last night in Dublin comes. Edward leaves the feasting men – quietly, watched by nobody, because he's no threat to anybody now. He goes to Joan's room. It's empty and coldly dark. He can't light a lamp, so he sits on the bed and waits for his eyes to adjust.

Did he even thank Grania? What was the last thing he said to her? God forgive him, he can't remember. He'd been so mad to be united with Joan at last that he forgot Grania was a real person.

He wishes he hadn't seen the hem of her skirt dragging through the puddles. He should have looked away, like he did in Oxford.

Oxford wasn't his fault.

This was his fault.

Grief comes; it presses the air out of him.

Kildare said Joan couldn't quiet herself, couldn't master herself. The idea of Joan crying out in pain is too much to bear.

He can see better now, a waxing moon lying over the floor like spilled milk. He folds back the bed coverings. There's an indentation in the stuffed mattress. Small, girl-shaped. He finds an apple core forgotten in a corner. A slipper lost under the bed. He picks it up – but he can't take it with him, so he puts it back.

Lying not far from the slipper, further under the bed, but gleaming, wanting to be found, is a silver and bone comb. He runs his fingers over the tines, imagining them pressed against her small, catlike skull, tilling the black hair, the blue-white brightness of skin revealed in the parting. He sniffs it: it smells of her, a perfume of clove and roses, and animal oils. He presses its points into his palm, harder and harder, leaving a row of indentations glowing white in red.

And then it's the morning of departure, walking in state through the town to the ships looming on the sparkling sea, a savage herd of wooden elephants, Kildare the Great Earl suddenly small on the dock as he waves them off, and the cries

God save the king

To Victory

Crom a Boo

ringing in his ears.

Crossing

Things Lincoln Says as They Cross

Oh, the abominable sea sickness has you! My poor cousin. Rest below decks.
Shall I read you some Bible passages?
Here is a little broth, and biscuits. They're not savoury but they're wonderly good for a crazed stomach. The absence of flavour is remarkable.
We will dine again on swan at your table.
Another Bible passage? A psalm? The Lord makes firm the steps of those who delight in Him.
You look weary, my cousin.
I've brought water for your brow, here.
Another psalm might help, mayhap?
Shall I let you sleep?
I'll let you sleep.

Things Thomas Fitzgerald Says as They Cross

Are you alright there, your grace?
Very white you look.
Has something more than sea quease troubled you? Is it the death of the lady Grania? Passing doleful it is to lose such a goodly lady, in such a way.
Her soul will be at the side of Christ now, by Jesus. A right merry lady.

We're to make land in Lancashire. I'll be seeing England for the first time!

Sure, I bet you can't wait to see your people again. Think of the open arms of the English girls... I hear the noble English demosels put your pintle in their mouth and say the Paternoster.

Did you hear the one about the English Lady and the Bawdy Baker? Still so white!

You should have seen it earlier, one of your York nobles was sick over the rail and the fish ate it.

It's a bad one, is it, your grace? No disworship in it.

Shall I leave you be?

I'll leave you be.

War

Lovell says,

'The usurper Henry is inquiet and marvellous mistrustful. My man in his service says he has no witting at all which of his nobles will side with him or against him. He's counting up all the estates he confiscated. The Marquess of Dorset tried to join him, and Henry put him in the Tower.'

And,

'He's proclaimed it in all the cities that anyone spreading false rumours of his imminent overhurling will be put in the pillory.'

And,

'He's noising it in the North that the Pope supports him. As if a papal bull can't be bought.'

And,

'He summoned the queen to be at his side at Kenilworth. He must be adread that she'll escape him.'

Each piece of news seems to increase Lovell, not in size or liveliness, but in substance, so that he seems to move through the men like a great ship carving water, steep waves driven up in his wake. When he speaks, everyone is silent.

They reach the Lancashire coast in early June. A noble named Sir Thomas Broughton meets them, embraces them with much cheer, and provisions the soldiers with food from the nearby abbey.

That night the men put up tents, make fires and burn pottage in iron pots over them. Edward marvels at the sight; so many curling shoots of smoke, rising up, commingling in the purple sky.

He doesn't mind the pottage. It reminds him of Jennott's cooking.

Sir Thomas Fitzgerald is surprised that so few other nobles accompanied Sir Thomas Broughton.

'I thought we had more love on these shores?' he says. 'Where are these English cunts?'

'English love is shy,' says Lovell. 'It hides until it knows it is safe to show itself. When the war is won you'll have your love.'

The army camps at Ulverston, then Cartmel, then Hornby Castle – owned by Sir Edward Stanley, the son of King Henry's stepfather, the Earl of Derby. The Stanleys being famous equivocators and bet-hedgers, as Lovell explains. They spun like weathervanes between York and Lancaster, and again at the Battle of Bosworth. And try getting one branch of the family to admit any witting of what the others are up to. Thus, the puissant Earl of Derby and his younger brother William, Henry's Lord Chamberlain, will have nothing to do with Sir Edward Stanley's misdoings if Henry wins, and will vow themselves true Yorkists if Edward wins.

From Hornby Castle they march toward York. A thousand Englishmen. Two thousand Swabians and Swiss *landsknechts* in their striped and slashed finery. Five thousand Irish. Edward was adread that he'd be called on to make speeches, but so few of them speak English. Which is differently inquieting. Edward doesn't talk much to the men. He mostly keeps company with Lincoln and the others. Sometimes he walks between the tents in the early night; the warm summer breeze sending him parts of conversations in divers languages, and an old song:

> *Western wind, when will thou blow,*
> *That the small rain down can rain?*
> *Christ, if my love were in my arms*
> *And I in my bed again.*

Edward thinks of Joan. Which he has tried not to do. In the same way that he tries not to cut his own arm off, or hold his hand in the fire.

The atmosphere is different with no women around. The boozing is harder and wilder. The japes are crueller. Edward sometimes sees common women leaving tents at dawn. Sometimes the women are weeping. When the men aren't singing ballads and playing dice games, they're arguing, or fighting. He passes an affray: shouting, pushing, then − unexpectedly − one man sticking his halberd in the other man's throat. A fine spray of blood goes up, patterning the ground. The body is carried away. Then the men go back to the dice, and Edward to let out his shocked tears in his tent.

There's a metallic tang in the air; he can feel it. Like swords being sharpened.

Like coming war.

One night he seeks out Lincoln and finds him sitting on the ground, leaning against a tent pole, his eyes voided of all sense and life. His body is curled up on itself like a woodlouse. Frightened, Edward touches him on his shoulder. Lincoln doesn't respond. But his chest moves quickly; the air hurrying in and out.

Afterwards he says, 'I had a lapse before you. Please forgive me.'

'What sickness is it?' Edward asks.

'I don't know. It does my body no harm. But my minds are removed back to a time I prefer not to— I hope you can excuse me.'

'Of course,' he says.

Please God, he prays, keep Lincoln from harm, he is devoted to Your service and − not to question Your wisdom − what good could it do You to take him off the earth?

Please let him remain heal and whole, amen.

They camp at Masham with the intention of marching to York, which had previously indicated that it was favourable to their cause.

Edward signs his first letter as King Edward VI to York's mayor, asking the city for lodging and provision. But York has lateward voted to support Henry, and the Earl of Northumberland is on his way to the city to defend it.

'A shit on York's head,' says Sir Thomas Fitzgerald.

'We move south,' Lovell says.

'Henry's marching toward Leicester,' Lincoln says. There's no sign of his earlier sickness on him; he's bright, almost feverish, as if the spirit has re-entered his body too hot. 'Soon we'll meet!'

A couple of thousand more troops join them; men in the service of various Yorkshire nobles including the two Lords Scrope. They are provisioned by Jervaulx Abbey, whose Abbot offers them his prayers.

'It's not enough men,' says Martin Swartz.

'It's enough men for what I've got in mind,' Lovell says.

Lord Clifford, a noble fighting for King Henry, is known to be in the area with four hundred men. So Lovell takes two thousand men to find him. Clifford and his soldiers are lodging for the night at Tadcaster when Lovell attacks them, making great affray; skirmishes brasting out in the streets and houses of the town. Clifford has to flee for his life. Lovell comes back laughing, running with other people's blood. His men are dragging trunks and coffers, stolen from Clifford's retinue, whom they encountered by good fortune on a bridge.

'A beautiful moonlit meeting,' Lovell says.

'None robbed from the townsfolk?' says Lincoln.

'Maybe some,' says Lovell. 'Soldiers do but naught according to their kind. And I thought we should let them have some merriness. But very few Tadcaster folk were slain or maimed, it was passing gentil.'

Clifford reaches York and shuts the gates. Lovell sends the two Lords Scrope to lead soldiers in an attack on the city. They can't breach it, but the attempt draws the Earl of Northumberland to help with the defence instead of joining Henry's army. Then, when Northumberland leaves the city, on the Feast of Corpus Christi, he goes northwards.

'He's riding *away* from Henry?' Edward asks.

'Northumberland knows we're going to win,' says Lovell. 'He'll find things to occupy himself with until that time.'

War is slightly delayed, on account of Henry getting lost near Nottingham. He and his men camp in a forest for the night. They can't find the city the next day either, and spend the next night in Radcliffe village.

'Shall we give them a map?' says Sir Thomas Fitzgerald. 'I thought this war would be done by now. I've got a wife and children at home.'

Lovell's men noise it among the people that Henry has already fought and lost. Several nobles on their way to fight for him decide to believe the rumour and go back home. Others go into sanctuary. Lord Welles deserts Henry's side and goes to London, where he procures great commotions by telling everyone that Henry is lost and dead, whereupon York supporters make affrays upon Henry's officials; beating and robbing them; shouting, *Long live King Edward*!

'If they're all waiting to see who will win, maybe no one will come to the war?' asks Edward, hopefully.

'Too many are here already,' says General Swartz. If he's regretting accepting this commission from Margaret, he doesn't noise it. But he doesn't participate in the mirth of their side either. He spends the nights alone, away from the japeful nobles. Edward envies him.

Lincoln and his men meet and fight a troop of lances led by Lord Scales. For three days they skirmish in and about Sherwood Forest. Edward worries about Lincoln, but the news comes back to the main camp: Lincoln has won. Scales is fallen back to Nottingham. Lincoln returns in a haze of gratitude to God, who saw fit to lift his affliction and allow him to dispatch many tens of men by sword.

'Praise God indeed,' Lovell says to Sir Thomas Fitzgerald. 'There's no killer like Lincoln in a holy fervour.'

The city of York, hearing of the victory, announced it was pledging itself to King Edward VI.

'York's going to give itself a neck-crick turning about so fast,' says Thomas Fitzgerald, jubilant.

'This side-fight was a mistake,' says Swartz. 'In these three days more men have joined Henry at Nottingham.'

'So he found it then.'

'The Earl of Derby has sent him six thousand men,' continues Swartz. 'He now has twelve thousand men at Nottingham.'

'By Jesus, what is this, a maths lesson?' says Thomas. 'Where's the cane?'

'Henry has it,' says Swartz. He bows to them all, and quits the room.

It's the night before the battle. Henry is approaching along the south bank of the Trent. Their own army crosses from the north and camps at East Stoke. It's another hot night, the calm air rippled by foxes and owls and the sleep stirrings of the men. Edward can't sleep. His stomach is cramped with terror, his eyelids fixed open. He goes to find Lincoln. He hears him before he sees him, standing outside his tent, talking to Swartz.

'More may join us tomorrow,' Lincoln says.

'There's no time,' says Swartz. His face is out of Edward's sight, but Edward can hear his expression. Contemptuous. Resigned.

'The great Vegetius says valour is greater than numbers,' Lincoln says.

Edward remembers himself, as Little John Collan, four years ago, thinking this about Gaspard the goat, and how it turned out that the goat not only had more mass than John but more valour too.

'It's true the nobles are more ware than we expected,' Lincoln says. 'But their hearts belong to us. I know this.'

Edward moves quietly away back to his own bed.

The day comes, against Edward's wishes.

The battle comes.

He, Lovell, Broughton and a few others are sitting on their horses at the top of a hill, the men arrayed before them. The sun is newly up; the scent of grass and wild camomile rises up to him as the horses shift about. The river is beside and behind them. The day is quiet, their men are quiet, but the sense of building pressure is loud in his ears.

In the distance, a glinting multitude of soldiers has come into view.

'There they are,' Lincoln says. 'But where are the rest?'

'Is Henry here?' Edward says, seeing a standard.

'Sure, right behind his men,' says Lovell. 'Only a mile away.'

'That's only half the men, just an advance guard,' says Lincoln. He turns to them. His face is like a sun. 'I say we engage them now! Before the rest can reach them.'

'We should retain the high ground,' says Swartz.

'And *you* should stay back here,' Lovell says to Lincoln, but Lincoln is already moving forward, shouting to the men. Swartz curses in German, follows, shouting commands to his own arbalestiers.

And in an enormous roll of drums and a screaming of *Crom a Boo*, the world loses its wits.

Edward's eyes, which wouldn't close last night for God nor man, shut themselves now. Lovell and Broughton are just behind him on their horses: his cowardice is hidden from their viewline. But, as they did in Oxford, the sounds persist in making their way into his ears. The war rebounds around his brain-pan. This is a good thing, he tells himself, a noble thing, like a Homeric epic:

> *And like a great flock of bronze-winged birds*
> *Taking as one to the sky when a bough*
> *Breaks beneath the hunter's unwary foot*
> *Brazen clamour rose from the men below,*
> *A clashing of sword and plated armour.*
> *The violent cracks of arquebuses*
> *Ring loud as the hammers of Hephaestus—*

'Henry's men are running!' Lovell says to Broughton. 'By God, the sight of those half-naked Gaelic savages must have astonied them.'

Blue-eyed Athene urged on the York host
As Eris walked among the Tudor throng
Raining fear upon the massed bright helmets
As hail assails the fierce horns of oxen
And drives them into terror—

'A curse on them, it's turned,' says Lovell. 'It's turned. They're real-ising they aren't overmatched. Lincoln's revealed our weakness of number. And arms. And horses. God damn him!'

The valiant kern, with their long knives drawn
Cut down the—

'The kern are distroubled,' Lovell says. 'They've got no armour. Henry's bowmen are slaughtering them.'

Furious was the Swabian vengeance—

'Swartz's men are overnumbered. They're wading through kern parts. They're being cut down! I can't see Swartz… If he has any sense, he's run already.'

Athene—

'They're running,' Lovell says. 'And now we hie, and quit the field. *Lincoln?*'

Edward opens his eyes. Lincoln, still on horseback, is galloping up toward them. Blood, not his own, is streaked up his breast plate and mail. Edward offers a prayer to God: Thank you, heavenly father, for keeping Lincoln safe. He doesn't look down the hill at the haze of brown and red and smoke. Swartz's horse canters up through it and past them toward the river.

'It's lost!' Lincoln shouts. 'It's lost.'

Lovell wheels his horse away. 'Fall back, then,' he shouts. 'What – what in hell are you doing?'

Lincoln is turning back, back down the hill.

'By Christ's bones! Leave him,' Lovell says. 'Come on, your grace. Quickly!'

He and Broughton start for the trees. Edward – not knowing what he's doing, his brain having left his body – urges his own horse after Lincoln, down the hill.

He hears Lovell behind him, screaming now:

'Fuck! Someone get him back! Catch him!'

Yes, thinks the only part of Edward's brain still halsing to his skull, yes, catch him. What is he doing? He can't save Lincoln. He's lost his wits.

But he must save Lincoln.

Stop him!

But now he's among them

the men running toward him, the kern and the *landsknechts*, chased by Henry's men

a horse collides with him, the world spins upsodown, and he's on the ground

the fighting moves around him like a wave of rocks; a sharp, heavy clattering

the ground torn into mud, clogged with old rain or blood, blanketing him, pulling him down

tries to sit up

a blow to the head, a foot or a hoof

shouting, screaming, strangled cryings out, grunts, gasping, groans on the ground, near, the scrape of sword against metal, clanging, dull thuds, a horse scream, a high human wail, ending short as if snipped off with scissors, the smell of blood and worse, entrails, brawn, like a butcher's shop, voice from the market crying out hock, rump, head, tripe, brawn, neck, sweetbread, but that's not here, that's a sound from inside, not outside, he raises his head, sees a man trip and land on his own sword, a snaking smell of shit weaving up through the smell of blood, his nose is so full of the smell of blood he thinks it's bleeding

the din passing over him, in the direction of the river

quieter now

He gets up.

There are people on the ground around him, mostly his own people, juddering, groaning, flat and still. He staggers in the direction he saw Lincoln go. He sees Sir Thomas Fitzgerald, half pinned under a dead horse, coated in a red paste of bloody mud. Edward runs to help him before he sees that Thomas isn't moving. Half his jaw is struck off, leaving a neat white line of teeth, intact tongue.

More of Henry's soldiers are coming up the hill toward them. Edward catches sight of Lincoln's horse, fallen and thrashing on the ground in the distance. He finds a sword, pries it from the grip of a severed arm, and runs toward it.

Lincoln is sitting on the ground next to his horse. There's a dead man next to him. Lincoln's legs are drawn in toward his body, his arms brought up to his chest. His face is unoccupied.

Tudor men are running toward Lincoln, closer than Edward. A Tudor knight on horseback rides through them, overtakes them.

'Take him alive!' shouts one. 'King's orders! Nobody kill him! The king wants him alive!'

The Tudor knight dismounts beside Lincoln.

Edward keeps running, hardly able to breathe, nearing them, near enough to see Lincoln blink, flinch, then smile at the knight. As if they're friends.

Maybe they are friends, because the knight drops to one knee, cradling Lincoln, to help him gently to his feet.

Then he takes a knife out of his boot and presses it into Lincoln's body.

He steps back. Lincoln falls to the ground. Edward can see the blood flowing out of him.

'He tried to kill me,' the knight shouts. 'The knave! He had a knife!'

Edward, reaching them, doesn't know what noise he makes, or who is around him, what is happening. A maddened wroth speeds him. He runs at the knight, sword raised—

—and is on the ground.

One of the soldiers has tripped him. He hears them saying, *it's the fucking pretender, no, it is aright, what the fuck, how in hell is he here* as another stands on his wrist and removes the sword from his grasp. Then they pick him up, twisting like a cat, and carry him between two of them, through a noise that sounds almost like trumpets.

It *is* trumpets, and Edward can't bear it, can't bear seeing and hearing and existing, can't bear that his body is whole and not broken apart with mourn, that his soul is still here, how does it have the shame to abide here, with the brave men gone – Swartz gone, Thomas Fitzgerald gone, and Lincoln, his cousin Lincoln, left face downward in the red mud.

He's in a bare cell.

He doesn't know where it is. He asks the guard, who won't tell him, and Edward calls him a cunt and now the guard brings him food, which he squashes first with his boot, but Edward doesn't give a shit because he doesn't want to eat anyway, if they won't kill him he'll quit himself, and when he's escaped this wretched world he'll go looking for the others

Lincoln Thomas Fitzgerald Grania

to say sorry, sorry, sorry, sorry, sorry, sorry, sorry, sorry

The guard isn't allowed to beat Edward, he says. A great shame. Henry forbade it. Instead, the guard torments him with tidings. Swartz's mercenaries were given quarter, and are to be sent home. Does Edward think any of his stinking Gaelic friends received mercy? Well, they did not. All of them were killed as they fled along a narrow gully toward the river; a natural trap, to be known ever after as Red Gutter for the blood that flowed down it. The kern who made it to the Trent mostly drowned. They were buried in a mass grave, all tumbled in like dead rats.

The guard takes Edward's fairy arrowhead and throws it out of the window. He stands on and crushes the tiny whittled ship.

At night Edward mutters syllogisms to himself:

All enemy men want Lincoln alive

Lincoln was killed

Only a friend would kill Lincoln

None are bocardos, but they are inescapable. They revolve in his head. The Tudor knight who killed Lincoln was a secret York ally – and Lincoln knew this, and smiled before he died, because he saw his friend coming to help him.

Why would the friend kill him? It must have been as Lovell said: to stop Lincoln giving up information on the secret Yorkists of England; their names, their hiding places. Edward remembers Margaret telling him that one of the secret Yorkists is a very high-up man, a close friend of Henry's. It must have been on his orders that Lincoln was killed.

Edward hopes Lovell got away from the field. He isn't longing for Lovell to come back and save him. He doesn't want to be the York hope anymore. Hope has no home in his body. But he wants Lovell to hear what was done to Lincoln, to find that wicked knight and his master, get his hands round their necks – like Edward wishes he could – and press as hard as he can.

Tears come to his eyes, flow out. He shouts curses; kicks the rough wall, the heavy wooden door. The sounds rebound in his brain-pan.

Maybe Edward's in the real Bocardo. The straw-stuffed mattress, the narrow high window, the outwardly bolted door; these could be the innards of a prison. He could be anywhere. Maybe he's in the Tower, where the other Earl of Warwick is kept. Maybe he's in a place like Bedlam, for people crazed in their wits.

Breath eludes him. It leaves his chest and he can only recover scraps of it. He starts to panic. Are his minds whole? Has any of this

303

happened? Oxford, Mechelen, Ireland, Stoke? Is the bleeding lump on his head from the battle? Or is he a farm boy who got kicked in the head by a cow?

His body feels like a stranger's. His soul races around it like a trapped spider.

Didn't they say the other Earl of Warwick had been in captivity so long that he'd been parted from his reason?

'Edward, Earl of Warwick!' he shouts. 'Are you there? Are you... *me*?'

No sound comes, from within or without.

Simnel

'… he shall yield life for life, eye for eye, tooth for tooth, hand for hand, foot for foot, burning for burning, wound for wound, sore for sore' –

Book of Exodus, 21:23–25

I

Eventually they take Edward out of the cell. Beyond his walls there had been celebrations, and Henry offering thanksgiving to God, and forgivings of various people, including many of the common rioters who had ransacked Tudor houses, and the two Lords Scrope, who claimed that they'd joined the rebellion not by their own design but by the will of their tenants.

And now it is time for Edward to be forgiven.

First he has to confess. He is taken before Henry's best friends, the Lord Chamberlain Sir William Stanley and the Lord Chancellor Bishop Morton. A grey beard and a white beard.

He stares at them with a hateful maugre.

'Who are you?' Stanley asks him. 'In *truth*.'

No point saying Edward, Earl of Warwick. He lets the name go; it falls easily away. But he won't give them the name Collan. He needs to keep his family-that-was safe.

'Lambert Simnel.'

'And who are your family? Where did you grow up?'

'In Oxford. My father was a joiner.'

'Was?'

'He and my mother died of sweating sickness.'

Morton stares at him for a moment, then shrugs. 'And you were got hold of and trained in doubleness by a priest—'

'He's dead too.'

'No, he's not. Priests are exempted from hanging. He made a full confession and was lateward pardoned.'

'Oh, I remember,' Simnel says. 'You got a fake priest to confess, or a real priest to make a fake confession, so you could proclaim my fraudulence.'

'Do you know the whereabouts of Viscount Lovell?'

'So you didn't catch him,' he says. 'That must be annoying.'

Stanley looks wroth at that. He raps on the arm of his chair.

'That's enough, you little shitpate. We've been gentle with you because you are a boy. But things can go much worse for you. Do you want to leave this Tower as a dead body, or a free man?'

He doesn't answer.

'So,' says Morton. 'Do you know who may be offering them shelter?'

Simnel shakes his head.

'I don't know,' he says. 'In truth, I don't.'

'That's a shame,' Morton says. 'Guards, take him back to his cell.'

They come back the next day, with more paper.

'I'm not telling tales of anyone,' Simnel says. 'So if you want me to do that, you should just kill me.'

Morton smiles.

'You misunderstand. Only threats to the throne are killed. *This* is your public confession. Which will be about how you were born to low people, before a greedy priest of no significance trained you as a pretender, and a few easily fooled nobles were tricked – but now they are dead, and nobody of importance betrayed their sovereign king, and the affair is entirely over.'

They've written it already.

He only has to copy it out in his own writing and sign it. As he holds the quill he remembers his dream of being another Julius Caesar, a king who writes history.

He signs.

'Well done,' says Stanley.

2

So here he is.

Not a dead body, and not a free man.

They put him to work in the kitchens, so they could say: *He was a pretender, and now he is a ladlewasher.*

Great mirth.

I am not a ladlewasher, Simnel corrects them. *I am a* spit turner.

Edward never saw these parts of a castle before. Up above is where he would have walked, attended upon by servants: the world controlled by Sir William Stanley, which Simnel is given to understand he will never see again.

The lower world is the *Domus Providencie*, controlled by a Lord Steward Simnel rarely meets, there are so many layers of servant-tiers between them. Here there are larders, a pastry kitchen, buttery, cellar, ewery, bakery and the kitchen. Pantlers, bakers, butchers, brewers, waferers, larderers, sauciers, dessert cooks, undercooks, scullions. The hundreds of servants rushing around these demesnes wear no livery, being below eyesight. They hand food and drink to the liveried servants who come from the great halls and chambers of the *Domus Magnificencie*: the upper world.

He's never seen anything like the kitchens. In Mechelen and Ireland those doors were closed to him. Now he walks through great halls, full of people and noise, as vast as an underground city, except everyone in this city is doing only one thing: making food for the city above.

The last time Simnel watched food being prepared was at the farm. The small room, small fire. Jennott and her burned bread; turning, laughing, *the goat got you again, did he?*

The thought of her doesn't make him cry. He hasn't cried since he left the cell. But there's a dull pain in his body, radiating out from the centre, like heat from a coal.

Simnel's own lord here is the master cook Simon Bricket, a man with a glistening face, who bowed ironically when Simnel arrived. Everyone else turned to watch and laugh at the jape. Simnel should have laughed too, to make friends, but the laugh wouldn't come. Bricket raised his eyebrows in a *we've got one here* way and indicated the two great fireplaces, one with cranes holding pots and cauldrons on hooks.

Ther other with a row of spits before it, and a little stool beside.

Your throne awaits, said Bricket.

Simnel took his place and the heat rose around him. A dizziness of body – no, of memory – overswept him. The clangs and dings and clashes of pots ladles tripods pokers pans graters kettles knives, a scraping hissing bubbling spitting banging shouting

Battlefield—

no

Bricket was staring at him, a wary alarm folding his damp forehead.

What did Simnel look like? Like… Lincoln?

no

A mistake to think of Lincoln.

Don't think of Joan either, or Grania, her dress in the mud—

no

He mastered himself. It's matter of clamping, and halsing. Containing all the dole and pain, then closing the lid. His chest a casket. His ribs iron bands. Nothing escaping.

What do I do? he asked.

Bricket said, Turn the spits slowly. And take the fat trays to John when they're full.

And left him to it.

During working hours the other servants hardly speak to Simnel. The kitchens might be the size of a city, but it isn't like Oxford, with each man and woman about their own doings, their own purposes, their own separate days; colliding, bartering, arguing, courting, competing. The servant world is more like a hive of bees. Everyone has a distinct role, which they sweat to perform, but they all have the same intent, they all fly as one, they all service the king.

This is what he had sensed in Mechelen. Simnel, Edward, even John – none of his selves were like these people. Servants aren't sib to village folk or nobles. They have their own rules and customs. Simnel goes about this new country as a foreigner. He could try to learn its ways – but then he realises that for the first time in his life, he doesn't have to. So he doesn't.

Once each of the two meals of the day are served to the several hundred denizens of the upper world, the kitchen folk find themselves with a small amount of time, and they use it to assay him. Some of them make japes, calling him 'your grace' and asking for his touch to cure the scrofula. Some ignore him. Some trip him, insult him, tell him he's going to hell for treason. He senses little real mislike behind it, and when he makes no reaction, the offences mostly stop, except for one committed pastry chef's boy, who calls him a milksop and pushes him so hard he almost lands in the fire, and then a dark wroth comes over Simnel and he picks up a poker for a sword and takes the boy's hat off, then winds him with the flat, and is lunging at him a third time when Bricket, who had been watching indulgently, steps in and knocks Simnel down with a waffle iron.

'That's enough,' he says.

A larger number than he expected try to be his friend. Some say, quietly, that they're right sorry for him.

This is the worst thing.

And all of them, every single one, whether they like him or no, have questions.

What was your displaying like? When you were brought before the court? Did they whip you?

He was not whipped. He was led in to receive his pardon as all the assembled nobles watched. The interest was so great that people were crowded out of the great hall and into the corridors, treading on each others' skirts and un-gentilly shoving each other, just to watch him pass. Beyond the range of Henry's ears, people were saying the wrong things, like,

'By God, he's a York in countenance aright.'

'And height.'

'A passing fair-faced lad.'

'The sib of the late Duke of Clarence.'

One girl gave him an inviting wink.

In the great hall, he notices the stonework is not so skilled, the carvings not so ornate, the paintings not so exquisite, as the hall in Mechelen that Margaret planned to pull down and rebuild.

Simnel doesn't say any of this to the people of the below world.

He says, 'I made my repentance, then humbly received the king's pardon, and am grateful of his mercy.'

What was the king like?

A narrow-bodied man within a large amount of coverings; fur, velvet, gold. Thin face. Thin untrusting eyes, the left one not quite straight. When Simnel appeared, making sure to bow his head, Henry gave a thin smile. Then Simnel had to fall on his knees, and Henry said, *Hereby I pronounce my great forgiveness*, or something like that.

Later, he thinks of the costumery and the pomp and assemblage, all to pardon a joiner's boy: Lovell was right.

Henry was frightened.

Simnel says: 'Richly dressed and wonderly puissant in demeaning.'

What was the queen like?

Beautiful. Tall. Blonde. Silent. A russet silk gown, ermine purfils, frontlets of gold on her veil. Her eyes sought no meetings.

Did she think: *is this is my cousin, or is he in the Tower, his wits gone – while my other cousin Lincoln is dead, my two brothers are dead, my father and uncles are dead, my mother is sent away, my half-brother is under watch.*

Maybe.

No wonder she was quiet.

'Modest and passing fair,' he says.

What was my lady the king's mother like?

A small woman, though her son is tall. She has his thin lips and high eyebones, high cheekbones. Bones are what come to mind when you look at their faces. She sat beside the king and it was hard to avoid her great, dark eyes, the dreadful weight of them.

He's heard she is a woman of large religion, but she seems to have an equal passion for jewels. She wears a gilded girdle, diamond and ruby rings. Her black damask gown has more ermine than the queen's.

At moments as Henry spoke her eyes filled with tears, but her mouth never trembled.

'Small of person. Formidable,' Simnel says.

What was Margaret of Burgundy, the despitous duchess, like?

He says, 'A lady of dignity and passing—'

He was going to say wisdom.

He remembers her laying her hand on his. Saying, *you have a sound nature.* Her wisdom failed her there.

'I expect she now regrets her demeaning.'

What was the Great Earl Kildare like?

... Simnel?

What was John de la Pole, the Earl of Lincoln like?

But he won't answer any more.

At night Simnel eats his supper: pottage or the lower crust of the bread, gritty from the floor of the oven. The kitchen is locked, to stop the servants stealing the fat and eating it. They should scrape it off the walls around the fire, he thinks: the inch of grease coating the stone reminds him of childhood, when his then-dad Will Collan used to chop at him for laying the butter too thick on his bread.

He misses butter.

Then he goes to bed, on a straw mattress in a room stuffed with servants, the smell of the day's cooking rising off them, a snoring from many throats creating a noise almost like the sea.

This is when he allows himself to think of them.

Joan first and Joan last. Her hair loose in the dark curtained space of her bed. *I say it is what one loves.* The unimaginable thought of her crying for Grania.

Death should be quiet and kind and come at the end of a long life. It should not be sudden and violent, a soul dislodged from the body by a great outrage.

What is meet for people who force the soul out before its natural ending day?

Death is meet.

Death for Plunket and Kildare, who killed Grania.

Death for the unknown knight who killed Lincoln.

Death for the unknown Yorkist close to Henry, the man who caused the death of Lincoln.

Death – by the same holy law – for Simnel.

And he will accept it, after he escapes, kills those four men, gets back to Ireland, and saves Joan from marriage.

Enough time to do that, he asks of God. (Kneeling in church, turning the spit, turning in his straw bed.) *By your leave.*

Amen.

3

In September the court, in a long train of packhorses, coaches, carts full of furniture and other goods, travels to Greenwich. The king and queen travel there on a royal barge, to spare their royal arses the pain of bouncing along England's heinous roads.

The palace stretches along the Thames, its red-brick face reflected in the sunlit water. Deer move in and out of the wooded grounds.

'Are you thinking about how this might have been *your* palace?' Beatrice asks Simnel.

Beatrice is a young housemaid he met one evening while the other servants were playing cards. Simnel went outside to look at the stars and plan his vengeance and nearly fell over Beatrice, sitting on the step eating a pie. She offered him some and he took it. He supposes she thinks they're friends now. Taking the pie, that was his mistake.

'I'm not thinking about aught other than how grateful I am to King Henry, my sovereign lord, for sparing me,' he says.

'You speak so prettily,' Beatrice says, sighing. 'But you're right boring.'

'You don't have to speak to me,' he says.

Beatrice looks at him. She has very pale brown hair, hardly even a colour. Her body is wonderly small. She pokes at people with her eyes in a way that says: do not call me small.

'It's alright,' she says. 'I suppose you have to be boring. We can talk on other things.'

Henry's parliament metes out its justice to the supporters of the rebellion. Some nobles are fined, others attainted, others pardoned. Several men, of little consequence, are hanged as a warning. Rumour-spreaders are also hanged.

Lovell is missing, still.

Kildare has apparently spent the months since Stoke in a warly state of opposition to both Henry and his enemies at Waterford, maintaining that Simnel was the true king. It took him until November to give in and send Henry a letter of submission. Henry allowed him to keep his deputyship on the promise that he would be loyal and obedient in future. He wasn't punished.

Simnel would have asked, if there were anyone he could talk to: What in the name of God would Kildare have to do to be punished?

What would Joan answer?

He knows my father rules Ireland, she told him.

Where is Joan now? Trapped at Maynooth, waiting for her marriage? Or making plans to get away?

He remembers the force with which she bestowed her kisses, her fingers digging into his shoulders, the unlikely softness of her lips.

Joan, he thinks, as fixedly as he can, in case she can sense it, somehow.

I won't be long here.
Don't leave without me.

Elizabeth of York is crowned at the end of November, on St Catherine's Day.

'Better late than not at all, by the Virgin,' says Beatrice. 'Shrewish, though, his waiting so long.'

Before then, though, Henry made time for a celebration of himself and his victory at Stoke. Apparently the king paraded through London, cheered by joyous civilians—

'They'll cheer anything, I wouldn't take it personally,' says Beatrice.

—before the *Te Deum* was sung in his honor at St Paul's.

'My aunt saw him very close,' Beatrice says. 'She said he had a French look about him. From living there so long.' She pats Lambert's arm, comfortingly. '*You* don't look in the least French.'

The ceremonials for Elizabeth's Coronation take three days, and noise of them rattles constantly through the kitchens.

'A pageant of boats all covered in banners or streamers or what have you, made of silk, rowed by men in livery!'

'A barge with the great red dragon of Cadwaladr on it, that spat fire all down the river!'

'Trumpets and minstrels and divers other musics.'

'They let the Marquess of Dorset out of the Tower for the day. But not the dowager queen Woodville.'

'Not the queen's cousin, the Earl of Warwick, either. He had to stay in the Tower.'

'They scrubbed the shit off the streets, even.'

'Her procession went from the Tower to Westminster.'

'That's a full grievous lot of shit to scrub.'

'Gold on her kirtle, gold trim, gold coif, gold crown. Gold hangings on her litter.'

'Eight white horses to draw it, and everything decorated with suns and white roses.'

'Children dressed as angels singing her along her way.'

'They laid out a bay cloth runner for her to walk on, and the crowds all piled on it behind her, snipping off pieces, and the ladies behind her were shoved about and affrighted, and some of those in the press were squashed or trodden upon, and died.'

'A right shame.'

'Villainous savages, Londoners.'

'And the Queen so beautiful in violet velvet.'

'The Duke and Duchess of Suffolk took part in the ceremonials. You wouldn't have known their son had just died in open rebellion of the crown.'

'That's what those nobles are like. One week they try to kill each other, the next they're all *my dearest well-beloved*.'

'You knew the Earl of Lincoln, Simnel. Was he as wicked a villain as is noised?'

'Simnel?'

For the feast they cook:

pheasants, swans, venison, crane, capons, lampreys, crane, pike, heron, carp, kid goat, perch, mutton, beef, roast peacock re-dressed in its own skin, bitterns, pheasants, egrets, cocks, partridge, sturgeon, plovers, rabbit, a whole seal on a bed of leeks, quails, larks, crayfish—

'It's like Noah's fucking ark,' says a server, sweating into his livery.

Beatrice comes to Simnel, looking wide-eyed.

'I've been asked to give you this,' she says. She looks around to see if anyone is watching, then puts a sealed note in his hand. The seal has no insignia on it.

'It's from a servant. I don't know him, but I know he's in the king's retinue. He was waiting for me in a corridor. They know I'm your friend.'

'You should noise it that we're not friends,' he says. 'Being friends with me is peril to you.'

She looks stubborn, and pats his arm. 'I don't mind.'

He sighs as she leaves.

The note says that certain unnamed Yorkists within the court are purposing to rescue Simnel. He is to wait until a second, blank note is delivered to him. On receipt of this he should bide awake as his fellow servants fall asleep, then meet his rescuers at the back of the kitchens, where no guards are stationed, at two hours past midnight.

No signature.

Feelings shoot through Simnel, each one fast behind another. Exultation, blindingly bright, at the thought of escape. Lovell's doings, Lovell's elegant purposing. In Ireland Simnel was ware of Lovell; now he gives grateful thanks for him. But then: suspicion. What if this *isn't* Lovell? If Henry has sent this note to assay him? Simnel's heard about the king's love of surveillance. Is this a trick? And now: horror. If it *isn't* a trick, and he doesn't meet his rescuers, he turns a spit forever and Joan goes to her wedding unsaved.

He has no idea what to do.

A week passes. He's in dread that any moment he'll be handed a blank note, and called on to act.

Please show me the right path, he prays to God. *Please send a sign to instruct me.*

Then his mood turns over, shows a dark belly.

God?

Are you even watching?

The next day, there is large commotion in the palace, reaching even the kitchens: four of the king's servants have been convicted of treason and are to be hanged at Tower Hill. Simnel is sore grieved to hear it. He didn't know these people, but they were his friends. The nearness of the chance of escape, now lost, is inexpressibly painful.

He's adread that one of the servants will give up Lovell's hiding place, but there are no more arrests, and Simnel feels stupid for his fear. As if Lovell would allow himself to be found so easily.

At the same time, Henry calls a parliament. He has discovered a problem with the existing laws. In that they allow for punishment of treason that has been *done*, but not treason that is only being *thought about*. Henry appoints three officers of the Household to investigate servants, find out any confederacy, compassings, conspiracies or imaginings concerning his own destruction, try them, and convict them.

Nobody in the kitchens knows what the servants did. They all ask Simnel, which alarms him.

'Why do you come to me?' he says. 'I've got nothing to do with it.'

'You're the Earl of Warwick, aren't you?' says a waferer, as if Simnel's stupid.

'No! I'm a pretender and a joiner's boy.'

'My dad was a joiner,' says a pantler. 'What's stronger, split timber or sawn? Explain a mortice and tenon joint.

'See,' says the waferer, when Simnel is silent. 'He's a fucking *earl*.'

'Probably compassing and conspiracing,' says a scullion.

'You villainous lusks,' Beatrice says to them. 'If you don't leave him alone, I'll go to the king and tell him I saw *you* compassing.'

When they're alone she says, 'I called them lusks! I was sore adread. But I'm just so relieved the king didn't hang you. Blessed be the Virgin! I asked her to watch over you, and she did aright.' She places her hands on her heart and sends a tender look skywards. 'Is this business to do with that—' she whispers '—*note*? I won't tell anyone, on my oath.'

Simnel, inquiet, rubs his face. It's slippery. He always has an oily coating these days, from the fire. He looks at Beatrice. He's never considered her as a woman before. She's so short, for one. His view of her face is usually at a steep slant. Her countenance is pleasant. None of that matters. If she looked like Helen of Troy it wouldn't matter. Whatever region of the minds are given over to love, a freezing shadow has fallen over his own.

He hopes she doesn't purpose anything other than friendship. Friendship is danger enough.

'You shouldn't defend me,' he says. 'I mean it. It'll work you wrack.'

'I'll do what I like,' she says.

She's nothing like Joan. But for a second, in her gathered-up fierceness, eyes hot, she reminds him of her. It's a compelling sorcery. He has to nod, and give way, and hope that his curse, which he sees as the mingled mud and blood staining Grania's skirt, covering Lincoln's body – that none of that foulness will get on her.

4

Simnel asks Beatrice if she knows of anyone who could take a letter to Ireland. She shakes her head.

'You were right,' she says. 'I asked around: you *are* under watch. They're ware you might try to quit here in the night or something. There are people in the kitchens earning extra wages to report on you. Hey, you're lucky I'm not one of them. Or that'd be a large mistake, telling me about letters.'

It is a mistake, for different reasons. Beatrice wants to know, now, who he's writing to.

'Is it a woman?' she guesses. He says nothing, looks no way – but she carries on. 'A woman you love? I can tell it is. I'm sorry, Simnel. You look right doleful, my eyes grieve to see it. You must sore miss her. Is she fair, and kind, and honourable?'

Simnel's in between despair and laughter now. He's almost tempted to tell her about Joan.

'I'm not sad,' he says to Beatrice. 'I'm regretful that now you're under watch too, when I warned you—'

Beatrice laughs. 'Oh, they can watch me all day if they like,' she says. 'Tidying rooms, making fires, carrying shitpots. By the Virgin, it'll be good to feel important! I run after the people who run after Henry, and now Henry's after his people to go after me. Round and round we go.' She puts her hand on his arm, and gives it a familiar squeeze. 'You can just tell me if you don't want to talk about your dole,' she says. 'You shouldn't lie that it doesn't exist. Lying puts your soul in danger.'

In her certainty she reminds him of John Collan, and of Lincoln. Both of them were certain; both of them are dead. Beatrice's faith in goodness annoys him.

'You should be more concerned about the danger *you're* in,' he says.

'Yes, yes. You talk about it so much that I'll actually yawn when the soldiers come to haul me off. You know, you'll be making more mourn than me if they do, because you won't know what to do without your beloved peril; when you don't have anyone to shush, and warn every five minutes, that their lives are in danger.'

The court stays at Greenwich for the Christmas festivities. The dowager queen Elizabeth Woodville is a guest, though not a well-beloved one. She and Henry are a queasy pairing of disloyal and distrustful. He's been treating to marry her to James III, King of Scotland, which would both give her due worship and put her many miles away.

The king's mother is also there, as she usually is. You'd think she wanted him back in the womb, said Beatrice. On Twelfth Day, when the king and queen wore their crowns, Margaret Beaufort wore an identical mantle and surcoat to her daughter-in-law, and a crown of her own.

'She won't have the queen ahead of her in worship,' says Anne, one of Beatrice's chambermaid friends. 'At state events she walks only a half-step behind the queen. She'll trip her up one of these days. She sits under her own cloth of estate in church! I never saw anything like it. Even the dowager queen didn't go so far, and she was a terror for inventing ceremony for herself. I remember when I first came to court as a girl, she made her own mother kneel for four hours while she ate her dinner.'

'King Henry's the same as his mother,' says Beatrice. 'He has the peers of the realm serve him his meals, not the household officers. And he can't walk anywhere without his little canopy.'

'For a miserly man, he spends large money on jewels and plate and clothes. Rebuilding all the palaces. Of course, we got no rise in pay.'

'It's the people with the least claim who spend the most,' Beatrice says. 'All these overdoings… He knows he's a nobody, just like the dowager queen was.'

'No blood, no substance,' agrees Anne.

'No king at all.'

'You mustn't talk like that,' Simnel says to Beatrice. 'I know you do it to be kind to me. But how well do you know Anne? What if she's watching me, and trying to lead us into treason?'

Beatrice looks confused. 'What? Oh! You've never been a servant. We've always talked like that. We talked like that about King Edward, we talked like that about King Richard, and now we talk like that about King Henry. If he makes a law against unflattering talk, he'll have no servants left.'

She pats his arm, then looks merry.

'How well do I know Anne?! By the Virgin! You're as suspicious as King Henry himself.'

King Henry himself sends for Simnel a few weeks later, early in the morning. Simnel walks with a guard down a series of cold corridors and halls, wondering if this is his ending day. Out of the windows the grass stretching down to the river is silver with frost; a white haze hangs over the water. It's not such an ill day to quit the earth. And the earth has come to feel like such a weight, with no more notes from wellwishers, his hope of escape and vengeance burning dimmer and dimmer as each day passes, with each turn of the spit.

Easier to...

... let go.

He only hopes Beatrice isn't under any suspicion.

He's brought into a more modest chamber than he was expecting. He can't be in Henry's rooms – though Henry is here, sitting behind a desk, and his chancellor Bishop Morton standing beside it. Simnel bows. It is indicated that he is to sit down with them.

A strange way to start his dying.

He takes the opportunity to inspect Henry. The king is dressed all in black. Up close he has the dull yellow skin of a melancholic. He isn't ugly, but no warmth or mirth rise from him, and the effect is flattening. His gaze on Simnel from his good eye is perfectly flat. But the left eye, looking sidewise as it does, seems whimsical, playful, almost conniving against its master. Maybe it's the result of not letting merriment have its way: it hides in one body part, and plots the overthrow of the whole.

'Treason among my servants,' Henry says. 'And treason lateward at Calais, with great ordnance needed to put it down. I thought the conspiracies would end with Stoke. But they continue. As do… you.'

'What we ask ourselves is: are the two things related?' Morton says.

'I have no witting of any of it,' Simnel says. 'I work in the kitchen all day. At night I sleep. I speak to nobody.'

'We know,' says Henry. 'We had a cook watching you. As you say, you're not in any position to engage in privy conversings. And we've been thinking on this. Would you like a better job, Simnel? One in which you can speak to nobles. And if any speak to you of treason, then you hie to Bishop Morton, and tell him what they said.'

'You want me to lure traitors?' Simnel says.

'This is how you address your sovereign king?' Morton says.

'My apologies, your grace,' Simnel says. 'But why me? You have spies already.'

'I am not all seeing, not all knowing,' Henry says. He looks irritated to be reminded of it. 'I know that there are men who are not loyal to me. The death of Lincoln caused me much dole. I wanted him to tell me who they were.'

'Who killed him?' Simnel asks.

'Who was it?' Henry asks Morton.

'A knight, Sir Hugh Cross.'

'Ah, yes. A goodly man. The treacherous Lincoln shammed illness, and then essayed to puncture him with a hidden knife.'

'A great disworship.'

'Like all traitors, Lincoln abandoned his gentilesse when he turned against his king,' Morton says. 'As Boethius says, he descended to the level of the animal. In this case, a mad lion.'

Simnel feels his own animal wroth rising in him. He tries to master it.

'Now we wonder what *you* are made of,' Morton says. 'Were you compelled by traitors, or is your own heart traitorous? If you are truly repentant of your earlier sins, you'll be eager to help eradicate the evil that has secret hold in this court.'

'But what, my lord, would you have me do?' Simnel asks.

'Nothing. At first. The villains will seek you out. You merely allow them to give themselves away. To unbridle their wanton tongues, which, without stricture, become loose and slippery, and in their wetness slide into an excess of words. And in this flood the evil-disposed will be drowned, and delivered to our justice.'

'A flood of... saliva, my lord?'

'A flood of God's creation, from which his grace the king, like Noah before him, will be preserved to fulfil his exalted destiny.'

'Uh. Amen,' says Simnel.

All this while Henry's flat right eye has been hard-trained on Simnel. 'He looks much older than the true Earl of Warwick,' he observes.

'I believe he is older than the earl,' Morton says. 'But then long confinement does have a pinching effect.' He squeezes his fingers together. 'Whereas this one has been running free.'

'Overfree,' Henry says.

'We purpose to make you a falconer,' Morton says. 'It's easy for nobles to speak with you privily when you take them their birds, and you'll have divers places out of doors in which to let them pour out their evil designs.'

Simnel's hunted with birds, as Edward, but he doesn't know how to care for them. Their little heads and large intent eyes inquiet him, even. It's the same with cats. The only reason they are agreeable is because he's too big to eat.

He thinks about the people he knows; divides them into predator and prey.

Kildare, Lovell, Margaret, Henry: predators.

Maister Richard, Bella, Beatrice, Lincoln: prey.

Jennott, Grania, Joan: both.

What is Simnel? Prey, before today.

Now they want to turn him into something sib to a falcon: a predator, owned by a bigger creature.

'I don't know anything about falconry,' he says.

'You'll be taught,' says Morton.

Betraying Yorkists. Is this what he's going to do? Turn friends over to enemies? But then he thinks of Sir Hugh Cross, and the high-up Yorkist whom Cross is serving. Simnel had purposed to get revenge on them by telling Lovell what they did. But Lovell might have had to flee. Lovell could be dead. And Simnel can't wait for him. He could send Cross to the chopblock himself – and then, during the frenzy of a hunt, he could slip like a roe deer into the trees, and never be seen in England again.

There are some heads here in need of a trim, Joan says.

He tries not to smile.

'I will be honoured to serve you,' he says. 'May I ask, humbly, for a small meed?'

'Look at him humbly dictating terms,' Morton says. 'Do you recall you *lost* the battle for the throne?'

'What is it?' Henry asks. 'Not pay. You are still in our debt for the cost of the men and arms we sent to Stoke.'

'I would beg his grace for a small allowance of paper and quills, and for books to read.'

'The *loan* of books,' says Henry. 'I will grant it.'

5

The court moves to Windsor for Easter. The palace is a great grey stone fortress, with a quadrangle for tourneys and a magnificent Gothic hall. It was last extended by Edward IV. Henry is planning more additions.

'He could knock London down and rebuild it and the people would still be nostalgic for King Edward,' says Beatrice. Her own mother, who was a cradle rocker back then, said Edward was the merriest, most beautiful man on God's earth; she was full enchanted when he squeezed her breast through her kirtle and ruled it the fairest breast of the day.

'What do the nobles think of Henry?' Simnel asks. 'What do they say in their bedrooms about him.'

'Not much, or they'd be put right off their swiving,' Beatrice says, and laughs for some time. 'That was a good jape, wasn't it? In seriousness, they say the same things we servants do. That he's strange, awkward and suspicious. A mean cleric in a king-costume. And tight as a frog's slot, if you'll excuse the large language.'

Simnel, new falconer, spends most of his time outside, watching spring come over the land. It reminds him of his childhood. Daffodils and crocuses; newly unrolled leaves. The high cries of lambs and fledglings. Bees purring over dandelions. The air is still sharp, his birds cut through it like knives. He's surprised how willingly they come back to the glove and the hood. Though now and then, one doesn't come back.

He wears a livery, which he mislikes.

But he isn't greasy. A good thing.

The head falconer, a man named Hobday, understands that Simnel is to be allowed to do mostly as he likes, as he's in the King's service. He doesn't know that Simnel is spying. He's been told that Simnel is for display only. Not functional.

The other falconers don't like him. Nothing strange about that. He's either a peasant or an earl (low blood or evil blood) and neither one should be taking honest men's falconry work. He could explain to them that he's not actually doing any work, but he senses this will win him no more love.

One of the falconers Simnel hates. Thomas Dauke.

Simnel's seen him striking the horses, which are afraid of him, and when they discovered a hatchling with a malformed foot, and Simnel said he'd take it and care for it, Dauke said, this isn't a shitting lazar-house, and flattened the bird under his boot.

Simnel has the pleasure, in his new position, of regularly seeing Henry proceed to his horse, swathed in furs, with eight footmen and eight knights attending him. He walks by Simnel with his right eye staring forward. Only the left eye acknowledges him.

I call for blackest mischief, says the eye.

Simnel swears to it: *I'll do what I can.*

He gets his pen and papers, but he can't write. The day of the battle, his words failed him.

No, that's not true.

They failed him many times before.

Not true.

Every time.

He'd try to express something, and it would slide off sidewise, or turn on him like an injured animal, snapping. Epic, ode, fable, *lai*, romance, *fabliau*: the shapes were wrong. He couldn't fit the thing he was trying to say into the vessel that was supposed to contain it.

He can't even fit *himself* into a vessel.

What is he: a peasant, an earl, a bastard? No one to answer him – and he wouldn't believe them if they did. He always wanted to write something true, but how can anything good flow from the quill of such an unknowable, untrue creature?

The first person who wants to speak to Simnel is Rodrigo de la Puebla, the Spanish Ambassador. He's been sent by King Ferdinand and Queen Isabella to check the baby Prince Arthur's beauty and gentilesse and report if he's a meet match for their daughter, the Infanta Katherine of Aragon.

Henry doesn't want de la Puebla and Simnel to talk. But his need for a Spanish alliance – confirmation of his right to rule – is desperate, and when de la Puebla says that Ferdinand and Isabella were already nervous of sending their daughter to a country in which kings have a shorter lifespan than robins, and lateward they are further inquieted by the thought of a Yorkist pretender being sheltered at court, and would like to be assured that, like a lion in the Tower, Simnel's claws have been filed down and his warly nature beaten out—

—well.

Henry resents him. But he can't refuse him.

De la Puebla, in truth, doesn't give a shit about the peril posed by Simnel. He's just curious. He's also full of grucches and plaints, and noises them freely.

'Why are there no courtesans here?' he asks. 'I'd heard that English women are renowned for their lechery. I thought it would be another Italy. But this is nothing like. It's just stews and dismal tavern whores – and after coupling with one of them my pintle was much distroubled with burning, even though I dipped it in vinegar after.'

'I don't have any advice,' Simnel says. 'I've never had ado with a woman.'

'Isn't that absurd!' de la Puebla says. 'Here I am, free and of means but marvellous ugly – ' (this is true) ' – and here you are with a face like a painting, and no way to exercise your wiles. God must be as fond of japes as humans are.'

He pours them more wine. They're in de la Puebla's own private chamber. Simnel's usual state of maugre and low dole is lightened somewhat by the fire, the taste of the wine, the silver bowl of candied figs, the cushioned chair under his arse. At some point between Mechelen and Ireland, he apparently got used to those things.

After the second cup of wine de la Puebla becomes romantic.

'I have never seen any woman so beautiful as the queen,' he says, sighing. 'It is a great pity how she is kept down by Henry. He is not her equal in gentilesse.'

After the third cup he is confiding:

'This is not so goodly as the wines of Burgundy, is it? No. Henry is remaking his palaces in the style of Mechelen, but he's never been there. And it shows. It is not so beautiful, the food not so savoury. And his banquets! Ah, me. Sixty courses of silence. There is no joy here.'

A memory of Margaret and Philip darts into Simnel's heart, making a little wound. De la Puebla doesn't notice, and continues, 'And the smell! You can't call yourself equal to the great courts of Europe when your most worshipful nobles are pissing into the fireplaces like stray dogs.'

'The kitchen servants do the same,' Simnel says.

'Abominable,' cries de la Puebla. He sighs. 'Nobody here gives me right worship. Ferdinand and Isabella accuse me of taking Henry's part in negotiations. Henry accuses me of guile, and threatens to house me in some loathly lodgings outside the palace. The English lords despise foreigners. They have never seen the splendour of Europe, and fancy everyone envies them. They think themselves superior to me. Me! Who never fouled in a chimney in his life!'

After his fourth cup de la Puebla slides into sleep, his grimly face fallen into a smile at last, and Simnel puts the rest of the candied figs into his sleeve, and shows himself out.

One of Morton's men brings him a book. Simnel is interested to see what they've chosen for him, until he realises it's obviously just the most worn and dirty volume in the library. He can barely make out the title.

The Consolation of Philosophy.

Ha.

'So you've found me at last,' he says to it.

'Are you talking to a book?' says Dauke, passing by. 'You daffish turd.'

Simnel watches Dauke's back, hieing itself away. Dauke never stays around for long after delivering an insult. He doesn't know he's in no peril. Simnel has privily kept up his sword practice with a piece of wood, and yearns to poke Dauke with the sharp end – but Henry wouldn't like him to be making affray, and he can't risk his position.

He sits down with the *Consolation* instead, on the steps outside his quarters. He wonders if any great personages have turned these finger-spotted pages over before him. He wonders if they were consoled.

Maybe if they were great personages, they would be. Lady Philosophy isn't interested in any other types of people. Her advice to Boethius is to be grateful for his achievements, his family and his fame. She explains that God bestows every fortune to reward or test good men, or to punish or correct evil men – and so every fortune is just and useful. As for whether the suffering on earth might seem, at times, a little *overmuch* – well, it is not right for a man to understand the workings of God.

Simnel wonders how Lady Philosophy would console a village girl who had been raped and murdered by a soldier. The girl has not been rewarded or tested. She's dead. So, is this about the soldier? If he repents afterwards, has her life ended purely in the service of his improvement? And what if he doesn't repent, and lives out a long and evil life? Why did the girl have to die?

No answer.

Of course not: Lady Philosophy doesn't answer the calls of illiterate dead village girls.

Maybe Lady Philosophy would come to Simnel if he were wearing his Edward clothes. The gold buttons might lure her in. And then – when she got close enough – he'd get hold of her, and ask if Grania died so that Simnel, or Joan, or fucking *Kildare* could learn something. And if she said yes, he'd push her into the nearest midden heap, goddess or no.

And God would be welcome to strike Simnel down for it. If He was watching.

If He gave a fuck.

6

In April, the Garter ceremonies are held. The king makes his mother a Lady of the Garter, and she and the queen, both wearing red gowns trimmed with white squirrel bellies and banded with gold, process through Windsor's grounds in a chariot covered with cloth of gold and drawn by six gold-harnessed horses.

The Burgundian Ambassador is one of the foreign nobles invited to the great feast. He requests an audience with Simnel, and is granted it. And so they have a miserable interview in which the ambassador, a gentil man, asks things such as, 'Are you well? Are they treating you respectably?'

And Simnel says, 'Yes, I am well, I want for nothing.'

(Almost able to feel the inevitable listener on the other side of the door; a pulsing, breathing body flattened against the wood.)

The ambassador says, 'Your aunt—'

'I pray you. She's not my aunt. I am a commoner, and I repent my treasonous doings.'

The ambassador bows his head.

'As you like. The Dowager Duchess of Burgundy and Philip, Lord of the Netherlands and Duke of Burgundy, send word that they think of you, and keep you in their prayers.'

A brightness leaves the room after the ambassador is gone; nothing physical, but a feeling, like the last of the sunset light withdrawing from a castle roof.

Simnel's starting to think that Henry is wrong and the court has run dry of compassings and conspiring, when a pale blonde noblewoman named Lady Catherine FitzAlan clutches his hand after he's brought her a falcon, and whispers, 'You are blessed in the eyes of God, your grace, and we are grateful for what you tried to do.'

He bows, astonied.

'It is I who should kneel,' she says. 'Know that there are many loyal subjects working for your freedom. But hush – the others are upon us.'

She rides away in the throng.

Simnel was waiting for Sir Hugh Cross, or his master. He didn't expect to be hand-pressed by a small-boned lady with a tremble in her voice. He mislikes the thought of handing her in to Henry to be interrogated, maybe hung. Much mislikes it.

But what if she's been sent by Henry, to test his loyalty? What if Simnel's the dupe of a skilled voice-trembler, and if he doesn't give her up, she'll give him up, and then he'll be hung or sent back to the kitchen and his chances of rescuing Joan will expire at the end of the rope, or melt, over the long years, into a puddle of fat.

So be it. He's not going to tell Henry.

Are you japing with me? Joan says. *Throw her to the fucking wolves.*

Joan is getting impatient, and he can't blame her.

I won't, he says. *It's strategy. But if we watch and wait, more puissant people may reveal themselves. If I snatch at the tail of the rabbit now it'll disappear into its burrow.*

Argue what you want, Joan replies. *The truth is, you're a wretched white-livered milksop.*

His sharp-beaked love; she doesn't spare him.

Each day after Lady FitzAlan pressed his hand is a stone laid on Simnel, an increasingly unbearable pressure. But by the time Whitsunday comes around – and Edward still unhanged – his dread leaves him.

The dowager queen, Elizabeth Woodville, is at court for the festival. Simnel sees her once, passing by with her attendant ladies. She has a face where beauty once lived, and now wroth is there instead.

He understands.

Beatrice wants to know what it was like living on a farm. Sharing a room with only a few other people. Walking to the local tavern for a beer and everybody there is your friend. Sowing carrots in the cold earth. Picking a strawberry from the tree—

'They grow on the ground, Beatrice.'

(Picking a strawberry and sitting in the sunlight and eating it: your own strawberry.)

'The farm was a long time ago, I can hardly remember it,' Simnel says. 'But, yes. It was good. Those were good years.'

He can see her watching him tenderly. He knows what she's thinking. God knows she tells him often enough. She thinks he's shut his dole up inside himself and it's not healthy: the black bile might build up inside him, brast his chest open, patter everywhere like a rain of ink. She prays to the Virgin often on this matter. She seems to believe that everything will be better if Simnel would only lay his head on her small yet capable shoulder, and weep.

But he's not tempted by the shoulder. His eyes have been dry since they led him out of his cell. One day maybe the tears will come back. Probably. Nobody dries up permanently, surely. And Simnel doesn't need tears right now anyway. He's got to fix his minds on his purposes.

'I want to live on a farm,' she says. 'My *own* farm – I mean, it'll be owned by the local lord aright, but at least that's only one lord over me, and not hundreds, like here.'

'Court is like a beehive,' Simnel says. 'Everyone stacked on top of each other.'

'That's exactly it!' Beatrice exclaims. 'You're so clever at meta-phor-making. That's what I am. A bee.' She makes a little buzz.

Simnel inclines his head, though he thinks that bees wouldn't call their rulers wind-eggs, or drasty shrews, or try to make their eyes go into different directions and – not having Jennott's skill in such matters – fail, and give themselves a headache, then say the headache was worth it, to make him, Simnel, smile.

The court spends the summer of 1488 at Woodstock Palace. Henry has spent large money upgrading the house, painting its gatehouses with red roses and rougedragons, and creating an interconnected drawing chamber between his and his mother's rooms. The parkland around the palace is verdant and full of game, and Simnel is busy serving nobles who want to hunt deer, roebuck, hare. Every day horns announce the kills.

It is under cover of the horns that a gentleman called Hextall says to Simnel, 'You have friends still, my lord.'

Simnel bows, but he says, 'If you haven't been sent by Henry, you will be able to name the friend who sent you.'

'Sir Hugh Cross,' Hextall says. 'Your most devoted supporter, and my great friend. But you may not know his name?'

Simnel smiles. He says, 'I know his name. I knew his worth at Stoke, when he acted to prevent the Earl of Lincoln from ruining us all.'

'God praise his quick demeaning,' says Hextall. 'And you can be sure that he was handsomely rewarded for it.'

By his master on high, the double friend of Henry's, thinks Simnel, and – made momentarily stupid by wroth – almost takes Hextall by the shoulders and demands *who*, before he realises he's already supposed to know.

He puts his smile back on.

'It's wonderly good to know that our most puissant friend has been protected,' he says, hoping that Hextall will name him.

'Yes,' says Hextall, smiling.

There is a short silence.

'Will Cross come to court anon?' Simnel asks.

'Sadly not soon, my lord. He tries to stay away. For obvious reasons. But I will attend the Christmas celebrations at Sheen, and should have further word for you then.'

'I thank you,' Simnel says. 'It is through your courage that we will triumph.'

'Amen,' says Hextall.

'Hextall is a traitor,' Simnel says to Morton.

He'd deliberated over this. The death of a man. Deaths have happened in his name – or his old name: Edward, Earl of Warwick. But this will be the first death he's planned himself. The first killing. This is a dark river to cross.

But he thought of Hextall saying: *God praise his quick demeaning.*

God praise Cross's quickness, at pretending to be Lincoln's friend, and stabbing him.

Wicked heads don't deserve bodies, says Joan.

If Simnel goes to hell for this, so be it. He'll meet Hextall there – and do him another evil turn if he can.

He's also considered strategy. It occurred to him that he could keep silent, let Hextall help him escape court, then escape Hextall. Or even bide with the rebels – let them kill Henry and make him, Simnel, into King Edward again. Whereupon King Edward would kill Hextall, Cross and Cross's unknown master. Then do as Lovell said, and bring Joan and her husband to court.

Joan didn't like that plan.

No husbands, she said.

Anyway, Simnel doesn't have faith in the Yorkists to succeed, or to not betray him. If he puts himself into the hands of known villains such as Cross, and they get caught, Simnel would without doubt be given up. Interrogated. Tortured. Hanged. Joan lost. Et cetera.

Better to earn Morton's trust this way, then escape himself. He doesn't trust any hands now, except his own.

'Glad tidings!' Morton says. 'I had begun to doubt your intentions. By Saint Leonard, this is timely, lad, full timely. It was my idea to have you become a spy. I was in peril of looking as stupid as you if you failed. Now, Hextall will be working for others. Do you have any witting of them?'

'Not yet,' Simnel says.

(Simnel wants to speak to Sir Hugh Cross himself, and then his master.)

'Keep talking with him,' Morton says.

'I will, and will listen as his tongue floats him away on a flood of sinful jangling,' Simnel says. Morton lofts his eyebrows approvingly.

'Very good,' he says, and Simnel goes back to his quarters with a fresh stack of paper, and Chaucer's *Parliament of Fowls*.

That year the famous Wool Earl of Ormond, Sir Thomas Butler, joins Henry's privy council. He's one of the richest men in Ireland – despite, as Kildare used to say, not considering the country worth dropping a turd on, and spending most of his fucking time in England.

One of Ormond's men, a Palesman named Patrick Madan, used to be in Kildare's father's service. Madan comes to find Simnel in the early autumn. Not to plot. He's only eighteen; merry; he says he wants them to blaver of Ireland like a pair of jangling wives at Mass. He's brought a flask of beer.

What Simnel wants is news of Joan, but Madan doesn't know her, or her sisters. He has tidings of Kildare.

Simnel's not heard about Kildare's pardon? By Jesus, this'll make him sore mirthful.

In June King Henry sent Sir Richard Edgecumbe to go about Ireland getting the nobles to swear oaths of loyalty, in exchange for formal pardons. But Kildare kept him waiting for nine days, on pretence of being away on a pilgrimage, and then for several days more, while he gathered the chief lords of the Pale for their agreement, then two days more, while the lords prevaricated. And then once they had agreed to be loyal to King Henry, and to never betray him, Edgecumbe presented them with the Bond of Nisi, meaning that they had to forfeit their estates if they were *not* faithful to the king. And this they wouldn't do. Rather than agree to it, they said they'd become Irish every one of them.

By which they meant, they'd join with the Gaelic lords, and Kildare would rule Ireland as its high king.

Which wouldn't be much change there.

And also at that moment word came that King Henry's ally James III, King of Scots was overthrown by his son, and had mishaply died in the process, which left Edgecumbe in a wonderly bad position, because it was obvious Henry would soon be sore pressed dealing with a new Scots king with no love for him.

And so the Bond of Nisi was abandoned, and Kildare and all the lords swore ceremonially upon the Holy Sacrament to be King Henry's true liegemen.

But not to lose their lands, if they weren't.

But here Madan stops himself – he's realised how stupid he was, because he noticed Simnel wasn't laughing in the right places, and that his brow was low, and it's only now Madan's realised what's troubling him, honestly, he's a terrible doddypoll, you should ask his mother, she'll tell Simnel what a gift Madan has for blavering and not thinking, and he's done it again, going on and on while Simnel must have been naturally adread to know what has happened to his other friends in Ireland!

Blessed be God, they're all still safe and well.

And all pardoned, save Keating, whose villainy was considered to go right to his bones. But the Chief Justice Thomas Plunket – a friend of Simnel's, Madan knows – was forgiven. Madan can see Simnel is relieved to hear it. By the Virgin! Sure, it's a savoury thing to bring good news. He hopes it's a comfort.

Madan left Simnel another bottle of beer. He said he wouldn't be drinking it. Rosy with the effort of trying not to seem pitying of Simnel's reduced condition.

The next day Simnel finds some writing in his bed. It's his own. A drunken, muddled debate poem in which a goose and a peacock argue over the nature of happiness. The goose thinks happiness is to be found in farmwork, repentance, humility. The peacock thinks happiness lies in power and money, which can, if lost, be won again. A cuckoo appears next, and says it thinks it might be happy, if only it knew what it was: peacock, goose, or some other bird.

Not exactly *The Parliament of Fowls*. Also: dangerous to keep. Simnel puts it in the fire. Wondering if one day he might find Lovell again, and ask him for the truth. Earl, peasant, bastard. Lovell must know which he is; Bishop Stillington would have told him.

Lovell's a practical man, as Joan once said, unmoved by love and pity. If he doesn't find it useful to tell Simnel, he won't. But maybe if Simnel explains that he won't be joining any further rebellions until Lovell tells him the truth – maybe then Simnel will find out exactly what he is.

7

The court resorts to Westminster for the autumn.

Westminster! Rich in history.

Situation chosen by Canute the Great.

Great hall built by William II.

Oak hammer beam roof added by Richard II

The whole rebuilt in the Gothic style by Henry III – who wanted a private chapel even more beautiful than the Sainte Chapelle de Paris, and so he gave it a hundred-foot-high ceiling of cerulean blue, covered with gold stars, and walls painted with kings and angels, in the colours of jewels.

(So says Beatrice, who got lost and ended up in there one day, before being chased out by a cleric.)

Simnel meets Henry and Morton at dawn again. The same grey light, the same small, empty chamber. He remembers sitting beside Margaret on her balcony, Kildare in his deafening great hall. The plotters in the open, while the plotted-against sits in a cupboard and shrinks from the touch of an eye.

Henry has fallen to strife with the French over the matter of Breton independence. Some very cutting poetry has been written on both sides and now war is inevitable.

Morton says to Simnel, 'I saw you talking to a young demosel yesterday. Did she speak of harm against the king's person?'

(The fair maiden had whispered to Simnel, I dreamed last night of you in my bed and though I was frightened of your male part I did not hesitate to give it shelter.)

'She didn't,' Simnel says, waxing red. 'But you know she's of a Lancastrian line. Why would she—'

'It's not just Yorkists who might work us wrack,' says Morton. 'It could be anyone. People are poorer. James III, our ally, is gone. The mood is queasy. The cruel eyes of nobles, like crows, are always circling, hoping to seize on a weaker creature.'

Henry has been silently watching Simnel – with the intention, Simnel guesses, of setting dread in his heart. But Simnel's heart is already full of maugre and despite. No room at the inn. How thin Henry's fingers are, Simnel thinks. Birds could make nests out of them.

Henry gives up the silence now, with a look of annoyance. He says, 'A weaker creature?'

'Not that the king is a weaker creature!' Morton cries. 'Anyone who says so, by Saint George, I'll have *their* eyes plucked out of their head.'

He stares at Simnel warningly.

Simnel wonders now if Morton could be the high-up Yorkist in Henry's employ. But he's too zealous. Sometimes his eyes fill with sympathetic tears when he talks about Henry's travail, his endless troubles. They threaten to now, as he continues talking, insisting that the taxes Henry's levied to pay for his war have annoyed no man; that last year's harvest may have been meagre, but Henry has a great stock of love.

Simnel is close to enjoying himself. He thinks if he were Henry he'd pray that Morton *was* a secret Yorkist, about to run off to Burgundy. He'd work Henry less wrack there than he does now, sticking loyally at his side.

Henry places his hands on the table, impatiently, and Morton stops his jangling.

'I want you to find out where Lovell is,' Henry says. 'He is still in England. Do you have any witting of who might shelter him? By God, the man creeps like an earwig.'

'I don't know where he is. Probably sheltering in some small room, keeping his face from the window,' Simnel says, and watches Henry's lips pinch. He adds, 'I have a question, if I may?'

Henry inclines his head.

'How many people know that I am spying for you?'

'Only the three of us,' says Morton.

'Then you should keep it that way. You don't want the Yorkists to find out that I'm double. As we don't know who the Yorkists are.'

Morton says, 'By the Saints, look at the little pretender now, telling us our business!' and Henry says nothing – which Simnel understood to mean: point taken.

At Christmas the caravan of the court bumps and tilts its way to Sheen Palace. Henry confiscated it from the dowager queen: he was passing taken with the timber-framed manor, the wide moat, the great donjon tower built of Caen stone, the privy lodgings with views of the Thames, the lions and antelopes and swans and harts cavorting in the ceiling mouldings.

Henry plans to modernise it.

Sheen is where Hextall finds Simnel again. He's back from a boar hunt and smells of sweat and earth. They stand behind a holly tree and Hextall says, 'How close are you to the cooks who prepare Henry's meals?'

'Why?'

'We were wondering if you might get something into his food.'

(Thus confirming Simnel's decision not to escape with Hextall and Cross and then kill the pair of them. They'd never have reached the escape stage.)

'Me? What about our ally, Henry's friend?' Simnel asks. 'He'll get closer to the king than I can.'

'I'd have to ask Cross about that,' Hextall says. 'You know how it is. I know that great men are for us, but I don't know their names.' He hesitates. 'They know *me*, of course. I am invaluable to them. I met Lovell once, and he told me I was a goodly fellow.'

'I recognised your worth immediately,' Simnel says. 'And Lovell is safe, I pray. Where is he now?'

Not that Simnel's going to tell Henry. This is for his own purposes. But Hextall has no idea. He really is a woodenpate. Nothing but a collection of arms and legs and body and head, in just-good-enough working order to be propelled around by his masters.

Like Edward was.

There's a crashing of branches and the falconer Dauke, horse-whipper and bird-treader, breaks into their conversation.

'You're in my pissing spot,' he says to Simnel, then sees Hextall, and bows. 'Beg forgiveness, my lord.'

Later that night Dauke kicks Simnel's pallet and murmurs, 'Mouth-work for the gentilhommes, is it? Don't worry, I'll keep your secret.'

'What secret?' says the man next to him.

'Simnel's been licking pintles,' Dauke says. 'That's how he can sit on his arse all day. He's saving it for his noble masters.'

'Hextall doesn't know who he's working for,' Simnel says to Morton. 'He said it was a puissant noble but whoever it is, he's ware and wily. He sends notes to Hextall using unwitting servants and laundresses and so on.'

'This grieves my ears to hear,' Morton says. 'We'll have to pick Hextall off the bough now, before he is ripe.'

'Also, a falconer named Dauke heard part of our talk,' Simnel says. 'He knows Hextall is plotting treason, and me too. He'll jangle it widewhere.'

'Devil take this Dauke churl! We'll need to be rid of him too.'

'I had an idea regarding that.' (Joan's idea: but no way to explain that.) 'If you kill Dauke secretly, but say he retired, and at the same time let it be known that Dauke was the one who brought Hextall's treachery to your notice, this will lead minds away from any suspicion that it could have been me.'

Morton looks at him contemplatively then, tapping his front teeth with the nail of one finger.

'Sharp-witted, aren't you?' he says, and smiles. 'And holding no lingering love for your former masters. All to the good.'

'I'm glad to be free of them, my lord,' Simnel says. 'I brought your Chaucer back.'

Morton gestures at the bookcases.

'Take what you want.'

In March the marriage between the Infanta Katherine of Aragon and Prince Arthur is agreed. The gentleman Edward Hextall of Dover confesses to charges of treason, and is executed. The falconer Dauke leaves court for a new position, below ground.

Edward goes to the mews, where the birds sit quietly, wearing their little leather hoods. They shift on their perches, sensing his entry. Their blindness reminds him of Confession, a place he hasn't been for a long time.

'Maybe I should confess to you,' he says to them. 'This season your young are safe from harm at falconers' hands. You could say the doing was dark, but if I saved something good, what do you say then? Hey? Aren't you going to debate it?'

But his own amusement has faded, stretched too far.

He bows to the birds, and leaves.

Dear Lord God, I killed two men.

    Because of me, because I wanted it to happen, two men are dead.

    I might kill more.

    I'm thinking heretical thoughts.

    Do you hear them?

    I'm not going to praise you, as Boethius did. And I don't believe you planned all the cruelty on earth.

    I don't believe you have a plan at all.

Simnel reads some satires he borrowed from Morton; considers trying to write one himself. Maybe here he could loose his wroth and pain.

But he can't bear to join the company of satirists. Catullus, Martial, Horace, Gower, Langland. They all write the same things. Kings are surrounded by bad advisers. Priests are corrupt. People give you large worship when you're rich and abandon you when you're poor. People like to wear ostentatious clothes. The newly rich fail to accurately replicate the manners of the nobility. The long-rich are misers. Adulterers lie. Drunks drink. People are self-interested, gluttonous, faithless, vain, cruel.

As Joan said once, it's just all so fucking *obvious*.

And who is Simnel to write satire, anyway? Satire is written by the noble, in service of the social order. It attacks the people who transgress the roles ordained by God. Women acting like men, men acting like women, nobles acting like slaves, slaves acting like nobles.

Simnel can't join in with the moral outrage. He's exactly the thing they're complaining about.

A noblewoman, young and newly married, comes to Simnel while the court's at Windsor to ask some questions about her peregrine falcon Athena, who she thinks might be a little crazed in her wits, because Athena has been lateward making large noise at Mass, and embarrassing her mistress – and then she makes her lady attendants leave them, and draws Simnel to a secluded place, with him saying, 'Please don't speak to me of treason,' and she saying, 'Treason?'

Then she kisses him.

'Oh, thank God,' he says (into her neck: he doesn't want to alarm her by saying *God* too loudly, at a time like this).

She takes off her gloves, unlaces his hose and lets his penis out into the April sunshine. She marvels at its quickness. She helps his own hand find a way through her great weight of skirts and onto her quoniam – and he wishes the skin on his fingertips hadn't hardened, so that he could feel completely the silkiness and tenderness of that place. Then she explains that she can't be seen with tree or ground stains on her clothing, and would he mind picking her up and cleping her while holding up her skirts, free-standing, thrusting with large vigour but not too much vigour, as that could overbalance them?

He assures her that he absolutely can. And for almost two minutes he does right well.

Afterwards, she isn't annoyed.

She says, 'Was that your first? I had no witting! That explains it. Here, give me your hand again. Look, this is what you can do for a lady if you go off too soon. See? And you move the fingers like… this. Yes, exactly, don't stop that, yes.'

Every day that week he hopes she might come back.

He would have thought, before it happened, that it – swiving – might have reminded him of Joan. But it's the only time he can remember *not* thinking about her.

Though now he's adread that he's broken something between them, some contract they never spoke, because never had to, and now he's betrayed it.

And yet he still

doesn't want to, but still wants—

—wishes that lady might come back.

Unexpectedly, it's the lady of the trembling voice he encounters next. Lady FitzAlan. He hadn't seen her since she pressed his hand and swore loyalty to her kingly idea of him. Now she comes to hunt with a few other ladies, and afterwards she wants to talk.

It occurs to him that she also might be looking for something in the line of amor, and not treason at all: she's so nervy, turning red then white – but no, it's a coup that's in her minds. She tells him that there will be trouble in the North, that certain men her husband knows are planning insurrection. They plan to put Simnel on the throne. She doesn't know any more details because her husband, Sir John FitzAlan, says it's not meet for her to know.

She speaks of her husband as a great and devout man and gives many examples of his greatness and devoutness, and in every example he sounds like a cunt.

The man goes before the woman, is one of his sayings. Guides her weaker brain, and rules her with right wisdom.

'He's very holy,' she says.

'Hmm,' Simnel says.

Kill him, says Joan.

But what about Lady FitzAlan? She trusts him and she looks timid but yearning, and something about her reminds him of Lincoln, so he won't be feeding her to any wolves, so stop asking.

Fine, Joan says. *Listen. This is a woman in want of love. If you do her reverence, and listen to her, she'll tell you all her shitsack husband's doings, and you can hand him to Henry. She'll be in no peril. Wives don't get hanged for their husband's treasons.*

So he puts on an earnest countenance, and tells Lady FitzAlan, 'I also see holiness in you.'

'Oh!' she says. 'No. I do the best I can to seek God's grace. I take much joy in pilgrimage. I have a collection of over one hundred badges from shrines. Here is one I wear always: St Michael trampling on the devil. They have healed my bodily sicknesses many a time, their magic powers are very strong. One saved me from a bridge collapse last year.'

He looks into her eyes steadily. He lets the moment draw out. Then he says:

'It was God who saved you, my lady. He knew you were a woman of passing worth, meet to carry out His will.'

Her eyes widen. Her cheeks turn red.

'... Oh!' she says. 'I... I have no speech.'

After she's gone, he looks at the sky. It's blue and calm. No trace of God's wroth, or His approval, or anything at all.

Beatrice approves. She's heard he's been talking with Lady FitzAlan. And before Simnel gets all affrighted, no, nobody else knows; Beatrice is friends with Lady FitzAlan's chambermaid, that's all. And Lady FitzAlan is such a goodly woman, so devout, always reading this book by Margery Kempe, another holy woman. Beatrice approves of women showing love to other women. She says, with a familiar gesture – hands clenched on her heart, gaze to sky – this is the rule of the Blessed Mary: her sacred law. (Simnel once began to say, he didn't think that was canonical, but Beatrice's eyes commenced jabbing the way they do when people call her small, so he dropped it.).

'I wondered if you might be going into the hudder-mudder heir-making business,' Beatrice says now. 'But Lady FitzAlan isn't like that. It's a shame: her husband is a knave, his seed should be stoppered up before it gets out of the spout.'

'Heir-making?' Simnel says.

'Oh, yes. Wives using servants the sib of their husband to get themselves babies, when the husbands can't do it. I even heard of a *husband* who asked a groom to do it. But then the husband asked to watch the doings, so I'm not sure what that one was about. Anyway. I'm right glad to see you finding hope in life again.'

'Good,' says Simnel, hoping that if he feeds it as few words as possible, the conversation will weaken, and give up the ghost.

'I expect this woman reminds you of your lost love,' says Beatrice. 'Was she very meek too? Often at prayer, was she?'

'I do remember catching her alone in church one day,' Simnel says.

'Well, I wish you good fortune. Her husband is an old barrel. Hopefully he'll die before she's too old to marry you.' She waxes red. 'Forgive me for saying it.'

'Forgive you? I pray God it happens before the year is out,' Simnel says, and Beatrice giggles.

'You're very japeful today,' she says. 'It lightens my heart! Oh, what a beautiful thing love is!'

8

Not long after the feast of St George, which the court kept at Windsor, word comes to Henry that the Earl of Northumberland had been in York collecting taxes for Henry's war on France, when a mob of cityfolk made affray on him and horribly slew him. He died of either a squashed head or a sword-piercing, possibly both.

The commoners of Yorkshire and Durham weren't only protesting the taxes, Morton tells Simnel. The Northmen were unreasonably loyal to King Richard. And the deviser of the rebellion, Sir John Egremont, is a Yorkist and has a larger plan to see Simnel on the throne.

Egremont attacks York next, but is defeated by Tudor troops. Henry goes North to oversee the punishment of the rebels. A two-storey scaffold is put up in the city for mass hangings. Egremont himself escapes, and goes straight to Mechelen.

'The king sees this as another shoot rising from a poisonous root, deep in the earth,' Morton says. 'It's the root we must dig out.'

'I will be vigilant,' Simnel says.

'I hope you will,' Morton says. 'Because what the king wonders is whether the number of treasons you prevent is less than the number that are carried out in your name. It is this calculation we apply when we consider the matter of your continued existence.'

At Simnel's request, Lady FitzAlan lends him Margery Kempe's autobiography, which she says is the holiest book she's read save the Bible. He finds the book — a bid for canonisation so obvious it should have been titled *If Saint Bridget Did It So Shall I* – amusing, but doesn't say so.

'By my faith, I don't understand why everyone finds her so annoying,' Lady FitzAlan says. 'But how pleasant it must be to be visited by Jesus each time people are cruel to you, and have Him tell you that you'll sit at His side in heaven. And look how He tells her to fast on Fridays, and then when her husband says he'll only let her live in chastity if she starts cooking on Fridays again, Jesus tells her she may leave off the fasting, and that this was His plan all along.'

Simnel's reminded of what Beatrice said about Margaret Beaufort, the king's mother: she spends all her time at religion so as to avoid her husband. Is it any wonder? said Beatrice. Married at twelve. Birthing Henry at thirteen. Who would want a man near them after that? She gave Simnel a small side look, then said, She probably prefers women now.

Right, said Simnel. Having no idea what she was talking about.

'I wonder what it would be like to hear Jesus,' Lady FitzAlan says. 'Can you imagine? To be relieved of all the fright, all the confusion. To *understand*. Have you ever heard Him? But you are his chosen king. I expect you must.'

No, is the answer.

'At times,' he says.

'I knew it would be so!' she says. 'But now I must hie. The other ladies will be waiting. But my husband's man Mayne is here to speak to you.'

'Good morning!' says a voice behind Simnel.

He turns, and is astonied.

It's one of the men who killed Maister Richard and Bella. Miles. The fat-bellied one. Last seen at the dock, saying, *'Bye then, lad.*

Simnel doesn't hesitate. 'What cheer?' he says.

'Right glad for seeing you!' Mayne says. 'I wouldn't have recognised you. What are you… sixteen, seventeen? And you remember *me* – now that joys my heart.'

'Well, you're still fat,' Simnel says, and Mayne laughs and clouts him on the back. Simnel asks him, 'So you're in FitzAlan's service?'

'I've been passed around like a fucking wineskin, lad. But I'm a York man, to my ending day. I went to that becursed shitheap France for King Edward. I fought for King Richard at Bosworth.'

Simnel asks, 'What happened to your friend, Jenkin?'

'That perilous cunt? He was caught years back. Got his pardon by informing on us. He told the king's men everything about your time in Oxford, though you were long gone by then, and then – do you know what they did? – they had him sham that he was that priest of yours, and make a confession to Henry's council! Ha.'

'So that's who their priest was,' Simnel says. 'So, do you know Lovell? How is he?'

'I don't know him, but I expect that fucker's in full good cheer. I hear he's heading off to Scotland soon, on the hospitality of the new king.'

'Blessed be God, and Lovell,' says Simnel, and Mayne inclines his head devoutly. 'Are you going North too?'

He's wondering whether to try to get a letter to Lovell through Mayne, to tell Lovell about Lincoln's death – that it wasn't an honourable last stand but a low thing in the mud; that the high-up friend of Henry's ordered it done, and the ordering and the doing must be avenged – but then he realises Mayne might be more loyal to Lovell's master than to Lovell.

'Oh, no, I'm biding here for the moment. Helping with your rescue, aren't I?'

'Again,' says Simnel.

'Again?' says Mayne. 'How's that now?'

'You rescued me in Oxford, remember?'

He doesn't remember because it wasn't true, says Joan. *Assay him. Do it.*

Simnel hesitates, then says, 'By which I mean, you made sure that the priest and his leman wouldn't be tempted to tell their story once I was gone.'

'Oh, yes, that turdish milksop,' Mayne says. Simnel's smile is cold and set on his face now, like yesterday's pottage. Mayne doesn't notice. He's in full billow. 'He talked too much. Then Morelle said he'd moved his whore in. Morelle said: who else might he jangle to? And let me tell you, nobody could ask for a more faithful man than me. Morelle says break some heads, I don't say *who*, I don't say *why*: I say *how many*. I broke over a hundred heads at Bosworth. I was as slender as a greyhound back then, aright. But I cracked brain-pans like eggs.'

He mimes an axe swing over his head.

'*Morelle?*' Simnel says.

'Heh,' Mayne says. 'Of course, you never spoke to him. The servant. The sham deaf mute. That's Morelle. My master. He did a good job, by Christ. Myself, I'm a talker. I'd have burned myself on a pot and said "fuck" or something but Morelle's wonderly good, wonderly good…' Then he starts laughing. 'Cock's bones, I couldn't resist showing the priest that sack of coin. He thought he had the pot by the handle then, aright. Tears of joy standing in his eyes at the sight of the money I'd been paid to kill him! Saying he'd be a fucking famous scholar or writer in London or some blaver. That was a full merry jape. Ha! Maybe he could have been a famous writer. I've no witting. But he threw it away the day he got a sniff of that jade's plum pie.'

'He was never a good writer,' Simnel says.

Mayne laughs, then shakes his head in marvelment.

'And to remember you, weeping and taking on about that bit of business. You've changed, lad. You're a killer yourself, now, aren't you? I can see it in your face, your demeanour. Maybe you haven't taken a head off yet, but you've got the right minds for it.'

'Maybe,' Simnel says, smiling. 'Anyway. I'm wonderly thankful for your service. And if I do reclaim what rightfully belongs to the Yorks, a fair portion of land and a pension will be yours.'

'You're a right goodly king,' Mayne says, bowing. 'I always fucking said it. God bless you.'

The hunting party departed, Simnel sits down on a stump. He holds his head, knots his hands in distress. His face, let free, runs through a pageant of grimaces: horror, grief, wroth. He can't speak or cry out. So he contorts, in silence.

Is this a shock?

He didn't know it, but it doesn't shock him. As if he always knew that Bella wasn't a spy who'd convinced Maister Richard to betray Simnel to King Henry. That Maister Richard was no murderer. But he knew this truth was unbearable, and so he put his hands over his eyes and ordered it out.

It's not surprise that strikes him now, but guilt.

Bella never liked him, but then she was so sad – he sees that now, she was sad and afraid. And he's sorry he never said anything kind to her, just misliked her back. He was sad and afraid too, aright. But she died and Simnel lived, so he should have fucking cheered up a bit and told her she was a goodly lady, something like that.

He doesn't weep, though the two of them deserve his tears. But weeping is beyond him. Each sadness now is just another weight, to add to the rest. Instead, clerkly, he makes his list:

Kildare
Plunket
Mayne
Morelle the deaf mute-that-was
Cross
Cross's unknown master

The people who lied to him, goaded him, gulled him, terrified him, confused him, drove him from place to place like Apuleius' ass; took away Will Collan, Tom, Oliver, Joan; killed Bella, Maister Richard, Grania, Lincoln – anyone he ever loved or might have loved, and left him alone; more alone than anyone, because they even parted him from his own self.

These people, say Joan and his heart with one voice, *must suffer*.

It's late autumn before Simnel sees Lady FitzAlan again, out for a walk, her skirts creating a wide path in the fallen gold leaves. She's accompanied by a servant, a woman who withdraws elegantly at the sight of Simnel.

He misses Grania, who never withdrew elegantly.

Simnel asks her about her recent pilgrimage to Canterbury, and admires her badge. He asks how her husband's plans are going. He's seen Sir John FitzAlan, of course. A thin-haired older man with orgulous black brows and the broad beak of a rook. Neither of them acknowledges the other.

'He wants to meet you,' she says. 'But he's ware. For him to be seen with you… it's great peril. It's different for me.'

'Different because a woman isn't suspected of strategy?'

'No. Because if someone sees me with you, they'll think – ah. You see, the ladies of the court talk about you… Uh. Not chastely.'

Her flush has overspilled her face and travelled down her neck.

'Anyway,' she says, 'he hasn't got the money yet for a rebellion. But he's raising it.'

'I'm right grateful,' Simnel says.

There's a short silence, and then she says, explosively, 'I'm sorry I did not tell those ladies not to talk of you so lightly. I was… afraid. And I did not do right.'

'It's no matter,' he says.

'I thought of Margery Kempe, who spoke so boldly against sinful talk. I wish that I could speak like that. But my husband says it is not fitting.' Then she laughs. 'Forgive me, I just imagined what he would do if I roared in church like Margery.'

She looks so transported at the thought.

'I see holiness in you,' Simnel says, moved. 'Whether you speak or not.'

She shakes her head, but she looks at him quickly, and he sees exposed fear and love in her eyes, and a tremble in her mouth.

He feels grieved at deceiving her, but thinks: *she'll be happier without her husband.* Without Simnel too. Just like Elaine tricking Lancelot into swiving her to father Galahad: an evil thing is being done, in the service of goodness.

Lady FitzAlan hies to him in a great commotion of parched, frost-stiffened leaves. When she gets closer he can see she's distressed, though she's out of breath when she reaches him, panting; eventually brasting out with, 'They're false, they're false!'

It emerges, between storms of weeping, that Sir John FitzAlan and his fellow conspirators have decided that the Earl of Warwick in the Tower is the real Earl of Warwick after all. They'd met with a gentleman named Edward Franke, who'd fought for King Richard and was lateward escaped from the Tower. Franke said it was passing easy to get out of there; they could pop the earl out like a cork. And then they got a letter from some puissant person, she doesn't know whom, telling them to forget Simnel. This person suspected Simnel of being under watch, because Hextall was caught so quickly, by a nosy falconer who later disappeared from court, no doubt on a spy's pension.

Simnel's first thought is of the secret Yorkist. *Iterum, you fucker.* Along with a burst of wroth, a flare from his hating heart.

Spies get pensions? is his second.

Also, said Lady FitzAlan, they said the noise of Simnel has died down; his name didn't ignite rebellion in the North like it was expected to; plus he wrote a confession that a true king would have gone to the block rather than put his name to; plus he's been a servant for over two years now, and feels like stale tidings.

This is more painful to hear than Simnel expected.

But Lady FitzAlan is in greater pain: a torment she sees as spiritual. She told her husband that what he was doing was great shame in the sight of God, and he knocked her to the ground. She can't hunt today because her hawking wrist is a little askew.

The wrist is swollen double.

'It is not hurt,' she says. 'It is his soul that must be sore hurt. I think the consciousness of his sin made him so warly. I say Masses for him every hour.'

Simnel says to Morton, 'You should have Sir John FitzAlan followed.'

'FitzAlan? Are you sure?'

'He's in full purpose to steal the Earl of Warwick from the Tower. He's meeting with the other conspirators this month. His man John Mayne is involved. Edward Franke. Others whose names I don't know.'

'FitzAlan!' says Morton. 'He was trusted. By God, these are heavy tidings. Sore heavy. And the queen about to give birth. How did you find out?'

'I saw Mayne escorting Sir John's wife, and recognised him as the Yorkists' man. He remembered me fondly. I also tried speaking to her, but she had no witting of any of it.'

'You've done well,' Morton says.

'She won't be punished, will she?'

'Who?'

'The wife.'

'No, of course not. The doings of wives aren't worth a gnat.'

That December Mayne, Franke, FitzAlan, and four others of their acquaintance, including one of Henry's own ambassadors, are arrested on charges of treason.

Morton assures Simnel that Mayne will hang. Simnel wonders where the souls of Maister Richard and Bella are. If – like him – they feel a dark, rich pleasure at the news.

If in the next moment – like him – they're dissatisfied.

Now find his masters, they say.

FitzAlan's name is to be kept quiet.

'Nobody needs to hear about loyal-seeming nobles turning on our king,' Morton says. 'It might put like ideas in the brains of the people.'

The court spends Christmas at Westminster, where an accursed air blows the measles into their midst. Divers courtiers die. More of the servants die.

On the day after Childermas the court flees the perilous air of Westminster for Greenwich, but the Christmas celebrations are weighed on by the fear of disease.

'No disguisings,' says Beatrice. 'And hardly any pageants, and the Abott of Misrule suggested a game in which people flung and swung each other about, and everyone said no.'

Then she starts to cry: her friend Anne was one of those taken.

On a lightly snowing January day, Franke, Mayne, and Sir John FitzAlan are put to death on Tower Hill. FitzAlan's extensive lands and manors are forfeit to the king.

'The ill wind blew us some good, as the saying goes,' says Morton.

The deceased Sir John FitzAlan's wife, newly poor, has to live on the mercy of relatives, who put her in a grimly abbey in the Marches.

Juvenal said that the punishment for parricide was to be sewn into a sack with a cock, a dog, a snake and a monkey, and the sack dropped into the sea.

At nights Simnel's stomach feels like that sack.

Leave it behind you, says Joan. *Think of me. You did right. If you win Henry's trust it'll be easier to escape. And FitzAlan was a marvellous turd. And Mayne would have given him up anyway.*

But he can't leave Lady FitzAlan behind him; she's followed him somehow, she's a ghostly presence, in a way that the real dead – Grania, Lincoln, Bella, Maister Richard – are not. She once said she would devote herself to him until her ending day, and maybe this is what that means: here she will be, halsing close, until she dies of misery or from the cold damp air.

9

February passes at Westminster. The king and queen and the king's mother celebrate Candlemas with a play in the White Hall.

'Are you not tempted to write something?' Beatrice says to Simnel. 'You read so much. I would have thought that inevitably leads to writing. It's like spending too long in infected air. Soon you become sick. Why don't you write a merry play of your own?'

'Plays, like stories, pretend to be merry but are never anything more than a buttressing of the status quo.'

'Right,' Beatrice says. 'Is this… about Lady FitzAlan?'

Simnel looks at her and sees, to his dismay, that she has her sympathetic countenance on. Her hand doubtless ready to reach out, pat. Beatrice is probably the kind of woman – decent, wise, kind – that John Collan would have married. For that reason sometimes Simnel finds her company hard to bear.

'You must miss her,' she says. 'I hope she's in good health. We should pray to the Virgin. Though this matter might be too large for the Holy Mary. We must pray to God.'

Pain arrives in his heart.

'For what?' he says. 'What's God good for but unlatching the clicket gates of holy ladies? He's no use to me now.'

(Joan laughs.)

Beatrice looks at him, her head on one side.

He sighs. 'I'm *japing*,' he says.

She holds her look. No laugh, no disapproval. Then she says, gently, 'Are you alright, Simnel?'

He feels stupid. Then he feels annoyed. What does Beatrice know, what has she suffered? Her family are decent, wise and kind, and alive in London. Who is she to try to make him feel so small and ashamed?

'I'm fine,' he says.

Spring comes: blue sky, glistening leaf buds, light-witted new flies dancing up and down in the sun beams. The fox-hunting season ends and the roebuck season begins. Simnel sees Henry riding out. His best friends, Morton and the Lord Chamberlain Sir William Stanley, are beside him. The welcoming party for Simnel's arrival at court. Morton and Stanley: greeting him, calling him *shitpate*, handing him his faited confession. Will they bid him good cheer today?

They see Simnel, aright, but they don't look at him.

Morton only acknowledges Simnel when they meet alone. These days he even smiles.

'Simnel, the mills of the king's justice need fresh grist,' he says. 'The last heads you gave them will only last so long.'

Simnel, in discussion with Joan, devises a plan. A treaty between the two of them. The main points of which are:

1. To remember the unintended afterclaps that may come of handing over traitors. In particular when it comes to their wives and children.
2. To refuse the overtures of honourable men. Or evil men with honourable wives.

(Joan rolls her eyes at that one. But she agrees to it).

For a few days Simnel worries that he won't be able to find a man and a wife sunk deep enough in wickedness.

Then he meets Richard White and his wife, Cecily.

He hears about them first from Beatrice, who's making mourn out of measure because some Yorkist lady called Cecily White slapped a laundress who was washing her hair, and called her a grubby hedgepig.

'Which she is not!' Beatrice says. 'She's so clean, and smells of Castile soap.'

'Who are these people?' Simnel asks.

'Elyn? A friend. Of sorts.'

'Not the laundress. The Yorkist nobles.'

'They're the Whites,' Beatrice says. 'Why? What's in your head? You look... I don't know. But I mislike it.'

The next day Simnel puts himself in the way of Richard White. They stand under an oak with raindrops tapping the ground around them. White is is a pleasant-looking gentilman with shiny hair, and is in temperament exactly as Simnel hoped. He congratulates Simnel on his fair face and prophesies an outbreak of yellow-haired Yorkish infants in the nearby villages. He himself has just had some nuisance of that sort. His wife had this little chambermaid, who drove White's wits in all directions, with her coy dodgings and hidings and 'you mustn't's! He only got a tumble by threatening to have her dismissed. 'Like Ovid and his dusky Cypassis,' he says. 'And I'm a newfangled Ovid aright.'

In the end he had to send the girl away because she was pregnant and ill-tempered. Talking of *raptus*, like she was a man of law! By Saint Verena, it was full mirthful. Who even taught her the word?

'How did you keep it from your wife?' Simnel asks.

'She found me out but didn't care. The wench was bad at her job anyway. She'll do better as a harlot in the stews.'

White knows of a plot to rescue Simnel, he says. He was approached, but hasn't committed himself yet. Speaking to Simnel now has convinced him that this is his rightful king, who would no doubt reward his loyal subjects in most plenteous wise. White proposes that, when the time comes, Simnel gets himself out of the palace grounds, then to White's estate at Thorpe.

White won't tell Simnel who else is involved in the plan. The king has lateward been hanging men for treason on the hour; his spies are everywhere, knowing about compassings before people have even compassed them. Dream of his death and he'll swoop in like an owl, and pluck you out of your bed. 'It's bad enough that you can give them *my* name if you're caught and tortured,' he says. 'Of course, I'd be on my way to France by that time.'

'The French are involved?'

White pinches his own lips shut with thumb and forefinger. 'I have jangled more than enough,' he says. 'And here comes my wife and the other ladies. She's the one riding the grey palfrey. People say my wife is as fair as the queen. It's not wise to say: *fairer*. But.'

'Undoubtedly' says Simnel.

He bows to the women as they pull up, feeling the fair Cecily White's dark eyes on him, and quits them. He lets another falconer bring out the birds to the party and stands out of sight to watch the group. She's still looking in the direction in which he left, head slightly lifted, eyes searching.

He recognises Cecily White's expression. He understands female expressions better now. And the rest. The squeeze of his fingers as a bird is handed from glove to glove. The closeness of a brush-by. The leanings in. The notes passed to him:

Meet me here in three hours.
I hardly dare to ask it.
My lord I do adore you!
Sir, if you be of my minds, please say.
I can think of nothing other than fucking you.

And yes, he's sad, and black, and sour of heart, but he's tall and almost seventeen and he can keep going for over ten minutes now. And also, what's he meant to do when a lady shows him her queynte's shining labia, the same clover pink as her nipples, but press his mouth against them? She was astonied – but she let him, and then she prayed him bide there a little longer.

Though that act brought a little wrack, too, because afterwards the lady, who was married – they were all married – seemed stricken by feeling. She started smiling tenderly in his direction, holding his hand too long. So he told her he was under watch by the king, at which she was adread, and said they must part for the sake of both their lives, but promise never to forget each other.

Goodbye, my love!

(And if he could just do that *mouth trick* one final time.)

After that, he thinks he'll swive like he spies. Confine it to people he mislikes, who wouldn't care if he lived or died.

And on that note…

Wouldn't it be both *dulce et decorum* to use the principles of Ovid, White's hero, to seduce his lady wife?

In Ireland Simnel's heart had withdrawn from Ovid in disgust. In the world of Ovid's elegies, women's faces can be scratched in anger, because their tears are never real, only sham ones to get money – and so it's fine, too, to pretend to cry yourself, to make them believe you love them. You can promise them gifts or loyalty and never deliver: it doesn't matter, because women are heartless. They're cheats, so you can cheat them; they're vain, so you can falsely flatter them; they're stupid, so you can pretend to agree with all their stupid opinions. Whatever it takes to fuck them, and if none of that works: force them, because they want to be forced.

The problem with Ovid, Joan once said, besides being a shrew, is that he didn't understand women. He thought they gave in to persistence, nauseating love letters, worshipful slavishness. While he himself was only aroused by indifference. *I flee the eager, I chase the coy.* But he didn't realise that most women are exactly the same. They can't bear not to be noticed. They seek what is elusive. They want what is wanted by other women. If you play it right, you shouldn't have to lift so much as a foot in their direction. Let alone a fucking *pen.* By the Virgin! Nobody wants a love poem. Nobody. Anyway, my point is: if you reverse all Ovid's advice, you have a powerful stock of ordnance.

Interesting, said Edward.

She laughed, and said, Of course, none of that will work if a man isn't rich, or good-looking, or celebrated. At least one of the three.

And I'm none, I suppose.

Edward. If you become king, you'll be all three. The only techniques you'll need will be how to get women out of your bedchamber in the morning.

This is a… compliment?

Not really, she said. She sent him an unnerving smile. You'll never know if it's love that we feel, or ambition.

361

The next time he sees Cecily White – looking, in the silver April light, like a beautiful dark otter, slender and avid – he makes her a dismissive, near-disworshipful bow. Then he walks away, and lets others serve her.

The same day, Simnel sees Sir Hugh Cross.

He's on horseback, in a group of men, and Simnel's view of him is sidewise, but he *knows* him. His blood knows him, understanding faster than Simnel's own brain, and it races into his head and feet and arms, urging him to run; go after; bludgeon; tear; destroy.

Drag his body through the forest until he breaks into parts.

No: demand of him, who told you to kill Lincoln?

Then the breaking into parts.

Yes.

He looks around him for a spear, or a thick branch.

Wait, says Joan. *Don't be stupid.*

He doesn't want to listen. The wroth grips him.

He's surrounded by archers. How are you going to help me if you're full of arrows?

Simnel hesitates. He stares at Cross's back. Cross is laughing about something. He turns to another man with a foolish expression, doggish: What a good jape I just made. It takes Simnel a moment to understand that the man Cross is talking to is Sir William Stanley, Henry's Lord Chamberlain. Stanley appears in good cheer. His thin arms are sticking out like pot handles; hands on hips; round belly forward. Simnel can make out a smile, nestled in his dark grey beard. Obviously nobody has any idea that Cross is a traitor.

If Simnel throws a rock at Cross, he might miss and hit Stanley. But then Stanley called Simnel a little shitpate, didn't he, when he was making him sign that sham confession?

He looks for a rock.

Stop it, Joan says. *Vengeance is an angry hound. It needs a cool master.*

Fine, he says. Alright.

There are no rocks, anyway.

Good. When the time is right, the hound will be fed.

362

'Your flesh is mine to despoil,' he says.

'Yes,' Cecily White says, 'I submit!'

'No place on your body is safe, my rough hands roam where they like,' he says. 'You have no choice but to yield to my boistous staff.'

'I am your obedient captive,' she whispers. Her teeth clench; her eyes press shut; a pulse runs through her body. It brings him to his own ending, prudently outside her, pattering against the mossy stones of the wall, the purple columbines.

One of his other lovers had told him about this ruin in the woods; of unknown origin, only three walls of it left and a worn stone bench. The bench is especially useful; he's been starting to get an ache in his back.

Cecily's straightening her skirts and smoothing her finger-marked breasts back into her bodice. What she likes is to come here while her husband is playing tennis, with her maid on guard, and have Simnel – as rebel peasant, grimly robber, itinerant soldier – happen upon her and force her elegant white body to his will.

Her husband doesn't understand her, she says. She's of an ancient family and his is new. There's a merchant within living memory. But she's a second daughter and he is rich, so. Anyway, Richard is a fine husband, but he never liked being asked to play the yeoman. She supposes it's too close to home.

'When can I see you next?' she asks. 'In two days he'll be hunting roebuck.'

Simnel, lacing his hose, takes his time about answering.

'I don't know. I'll send word,' he says, giving her a short bow. 'I have to go. You should bide here for a moment longer.'

'Of course,' she says. She's a beautiful woman, especially now, radiating velvety satisfaction. He turns his back on her and quits the ruin, passing the maid as he goes.

Who gives him a look.

There are so many different kinds of treachery.

Morton asks again if there have been any tidings of Lovell. Simnel has been wondering the same thing.

'Does he have any former friends at court?' he asks Morton. 'People who may still privily be his friend.'

'That's a sapient idea,' Morton says. 'I'll ask Sir William Stanley who Lovell's friends were.'

'Why would the Lord Chamberlain know?' Simnel asks.

'Stanley was Lovell's stepfather. His second wife was Lovell's mother.'

'Huh,' says Simnel.

He's only spoken to Stanley once, when the man called him a little shitpate. Could that have been pageantry? Since then he's seen Stanley, and Stanley has full ignored him.

'*Huh*,' he says again.

At the end of July Henry writes to Kildare, who was meant to appear before him after the rebellion, but had made divers excuses not to. Henry orders him to present himself in England within ten months, or Henry will not pardon him from his many recent infringements of the laws regarding retinues, arms, and livery.

By which to say, Henry makes out a general pardon for the Great Earl in the meantime. And in exchange Kildare must appear within ten months.

Kildare tells Henry he most faithfully will.

'I heard you're having ado with Cecily White,' says Beatrice. 'How could you? She's a heinous shrew.'

He can't tell her the truth.

'It's just sport. It's not love.'

'Not love, you say? Oh, I'm *full* astonied at that, that it's not love. By the Virgin! That woman has no kindness in her heart. Did you not listen when I told you about the laundress?'

'Is the laundress permanently disfigured?' he asks. 'Well? Or did she recover?'

Beatrice is silent. Her small fists are bunched in her skirt.

'How many people know about these doings?' he asks her.

'The hitting of the laundress?'

'No! Enough with the laundress! Who knows I'm meeting Cecily White?'

'Only servants. None of your kind.'

'Good. Now, I have a question for you: what do you know of the Lord Chamberlain? Sir William Stanley?'

'He's a goodly man,' says Beatrice. 'He's kind to servants, anyway. Not that you care about that.

Why are you asking about Stanley? Do you want to have ado with him now? Well, forget it, he's too pleasant, he's none of *your* type.'

'How are we talking about sodomy now?' Simnel says. 'You're japing with me.'

She makes a face. 'You think you're so old in guile, but you can never tell when men are having ado with men and women with women.'

'Why would I want to? None of that has anything to do with me. And women can't even do such a thing. Nature hasn't given them the means. But is Stanley a bottom-hole belabourer? Is that what you're telling me?'

'*No*,' she says, irous, and hits him on the arm.

'Ow,' he says, exaggeratedly clasping himself. 'Why are you so warly today? Your choler must be too high. My aunt-that-was, Margaret of Burgundy, used to be bled to keep her minds serene and rational. We can't afford a leech, but I could stick you with a pin, if you like.'

'Shut up, you doddypoll,' says Beatrice, but she's laughing now, and he's pleased to see it.

Cecily White doesn't know Stanley, and isn't interested in talking about him. Other people bore her. Her husband's plot, in particular, bores her. It reminds her of a day when she won't have Simnel the falconer anymore. She says sadly that she once got a gardener involved in some bedroom pageantry, but he was too grimly for her. He wiped his nose on his sleeve and called her 'yer ladyship' in a parlous accent.

And then she couldn't walk in the gardens! Well, she could, once she'd sent him away.

Quite the exemplum, Simnel said. (He never has trouble following Ovid's advice. It's not hard to scorn her; mock her; avoid her).

But then, he wonders how different he is from Cecily White. Not long ago the court convoy passed some farmers and they seemed so... crude. Like they'd been whittled by a labourer's hand. He remembers, uncomfortably, the beloved people of his childhood. Were they like this? Straw sleepers, ball scratchers, one eye to the sky, muttering about the soil.

And his nose has changed. When did that happen? The smell of the farms doesn't say *home* anymore.

It says, *Simnel, you have no home.*

No hearth for you, no place in all the world that will know you.

He finds out more about Stanley. The brother of King Henry's step-father, he was loyal to the Yorks in their wars with the Lancasters, but then before Bosworth he secretly changed sides and fought against King Richard.

Treacherous, thinks Simnel. He remembers Lovell saying the Stanleys were marvellous side-switchers. What if Stanley has switched back again?

Simnel's encountered so many court men as he brings them their falcons. The former Yorkists seem almost afraid of him; they mutter and duck until he's gone. The Tudor loyalists ignore him more ostentatiously. Or they make witty remarks to their friends about him, or sneer at him. One man, after a rainy hunt, shook the wet dirt off his cloak in Simnel's direction, then laughed. That moment came back to Simnel later – Simnel's cock deep inside the queynte of the man's fair wife – and the pleasure he felt then was wonderly increased.

Stanley doesn't dramatically ignore Simnel, remark on him, sneer. He keeps his eyes away, almost shyly.

To test him, Simnel drifts toward Stanley one day. Stanley, as if he had always wanted to be on the other side of his horse, moves away. Simnel tries it again. Stanley now wanders in the other direction. The two of them move around the horses and men in a strange, slow dance. A weasel rondelet.

So, Stanley is ware of him. And no reason at all to be, unless Stanley is a traitor. The high friend of Henry's, the secret friend of the Yorks. This explains why Sir Hugh Cross was sniffing around his hindquarters. Stanley must be the man who ordered the death of Lincoln, to protect his own miserable corpus. Not that Simnel can prove it yet. He couldn't even say he knows.

But he *knows*.

And through Cecily White, Simnel is going to get hold of that corpus, flay it into bloody streamers, hang it over every wall in London.

Metaphorically speaking.

August comes. The nights are rose-coloured but soon they'll cool. He pushes Cecily White too far, asking her questions about his rescue. She becomes distant, and says Simnel's becoming over-needful. So he writes himself a love note from another woman and lets it drop out of his clothes the next time he's fucking her.

She notices it, snatches it up before him, reads it, and turns rosy with wroth. Her small teeth show. Her breasts are resplendent in the sunshine. For a moment he almost likes her.

He tries not to smile as she rages, quietly, so as not to be heard by her maid.

Villainous, heinous, faithless, pernicious!

All these things and more. How could he? He is a low knave, a coward ape, a bawdy churl. She never wants to see him again.

He remembers Ovid: 'The man who piles remonstrance on a woman is begging to be proved wrong.' Reverses it, as Joan taught.

'You're right,' he says cheerfully. 'You are too good for me. I can only make you full and humble apology, and wish you better luck of your loves hereafter.'

'Hereafter? You're letting me leave?'

'My dear lady, the wounds of Cupid's arrows rarely overlive a summer. And I've thought lateward that our sport, while merry, was reaching a natural end. Had you… not?'

She stares at him. For the first time he sees tears in her eyes. They don't move him.

'Don't say these things!' she says. 'You were full affectionate just now. How can you forget that?'

'I never would,' he says. 'But pleasure grows dull without right worship. I do not accuse *you*. But I suspect your husband of light-mindedness. I don't trust that he truly means to help me attain my kingship.'

'But he does! In God's sight, I swear it.'

Simnel wonders what God would make of the sight of her small brown nipples, still exposed; the twinkle of Simnel's spilled seed on the ground.

But God, as usual, isn't paying attention.

Simnel pretends to be unconvinced, until she tells him the plot is advanced, they are in company with Sir Robert Chamberlain, King Richard's former knight of the body. Sir Hugh Cross. Others even more important than them. Someone very high; close to Henry. She doesn't know his name because he's passing ware. And all of them are in the service of the King of France, who is waiting to welcome the York heir.

'France? Not Burgundy?'

'No, France. King Charles.'

Well, and why not? Simnel thinks. The French must have been sore grieved to miss out on the last invasion attempt. Let them have a turn.

'And Lovell?' he asks. 'Have you heard his name?'

But Cecily hasn't, and he has to put thinking aside for the moment, because the quarrel is over and Cecily White has extended her hands, eyes pleading, expecting a passionate reuniting, and he has to come up with some fitting talk. He resorts to the use of the sermon from yesterday's Mass, in which they were exhorted to accept the punishments of God like His good child; to give themselves to His command; to kiss the stick with which He has beaten them.

Cecily White is brought off so exuberantly a sob brasts out from her, echoing, sending a brace of woodpigeons clap-clapping out of the trees.

His work is done.

Simnel considers taking this as his opportunity to escape. Stealing money from somewhere. Travelling off the roads, through fields and copses. Living on hedgerow berries and river water. Heading for Richard White's manor.

But at the end of this imaginary journey, the Yorkists wait. Richard White. Sir Hugh Cross. Sir William Stanley. And the King of France.

He realises he'll never be able to escape with any Yorkists.

These are people who kill their friends. Who would happily swap Simnel for the Earl in the Tower, should an Earl in the Tower become available. No doubt they'd sell him back to Henry for a pardon.

If it were only a matter of one or two, Simnel might have tried to sham friendship then work out a way to escape them or kill them. But he could never escape them all, or kill them all at once.

He has to stay here for now, and settle for only killing one at a time.

'Good *lad*,' says Morton, when he is told about Richard White – and Simnel is reminded of God, laying down His beating-stick. Beaming much like Morton is doing now.

My good child.

Simnel doesn't tell Morton about his suspicion of Sir William Stanley. He needs to think that information over more, and decide how best to use it.

Richard White is arrested and charged with engaging in conspiracy. Cecily White is kept under guard in her quarters, then sent back to her estate in Norfolk. Before she leaves she sends Simnel a letter via her maid,

We are undone – Richard thinks I betrayed him – He caught me in a lie about where I was that day I saw you – I am in much peril of my life. You must help me.

369

Simnel can't reply to her, and he can't help her. But she'll be fine, he thinks. Her husband and his friends will be beheaded soon. She'll lose her estates, which is a good thing. Fewer gardeners to bother. And she'll have to be kinder to maids and laundresses.

The king's men go after Sir Robert Chamberlain, but he flees with his sons and is only captured some months later, January 1491, in Hartlepool. (Morton says Chamberlain had taken sanctuary at Durham Cathedral, but the Bishop of Durham handed him to Henry on the understanding that he could keep the fugitives' goods.)

In March, to the accompaniment of courting birds, Chamberlain is beheaded on Tower Hill. Richard White is due to hang. When his own ending day comes he's led onto the scaffold, then pardoned, at which he drops to his knees, weeping and taking on marvellously. The crowd is very impressed with the spectacle.

'Oh, yes, he bargained for his life, and the terms were favourable,' Morton says. 'He told us where Chamberlain was to be found. Some traitors move around foxlike. For example: Lovell. But Chamberlain sat in the same spot like a toad under a rock.'

White didn't betray Stanley. Of course he didn't. It was probably Stanley who'd got him his pardon.

'Were *you* in favour of his being freed?' Simnel asks Morton. 'It seems overlarge generosity for such a man. I'd have pressed the information out of him with stones, then hanged him.'

Morton looks tenderly approving at this.

'You are a stern lad,' he says. He looks almost as if he might be about to pat Simnel's hand. Simnel places his hands on his knees. 'And, by Saint Sebastian, no, I said he ought to die. But Sir William Stanley argued for him. He can be soft-hearted.'

Soft-hearted to knaves. Kind to servants. But not soft or kind to Lincoln, thinks Simnel. Hatred moves him; he feels his face twitch, darken.

Morton misunderstands his expression. 'I know,' he sighs. 'You think as I do: to skimp on God's justice is unwise. Other traitors may be encouraged. But then I argued for *your* death, and look how useful you are now. You almost make me wish I'd had a son.'

To which Simnel is too astonied to reply.

Then a dreadful thought comes to him.

'Cecily White,' he says. 'Where is she? Where is Richard White?'

'Celebrating together, I would guess,' Morton says. 'We sent him home days ago. Though their celebrations will be of a straitened nature, without large nobley. Ale and pottage, perhaps.'

And he laughs his dry old laugh.

Tidings come later that month: Cecily White has died of a fever. Which was strange because there was no outbreak in her part of the country.

Forgive me, Cecily, I never meant to—

But is that true? He'd meant for her to be unharmed, he'd believed she would be unharmed, but now he wonders: did he truly believe it, or did he decide to believe it, or did he just not care?

This is the truth.

It's not Cecily he wishes he could speak to. It's Joan.

What do you think, Joan? You thought I couldn't do this, but I did.

Are you glad?

11

Summer is here. Simnel walks with Beatrice to the edge of the deer park, and they sit with a bottle of ale, overlooking a slope of fields. Jack hares are fighting in the long grass, a honeysuckle scent loads the warm air.

When the ale is finished, he thinks, he could just walk away. There's smoke rising beyond the tree line, pinkish in the sky. What would the people living there say if he walked up to their door – and said what? Good people, please can you provide me with shelter, and a change of clothes, and enough money to fund a passage to Ireland?

Ha, ha, ha, ha, is what the good people would say.

And even if they gave him all their bread and their own clothes, is he really going to walk away from Stanley, and Cross, and Lovell? Any day now the Yorkists could send a new plotter, give him the means to get to these men. Though he's passing tired of waiting.

'You look grimly,' Beatrice says.

'Sorry. I can be more merry. We could play cards?'

'It's alright. I'm feeling grimly myself, in truth.'

'Why?'

'I can't say. No, I will say. I'm sore sick of not saying anything. The laundress I spoke of before, Elyn. Is my... Uh. I love her.' She doesn't look at him as she says any of this. She stares warly at the horizon, like she's daring it to speak.

Simnel waits for her to finish. Words must be missing. But she doesn't say anything else.

'You love her? What's wrong with that?'

'I love her like a woman loves a man. The wedded kind of love.'

'What? Is that *possible*? Are you japing me?'

She shakes her head no.

'Is that… is it even a sin? I never heard of it at any law proceedings. Or saw it in the Bible. I know, uh, tribadism happened in ancient times. I thought the practice long dead.'

'It's not in the Bible – Elyn says. Or in any sermon, or anywhere.'

'So you won't go to hell,' he says. (Thinking: *If there is one*). 'Well! Now I think about it, it makes sense. A woman is more beauteous than a man. And does she love you back?'

'Yes. For a year now.' Her hand goes to her heart; curls there as if in prayer to the Virgin.

'Then why are you making dole?'

She makes a noise of exasperation. 'Because how am I going to leave here and have a house of my own and a family with a *woman* as my husband?'

And there's no answer to that.

Eleven months after Kildare was ordered to present himself before Henry within ten months, he sends a letter.

He's very sorry; remains Henry's truest, most loyal subject, but has been prevented from coming by divers grave and mishaply events, such as attacks on his allies, whom he had to assist, and also he has had a cold.

He full intends to come as soon as he is able, in token of his most devoted faithfulness, and right worship et cetera.

At the end of June the queen gives birth to her second son, a large redheaded infant named Henry. He's borne off to his baptism in a procession of two hundred torch-carrying men, from Greenwich Palace to the church, his outraged screams echoing all around the courtyard.

Everything is quiet, plot-wise, until late autumn. No Yorkists approach Simnel. The women come to him, as usual. He turns away from the ones who curtsey. Doesn't talk to them long enough to find out if they purpose war or amor. Their tender expressions alarm him: tears standing in their eyes, pitying his condition when they should be fearful for their own.

Annoy him, even.

Get out of here, he wants to say. Unless you want to be murdered by your husbands. Or poisoned, slowly, by the malodorous Welsh air.

In November Simnel hears about the next treasonous doings. Not from a Yorkist, but from Morton.

Some priest named John Hayes has been charged with misprision, for receiving a letter from John Taylor, a Yorkist exile living in Normandy.

'But hold on, you'll find this amusing,' Morton says. 'Taylor is the man the Duke of Clarence trusted with hiding his baby son – the Earl of Warwick – from his brother King Edward. Which of course Taylor failed in doing. Though your old friends pretended not to believe *that*.'

The old pain, of having no self, rises in Simnel again. He can't see an end to that particular pain. He didn't realise Taylor was alive – one of the only men who must know which earl is which. But Taylor is in France.

'Very amusing,' he says.

'Anyway. Taylor told Hayes to get hold of the Earl of Warwick and bring him to France.'

'Did he say which Earl of Warwick? I mean, the real one in the Tower, or me?'

'I don't know. But it seems France and Burgundy's mutual mislike of England has made them friends. And Ireland too, that home of boistous wretches. Taylor promised that all three would provide the escaped earl with troops, coin and ships. Hayes threw the letter on the fire, and didn't report any treason to the king.'

'How did the letter get read if it was thrown in the fire?'

'Oh, the letter was read already. Hayes was betrayed by one of his own. This is what the Yorkists are like. Faithless even to each other. I exclude you from that: I know you were an unwilling victim of their schemes.'

He smiles at Simnel. He's been doing this a lot lateward. Simnel smiles back. The smile floats on his body like a feather on water, never dropping below the surface. It's good that Morton has gone from execution-minded to fatherly. But Simnel isn't in the market for dad number three.

He wonders which earl had been chosen for rescue. Has even Margaret given up his cause? What did she say in Mechelen: *A wheel comes off the cart, you replace the wheel.*

There's always another Earl of Warwick.

The jape of course is: both Edward, Earl of Warwicks have been abandoned. Surplus heirs. By December it's known widewhere that the rebels have somehow acquired a living York prince.

Simnel is called to a meeting with Morton. Henry is there, wearing his cold stare. Half a cold stare, anyway. Simnel wonders if Henry realises that Simnel knows that Henry being present is a sign that he's sore distroubled. Henry tries to look as unreadable as Margaret of Burgundy, but his fears brast out all over his body: tight fingers, clenched lips, awkward-sitting head, and then that rogue eye, even wilder than usual.

A young man, lateward seen in Cork: looking exactly like King Edward's younger son Richard, Duke of York would if he were still alive and not killed by King Richard in the Tower. The noise is the man's not handsome, but is undeniably Edward-like. And the French are backing him. John Taylor is backing him. The French King, desperate to fund someone's, anyone's invasion of England, is backing him.

Margaret of Burgundy is backing him.

Simnel had expected to hear something like this about Margaret. He'd expected it to be painful, and it's exactly as painful as he'd expected. The wheel has been replaced.

'Of course she would do this,' Morton says, furiously. 'The angry woman is a wolf in God's sight. The madness of Margaret's wroth has transformed her into a crazed beast, snapping blindly all about.'

Simnel bows his head to indicate agreement. Though he doesn't think crazed wolves would talk so much about trade routes. Or present so much paperwork to be signed.

Morton, inspired by the presence of Henry, is in a fervour of metaphorisings. 'Just as eagles in their mountain eyries are buffeted by large tempests,' he says, 'kings are made inquiet by cruel fortune. How can his grace sleep a whole night through, disordered as he is in his—'

'I am not inquiet,' says Henry, now. His chilly eye rolls toward Morton.

'No, your grace, forgive me, that was mis-said! Our great Lord Henry's sleep is full untroubled. Everyone admires his unwrinkled countenance. And his excretions! Regular and smoothly produced; they are the marvel of the court.'

Simnel doesn't wonder any more if Morton is cunningly japing Henry. The man is horribly sincere. But he can't find this – or Henry's look of withheld anger – funny. His own low nest is in peril.

'Has anyone heard anything of Lovell?' he asks. (His last hope of escape, of getting the truth about himself, of vengeance on Stanley and Cross.)

But nothing.

'I'm not sure you'll learn anything of use,' Morton says. 'But keep vigilant all the same. By God! Why are we so bedevilled? Another pretender. The world has lost its minds.'

Noise of the supposed Richard, Duke of York is loud at court that Christmas. Strangely enough, the ladies of the court don't seem to sense that Simnel is yesterday's bread. He wants to say to Joan: *You warned me that I'd never be able to trust a woman's intentions, and yet here I am, no prospect of a throne, and still they come, not for ambition but for pure lechery.*

The frost covering the woods is no obstacle. Simnel's ascended to bedchambers: feather mattresses, ewers to wash in, wine, useful servants or guards keeping watch. The upper world opened up to him when he realised he could get around almost anywhere in the palace dressed as a liveried servant. For the first time he experiences true invisibility. Only when the clothes come off does he turn, gratifyingly, back into a man.

And so he's taken aback when he walks into a lady's chamber and she gives him a gold coin. Then he puts it in his purse. It sits where the small ship and the fairy arrowhead used to be.

'You're more gentil than I expected,' says the lady. 'How did you speak back in the blacksmith's or wherever you were raised? I bet they told dirty stories. Tell me one.'

Simnel can't remember how he spoke. He can't remember why he's here, what made him hot to visit this woman. He undresses himself but he's thinking the wrong things: how it's been months that he's been waiting for Cross to come, or anybody; he's been thwarted of his means to threaten someone, hit someone, kill someone; because of some fucking new pretender he's watching as his chances of vengeance and escape twirl leisurely past him like sycamore keys.

Joan, he's losing Joan.

The woman is waiting on the bed, naked. He stands unmoving and looks at her, making her bide even longer, until tiny bumps of cold appear on her exposed skin. His own annoyance has taken hold of him. When he does fuck her, he moves her around on the bed like an animal he's herding, a push to her rear quarters, a pull downwards on her neck; she looks surprised, like she's never sucked a penis before, and probably she hasn't.

He's surprised that any of this arouses him: he mislikes that it does, he mislikes her, for bringing this to his attention. More than anything he feels a great hatred for himself. His self? What is that? What part of him is this? Does it come from John Collan, or Lambert, or Edward, or Simnel? Is he any of them, even? Who the fuck is he?

She gasps then, moves convulsively, goes still. It's over, for both of them. He didn't reach his own ending, but he's suddenly so limp, and she's so wet, that she has no idea.

Afterwards she asks to see him again. He's astonied. He doesn't know if she liked what happened because she doesn't usually get treated like that – or because that's the only way she gets treated, and she doesn't expect anything else.

He doesn't go back.

Not to her, not to anyone.

Simnel thinks of Joan, the time when they lay under the tree and looked up through the leaves at the blazing blue sky.

Except this time Joan turns to him and says: *You aren't the same.*

Well, no, he admits. *It's this poisonous wroth in me. But once the people that wronged us are dead, I'll be kind and tender again, and you'll laugh at me for it.*

She says: *Your love isn't the same.*

He says: *My love for you exists outside time. See, it looks exactly as it should, as bright and fresh as an apple.*

The sky is darkening. Fear comes over him.

She doesn't reply.

12

The supposed Duke of York has left Ireland for France. When he arrives he's given royal apartments, a retinue and a guard of honour. Divers Englishmen – over a hundred of them – make their way over to support him: among them Henry's French secretary Fryon, and Sir George Neville, who had been knighted by Henry himself at Stoke. Which is passing embarrassing for Henry.

(Simnel takes his satisfactions where he can.)

Kildare, however, holds off from open support of the supposed duke. His ally the Earl of Desmond made open cause for the new pretender, but Henry couldn't find evidence that the Great Earl was helping the rebels. As a warning, he gave Kildare's great enemy, a bastard Butler by the name of Sir James Ormond, divers castles, powers and royal commissions.

'That should keep the Irish busy,' says Morton. 'They'll be in fierce enmity, biting at each other's tails like rats.'

(Simnel thinks that, unlike Morton, he's seen how rats live – and unlike humans, rats never make war on their own families.)

'I doubt any alliance between Burgundy and France will last,' Morton continues. 'Charles of France has just married – by force – Anne of Brittany, the bride of Maximilian, King of the Romans.'

(The less Simnel says, the more Morton forgets to stop talking.)

'The common people seem to have overmuch love for this pretender,' Morton muses. 'But low people are lightwitted and changeable. Right now they are taken with the idea of a lost prince. Did you hear his story? That the older brother was murdered, but then the assassins were overcome with remorse and couldn't kill the younger boy. They gave him to another of their number who protected him afterwards, in exchange for his word that he wouldn't tell anyone his lineage for a certain period of years.'

'Did he say who the murderers were?'

'He refuses to name them. Lateward he lived with Sir Edward Brampton. A loathly old Yorkist, in exile since Bosworth. Brampton must have schooled him. Though I wouldn't be surprised if this York were a bastard of King Edward's. God knows, there were enough of them.'

'It's a stupid story,' Simnel says. 'Why would the murderers kill one and save the other? Knowing that he could name them later? But of course he can't name them, because he's a faiter.'

He doesn't know why the matter of the York pretender annoys him so much.

'It is indeed passing stupid,' says Morton. He shakes his head, and says, 'It won't last.'

Beatrice thinks the new pretender is most likely a bastard of King Edward's. There were enough of *them* to supply pretender after pretender, one for every year of Henry's reign.

'I don't see why a bastard can't be a king,' she says. 'That Breton bastard of Henry's is good enough to keep at court, but he can never sit on the throne. It's strange to me.'

'Henry has a bastard?' Simnel is astonied. 'Not that skinny teenager who sits beside him in the hunt?' Beatrice nods. 'By Saint Verena. He *does* look like his father. Like a bundle of sticks, tied up wrong.'

It must have been Henry's naughty eye that fell on the boy's Breton mother, while the straight one closed itself in dismay.

'Proof of passion in Henry,' Simnel marvels. 'The world is full upsodown.'

'I don't know about passion. He loves pomp and nobley so much, he probably has two officials holding a little canopy over his upstand-ing pintle as he proceeds toward the bed,' Beatrice says. 'The poor queen. She must go in dread of his visits. That's one pleasant thing about being a servant. There's a better chance of marrying someone you'd want to share a bed with. Well. For most servants. Probably not for me.'

The dowager queen and the Pope both die that summer. The Pope's death is no surprise. By the end he was too weak to sup anything more than a couple of drops of milk from a young lady's breast. Elizabeth Woodville died of illness – which Beatrice put down to her having been made to live at Bermondsey Abbey, with its wet and rotten air, to save Henry the money of her keep. And the funeral! It was a disgrace. The queen was confined ahead of the birth of her second daughter, at least, so she didn't have to see how outrageously Henry short-spent on her mother; no bells, no cloth offerings, no dirge, no Mass.

'They even burned old candles,' Beatrice says. 'He always had a maugre against her.'

'Did you or Elyn ever meet her?' Simnel asked.

(He's met Elyn now. He was struck by her unfriendly manner and fierce set of eyebrows. The eyebrows said she didn't think much of Simnel.)

'No. I heard that she was a marvellous shrew. But still. Old candles. It's not right.'

In Ireland, the rats that were supposed to be biting each other's tails have armed themselves. Men had to choose whether they were for Ormond or Kildare. Frays brast out all over. Men died. Cashel Cathedral was burned. A mob of Dublin civilians, in pursuit of Sir James Ormond, stormed St Patrick's Cathedral and shot arrows hab nab everywhere, not sparing the images of Jesus or His mother or any of the Saints.

Kildare, in one of his fits of affection, made peace with Ormond, taking his hand through a hole in the door of the chapter house Ormond was hiding in. But they fell back to maugre shortly after, and in June Henry removed Kildare from the Deputyship and replaced him with his former friend Archbishop Walter Fitzsimons. Kildare's father-in-law Lord Portlester was replaced as High Treasurer of Ireland by Sir James Ormond.

Morton, who thinks the time for beskifting Kildare is long over-passed, is delighted. 'Peace will come to Ireland now,' he says. Henry's prophecy-man, Cornish, has promised as much. The war and ravage-ments that had lateward broken out in Meath are the last spark of a dying fire.

'Kildare's time is over,' Morton says.

Simnel doesn't think either the Great Earl or the York pretender is going to oblige Morton by quietly disappearing. And he has to consider his own situation. No rebels are going to come to him with conspiracies when there's a newfangled imposter preening around Europe. Lateward he's only been able to give Morton a few committers of secret murder or *raptus* or fraud – the villains of stories told by his former lovers. This allows Henry to confiscate lands, which he likes. But soon he will wonder what Simnel's value is. And none of this brings Simnel closer to finding Lovell, or getting vengeance against Cross and Stanley. His hands there are empty. He doesn't even have any proof of Stanley's doings.

If the conspiracies won't come to him, he'll have to start his own.

He asks Morton if there are any other good spies in Henry's employ.

'Not many as good as you,' Morton says. 'Why?'

'I have a plan that goes beyond sitting and waiting,' Simnel says. 'If you'll trust me to take charge of it. But I need someone else. Is there a skilled man available?'

'Sir Robert Clifford comes into my head,' Morton says, wagging his head dolefully. 'But his divers talents are sitting like ripe apples on the bough of a tree growing from a cliff. Unharvestable. And perilous to try. He used to be a spy for Richard, but since he transferred his loyalties to Henry he hasn't been trusted by Yorkist traitors.'

'I have an idea of how to change that,' Simnel says.

'Well! I'll ask His Grace the King for permission. I feel sure he'll grant it. God bless these ideas of yours, Simnel. I want nothing more than for you and me to get back to doing His work.'

I work as you taught me, he says to Joan. *Are you proud?*

Joan doesn't answer.

It doesn't matter. He knows what he needs to do.

In October Henry leaves England to invade France. He takes seven hundred ships and fifteen thousand men, and besieges Boulogne with engines of war.

The queen and the royal household abide his return at Eltham Palace. Eltham was beloved by King Edward, who added battlements, a newfangled pleasure gallery for divers sports, and a great hall with a gilded hammer beam roof and walls covered in badges of the sun in splendour and the white rose – which surely Henry, who has already been at his own improvements, won't let stand for long.

The palace stands on a tall hill. Below it the gardens, the trees of the hunting park. Then London. Roofs and spires and columns of rising smoke and masts of the ships on the wide Thames.

Simnel looks over it.

He would be so tiny in those streets. Undetectable. He has a piece of gold. He could slip in, enter a busy market, and that would be it. Freedom.

But then he could have slipped away so many times. They stopped watching him long ago. He could have Robin Hooded his way to Ireland, robbing rich men on the road. Maybe got caught and killed. Maybe reached Joan.

But he hasn't done it. He doesn't want to arrive as an outlaw, a beggar. He wants to bring gifts.

He wants to come to her and say, *Here: the heads of our enemies.*

So he bides.

After less than a month of besiegement, Charles VIII of France and Henry agree a peace treaty in early November. Charles wants beskift of Henry so he can be free to invade Italy. Henry wants the pension of 50,000 crowns a year that Charles agrees to pay him. As part of the agreement, the York pretender is to be expelled from France.

Henry is satisfied with this.

Nobody else is.

Margaret's stepson Maximilian is wonderly wroth because he and Henry had lateward agreed to jointly oppose France, but now Maximilian has been left out of the treaty altogether, with no pension.

The only prize he won was the York pretender, who has now arrived at Mechelen, to tell and retell his stupid story of wandering Europe in disguise.

(Not that Simnel's got a maugre about it.)

The English soldiers grucched in taverns that they'd been sat about pulling their pizzles for weeks, and now had to go home with no chance of any fighting, swiving or looting.

The commons were irous that they'd paid for this war with their taxes, but now the war was not happening and the French King's *casse-toi* money was going straight into Henry's strongboxes.

A triumph of diplomacy, said Morton, looking inquiet. Blessed be God.

A market trader's trick, said one of the nobles departing for the hunt.

A turd in his teeth, said a falconer. Fucking tight-fisted cunt.

Sir Robert Clifford meets Simnel before Christmas. Simnel has devised a piece of pageantry in which Clifford and he talk, and are seen talking; leading to Clifford's arrest and interrogation on suspicion of traitorous compassings, Yorkist loyalties, and purposing to help Simnel escape.

The faiting works. Soon Clifford has a new set of friends: low-level Yorkist traitors.

Clifford is delighted to resume business. He embraces Simnel with gratitude. 'I've been at home, speaking nothing but the truth,' he says. 'I've been so grievously *bored*.'

Simnel thinks of his maybe-father, George, Duke of Clarence. The lord of sleights and wiles. But he finds he doesn't have much room in his brain-pan to worry about blood – and not just because he doesn't know anymore if Clarence is his father. It was Edward, that godly boy, who wanted so painfully to be honest where Clarence was untrue.

Simnel's plan is to be better at untruth, and not get drowned in a barrel.

Clifford doesn't mention Sir William Stanley when he's listing traitors. Stanley is wonderly ware, Simnel thinks, irously. He still holds himself above all their heads, circling above the cloudline. But if he dips so much as a wing toward the ground, Simnel's going to catch it, and pull him down.

'I asked about Lovell,' Clifford says. 'But that seems to make people suspicious.'

'Better to forget it for now, then,' Simnel says. 'But keep your ears ready.'

'I will aright,' says Clifford, smiling. His rosy cheeks are like the apples Morton longed to pluck.

'Tell me, my lord,' Simnel asks. 'Have you ever wanted to see Burgundy?'

13

The Wool Earl's squire Patrick Madan, the merry tidings-bringer from Ireland, comes by in spring to see Simnel.

'I brought beer!' he says. 'Let's sit among the daffodils.'

Things in Ireland have not gone as prophesied. Peace is not come. King Henry is suspicious of Kildare, who has lateward hanged the son of the king's commissioner. Kildare sent messengers to the king to explain that the hanging was on a matter unrelated to the York pretender, whom Kildare was not after joining, and assured Henry of his loyalty.

None of this contented the king's minds. He even took Kildare's messengers prisoner.

'Poor demeaning, that,' says Madan. 'Your king is right suspicious, isn't he? Sees threating everywhere. Henry told Kildare he has to present himself at court before Hallowmas. Do you like a bet, Simnel? Shall we bet on whether Kildare will come?'

Madan takes a long drink of beer. 'This stuff is shite, isn't it? I wish I was home. Oh, talking of. How could I not have mentioned this earlier? I asked after the Great Earl's wife and children for you. They're all right well. His son is a hardy boy. His daughter Margaret is producing a tremendous many babies. All female, sadly. Two other daughters have lateward married Gaelic lords. 'Tis good policy. Eleanor is married to Domnhall MacCarthy the Swarthy, Prince of Carbery – you know him? No? And what's the other daughter's name… Joan. Yes. A beauty, I heard. Joan married Maolroona O'Carroll, Prince of Eile. You know him? No? Ah, he's one of the finest men in Ireland. There's none braver, more generous, or better read.

'Now, Simnel, by Jesus! Is that a tear I see in your eye? Don't sham, it is! Ah, I myself have a weep after a few drinks when I remember the hills of home. But *you* can sleep sweeter, at least, knowing the Great Earl's daughters have made good marriages.'

Joan? Simnel asks. *You've been quiet, lateward. Do you still love me?*
(silence)
I hear of your marriage, and I hear the man is a good one. And I wonder…
    if you might be happy with him.
(silence)
It's been six years. And it's wonderly hard, when I don't know your minds.
(silence)
But I'll still come. Even if when I arrive you don't know me anymore.
(silence)
I don't know anything about heaven. But I think it works this way: when
    you arrive, their test is to ask, Would you renounce this place, for
    your love?
And I will say: yes.

14

'Would the king consider letting me leave?' Simnel asks. 'Now that I'm no threat?'

'Leave *court*?' Morton seems genuinely mystified. 'What would you *do*?'

'Farm,' he says.

'Really? I suppose that would be a fitting life. But I'm not sure the king will allow it. Like a noble hawk that has been mobbed by heinous crows, he now sees threat where most men would not.'

'May I propose something?' Simnel asks. 'If I can prove someone both high up and close to the king is a traitor, would he give me a pension and let me go free?'

'Do you know who this person is? If so it's treason to withhold it.'

'It isn't proved yet.'

'He might say, you should find out traitors without asking for reward, on account of your great debt to him in sparing your life,' Morton says. Then he sighs, and says, more gently: 'I'll ask.'

I don't know what to do, Simnel says to Joan. *I wanted to come to you and tell you that justice was done, for Grania and Lincoln and you and me. But now you're married. There's no more time. I can give Cross and Stanley to that undeserving shitpate Henry, and quit court. But then Plunket and your father might never answer for Grania's death. But if I don't leave soon and help you, you might end up with children, and I don't want you to throw them in the sea. Or worse, keep them and love them, and love the father that gave you them.*

Joan doesn't answer. She's as silent as God these days.

Simnel wonders, for the first time, if he got it wrong. He thought she'd wanted him to work great wrack. But what if she'd only ever wanted him to come to her? Empty-handed: no victories, no heads.

If it was only Simnel that needed vengeance.

Please, Joan: tell me what you want.

No answer.

Simnel is escorted by Morton, very early in the morning, to meet Henry. Most of the palace is still asleep; the halls and cloisters and gardens strangely quiet, in the hazy light of not-yet-dawn. Their footsteps echo on the tiles.

Henry is waiting for them in a chamber with guards outside the door, but no servants within. It occurs to Simnel, as he and Morton bow and sit at the table, that it wouldn't be difficult to kill Morton (old) and Henry (weak, clerkly-bodied) right now. But then he'd die too. And he hasn't found out if Joan still loves him.

Henry looks tired. Simnel wonders if he's been to bed. The noise around court (a noise Henry has failed to smother) is all of assassination plots; poison on doorknobs; ambushes outside Mass; angry commoners; flybills calling for uprisings passed around the streets and nailed to church doors; a small but steady flow of nobles joining the new pretender in Mechelen. And here's Simnel, wondering if a quill thrust hard enough into the eye could reach the man's brain.

Such is the life of a king, says Boethius.

'I acknowledge your great services to us,' Henry says, 'which have much outweighed your grievous early offences.'

'Committed when he was only a boy, compelled by others,' Morton adds.

'Indeed,' Henry says. 'I am minded therefore to award you a pension.'

The king leaves a pause here, for Simnel to humbly make his thanks, which he does.

'But,' says Henry, 'not yet. Rewards follow results. You can retire when the person you speak of is found guilty at trial, and I am content in my minds that the York threat is dead.'

You miserable market trader, thinks Simnel. Buying himself indefinite servitude. Simnel looks at the quills on the table with longing, then at Henry.

Obey me, says Henry's straight eye.

Put a quill in me, says Henry's crazed eye. *Go on. Do it.*

Simnel says, 'Thank you, your grace.'

He can always escape without the pension if need be.

'Now,' says Henry, 'who is this great noble about whom you are making such strong accusations?'

'I want to prepare Sir Robert Clifford to approach Sir William Stanley, your Lord Chamberlain. Maybe you also ought to have Stanley watched.'

'*Stanley!*' Henry says. 'This is not so. You... you are mistaken.'

Each word is less and less fierce, and *mistaken* comes out very small. His brain is already turning on it, Simnel can tell. He sits back in his chair and his eyes seem to sink even deeper into his head. Only his fingers move, twisting inquietly.

'Stanley,' he says. 'God help us.'

They sit in silence for a moment, then Henry gets up abruptly and quits the chamber. Morton and Simnel stand, look at each other.

'By Saint Omer,' Morton says. 'Stanley is his trusted friend. He's brother by marriage to my lady the king's mother. This will be a spear to the king's heart.' He shakes his head. 'Still, let nobody say you didn't earn your pension.'

Simnel hesitates before laying out the next part of his plan. But not for long.

He tells Morton that Sir Robert Clifford should fait an escape to Mechelen, for fear of King Henry. This should convince Stanley – shy as a jay thus far – of Clifford's true loyalty to the York pretender, and attract more traitors to the cause.

Morton looks surprised, then pleased.

'The court of the wolf herself, Margaret of Burgundy,' he says. 'An excellent idea. I pity Clifford; he's descending into hell aright.'

Simnel thinks of the exquisitely painted halls of Mechelen, the immaculate streets of the town, the sunlit courtyards where he played by the fountain with Philip.

He remembers the word: *sehnsucht*.

He knows he's betraying his maybe-aunt Margaret. But Margaret won't be harmed by any of this. She's too powerful. The only thing that might fail is the new pretender's planned invasion, and Simnel doesn't give a shit about that. Whether a Richard, Duke of York rules or Henry makes no difference. York, Lancaster, Tudor. He'll ally with whoever looks after him: Simnel. And Margaret would see it the same way. She'd full merrily join up with her enemies the French against Henry, or her enemy Henry against the French.

It's just business.

The thought of Philip pains him. They'll never be kings and friends now. But then, they never could. This will be a good learning for Philip.

In July Henry announces that he's discovered the truth about the supposed Duke of York. Simnel isn't sure where this truth was procured from. It didn't come from Clifford. The spy had successfully lured Stanley into revealing his York sympathy, but he couldn't find out the identity of the new pretender.

Being a woman, and one disordered by wroth, I thought Margaret would jangle the truth immediately, Clifford wrote. *But she's wonderly miserly when it comes to secrets.*

(At which a *sehnsuchtian* affection for his former aunt lights Simnel's heart.)

Henry proclaims that the pretender is a Perkin Warbeck. Son of a bargee. Low-level mercantile employee. Had worked, for a time, for Sir Edward Brampton, before being picked up in Cork by the Yorkist traitors.

But the more Henry proclaims it, the less people believe it.

'We're not such doddypolls as to believe a York-looking man just happed upon the Yorkist rebels in an Irish harbour, and the plan was made on the spot,' says Beatrice.

Henry sets a patrol of ships on the North Sea, and has the ports and coastline guarded. He sends more men to Ireland – which is still distroubled, with fighting in Dublin, Sheep Street burned, men massacred in Oxmantown Green and slaughter throughout the Pale. He punishes Margaret and Maximilian for their support of Warbeck by banning trade and expelling the Flemish from London. The after-claps of that are heaps of unexported wool and cloth in London warehouses; affrays; riots.

Henry has been spending his nights gnawing over policy, Morton says. So much betrayal, such large infamy. So many divers things laying heavy on his heart. It's a miracle it doesn't brast.

So now as Simnel lies unsleeping past midnight, in misery and wroth, he wonders if Henry – far on the other side of the castle, up the stairs, through the guarded door, through a series of chambers, below the velvet curtains, under his gold-embroidered coverlet – is doing the same.

Simnel allows himself the pleasure of imagining Henry's down-fall. He's been reading Dante's *Commedia*, in which the poet placed several of his own personal enemies – both dead and still living – in hell.

Simnel imagines Henry in the fourth circle of hell, being crushed under a great weight of account books. It's not satisfying.

Simnel doesn't care, that's why. It means nothing much to him if Henry lives or dies.

He imagines, instead, himself as a demon in hell, with a long sword. Prisoners are brought to him one at a time:

Plunket, who caused the death of Grania.

Kildare, who killed Grania.

Sir William Stanley, who caused the death of Lincoln.

Cross, who killed Lincoln.

The sham deaf mute Morelle, who caused the death of Maister Richard and Bella.

Mayne and his friend, who killed them, are both dead, but Simnel imagines their necks stretched out under the sword anyway. And when they're all beheaded, their blood pouring off the scaffold, he starts again.

This time with fire.

15

Simnel hears that Bernard André, Henry's sycophant poet laureate, is working on an official history of Henry's regime. Using the gold piece given to him by the last of his lovers, he pays one of André's clerks a bribe to secretly copy out the work so far and bring it to him.

The clerk doesn't go away immediately. He's bored with his travail under the poet, and lingers around chatting to Simnel.

'Look, you're in the book,' the clerk says. 'I thought, as with Herostratus, they might have tried to excise your name from history. But here it is.'

(The clerk thinks his name is Lambert Simnel.)

'"A wretched lad, a princeling of rascals, a whip scoundrel,"' Simnel reads. '"Born to low people, of low occupations."'

He looks through the rest, which is in full hagiographic style: the child Henry's holiness causing wonder in all, virtue shining from him, everyone agreeing that he was destined to be a glorious king, just as his ancestor Saint Cadwaladr was, and so on and so on.

'God spare us, he's written a poem,' says Simnel. '"Descend, Calliope from your sacred mount…" By Christ.'

'Think of me, having to transcribe this ballocks all day,' says the clerk.

'I once wanted to be a king who wrote history. Now I realise *only* kings write history,' Simnel says. 'Is anything true written anymore?'

'Probably not,' says the clerk cheerfully. 'But we all know it's lies. When King Richard was alive the historian Rous called him a good lord and a punisher of oppressors. But now Rous has evil Richard in the womb two years; born with teeth and hair; misaligned in the body.'

'A goodly point,' says Simnel. 'Thank you.'

'Worth a little extra gold?' says the clerk hopefully.

'You had it all.'

'Then I bid you goodbye. Happy reading.'

But it isn't happy, and later, when Simnel's with Beatrice, he returns to his maugre against history.

'*We* might know the truth,' he says. 'But in a few hundred years, Richard will be a hunchback and I'll be a scoundrel. Those people won't know anything else.'

'Write your own history then,' she says.

'I'd be writing my own head onto the block.'

'Then write it in cipher, and bury it in a lead casket. Maybe some-one will dig it up a thousand years from now and puzzle it out.'

'I wonder what those people will be like,' he muses. 'Do you?'

'No. I'll be dead. I don't care who they are.'

'You're the one who wants me to write them a fucking book!'

'Only so you'll cheer up and stop making dole about stupid things. People in the future… By Saint Mary! As if there isn't enough to worry about in this life without worrying about the next thousand years too.'

Toward the end of the year, Henry insists again that Kildare come right anon to court, with no further delay or excusings.

Kildare says he'll come.

'And if you believe *that*'ll happen,' Madan says, 'then I've got a twelve-inch cock, and an ointment to sell you that guarantees like increase.'

But Madan is wrong.

In December 1493, six years after he was meant to present himself to the king: Kildare arrives.

Simnel gets an audience with Kildare easily. Morton, who sore mislikes Kildare's ability to get away with everything, like a fly you clap in your hand that flies out again when the hand opens, wants him to lead Kildare into unwise confidences. Simnel doesn't tell Morton that his dream of Kildare blavering himself into a beheading is hopeless. But Simnel wants tidings of Joan, and Kildare has them.

Kildare's personal guards are standing outside his chamber door.

'You can go right in,' says a guard. 'He's been looking forward to seeing you.'

And then, somehow sooner than he expected, Simnel's in front of Kildare: the Great Earl, bright as a burning fire – Simnel forgot the intense energy of the man – springing up from behind his table to embrace him.

'What cheer!' Kildare says. As he returns to his seat, Simnel takes one of the papers heaped on the table and puts it into his sleeve.

Kildare continues, 'Sit down, I pray you. By Jesus, it's been a long time. I gather you're here because they want me to jangle to you in the hearing of their spies. Marvellous mistrustful, I call that. But still, any reunion is better than no reunion. It lightens my heart to see you, grown into a passing manly-looking man. Nearly taller than me now. Well done, lad.'

Simnel says, 'Where's Joan?'

'Ah,' Kildare says. 'Is it like that?'

Simnel stares at him.

'It is then. Alright. I married her well, to the O'Carroll prince. A goodly gentil man. Too much of a man for her to work him any wrack, was what I thought. Now she seems to have him bent to her minds and the pair of them are causing me divers kinds of problems. And no children yet. I fear she's done some sorcery there. Cursed his balls, put a drought on them. Or else the seed withered away with fright.' His gaze moves to the middle distance, amused and affection-ate. 'Sure I'd put nothing past her.'

Simnel doesn't know what he wanted to hear, or if this is it. Words elude him.

Kildare takes his silence for ire.

'Wroth, still?' he says. ''Tis a strange maugre to hold. Think of *your* balls, lad. You should be grateful to Lovell for saving you from her, when you two purposed to escape my household.'

'Lovell?'

'You remember our friend Lovell, don't you?' Kildare looks at him closely. 'How have they kept you? Free or cell-bound? Do you have your wits?'

'It wasn't Lovell who gave us away. It was Plunket who hated us – spied on the two of us. Plunket who told you our plans—'

'Plunket! He did have a maugre regarding Joan, I recall now. But sure, the fellow couldn't tell you his own arsehole's plans. I love the man. But he's of no great wit. Where did you hear it was Plunket who undid you?'

Simnel doesn't want to say: from Lovell. He's beginning to see how stupid he's been, and he'd rather Kildare didn't see it too.

'Ah. I suppose it was Lovell told you that, was it?' Kildare says. 'He's a full wily fucker. In Dublin he had you under watch every minute of every day. He saw you two stealing my treasure, and he told me your doings. By Jesus, do you think he'd let you get away? *You?* His York heir? Hid by him, fed by him, raised by him. His investment! His only chance of getting his lands and position back?'

Lovell, thinks Simnel.

'Are you alright?' says Kildare. 'You've waxed wonderly white.'

'Where is Lovell?' Simnel demands.

But Kildare, smiling, shakes his head.

Simnel is full, crop to root, of wroth and shame and hatred, rushing up to meet a man who isn't here.

Only Kildare, who takes a part, is here.

'People have been killed because of me,' Simnel says. His throat is so pinched with anger it's hard to get the words out. He holds his hands at his sides. 'I've had people executed. And now I can't sleep. Is it the same for you? Do you lie awake and see the ghosts you made? Do they speak, do they lay their charges on you? Does Grania come?'

'Who?' says Kildare.

As Simnel leaves Kildare's rooms – no bow, no worship; brasting open the doors and startling his guards – he sees a valet coming toward him down the corridor. The valet sees him, turns around, and moves quickly away.

Simnel follows, as quietly as he can. The two of them walk beyond the press around Kildare's room into a quieter corridor, a quieter corridor still; Simnel trying to identify the man from his liveried back, slender, slightly jerky, moving quickly.

It's only when the valet steps into a large garderobe, leaving the door open, and turns to face him that Simnel recognises Morelle: the sham deaf mute. Looking straighter now, younger, more despitous of eye.

Simnel is astonied.

Morelle looks nothing so much as annoyed. He draws Simnel inside, then pulls the door shut behind them both.

'What?' Morelle says, in a whisper. 'What business do you have with me? You'll expose both of us, following me like this.'

'Don't we have shared interests?' Simnel says. 'Shared friends? Sir Hugh Cross? Sir William Stanley?'

Morelle's frown gathers tighter. Simnel feels his own body tightening in response. Peril, he thinks. 'You shouldn't know *his* name,' Morelle says. 'Are you a spy?'

'Lincoln told me,' Simnel says.

But Morelle says, 'Lincoln never knew.'

Understanding passes, blindingly quick, between them. Then Simnel headbutts Morelle. The man stumbles back, with a grunt. Blood runs out of his nose, through his hands onto his livery. Simnel takes his knife out and puts the point against Morelle's throat.

He's working against his own shock, which wants him to stand still and gape. To slowly comprehend what Morelle is saying. *Lincoln didn't know.* So Cross didn't murder him for Stanley's sake. He did it for Lovell. To protect the escape route Lovell had talked about, his network of Yorkist foxholes.

Lovell, he thinks.

But there's no time to contemplate Lovell. Morelle has straightened up, and regained some confidence.

'You wouldn't do that here,' he says.

'But I'm under Henry's protection,' Simnel says. 'You were right. So, yes, I would do that here.'

Now Morelle, suddenly nostalgic, waxes mute.

'Hey, how about you give me a spiced bun and I'll let you go?' Simnel says. 'No? No buns today? You fucking weaselfucker.'

'Listen,' Morelle says. 'You work for Henry. I know it's peril to you if you let me go. So I'll put myself in the same amount of peril, I'll tell you everything I know. Then we both have knowledge of each other, and surety therein. You want names? I can tell you which courtiers are writing to Burgundy.'

'I have those names,' Simnel says. 'Tell me about Lovell.'

Morelle, already pale from bleeding, loses more of his colour. He shakes his head. Simnel digs the knife in.

'Is Lovell your master?'

'He was. Up until lateward. Now I work for Stanley, while Stanley works for Lovell.'

'So it was Lovell who had Maister Richard and Bella killed. And for Lovell's sake that Lincoln died?'

Morelle nods.

'Where is he?'

'I don't know where, I swear it on the Virgin. Only Stanley knows – might not even know anymore. He was getting letters from Lovell, for a time, but Lovell didn't want to be part of this new rebellion. Said he doesn't trust the French. The last I heard, he was going to Scotland.'

'Alright,' Simnel says. He's disappointed, but he doesn't think Morelle has any more to give.

'So you'll let me go?' Morelle says.

'I never said what I would do,' Simnel says. 'But I won't kill you. I'm going to hand you to King Henry's men. You'll love Bishop Morton.'

'But they'll torture me, find out I don't know anything other than what I've told you, then hang, draw and quarter me.'

'That does sound likely, aright,' Simnel agrees. 'God's bones, you were wasted as a murderer! You should have sold prophecies to—'

Morelle, in a quick movement, takes hold of the back of Simnel's neck – as if he's about to kiss him – and pulls. Their bodies collide. The knife breaks through Morelle's skin and disappears into his throat. Simnel can feel it. Blood, hot as soup, rushes over his hands.

He steps back, astonied, and Morelle falls backwards against the wall, then slides down onto the ground. He makes terrible sounds, but not for long, and then his eyes become still and calm, his head tips backwards, and Simnel is left alone.

I should have known, he thinks, as he pushes Morelle's body to the back of the privy; inspects his own livery; decides the wet blood against the dark red cloth could be anything, could be soup; wipes the splashes off his bright buttons using his sleeve; leaves; shuts the door; heads to Morton, to explain the situation.

Should have known:

everything is Lovell.

Lovell oversaw Simnel's childhood. Took him from the farm. Had Maister Richard and Bella murdered. Had Joan taken away. Had Grania murdered. Had Lincoln murdered.

This shouldn't be a surprise. And yet somehow, it is. Simnel thought he had the measure of him. He knew Lovell was calculating and cold. What did Joan say? *Lovell is practical.* But Simnel didn't imagine how far practicality would go, without any human feeling to curb it.

The day John Collan saw him arrive at the farm in his drab hat, he should have run from sight, like a mouse in the shadow of a barn owl.

No, he should have leaped at him, like a rat, and bitten through his throat.

16

Kildare stays on at court until early May. Simnel expects not to see the Great Earl again – is glad not to – but then Morton sends for him.

Simnel notices the pile of livery on the table before Morton. It looks like some kind of table-servant's costume. Morton appears full of some privy delight.

'Our sovereign lord is planning a jape at the expense of the Irish lords,' he says. 'As we know, the king never japes without serious purpose, and his moral lesson here is to warn the Irish not to support the pretender Warbeck. While also embarassing and shaming the Lord Kildare for his heinous demeaning in the matter of your crowning. You may have heard Henry said to them, "My masters of Ireland, you will crown apes at length."'

'Very witty,' Simnel says.

'Wonderly mirthful! And on this note, the king has a task for you.'

And so here is Simnel, in a cupbearer's livery, making his entry into the great chamber at Greenwich – currently occupied by six hundred nobles at dinner, their tables laid out below the raised dais on which the king and queen sit at their own tables. The grace is done, food is being eaten, and the hall is loud with voices, Kildare's uppermost among them. He's sitting at the king's table, higher in precedence than even the Wool Earl.

Simnel, as instructed, fills a cup with wine. A strange combination of fear and hatred bears him, almost levitating, to the king's table.

Only a few of the Irish lords notice him at first, and the ones who glance at him don't recognise him, and then Henry says, 'Look here, my lords, your king Lambert Simnel has brought you wine to drink, and drinks to you all likewise.'

A silence drops onto them. The feeling of being in a dream thickens. Simnel's vision is shimmering like the torchlight. He is aware of Kildare, several seats down, looking at him.

Simnel offers the cup to the nearest man, Lord Killeen. Last seen at Simnel's – Edward's – Coronation in Dublin. Killeen avoids Simnel's eye. He grimaces and waves the cup gone. But the man next to him – Simnel guesses this must be Lord Howth, who never joined the rebellion, and is the only man laughing – says, 'By the Virgin, if the wine is good, I'll gladly take it from you.'

Simnel notices then, as Howth is drinking, a man sitting on the far side of the king who has a different demeaning to the rest of the guests.

Simnel knows who this is.

Yes, his skin is whiter, his hair more mouse-colour than blond, his body slighter, a couple of years younger – but it's *him*.

The other Earl of Warwick.

They must have brought him out of the Tower, for a day of display. His presence is intended to humiliate the Irish lords. Yet it's obvious he's not fit for purpose. The earl is finely dressed but his hands tremble and his minds seem buckish; his eyes jump around, he turns his head this way and that like people are talking to him, when nobody is. The men to either side of him are both ignoring him. Once he says something to one of them, stammering, but his neighbour keeps his face turned determinedly away.

Simnel, horrified and fascinated, progresses down the table toward Warwick. He almost doesn't remember the fact of Kildare's existence until Kildare calls for him to stop. His hand is out, for the cup.

The lines from Juvenal come into Simnel's head then: the man guilty of a crime who can't enjoy his dinner because his dry throat chokes on the food, and the finest wine tastes of vinegar.

He hands Kildare the cup. Every face is turned to them. Kildare takes a deep draught.

'Marvellous savoury,' he says, smiling. 'Thank you, your grace.'

Everyone laughs.

Henry looks sore disappointed, and privily wroth – but Simnel gets no pleasure from the sight.

He can see Warwick looking directly at him. He has an *asking* look now. As if he needs Simnel to answer a question: which of them is which, maybe. Who is real, who a sham?

But Simnel doesn't know.

He moves toward Warwick, not even knowing why – but Morton, beside the king, is speaking. Saying, 'That's all now, Simnel. You may quit us.'

Within the week Kildare is gone back to Ireland, full merry, having had payment for his expenses during his stay, and two of his men knighted.

Simnel wishes he hadn't seen Warwick. The sight of the earl's quaking hands comes back and back to him, each time no less painful than the last. He'd heard the boy was weak-witted after spending so long alone in the Tower, but the sight is harder than the hearing. How can Henry stand it? But he probably notes each sign of degradation in his account book, with satisfaction. Twitching, trembling, fearfulness. Look, he'd say, this is no king. Count the number of crosses in the crazed column. And see: none at all in my own.

Beatrice says, 'Do you think the earl would have been let out sooner if people didn't keep rebelling in his name? Uh, I mean, it's not *your* fault. Sorry.'

At night they come to join him:
Bella
Maister Richard
Grania
Lincoln
Lady FitzAlan (dead last year, of a fever)
And now:
Edward, Earl of Warwick

402

Sometimes Mayne comes, his expression ghastly, grimacing; eyes staring out from the level of his fat belly, where his arms cradle his bloodless head.

You did this, he says.

It's Simnel's one comfort.

17

All that summer England and Flanders quarrel over the new pretender. To leads to fro, this leads to that.

Maximilian continues to proclaim the miraculous return of the Duke of York, who he says has three birthmarks as proof of his identity.

Henry sends his Garter King of Arms to Flanders to inform them their York is a Warbeck.

The Flanders nobles ignore him.

The Garter gives up on the nobility and walks the streets of Mechelen, shouting that the York prince is a faiter and a sham.

The people ignore him.

Henry noises it that Maximilian doesn't have enough money to help Warbeck.

Maximilian gives the Duke of York lavish lodgings, a retinue of English gentlemen and a guard of twenty archers, all wearing the white rose.

Two Englishmen throw a chamber pot at the shield above Warbeck's door.

A warly crowd chases the Englishmen off. An English bystander is killed in the affray.

Henry becomes more mistrustful and ware by the day. The news of Sir William Stanley's treachery is wearing at him, Morton says. Then there's the King of France, who – despite the peace treaty – has offered to lend Warbeck ships to invade England.

Can you blame Henry then, for instigating nightly identity checks of servants? For creating an even more privy privy chamber, with only a few grooms in attendance, and an extra set of guards?

'I hear his turds have their own guard these days,' says Madan. 'And are watched on their way to the midden, in case they plot treason.'

Kildare is back in Ireland, which he still has the rule of – says Madan – even without his Lord Deputyship.

Simnel asks Beatrice to get him a piece of thin pig intestine.

'Why would you need that?' she asks. 'It's nothing bad, is it? I worry for your soul. Is this some evildoing, some dishonesty?'

'Why would you suspect that?'

'Because I'm not an idiot,' she says.

'No evil, no dishonesty,' he says. She looks hesitant. 'Beatrice, I swear it. On the Saints. No, on the Virgin. Content your minds.'

She watches as he travails with his quills and paper, and the letter he stole from Kildare's desk. Tracing the handwriting through the translucent gut to write himself a regretful note.

In which Kildare wishes Simnel good fortune, but will not help him again in any rebellion, because Simnel is fallen much out of mind these days, while Richard of York has the love of the people and has promised to restore Kildare's Lord Deputyship.

He realises Beatrice is a little too close.

'Can you read?' he asks her.

'No. And Elyn disapproves of it.'

'Disapproves of *reading*?'

'You can be very noble-ish sometimes,' she says, frowning. 'Not everyone thinks reading is the best thing on God's earth and anyone who can't read might as well be dead.'

She picks up the papers and squints at them. Simnel almost feels alarmed. As if she might suddenly, miraculously, make sense of what she's seeing.

'No sin?' she asks, again.

Is it sinful, to force Justice's hand to administer a slap to Kildare's face?

A slap long overdue?

'Beatrice! Why won't you believe me?'

She looks hesitant. Then says, 'Sorry. I don't mean to sound untrusting. You just look so…'

'Doleful? You always say I look doleful. You should expect me to look doleful, and then there'd be no surprise in it.'

'No. You used to look doleful. And wroth. Now you look…' She hesitates. 'Not *kind*.'

Simnel thinks of Maister Richard saying, about Margaret of Burgundy: *She's a Duchess. I don't know that kind or not kind is of any significance.*

Has his kindness gone? Maybe. Each of his selves took something from him as they fell away. He left his confidence on the farm with John Collan. His innocence drowned on the floor of the house in Oxford, as Lambert Simons covered his eyes. His happiness is still locked in Edward, Earl of Warwick's bedchamber in Dublin. When Simnel quits here, his goodness and his faith will be left in one of Henry's strongboxes.

What has he got now? His hatred, and his love. It's all he needs. The rest is chaff. Like Joan said, he's better off without. He should have brushed it off sooner.

Morton holds the Kildare-looking notes in his hands like the Holy Grail.

'Oh, my boy,' he says to Simnel. 'I think we have him.'

That autumn Henry appoints the diplomat and prodigious swiver Sir Edward Poynings to the post of Lord Deputy of Ireland. Kildare's former position. It isn't long before Sir James Ormond accuses Kildare of trying to assassinate Poynings. Kildare, realising the peril he's in, hies himself away into hiding, most likely sheltered by one of his allies in the lands far beyond the Pale.

Poynings' parliament meets in December and attaints the absent Kildare for 'great and manifold treasons', including inciting war, planning the personal destruction of Poynings, and divers other offences. Poynings also begins to re-Anglicise Ireland, which he sees as having sunk into a greasy black bog of Gaelicism. The war cries 'Crom a Boo' and 'Butler a Boo' are outlawed. 'To Saint George' or 'To King Henry' are suggested as replacements.

According to Madan, the new fashion among the Wool Earl's men is, when they take a shit, to cry: *To King Henry*.

Simnel's sorry for the Irish.

But.

But fuck you, Kildare, fuck you, and your Grania who, *and your* Thank you, your grace: *this is full rightly done, and not God's vengeance but my own.*

Does it make him happy?

Not yet.

The deaths of Cross and Kildare and Stanley and Lovell…

Above all, Lovell.

That will make him happy.

One part of the miserable poet Bernard André's miserable book sticks in Simnel's pate. It's entitled

'The Tearful Outcry of the Author', and addressed to God: in which André dwells on the wars between York and Lancaster; wonders why God would stand by as the Lancaster king was murdered; why he would allow others to work evil for many years, unchecked; warns God that *some people* wonder at His decision-making process – not only that, might even suspect Him of not paying attention to human affairs.

André seems to have forgotten that, a few pages earlier, God's Divine Providence gave Henry his victory at Bosworth.

How does that work? Simnel wonders.

No answer from André, and none from God.

By now Simnel's stopped expecting anything from the latter. If there ever was a God, He's gone. His children were so wicked that they've been cast off the whole earth. There isn't going to be a hell or a heaven. But nobody's realised it yet. They're all just carrying on, talking and working and fighting each other in the emptiness. And not the good but the strongest will survive.

18

Sir Robert Clifford, their spy in Mechelen, is coming back. He has, he writes jubilantly, a long list of names for them. Henry issues Clifford with a formal pardon for his 'treason' at the start of December, and Clifford promptly flees Mechelen. He's sailing back to England anon.

In the last year Henry has had spies resorting in and out of the household of his treacherous Lord Chamberlain, Sir William Stanley. Stanley's confessor, chaplain, servants and retainers have been interrogated. Several of them informed on him, and were paid well for it.

Simnel knows that once Clifford gets back, Stanley's arrest will happen quickly. He sends Stanley a note (*A Warning from a Friend*) and begs a secret audience with the man alone.

Simnel tells Beatrice and Elyn that he expects to have his freedom soon — and enough money to buy a house, maybe some land. He could farm or take up a trade. He says if Beatrice and Elyn want to leave court, Simnel could marry Beatrice. Elyn, to the world, would be Simnel's maiden sister, but behind closed shutters, Elyn and Beatrice would sleep in one room and Simnel in another.

'The Holy Virgin bless you,' Beatrice says, hands tight to heart, tears standing in her eyes. 'It would be my fondest—'

'I mislike it,' says Elyn.

'What?' Simnel says. '*Why?*'

'You are not to be trusted,' Elyn says. 'You're a liar, a secret-keeper and a courtly schemer.'

'Elyn!' Beatrice says. 'He's not a liar. Simnel is my friend.'

Simnel's conscience hasn't seen much light lateward; it sleeps among tree roots, seeing out a long winter. But it shifts now, stung.

Elyn says, 'If you know Simnel so well, where is he getting this money? Why is he *free*, suddenly?'

Beatrice opens her mouth, finds no answer inside, and turns to Simnel. Who has no answer either.

'He's up to mischief, and he'll bring trouble to our home,' Elyn says.

'But it would *be* a home,' he says. 'You're right that I'm a faiter. I have this money because of misdoings and secrets. But it comes from the king. So it's safe. But if you don't want it, if you want to be servants until your ending days, no beds of your own, seeing each other hudder mudder, I won't argue with you.'

'*Elyn*,' says Beatrice. 'It's from the *king*.'

'That cunt,' says Elyn. She sighs. Then she turns to Simnel. 'I still don't trust you. And don't expect any gratitude. I'm sure this is to your benefit in some way.'

'You're welcome,' he says.

Her eyebrows move angrily. 'I said, I *wasn't* thanking you.'

'Yes, and I was making a jape in the hope of causing you annoyance.'

He smiles at her. He's been floating in a strange kind of lightness – not a joyous, holy kind of lightness but a malicious, untethered kind of lightness – since he got a note from Stanley, agreeing to meet him. He's in the mood for merriment.

Elyn shrugs, and turns away.

Beatrice, not having listened to them, has clasped her hands together in prayer.

'I have to write to my mother!' she says. 'This is her dearest wish. Blessed be God, I am the merriest woman in the world!'

Simnel meets Sir William Stanley at the ruin in the woods. Feeling a strange, unspeakable pleasure at bringing him to this place of bawdy doings. Stanley in his furred velvet and neat grey beard; standing frowning, then astonied, at the sight of Simnel approaching, crack-crackling through the frosted trees.

'*You*? What is this?' he asks. 'What in God's name are you—'

Simnel wants to say: *Yes, it is I, the little shitpate, now come to shit all over* your *pate.* He nearly laughs, but makes his face heavy. A smile now would be a crack through which the cruel lightness could brast out, like the sun through a shutter edge, and give him away.

'That letter came from me, my lord,' he says. 'I am your supporter. Nobody else is. Your household is under watch and your friend Sir Robert Clifford has betrayed you. Henry knows you are sympathetic to the Duke of York, and it won't be long before you're arrested.'

Stanley is silent now, and white as the sky.

'I've been spying for Henry,' Simnel says. 'I had no choice. But I'm loyal to the Dowager Duchess Margaret of Burgundy and Viscount Lovell. I know no other friends. I've known for years that you keep faith with Lovell, and Sir Hugh Cross. But I never gave you or Cross away. Your mistake was making friends with Clifford. He was always the king's man. My lord, I need you to trust me now. Henry doesn't have enough evidence of wrongdoing to kill you, and he doesn't *want* to kill you. He loves you as a friend. Your brother is married to his mother. You'll be put in the Tower for a while, but they'll let you out again.'

Stanley remains wonderly composed. He doesn't move at all. His hands hang still at his sides. His gaze moves off and through Simnel, his brain hurrying to make its calculations. Eventually he says,

'So why are you telling me this? If I can't escape arrest, and I won't be killed?'

'Because we can save Cross, and Lovell. They're watching Cross now because they know he serves you. You can't warn him to escape: you can't use any of your people. But I can warn him, and Lovell too. Tell me where both of them are, and I'll get word to them that they need to flee.'

'What if you betray them?' Stanley asks. 'How can I trust you?'

'If I wanted to betray Cross, I could have done it years ago. If I wanted to see him captured now, I wouldn't have spoken to you. Think about it. If I do nothing, the king's men will arrest him, and in the meantime if he sends anything to Lovell, they'll know where Lovell is and send assassins. This is the only opportunity you have to stop any of this. I'm going to hie away from court anon myself and take a boat to Mechelen. Where I'll pray that we can meet as friends on the other side of this, with Richard, Duke of York as our king. I can speak to Lovell and Cross before I go. Or not.'

Again Stanley calculates. There's not much room in it. Only one conclusion. It's not long before he reaches it, and says, 'Lovell's in Scotland. In Edinburgh, on Drygate. He's waiting there for invasion, after which he hopes to return to his lands. Cross is at his own estate.'

'I'll go now and tell him myself,' Simnel says. He bows.

Stanley lets his breath out with a tiny hissing noise. Relief is visible in his face.

'God keep you,' he says, and bows.

Simnel exults in his success that night. Joan doesn't come to celebrate with him, so he goes over it alone. Lovell's address! Lovell's plans!

Though Simnel wishes Stanley hadn't bowed.

He knows now the kinds of details that attach themselves to him, that he comes back to at night. Lady FitzAlan's trembling voice. Cecily White's desperate letter: *You must help me.* The Earl of Warwick's shaking hand at the banquet table.

And now a sincere bow, given to a friend offering help.

Stanley was in evil company, Simnel says to Joan. *If you go to bed with evil men, you can't be surprised if you have to eat an evil breakfast alongside them.*

No reply.

Reluctantly, Simnel tells Morton about Sir Hugh Cross. He'd have loved to kill Cross himself, but the man's estate has its own squires and retinue and guards. Simnel could talk his way in, but not out again.

Knowing the limits of his own power. That's important. Eyes seeing clearly. Wroth controlled. Wits in his head.

Better that *someone* kills him, even if it has to be Henry.

Lovell he keeps for himself.

He says to Joan: *I'll go to Scotland, make him tell me who I am, and kill him. What do you think? Never mind.*

I know you won't answer. Maybe it's because you don't have to anymore.
We are of the same minds. Whatever you'd say, I know it already.
We go together, and we find the man who betrayed us.

In early January 1495, Clifford arrives in England.

He comes to Simnel first. Unexpectedly, he brings a letter from Philip.

'I told him it was peril to me to bring it. He was most insistent. By God, I think there were tears in his eyes.'

'What is Philip like now?' Simnel asks.

'I hardly spoke to him. He was occupied with reforms and swiving, like all new kings. In person he's nearly as pretty as you. Though not so grimly-looking. You've won yourself great worship now, don't you know that? No need to wrinkle your countenance with this frowning.'

'Thank you for the advice. The letter?'

Clifford hands it to him. Simnel doesn't recognise the seal, or the hand – more refined than that of Philip's last letter – but then Philip is in his majority now, and has a scribe to write for him.

Well-beloved Edward,

I am wonderly sorry that you were robbed of your glorious ending day. I remember how you went to war so gladly, facing torture and death, ready to stand as king 'til the last. I made mourn out of measure for you when I heard a confession of faiting and lowness was signed – and all was lost, forever! I did not understand at first. But the Lady Margaret said it was those peasant years that put you in the habit of submission. It is not your fault. Alexander never had to live as a peasant. You must not feel ashamed. You are alive at least! It is a consolation to be alive, if you cannot die in glory.

And with the old habit of being a peasant, you can accustom yourself back to low living in a way that a nobler man could never withstand.

And, God be thanked, we may rejoice that the York cause will prevail, now that the Lady Margaret has discovered Edward's lost son, Richard,

Duke of York. This must have been God's hidden purpose, unperceived by us until now.

You will have heard that I am now King of the Romans. Everyone has great love for me. It turns out that they did not have large love for my father's war-making. And Busleyden and Margaret say puissance grows in peacetime. Remember as a child I inclined to peace? My heart knew a truth beyond the reach of my brains – and now I am grown, I perceive my inwit fully, and see that I was wise all this time.

Sadly, my father did not come to my inauguration but at least he will be at my wedding. He wants to marry me to Juana, the daughter of King Ferdinand and Queen Isabella – a third child, and so I won't ever have to go to Spain and be a strange creature, like a bird in a pond, or a fish in a tree: a Habsburg king in Castile!

I pray for the success of your cousin Richard. I do not know him well. But the blood of York colours his cheeks most rosy. God praise him! And bring your house to rightful victory.

And yet I do feel a persisting, pointed sorrow in my heart, when I think of how we played at quilles and read our books – remember? – and swore that we would be brother kings forever. Remember how you longed to own an automated giraffe? What daffish boys we were. And yet I feel that old loneliness now – remember how it crept about after me? – as close as if it was that time again, knowing you misplaced and gone evermo.

Simnel holds the letter for a little longer. He wishes he hadn't read it. When he broke the seal he let the Philip in his minds out, like he cracked open something in the soul realm, the land of memory and ideas – and now the boy throwing nutshells in the courtyard is gone and this paper is all that's left.

Clifford has been watching Simnel with a look of weighing up. Sales, credit, debts, prices.

Simnel hands him the letter.

'Give it to Morton,' he says. 'I hold nothing privy.'

Henry has Clifford brought to the Tower for a sham interrogation, during which Clifford formally gives up Sir William Stanley; Sir

Humphrey Savage, Stanley's brother-in-law; Lord Fitzwalter, an official in the Royal household; Sir Gilbert Debenham, a Knight of the King's Body; and many more nobles and clergymen.

The men are all arrrested.

Henry was almost without words, Morton says, at the extent of it. It grieved his heart to see the king so stricken. That so many men had fought at Bosworth not for love of him, but against King Richard. To think that Stanley, so generously rewarded, could have been so faithless.

Of course, Morton says, this cannot be allowed to reflect on the king's person. As a *judgement* of any sort. We'll noise it that Stanley had a maugre against the king because he was refused a position.

Henry's men found a fortune in gold coins hidden by Stanley at Holt Castle, to fund the uprising.

'The coins will soften the bad tidings,' Morton says. 'Henry will appreciate that when he's in cheerier spirit.'

Clifford also claimed – helpfully, he must have thought – that Warbeck was the natural son of Margaret of Burgundy and the Bishop of Cambrai.

'We'll need to quiet that,' Morton says. 'It implies he looks like a York, and disagrees with our own proclaimings.'

'What about Cross?' Simnel asks. 'Has he been arrested?'

Morton frowns.

'Now,' he says, '*that* was unfortunate. Cross saw our men coming from a window and escaped. It was so close he left a cup of beer half-finished. It seems he dressed as a labourer and walked right past everybody. By Saint Euphrasia! He's Lovell's man aright.'

Simnel tries to find out where Cross has fled to. He approaches a younger relative of Sir William Stanley's privily, with a smile, but the man steps back. He looks angry and fearful, like an animal. Too fearful to attack Simnel, but too angry not to show his minds.

'I don't know Sir Hugh Cross,' he says. 'My cousin kept me from knowing. He foresaw a devil like you would come to torture me one day. So do it! The answer will be the same.'

They know it was me then, thinks Simnel.

'How could you?' the man brasts out. 'Stanley fought for you!'

'Oh? I didn't see him on the battlefield,' Simnel says. 'In fact, I only met him once. He called me a little shitpate. That was good faiting, I suppose? It was just as if he didn't care if they hanged me. As if I was a useful shitpate, and then I was a surplus shitpate.'

'He believed in you! He believes in the Duke of York, lately returned to us.'

'He believed in King Richard once, then turned about on him.'

'Because Richard killed the princes!'

'He let Lovell order the death of Lincoln.'

The man gives a bitter laugh. 'Tell me,' he says, 'how any man on earth might *let* or *not let* the Lord Lovell do a thing.'

Simnel has the sense that he's losing hold of the argument.

'We loved Lincoln as you did,' the man says. 'As we love your noble aunt Margaret of Burgundy! As we love the Duke of York! He's your cousin. He could have saved you! And you betrayed them all. Your own people.' There are tears of wroth in his eyes. He gets the words out with difficulty. 'He's a true York friend. And you call yourself a—'

'I call myself nothing,' Simnel says. 'Maybe they're my people. Maybe not. York, Tudor: you can all fuck yourselves.'

'Are you going to have me killed too?'

'Not today,' says Simnel.

He leaves the wretched man where he stands, weeping on.

That kinsman of Stanley's was lying, Simnel says to Joan. *Stanley deserves to die.*

He was lying, Simnel says.

(Not sure whom he's telling, this time.)

At the end of January some men are beheaded, others pardoned. Stanley is tried, found guilty and condemned to be hanged, drawn and quartered. Henry changes this at the last minute to beheading, and pays the axe-man ten pounds to do it cleanly.

Sentimental, says Morton.

Sir Robert Clifford was paid five hundred pounds, and retired from court. He wanted a manor by a river, and a walled pear orchard: he said he had a fancy to make perry.

'*You* won't get five hundred pounds,' Henry says to Simnel. This is their goodbye meeting. 'Clifford is a gentil man, and the payment has to be proportionate to the person. But you'll get a fitting sum.'

'And the knowledge that you've have done our Lord King a great service,' Morton adds. 'In a sea of iniquity and faithlessness, duty done is a pearl beyond price.'

Simnel doesn't say: I'd rather have a real pearl.

'I am honoured, your grace, my lord,' he says.

'You're our best spymaster,' Morton continues. 'Of course, I pride myself on recognising your value, so many years ago. It grieves me that the traitors now know your doubleness.'

Simnel has told Morton that the Yorkists found him out. Just in case Henry was tempted to keep his best spymaster.

'I am content in my minds that you won't be sought out by any more Yorkists,' Henry says now. 'Well, unless they're purposing revenge. You should keep your head low when you do leave.' Then he pauses, and does a small, untrue-sounding laugh. 'My ears were also gladdened to hear of your planned wedding – to a servant girl, yes? Blessed be God, I've secured goodly grooms for the queen's sisters, and now here is another full meet match.'

What he means is: a low marriage, between low people.

There won't be any coming back after that.

Malice puts Simnel in mind to say, 'Any tidings of Lovell?'

Morton makes a noise of exasperation and says, 'It is our great misfortune that he still escapes us. By God, I'd love to get hold of him. He made us look wonderly stupid at Portsmouth, before he fled to join you in Ireland – ah, seven of Henry's men had him and asked him questions, and they had no witting it was that fell Lovell himself they were talking to. Our failure still torments—'

'No failure,' Henry says coldly, and Morton stops, and bows his head. 'It's not over, so how can there be failure?'

There have been times at which Simnel, being stricken and injured himself, has not been able to enjoy the sight of Henry's distroublement.

This is not one of them.

Henry's good eye is flatly wroth; his naughty eye seems amused, as if saying, *What a turd, eh? Think of me. I have to be attached to this dullard.*

Me too, Simnel answers it. *But soon I will be free.*

He entertains a small phantasm in which he pops Henry's eye out of his head with his finger, and the eye is wonderly grateful, and Simnel and the eye go rolling loose and wicked around the world, looking for wrack to work.

He leaves lively-footed, gripped by an excitement that's wild and high-pitched, like drunkenness.

Lovell is mine, he thinks, not Henry's. Lovell hasn't taken anything from Henry except pride. He's taken everything from Simnel. And whatever Lovell didn't take, Simnel himself gave up in his pursuit. (He thinks of Sir William Stanley, no doubt soon to be among the party who call on Simnel at night.) So: Simnel will kill Lovell, and if the body is ever found, let Henry have his pet historians exalt it as his own doings, a purely clerical victory, his heart's desire.

What is Simnel's heart's desire?

In this moment – and how many people on earth can say this? – it's exactly what he has.

Henry's maugre, and Lovell's address.

Beatrice comes to Simnel. She's white with wroth. He's never seen her look like this.

'Has Elyn done something?' he asks.

'You!' she cries. 'You've done something. Tell me you didn't? That poor William Stanley. So kind, he couldn't even see a horse whipped, and there were others too, honourable men – I told you! I said Stanley was a good man, and you didn't listen to me!'

Simnel can't make any defence of himself. He tries to calm her; he reaches out, but she knocks his hands away.

'How did you know I was involved?' he asks.

'*That's* your first question!' she says. 'All the servants know, that's how. They're terrified of you. You sleep with ladies or talk to men, and then they die. They think you have fairy blood, or you're a sorcerer.'

She puts her hands to her head. 'I kept defending you when they chopped at you! I said Henry must have spies watching you, but *you're* the spy! Tell me that's not true?'

There is a long silence. She turns angrily to leave.

'Wait,' he says. 'These servants' masters – do they know? Is the truth out widewhere?'

He's worried that Lovell will hear that Simnel's on his way.

'Most of the nobles don't know,' Beatrice says, with scorn. Another thing he's never seen in her. 'I suppose that's the only thing distroubling you. You can sleep peaceful now.'

Simnel reaches for some tender words. 'Beatrice, I'm sorry that good men died,' he says. 'But it was for a greater good: to stop more evil men, who would have killed even more people.'

'Are you stopping these men for the common good, or are you stopping them because you hate them?'

Simnel gives up arguing. He sits down on the ground. Beatrice stays standing.

'Look,' he says. 'I told you from the start that you shouldn't be my friend. I've told lies, but I never told you I was a good person. That was your mistake. It's better that you know what I am. I'll give you money so you and Elyn can live happily, far away from me. But I want my revenge, and I'm going to get it. That's all. There's nothing else left in me. I don't even believe in God.'

She doesn't take a backward step at that, or even look astonied. She says, 'Oh, neither does Elyn. But she's not such a turd about it.'

'I am sorry, Beatrice. I didn't want to grieve you. But this is who I am.'

'You're still lying,' she says.

'I *am* sorry—'

'No, I mean, you're lying about not being good. You *were* a good person before.'

Simnel thinks of John Collan. Enchanted by kittens, brought to tears by a whittled ship, frightened by a goat. He seems as foreign as a Roman.

'I tried to be good. I used to think I'd be good again one day, once I'd finished killing people. I don't believe that anymore.'

'I'm not taking your money,' Beatrice says. 'You can't pay me to leave you alone. You're a full knave now, it's true. But I'm going to keep being your friend because otherwise you'll forget what you used to be, and then you'll never be able to come back.'

19

Beatrice and Elyn find a farm in a village. It has a decent amount of land, where they can keep cows and sheep. Elyn knows cows, she says, which is useful because Beatrice doesn't know anything besides chambermaiding, and there won't be any tapestries to dust here.

Besides buying the land they can afford farm hands, even a dairy maid. Morton made Simnel an additional gift of money – for his wedding, he said, patting his shoulder, and wishing him great joy in his new life.

Beatrice and Elyn give notice; they're going to travel on ahead of him. He has to make a journey, he tells them, and then he'll be back to join them.

'Another hudder mudder doing,' Elyn says.

'Content your minds: I won't be back for long,' he says. 'I'll help you set up, then I'll disappear. Maybe run away with some strumpet, maybe drown at sea.'

Elyn says she looks forward to it.

Beatrice comes to him.

'Don't do this,' she says. 'Whatever you're purposing. Leave with us instead.'

'Do you think that will save my soul?' he says. 'It's gone too far for that.'

'Your soul is salvageable until your ending day,' she says.

'Huh,' he says. 'That reminds me of a morality play I saw when I was a boy. In Banbury. With Mercy, and Mankind, and… well. That was a wonderly stupid play.'

But he's remembering Jennott eating a pie, getting oily crumbs on her goodliest kirtle. The smell of ale, the press, the sun. Will Collan's hand on his shoulder. The cart at night, slowly bumping home.

He feels a pain that comes too quickly. He can't barricade himself against it. The door flies open; the feeling comes in and takes him over.

Beatrice, ever-watching for this moment, moves in. She seizes his hand, and presses it. He allows it. He can't find the energy to stop her.

'John,' she says. He told her once that this used to be his name. 'Please. I know you want vengeance, but it will only work you wrack. By the Virgin, I know you're sore grieved at what's been lost. But it *is* lost, on earth. The people who are dead – you can't change anything for them. They're in heaven now, biding there for you. They don't want you going to hell, not for them. Your friend Lincoln – how do you think he'd feel? Would he want you to lie and murder? Or would it hurt him to see it?'

He thinks of Lincoln's beautiful eyes, full of God's grace. Made sad by him, Simnel.

'It would,' he says.

'I know you aren't happy. You haven't been happy since the day I met you. Not any good kind of happiness. Remember being a boy on your farm? Who was made glad by love, his kin and his friends. Not by vengeance. *He* would never do this. He would see that there's a farm, here, now, and people who love you – well, maybe not Elyn, but I do, and soon she will too – and maybe you can even rescue your lost mistress, and she can live with us. And we can lie in the sun and eat strawberries together, and you can be happy again. I know there are people who wronged you, John. But for Lincoln's sake, for your soul, for your happiness here on earth, you have to forgive them, and free yourself.'

He finds it hard to speak. He puts his other hand over hers, enclosing it between his own, warm as a sleeping dove. He strokes it briefly, gently.

'Thank you, Beatrice.' He returns her hand to her lap; stands up. 'But I'm going to destroy them all.'

Beatrice and Elyn leave court in February. Simnel packs his own things, then remembers he wants to say goodbye to Madan, and goes to find him.

He discovers Ormond's men in a high state of commotion. Kildare, they say, has been taken! Arrested in Dublin! Tricked out of hiding, by a false pardon!

Is on his way to England!

Simnel unpacks.

He can stay another few days.

By the time Simnel rejoins Beatrice and Elyn, there will be snow-drops, celandine, maybe lambs. The air will be ballock-freezing, but there will be something relenting in it too: the earliest idea of spring. Smoke will be rising from his own chimney. A cake in the oven? Yes, spiced with something. His heart, freshly fed with revenge, will be warm and fat. He'll stay a little while as the husband of Beatrice – for the sake of these two women, who are good (if not, in the case of Elyn, lovable) – and then he and Joan will get on a boat, and go somewhere where they aren't Joan Fitzgerald Joan O'Carroll John Collan Lambert Simons Edward, Earl of Warwick Simnel; where they are only known by the locals of whatever place they end up in as *those two, those lovers, who love each other above anything else.*

Simnel can't say to Kildare: *I had a part in this.* But it will be sweet to see him brought low, and know: *This was me.*

He's allowed to visit the Great Earl in the Tower, which he hasn't seen before. Morton goes with him, taking him over the bridge, passing the great donjon, built out of French stone by William the Conqueror; the mint producing Henry's money; the lions roaring in their dark alcoves; the Earl of Warwick, somewhere – alone again.

At the thought of his double Simnel's exultation drops away. But by the time he's at Kildare's door it's leaping high, flaming and greedy. He wants to drink up Kildare's misery like mead. And it *is* his meed, his deserved reward.

'I fear Henry might be minded to let Kildare off,' Morton says. He pats Simnel on the back. 'See if you can squeeze some more treason out of him.'

Simnel is shown in to Kildare's chamber – not the grimly cell he expected (hoped for), but a well- appointed chamber with a curtained bed, cushioned chairs, rushes on the floor and beautifully painted walls. In one corner sits Kildare, not getting up to greet him, and now Simnel's heart lightens: the Great Earl looks sunk in a wanhope deeper than Simnel could ever have dreamed.

He looks up at Simnel.

'What are you after?' he says, flatly. 'I'm not feeling hospitable.'

'I can see that,' Simnel says. 'I thought I'd come to offer my sympathies, from a king-that-never-was, to the uncrowned king of Ireland-that-was.'

'Ah. You want to enjoy your victory, such as it is,' Kildare says. 'I see you have the rights to the Tower these days. Is my present state of mischance your doings, too?'

He doesn't say it seriously, but when he looks at Simnel, who hasn't bothered to hide his expression of pleasure, he blinks, and understands. 'By Jesus,' he says, with a flaring up of maugre. 'What a despitous, shamming serpent you've become.' Then he sighs, and that sense of his old self leaves him in the exhale. 'I suppose that's part my fault – well, good fortune to you. We've all got our hills to climb. Though none of those summits seem so important, in the end.'

Simnel is confused. Kildare doesn't seem wroth. He just looks tired; heavy-eyed. Then he says, 'I don't suppose you feel like telling me news of my wife? Of my son?'

'What? What's happened to them?'

'Alison is ill, back in Ireland. They have my son prisoner.'

Simnel's pleasure leaves him. He loved Lady Kildare; she was a truly goodly lady. And Kildare's son Gerald isn't even ten. Younger than Simnel was when he was taken somewhere new and unfriendly. The idea of tormenting Kildare slips out of his heart.

'I didn't know,' he says. 'I could ask after them.'

'They won't let you come back just to bring me news,' Kildare says. 'I don't know when I'll hear of them. Who here is friend enough to tell me? Will I ever see my wife again? Are they being kind to my boy, or is he frightened?'

There are tears in his eyes.

Simnel doesn't want to hurt Kildare further, but neither can he offer an apology, or any soothing words. Kildare wipes his eyes and looks at Simnel, level and open, as if considering something.

And it seems, now, as if there is a darkness around them. That Simnel made a mistake walking into it.

'You should know,' Kildare says, 'Joan is dead.'

This is the darkness.

'No,' Simnel says.

'I'm sorry.'

'You're lying. To injure me.'

'I've never wanted to injure you, lad,' Kildare says. 'I'm passing sorry, for us both. She had a baby. She didn't live. It was Christmas Eve. I'll never celebrate it again. I'm telling you because I know you loved her. 'Tis true I was sore wroth at the pair of you, for nearly ruining our rebellion, but now I'm here, I think: what the fuck does all that matter? I should have let you go. The two of you wed and living in some insignificant castle, that would have been better than this. Look where we are now. I never told anyone—' his voice all in pieces '—my Joan, she was my favourite daughter, and I treated her the worst—'

Simnel can't bear to listen. Can't bear to be here.

Can't bear.

He gets up, bangs on the door to drown out Kildare; cries like a child, to be let out. As if he can be let out of hell, but that's not possible, because the hell now is in his own self.

Scotland

Simnel stands in a fine grey mist of rain, looking up at a grey stone house. The sky is grey; the sea beyond the harbour is grey. The birds caw-cawing in circles above the water: grey.

Simnel had gone to Lovell's address in Edinburgh, but Lovell had left. Maybe he heard Simnel was coming after him. Simnel did his best to convince the landlords of the lodgings that he was a friend of Lovell's and an enemy of King Henry, which they said they believed, but also, didn't care overmuch about. The last friend of Lovell's gave us a gold ring, said the woman. So Simnel gave them all his money, and they told him Lovell and his friend Cross were at Irvine harbour, there to get the next boat out.

He rode overnight, reaching Irvine at dawn, and asked at the Mermaid Inn where a man of Lovell's description was staying, and the man pointed across the street: there.

And now he is here.

Marco Polo told a story of Alaodin, the Sheikh of the Mountain, who built a sham Paradise with fountains and gardens and beautiful young demosels, then drugged young men and brought them to this place. The men believed they were in heaven. Alaodin told them that they needed to go back to earth for a short time, to assassinate people, but after that they would come back to Paradise (all the quicker if they died in the doing).

The men, enamoured with the demosels, made the best assassins anyone had ever seen.

Simnel wonders what would happen if the men ever found out that they'd been lied to.

An assassin in pursuit of Alaodin himself: how good would he be?

What makes a better killer: love or hatred?

Remember Joan's downfall only came when she allowed love (the love of him) to enter her heart.

He remembers thinking he only had his love and his hatred – and now he just has his hatred. It's eaten the love and now it's stronger.

He'd bought a sword, not knowing if he'd remember his Mechelen training; a small boy in a metal suit. But on the road to Scotland a man with a mace ambushed and tried to rob him, and first Simnel cut off the arm that was holding the mace, then beat the man to the ground with the flat of his sword. Not enough to kill him. Or at least, the man wasn't dead when Simnel rode away and left him. Someone would find him. Or not. Like the Edinburgh landlords, he doesn't give much of a shit either way.

He debates divers ways of entering Lovell's house, and can't think of anything better than kicking the door open without knocking. Lovell is in the hall, sitting in a chair by the fire reading a book, which falls out of his hand at the sight of Simnel.

Lovell looks nearly the same, only more grey, as if the weather of the harbour has begun to work on him. He doesn't get up. He looks astonied.

'What the fuck are *you* doing here?' he says.

There were nights when Simnel would imagine all the things he'd say to Lovell: how Simnel would inquiet him; make him tell the truth; make him afraid for his life, which he (ha!) never had a hope of keeping – something that he would gradually realise, and be sore sorry over.

Now Simnel's here, there's no savour in any of it.

He lifts the sword and points it at Lovell. It doesn't feel real. He says what he planned to say by dull rote, that he's here to avenge the deaths of people he loved, who Lovell killed, blah, blah.

'Wait,' Lovell says, as Simnel knew he would. The shock has dropped off him; he's looking more himself, more sure, more assessing. 'At least tell me whose death I'm responsible for.'

'How about Joan Fitzgerald and the lady Grania?' Simnel says. 'After you told Kildare what we were planning.'

Lovell raises his eyebrows. His brows say, *We are master of this situation.*

'That was Plunket,' he said. 'Don't you remember?'

'Kildare told me it was you.'

'You trust Kildare?' Lovell says, looking incredulous. It's so exactly what Simnel expected – the lying, the turnings around – that he's almost bored by it, like a morality play he's had to act a hundred times, in a hundred villages.

But then Lovell says, 'You trust his daughter? How well did you know *her*? I heard she was a famous liar. I heard you were to abandon the gold under a bush and go to bed before your meeting hour. Does that not strike you as strange? I know you loved her, but come on. Do you truly believe she'd have been there to meet you?'

He remembers Joan saying, *The gentil bird outwits the peasant, and he lets her out of her cage.*

A darkness comes into him. A fear.

But he can't think of that now.

He returns to the script. His best chance of wrongfooting Lovell. (Knowing, too, that Lovell himself has been wrongfooting people since before Simnel was born.)

He says, 'Then the evil priest and his mistress you put me in the care of – where were you when they sold me to the king? You were going to let them escape. It was only your man Mayne that saved me by killing them.'

Lovell doesn't hesitate.

'My men killed them on my command,' he says. 'I always protected you.'

'That's a lie: they didn't sell me to the king.'

Lovell makes a noise of exasperation.

'Fine. They were killed because they were a greedy pair of nobodies. Do you really give a gnat's shit about that? Or do you disapprove of my lying? I'm at swordpoint, what do you expect? I'll say what you want me to say. That's how swordpoint works. What do you *want*? I have gold here: I'll share it with you. What are you now, a servant? A peasant again? Do you want to be king? Come with me to Mechelen and we'll make it happen.'

'Why don't you tell me what I am?' Simnel says. 'You're the one who knows.'

'You're the Earl of Warwick,' says Lovell.

'I wasn't the Earl of Warwick when you were plotting to free the Earl in the Tower.'

Lovell shrugs. He radiates authority now. Lord of the situation. He says, 'The earl I serve is the earl who will serve my purpose. Stop looking so holy and be honest. Do you really care which is which?'

And strangely, Simnel realises he doesn't. Peasant, bastard, earl: none of them have Joan. Any of them can kill Lovell.

They stare at each other. He can see Lovell reading him, understanding him.

'You can get your own sword,' Simnel says.

'No,' Lovell says. 'I'm too old for affray. You'll win. If you're going to kill me, you'll have to do it with me sitting in this chair, unarmed.'

His eyes go to the door, very briefly, as he says it. Simnel needs to hie things along, or Cross is going to get back and he'll be outnumbered.

'Your man Cross is dead outside,' Simnel says. 'In payment for Lincoln.'

Lovell makes another noise of exasperation. 'Listen,' he says. As he says it, his hand leaps out from below his robe, and a knife flies out of it. It just misses Simnel's head and embeds itself in the wood of the door, thrumming.

Simnel steps forward.

It feels like such a small, usual kind of step, the sword leading the way, straight forward, a very short distance. And then the meeting, very natural, the sword entering Lovell's upheld hand, passing through it into his chest, through the chest – stopping, with a cracking noise, at the chair back.

Lovell's hand is pinioned over his heart. Blood wells up through his fingers. The sight of the blood, so quick, so plenteous, is what shocks Simnel – and he looks at Lovell, to see if he's shocked too.

But Lovell's eyes aren't on Simnel. He's seeing something else. His mouth moves in outrage, his eyes blink, his fingers curl and uncurl, a watery noise comes out of him. Then Simnel pulls the sword out and Lovell slides down in the seat, head back, as if his soul has left via his open mouth, leaving his body slumped behind.

So.

Simnel waits for feelings to rise up. Nothing happens.

He stands in an absence of feeling.

He works practically instead. He goes upstairs and looks around. There are two chambers in the solar, each with men's clothes in. Fur, good woollen cloth, fine white shirts. Knight-clothes. In one chamber there are two saddlebags of gold coins under the bed. He brings them out, pulls a sheet off one of the beds, and takes everything back downstairs.

'You know I might never have seen stairs, if it wasn't for you,' he says pleasantly to Lovell, as he shrouds his outraged face in the sheet. Blood is pattering beneath the body onto the rushes, over the fallen book. Simnel can still make out the title.

Juvenal.

Of course.

There aren't any other books to read, ones that aren't covered in blood, so he sits and spins his sword as he waits for Cross to get back. Ten minutes or so passes. The grey outside brightens. Maybe the rain's stopped.

No feelings, still. This surprises him. He's killed his first man. Does his heart have nothing to say? Any guilt, any joy, any relief, anything at all?

His heart, which is like all hearts, frightened and stupid, only wants to know if Joan really loved him.

When there's no answer to that question.

What does it matter now? Simnel answers. *Be silent, then, if you can't be useful.*

And here's Cross, at the door.

Cross draws his sword immediately. 'You? What is this?' he says. He stands, confused but bright and ware, staring at Simnel and the grey-lit room. The sight of covered-over Lovell, now a soaked red chrysalis, confuses him more.

433

'I thought you were one of us,' he says. 'What are you – Henry's man, now? Fuck, of course you are. Am I taken? If so I'll surrender peacefully. I seek merciful pardon! In exchange for information. Wait—' Cross's grip on his sword shifts, better securing itself. 'Where are the rest of your men? Are you alone?'

'I'm not here on Henry's business,' Simnel says. 'I was a friend of the Earl of Lincoln. You may remember murdering him as he knelt defenceless.'

'Lincoln? I swear it on the Virgin, that was on orders from Lovell. And you've killed Lovell. Is that not enough?'

As he says *enough*, he darts forward with his sword.

Lovell's knight, Lovell's tricks: it's like the man isn't even dead.

Simnel parries, attacks, and they fight for a short while: Liechtenauer in a confined space – *Zornhau* into a chair, *Mittelhau* gouging the wall-plaster, *Abschneiden* slicing across Simnel's leather jerkin and into his skin, a non-textbook headbutt in the nose from Simnel that knocks Cross back, only for a moment, before a violent *Stechen* from Cross: an unbalanced thrust that lodges his sword in the wall. Cross tugs at it; stumbles clumsily backwards into Simnel, who has pulled Lovell's knife out of the door, puts his arms around Cross – an embracing, like a gentle parent – and forces the knife into the yielding skin of his throat.

In. Across.

And a letting go.

No feelings now, either.

Blankly loading his horse, leading Lovell and Cross's horses with him, leaving the port town. Thinking nothing more than:

It's done.

After

He's lying under the cherry tree.

He being, at this moment: John Crossey.

Crossey: Elyn's surname, taken so they could all have the same name. (His sister Elyn, his wife Beatrice.)

John because he couldn't think of anything else.

In the earth a couple of feet below him are two heavy bags of gold. They said Will Collan, his father that was, stole his gold from a fairy king. They could say it now, more accurately, of John.

Through the blossom-covered branches, clouds hie across the pale blue sky. There are goldfinches busy in the tree above him. Everything he pictured before he left court is here. The celandines, the baby lambs butting their mothers in the field, the smoke rising from the chimney of the long, low house. The bed stuffed with feathers in its own quiet room. Even a goat: one of a gentil disposition.

None of it means anything.

Finding Joan, killing the men who took her away, who stole John's life, who killed Lincoln and Grania and the others. Everything he did after he left Ireland was to those ends. Now the ends are sheared away, like a road ending in a bottomless drop.

He looks up through the blossom, trying to remember what it was like to lie next to Joan in Maynooth, transported with love of her, praying to God to allow him to love her.

God now gone.

Joan now gone.

If someone said to him, *You can only have one of them back*, he wouldn't even think about it.

He thinks of the unbelievers he's heard of. The Holy Roman Emperor Frederick II, who called Jesus Christ a charlatan. Pietro della Vigna's lost book, which said that Moses, Christ and Mohammed were three imposters. The aristocrat Farinata, exhumed by a Franciscan inquisition twenty years after his death and put on trial for saying Epicurus was right that life dies when the body does – whereupon he was convicted of heresy and his corpse was executed. A farmer friend of Will Collan, fined for saying that God didn't care about farmers. The Englishman Thomas Tailour, hanged a couple of years ago for teaching that the soul is like a candle, and the candle goes out.

Joan, where are you now?

He should have killed Lovell before the man could open his mouth and say, *how well did you know Kildare's daughter?*

Things come back to him, like the churl and bird. Like the tenderness of her final kiss, so uncharacteristic of her. Was she pitying his coming abandonment?

Last night he had a dream like a poem, a dream vision; a quiet courtyard with white flagstones, marble statues of the gods, a gold fountain, a simple sky overhead and Joan sitting on the lip of the fountain with a piece of embroidery, the needle stabbing in and out. Looking up at him with malice.

No, with love.

It was love, it was love.

He can't picture it.

He remembers going to her room at the Abbey Court, after she'd been taken away. Wondering if

he could make her again from the shapes she left. Sculpt her from the empty room. The length of the hollowed shape in the bed, the measurements of the jaw and teeth that scooped the abandoned apple core. The discarded slipper under the bed with a faint darkening for each toe, like a bruise in the leather. The decisive butt of her heel.

He stares up at the sky. Even thinking about her, he can't cry. He hasn't felt anything since Scotland.

Joan said, *A man's heart shrinks, when disaster strikes, but when he gets revenge it grows again.* But John's heart hasn't regrown. Not that he expected, or even wanted it to. His revenge was meant to be a gift to her. Then she died, and he imagined his revenge differently: hoped it would destroy everything, including him, feeding on his human life and turning him bit by bit into something small, dry and black, burned from the inside out, a sooty husk, light and rattling, blowing across the roofs, over the fields, snatched at by a kestrel, swatted by a gardener – crunched, at last, underfoot.

The End.

He thought maybe Lovell or Cross would kill him; they'd all die together. Lincoln believed in *dulce et decorum est*, and maybe Lincoln *was* the lucky one, leaving before he could know the hopelessness of their rebellion, the long, sad afterclaps. Lincoln died in the belief that he was in the service of something good, and that God awaited him.

Not so for John.

The prospect of his own continuation is a question he can't answer.

He lies on the grass in the garden with his eyes dry as stones.

After a while, he realises Elyn has come to sit next to him. He doesn't know when she arrived. He closes his eyes and doesn't move, for a long time, and all that time she sits silently with him.

In the absence of any guiding principle, he decides to make himself useful to Elyn and Beatrice. He's been telling them farm wisdom, what he remembers of it. Not much, and it's all told now.

'Do you want me to teach you to read?' he asks them.

'Oh, yes, thank you,' Beatrice says. 'What a wonderly thing!'

'Absolutely not,' says Elyn.

'Is this some kind of heathen thing?' he asks. He's seen her conducting odd rites. Burying a bundle of bones (human or animal, he didn't want to ask) at the threshold of their farm. Making offerings of broken pots to water. He trod on a shard of earthenware the other day in the stream and cut his foot. He asked her early on if she was in league with the devil – just to check, it was important to check – and she got wroth and wouldn't answer any more questions.

'Elyn isn't a heathen,' Beatrice says.

'I am,' says Elyn. 'You just like to pretend I'm not so you can imagine us in heaven together.'

John asks, 'Why don't heathens like writing?'

'Writing's fine for letters of business and bills and so on,' Elyn says. 'But you book people take it too far.'

'I want John to write a book about his own self,' Beatrice tells her. 'Then, when I know how, I'll read it.'

'By Saint Paul, no,' John says.

Beatrice says self like it's one thing. He thinks of Little John, Lambert, Edward, Simnel. All clamouring at once, like the seven heads of the horned, leopard-bodied, bear-footed beast of *Revelation* that came out of the sea, making a hideous wailing and whistling and growling.

Nobody looked upon that beast and said:

'Ho: you should write a book.'

But later, he thinks about it.

John's dismissed the practice of autobiographising before. Kempe, Hoccleve, Boethius: it was so obvious to him what they were up to. They weren't writing a story; they were making an argument for their *selves*. Boethius has the last word on his persecution: it was ordained so that he might help attain the greatest wisdom, the highest holiness, and rise above all his miserable enemies. Hoccleve wants everyone to know that he was crazed in his wits once, but not anymore – that God afflicted him only because God holds him so dear, and now he would like to be invited to dinner again. Margery Kempe, more favoured than any other, didn't have to travail to puzzle out what God's plan for her was. She was told. Whenever something bad happened, Jesus would appear right anon to explain it, and remind her that her suffering was all on account of her being his beloved bride.

Poor Bernard André, John thinks, wondering where God is, why he isn't paying attention. Someone should have told him: It's because God's spending all his time with Margery.

Augustine, Boethius, Hoccleve and Kempe wrote to place themselves in history, in God's grace. They were writing for other people, to say: see, worship to God must mean worship to me.

But John has nothing to say to *the people*. He did once. He used to long to tell the people things. To grasp the cloak of the people, cry truth in their ears.

But now he thinks: *Let André write him, and all Henry's other chroniclers.* The written Simnel – a pretender, a silly boy, a rascal, a low-born puppet – has replaced the real one. Nothing he writes would change that.

And what is an autobiography, if nobody reads it?

Maybe nothing but a way to live life again.

Joan was right that writing is done by those *without*. John wants what is lost. Writing is his way back to the past, where Grania is having ado with her chaplain, and Lincoln is delighting in God, and Edward and Joan are lying under a tree, arguing, under a blue sky.

All of that.

Then – as Beatrice said – bury it.

May Day comes, and the village celebrates: a ribboned pole goes up on the green; the blacksmith runs about dressed as King Henry; Beatrice and Elyn, merry on ale, go to the dancing in the churchyard.

A few days later, they come to John, looking so strange and hesitating, and so different from usual (which is: Beatrice cheerful, Elyn not) that alarm comes over him.

'What tidings?' he asks, looking over them for signs of ill health or injury.

But it's nothing like that. It turns out they want a child. Well, Beatrice has always wanted children, and Elyn wasn't sure, but Beatrice said she'd be the one bearing it and suckling it and so on and now Elyn's in favour of the idea and so they'd like to get started on the business of family-making.

'An excellent idea, your child will be truly blessed with two such mothers,' he says, relieved. 'But wait. How are you going to *get* a child?'

They look at him.

'Ah,' he says.

He won't write of the *how*, and not just because Elyn said she'd flatten his plums with a millstone if he did. He isn't inclined to. Except to say, Beatrice wasn't frightened; in fact she kept giggling, and then apologising, and afterwards she said, *Well, that was really nothing at all.* But for John it was a strange, and distinctly sad, episode. He thought maybe she guessed at that, later. She said, *This won't inquiet things, will it? We'll be the same as before? You're my best friend.*

And he *is* still her best friend.

But also, it's not the same as before.

John's in another couple's love, that's the problem. He's an unnecessary presence already: they know how to milk cows, sow vegetables, harvest a field, bake and brew – but the idea of himself and his dole, hanging over a new, tender-skinned baby… He worries he'll do it some subtle damage. Bad air will get into it, a poisonous melancholy.

He considers farming somewhere else. But farming itself doesn't work. It isn't right anymore. The people of the village are friendly with Beatrice – even with Elyn, as rude and grucching as she is – but they don't talk naturally to John. They seem wary, or defensive, or hostile. He remembers the stories of stolen people, who spend a night in the land of Fairy then come home and find that a year has passed. By that calculation he's spent hundreds of years away. The farming people can tell: he's different now.

'You don't have to leave,' Elyn says to him. 'This is your home. We're your family.'

'What makes you think I want to leave?' he says.

'Do you want to leave?'

He can't reply.

'That's a yes, then. Where would you go?' she asks.

'I don't know. I've only just realised that I want to leave. Where would you go, if you were me?'

'Fuck knows,' she says. 'I diagnose. I don't cure.'

He sits under the cherry tree. Across the lawn, Elyn is shelling peas into a bowl. Beatrice is spreading laundry on the bushes to dry

Joan's soul: where is it?

He speaks to Joan: *I'm here.*

Please

Joan? Where are you?

It's been eight years since he saw her under the yew in Ireland. He can't even bring a whole image of her to mind anymore. Just parts – dark hair, white skin, blue eyes. Her face has followed her voice, receding into the darkness.

He doesn't believe in a God, but he thinks there must be a heaven and a hell, because Joan's soul is not with him, and it has to be somewhere.

He thinks of his father-that-was, Will Collan, who loved his mother-that-was, and Jennott, and maybe the Widow Mylton. But maybe they only got a third each of his love – and what happens when those two wives meet in heaven?

John loves only Joan. Nobody else will divide up that portion. When he reaches the gates of the afterwards, whatever that is, he'll show it, and say: *let me be with her.* Here as it never was on earth.

But then he thinks, what if he gets there and her husband O'Carroll, the man she maybe loved, is there beside her?

What if there are a host of blue-eyed, dark-haired, white-skinned women, and he can't recognise her among them?

What is this feeling that rises up now – no, he knows it, he doesn't want it—

—grief—

A contraction of pain grips his chest; tightens, cracks.

Beatrice is by his side – of course she is, she sensed the tears coming like an animal senses rain – she must have run across the grass, and now here she is, cradling him, no doubt having the time of her life.

(wouldn't want her to let go)

A sound comes out of his mouth.

—loss—

the sound of loss so long and angry and mournful out of measure, tears flowing with it, on and on, rising and falling

Part of him watching it thinking stop shut up stop it

Other part, more animal, howling back:

no

He curls up, and lets it overtake him. It can have him.

What is he, but this.

It's still warm after dinner, so they take cups of ale outside, where the sky is a pearly lavender, and a hedgepig is making a commotion in the blackberry bushes. They sit under the tree: John, Beatrice, Elyn, maybe a small child of his half-making in Beatrice's stomach. Beatrice did something involving the moon and a bowl of water and a silver coin and an invocation to the Virgin, who gave it to Beatrice to know – via the silver or the water, John isn't sure – that she is carrying a baby, and it will have Mary's own special protection.

'If the child asks who his grandparents are, what will you say?' he asks them. 'Peasant or noble? Will you say his father was legitimate, or a bastard?'

'I'm not even sure the baby Crossey is legitimate under God's law,' Beatrice says cheerfully. 'The marriage is a sham after all.'

It's when John pictures that small baby that he thinks: *how stupid it all is.*

John used to want to know what he was. At the end of every *lai* and romance, the lost babies find out who their parents are, the princes in disguise reveal themselves, the lovers recognise each other. An ending means knowing what you are. Taking your rightful place in the social order, layers of people, stacked on top of each other: peasant, yeoman, gentleman, knight, duke, king. If you don't know who is what, all the layers tumble into unholy chaos.

The knowing just isn't something John needs anymore. He used to think his old selves had fallen away – fled or forced out – taking his old qualities with them. Now he realises they're all here; he's all of them, and also some new and unknowable thing.

And is inclined to the view that an existence *outside* order is a rare kind of good fortune. To not have to be a king, or a farmer.

He uses some of his gold to buy books about far-off lands.

In the *Morte*, Merlin would warn Arthur and his knights that their actions would lead to their downfall. They all, without exception, ignored him. John knows why, now. What would he do, standing

444

there in front of the sword in the stone? Merlin saying: If you take this sword, you'll have a few months of glory, then six years of servitude. If you follow the Lady of the Lake – that beautiful magpie-looking woman there, with the blue eyes, the despitous tongue – you and she will have a year of bliss, then you'll lose her and mourn her the rest of your life.

He'd do it. Of course he would. Push Merlin out of the way, snatch it up. Bright joy, black grief. He'd take them both together.

He even misses people he hated; wishes them back, just to talk to them about the old days. He'd welcome Kildare now, bid him good cheer, say: *Remember Christmas at Maynooth?*

The bawdy stories about Plunket's wife; the dancing; the chaplain in Grania's dress; Edward in ecstatic pain, watching Joan across the room.

Remember Joan, he'd say to Kildare. *How we loved her. Even when she was killing people. Nobody here remembers her. But we do.*

How can he be wroth at Kildare – at Lovell, even – for ruining his life, when they gave him that life?

'I'm going East,' John says to Beatrice and Elyn.

'What?' Beatrice cries. 'No!'

'You're pregnant and you can read,' Elyn says to her. 'Hasn't the man done enough? Let him go.'

'You're pregnant?' John asks.

'I think so,' Beatrice says, brightening. 'But if you go you won't meet the baby.'

'I'll come back.'

'What's East?' Elyn asks.

Japan, where the palaces are roofed with gold and every dead man is buried with a pearl in his mouth. Peace-loving Kinsai with its famous pleasure barges. Yachi, where shells are money. Kara-jang, where crocodiles can be found. Hot Quilon, where the people and the lions are black, parrots live wild and no love is regarded as a sin.

'I just don't see what's wrong with going to Canterbury,' Beatrice says. 'Or the Holy Land. Where people have their clothes on. Why don't you visit your people?'

He won't visit Will Collan. Either Will Collan wasn't his father, or Will Collan was a father who sold his youngest son. Either way, Will is done with John, and John with Will.

'I might see a friend called Jennott before I go,' he says. 'Would you like a parrot, Beatrice? I'll bring you a parrot.'

'I don't know what a parrot is and I don't want one. I want you to be safe. Take some amulets for protection. Don't burn your pintle having ado in the sun. Be ware of mermaids and the French. I'll pray for you here, of course. I'll ask the priest for some holy water we can sprinkle on your shoes.'

'What? That's not even a custom,' says Elyn.

Beatrice starts crying; puts her arms out and rushes at John; stepping on his foot, hardly able to see through her tears. He pats her head. Feels, unexpectedly, tears rising into his own eyes.

His feelings are back, then. He isn't sure he's ready for them. But here they are. It's time to rejoin all the other havers of feelings. The havers of lives. Is he ready for a life? No. But here it is.

Plutarch wrote about how Alexander met the naked philosophers. They lived in a land of plenty. They ate fruit from the trees, tended their flocks, and drank water from the river. Each husband and wife had two children only, to replace them. They had no king.

Which is the wickedest of all the creatures? Alexander asked them.

The philosophers replied: Man.

Why? he asked.

They replied: Look at yourself. You are a wild beast, taking the lives of other beasts.

Then Alexander asked: What is kingship?

They replied: Unfair power used against other men; presumption supported by chance; a glittering gold burden.

Alexander wasn't angry with these answers. Instead he told the philosophers he'd give them whatever they asked for. But they asked for immortality. He told them he was mortal: he had no power to gift such a thing.

If you are mortal, they said, why do you wage war? Why do you collect lands and riches if you have to leave it all behind?

Alexander said, I am directed by divine providence above. If it were up to me I would prefer not to go to war. But my soul's master, providence, does not permit me to refuse.

John thinks:

Fuck divine providence.

I refuse.

He'll go to find the naked philosophers, if they still exist. Maybe they're long gone, like King Arthur, the giants of England, the giraffes of Mechelen.

But he'll find something anyway.

Something new to him.

At the end of June, Perkin Warbeck, several English gentilmen and one thousand soldiers sailed to England to invade. Their ships were blown off course and ended up in Deal. Warbeck stayed on his ship and sent a few hundred soldiers to make landings, but the loyal and heroic people of Deal hardily fought off the invaders.

So Henry's proclamation goes.

John's neighbour Miller Adam, who has kin in Deal, says in fact the men of the town couldn't decide what to do. They argued over it for a few hours, in which the compelling points were made that previous rebellions had failed, and this one seemed smaller in size, and the supporters of failed rebellions get punished, and so they mounted an attack on the soldiers, with arrows and bills. A hundred and fifty of Warbeck's men were killed, a hundred and fifty captured, and the rest escaped back to their ships.

At the end of July the captured men were executed and hung on tall gallows along the coastline, where they could be seen from the sea.

Imagine that grimly welcome, said Miller Adam.

I don't want to, said Beatrice, both hands on her belly, as if covering the child's ears.

And then Warbeck went on to Ireland, where he sheltered with the Earl of Desmond, and attacked Waterford, until Poynings' fleet chased them to Scotland, where he is now, sheltered by King James, and...

John finds himself losing the sense of the rest of it, as if his ears have been invisibly covered. But he knows the rudiments. Hide, seek, attack, retreat. It's all so familiar that it's like something going on in a childhood story; he feels it's happened already, he knows the ending.

He imagines Morton, exulting in his study over the news. Margaret, receiving it calmly. Kildare, penned lionlike and furious in the Tower. Henry, sitting at his great table, updating his lists of men's names, his rolls of who betrayed him, who might betray him, who is now betraying him.

Familiar, all of it, and yet so far away. His own minds withdrawn from them, pointing: East.

He digs up a portion of the gold for himself and gives some to Elyn and Beatrice. They are alarmed.

'What are we meant to do with this?' Beatrice says. 'We're not ladies. This is lady money.'

'It'll put us in peril,' Elyn says. 'When whoever you stole it from comes to look for it.'

'They won't be doing that,' he says.

'Fine. I don't want to know why. We'll use it hudder mudder. For the child Crossey.'

John has booked a passage to Spain.

He's going to be leaving the village on Lammas Day. For the first time in his life he'll be his own man. Everyone in the layers of society, even the king, is constrained. But John has money and nobody knows him. *He* doesn't know him.

He could be anything.

The thought is not without its terrors.

And, his minds go on, he's alone. In the absence of providence. Nobody watching, nobody teaching. No father God with a plan especially for him.

For a moment the terror overtakes him. The door is too open. The sky is too large. He's going to drown in the vast world like a fly in a bathtub.

Well then, he thinks, he'll be with Joan again.

And maybe he'll have seen a crocodile in the meantime.

He thinks on to the moment of leaving, riding through the garlanded village as the first loaf of bread made with the year's harvest is presented in church to receive its blessing. There will be a Lammas Fair, musicians, travelling performers to delight Beatrice and maybe even Elyn. His neighbours will fill the streets. They'll wave and wonder where he's going. Then they'll go back to celebrating, with candle-lit processions and feasting. Later, Elyn will kiss Beatrice and they'll go to bed. They'll say it's strange how not-different the house feels without John in it. They'll lay hands on Beatrice's stomach. Beatrice will worry that he's not safe from robbers; say a prayer, tipsy on mead; fall quickly asleep.

Elyn will think on, maybe picturing him, riding on a darkening road, past other riders and carts, through villages and towns, ever passing, not quite one of the living, accompanied always by the people of his memory: Grania, Lincoln, Joan.

But riding on, still, hoping to come to a place where he can live again.

Family Trees

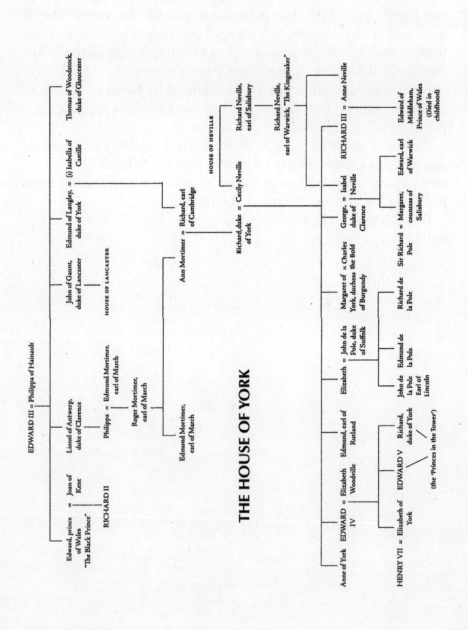

THE HOUSE OF YORK

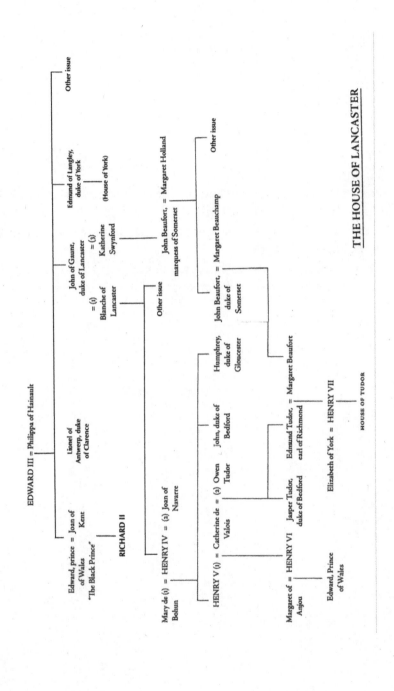

THE HOUSE OF LANCASTER

Acknowledgments

With enormous thanks to...

Early readers Bibby, Cian and Shelley. Felicity, Flo, Rosie, and Lisa at Curtis Brown. Christy at United Talent. Allegra, Lauren, Lynn and the team at Bloomsbury. And Jordan, Izzy, Matthew, Andrea and the team at Alfred A Knopf.

This book could never have happened without your wisdom, hard work and support, and I'm so grateful.

A Note on the Author

Jo Harkin studied literature at university. She daydreamed her way through various jobs in her twenties before becoming a full-time writer. Her debut novel *Tell Me an Ending* was a *New York Times* book of the year. She lives in Berkshire, England.

A Note on the Type

The text of this book is set in Bembo, which was first used in 1495 by the Venetian printer Aldus Manutius for Cardinal Bembo's *De Aetna*. The original types were cut for Manutius by Francesco Griffo. Bembo was one of the types used by Claude Garamond (1480–1561) as a model for his Romain de l'Université, and so it was a forerunner of what became the standard European type for the following two centuries. Its modern form follows the original types and was designed for Monotype in 1929.